F   Hynd, Noel
HYN

        Rage of spirits

DEMCO

RAGE OF SPIRITS

NOEL HYND

RAGE OF SPIRITS

Kensington Books

http://www.kensingtonbooks.com

Readers can reach Noel Hynd at: NHy1212@AOL.com

KENSINGTON BOOKS are published by

Kensington Publishing Corp.
850 Third Avenue
New York, NY 10022

Copyright © 1997 by Noel Hynd

Library of Congress Card Catalog Number: 96-077846
ISBN 1-57566-127-6

First Printing: February, 1997
10 9 8 7 6 5 4 3 2 1

Printed in the United States of America

This book is dedicated to
our many friends
on the faculty and staff of
St. Peter's School
Philadelphia
September 1987–June 1996
with thanks and appreciation
for something priceless.

And I heard a voice at the banks
of the U'Lai. And it called, "Gabriel!
Gabriel! Make this man understand
this vision."

—*Revelations 16:12*

"It was well known in Washington
that Nancy Reagan employed an astrologer.
Mrs. Reagan regularly conveyed the
astrologer's findings to her husband.
Often decisions of state were subject to
the alignment of planets."

News item

PART
ONE

1

The year was 2003 and the month was November.

William Cochrane sat in an uncrowded, desolate departure lounge of a charmless Midwestern airport, listening to the rumble of distant jets taking off and landing in the night. He was a solitary male traveler with a single piece of carry-on luggage on the plastic seat next to him. He was too tired to read an evening newspaper, his soul too laden with grief to even thumb through a magazine or listen to music on his headset. In more ways than he dared to imagine, he was a voyager in the midst of a journey, the destination as unclear as the itinerary.

On this evening in November, which was about to turn into early morning, Bill Cochrane waited only for the immediate things:

The elusive boarding call for his long-delayed flight, a red-eye out of Detroit that would take him back to Washington, D.C., and the strange new place that he now called home.

The instructions to buckle into his seat belt.

The takeoff into a night sky that was as wide and black as his mood.

Still, he waited. No movement. He was a man frozen in place. In time. In many ways, terrified. For the more distant things—like the subsiding of pain and fears within him—he would have to wait much longer.

Outside, it was raining. Cochrane hated flying in the rain. As was frequently the case, he consoled himself with things that weren't present. At least, he told himself, there was no ice.

Within the hour, hopefully, another lonely eastbound jet with a handful of late stranded voyagers would rumble down a secondary runway and he would be on it. Not a moment too soon. Anything to get him out of where he was.

Earlier that day he had attended the funeral of his final living parent. His father. A once-dignified human being who had had the same name.

William Cochrane.

Today the son had come face to face with the coffin that was generationally only once removed from his own. Just hours earlier, he had seen what remained of the body of the man he once loved so dearly lowered into a dirt chamber without windows.

They had brought him to a cemetery and a graveside ceremony that had been as lonely as the final years of his life. The cemetery was new and antiseptic. Like the lawns in front of a warehouse in an industrial park. The tombstones were packed together so tightly that the living could barely pass between them. There was no sense of rest. No atmosphere. This might have been a municipal golf course. Cochrane wondered if someday it would be.

There was a short service for Bill Cochrane's father. It was conducted by a young Lutheran minister who had met the deceased in his final hours. Hi and goodbye at the same time. Sorry you have to leave, shame I couldn't get to know you. Tomorrow I'll process someone else.

Who cared anyway? Nothing personal, in the good and bad senses of the concept.

And all the time at graveside, before the coffin sank into the earth like a bronze submarine, Bill Cochrane stood there besieged by thoughts. He wondered what he could have done differently, how he might have helped his father and was not able to think of anything. Nothing. Then the funeral staff had lowered the other William Cochrane into the ground.

Now, hours later in an airport, all he wanted to do was turn a corner and approach the second half of his life with as little pain as possible.

Hopefully without looking back. As if he could ever go forward without looking back. It felt so strange to have no living parent, and yet no wife or child either. It was as if he were coming from nowhere and going to nowhere.

Sometimes numbers troubled him. His father had spent ten years in a state hospital. His mother had died fifteen years ago. He would soon be looking at a fortieth birthday.

Forty.

Say it loud. I ain't proud.

Turning forty also meant gaining a foothold into a stolid resolute middle age. And middle age meant taking stock.

Looking ahead.

Looking back.

Hell, he reminded himself. He wasn't even forty. He was thirty-seven, exactly half his father's age when his father had died two days earlier. Herein was another quirk of numbers that had its own strange geometry and subtext. But he felt as if he had lived forty years two or three times. Maybe, he told himself foolishly, he had—all in the last twenty.

Certain words, certain questions, came back to him like a little catechism, a minirefrain of blank verse that haunted him constantly:

What is your worst fear now, Bill Cochrane? Death? No. Something worse than death. Something that had already happened. Something to which he had borne witness for a decade. Since it had first happened in 1993.

Two jobs and two nervous breakdowns ago.

Cochrane felt uncomfortable. He coughed. There was a small woman with bad skin at the check-in counter for the airline. She looked up when he coughed, as if she had forgotten there was anyone there. She gave him a perfunctory smile and went back to whatever she was doing.

Then his eyes drifted. He saw himself in reflection in a plate glass windowpane.

He still had a handsome face. But it was a lined face, weathered, with sad eyes, particularly today when circles hung beneath them. The eyes were a window on a tortured soul. The lines around the eyes—age creeping in on little crow's feet—were like a road map to places better left unvisited. And his jittery hands with bitten fingernails, which no observer noticed, seemed to conduct a nervous but silent symphony.

He wasn't on drugs, but sometimes felt as if he should have been. Or had been. Or someday would be. Like so many other aspects of his life, this, too, didn't make sense.

Someday, he wondered, could he please have a rational explanation for everything? Pretty please? Whom should he ask for same?

One of the bitterest lessons he had learned was sometimes in life the rational explanation just wasn't there, no matter how hard one searched.

Why had his father gone crazy, for example? A decade of psychiatric study had been unable to yield such an answer.

Cochrane closed his eyes tightly in the airport lounge. The fluorescent lights were committing bloody homicide on his eyes. But in his besieged head there was an arrangement of chaotic words and music.

A series of images. Himself as a child. His mother scolding him a day before her death fifteen years ago. His father's resolute descent into depression and then irrationality following her passing. A decade in a state mental hospital in Michigan because the family could not afford private care.

He remembered his last visit to his father two months earlier—a rail-thin gray-haired man, bent slightly but still standing almost six feet tall, white hair, wearing stained khakis and a maroon cardigan, improperly buttoned. His father had been outside raking leaves when Bill Cochrane had spotted him from the lobby of the hospital.

"How's Dad?" Cochrane had asked a doctor who was nearby.

"Well," a twenty-something male psychiatrist had airily answered, "he's well enough today to rake leaves. And it's a nice day. So maybe we should be pleased."

"He used to lecture in economics and political theories at Amherst," Cochrane had seen fit to answer. He felt like hitting the young shrink.

The doctor shrugged. "I know. And today he's well enough to rake leaves." He paused. A little wave seemed to pass over him and a touch of humanity emerged. "Go say hello. Maybe it will help when he sees you."

Bill Cochrane went outside to speak. But his father had said barely anything, failing to recognizing his only son. Or not choosing to. No one knew which.

The problem with psychiatrists, Cochrane concluded, was that they had all been in analysis themselves. That, and the fact that over the course of a decade they had done nothing to help his father. All they had done was preside over the slow inexorable decline of a once vital man into an automaton who, on a good, day, could rake leaves and shuffle around like a zombie in a pharmaceutical haze.

Ten years at the State Nut House, Cochrane ached. And what good had it done? Bill Cochrane would never see his father alive again, if he conceded that he had even been alive that day.

In the airport, the pain returned to Cochrane's soul. It was like a car door slamming on his hand. Repeatedly. He wondered if there was anyone else in the world who felt something similar.

A legion of *maybes* attacked him.

Maybe if he had spent more time at home after his mother's death, maybe if he had earned more money, maybe if he hadn't been so unstable himself . . .

. . . maybe if he had been a better son . . .

. . . maybe *something* could have turned out more favorably for a man he had once idolized.

Maybe.

He wondered. He looked out the window from the airport lounge. Still raining. Long wide streaks of water against the dark glass. It was so black out there that Cochrane couldn't even see the aircraft at his gate. His flight was already an hour late. He wondered if he'd be able to get out that night. He hated flying in and out of Detroit. It always seemed to be this way coming in and going out of this city.

The wind must have shifted because suddenly he was even more aware of the water hitting the glass.

Windows. Windows and doors. Physical and psychic. Sometimes, Bill Cochrane suspected, that's all life revolved around. Passageways from one place to another.

Sometimes he suspected. Other times he knew.

Windows and doors. Tunnels. Flights. Stairs. Up. Down.

Light to dark, then back again.

Conscious to unconscious, then back again.

Waking to sleeping, then back again.

Life to death, then—

No. That was the final trip.

You didn't come back from that one, did you?

And for that matter, where did you go?

He asked himself again, though he knew the answer.

What is your worst fear? Death? No. Something worse than death. Something that had already happened.

What is your worst fear?

A living death.

In the airport, Cochrane spoke the words aloud. "A descent into insanity, like my father."

And he found himself thinking, "I am running away from it and approaching it at the same time. The faster I run, the closer I get. God!"

Bill Cochrane bore the same name. He wondered if he bore the same cross. The same future. The same end.

Already there were signs. Only he knew how unsteady he was. How fragile his emotions were. It wouldn't take much to push him over the brink.

Not much at all. He knew this as a fact.

He had worked as a newspaperman in Springfield, Massachusetts. He had covered local crime and local politics. Sometimes the two intersected. He reported it cheerfully in his newspaper.

One day someone took a shotgun and blew out all the windows in his car. Luckily he wasn't in it at the time. It was meant as a message. The senders had skipped Western Union for something twelve gauge and more direct.

His first nervous breakdown had followed six weeks later, though the hospital had been generous enough to call it "exhaustion." He had resigned thereafter, had gone to California and found another job in journalism.

He had worn his nerves raw there, too, poking into things best left unpoked-into. This time he had been slyer. His father had been in a mental hospital by then and Bill Cochrane rather wished to stay out of one himself. There were plenty of stories he could have run if he wanted to live eternally with the possibility of a gasoline bomb coming through his window some night. So in his thirties, he had learned when to lay off and how to play politics. He had even parlayed the situation into a good political job when the United States Senator from California, Gabriel Lang, had come east and been elected Vice President in the year 2000.

Now it might have seemed all cozy and secure. Good job. Sharp professional profile. Part of the government. The recent write-up done of him in his college alumni magazine was impressive.

But somehow it wasn't cozy and secure.

He knew the truth. Or what he felt was the truth.

He thought of himself as a fraud. A sellout.

Not so much a failure, but as a man who could have done much better. At everything. He had set out to do serious work. Instead, he ran second line press briefings. Deep in his soul he would have begun any autobiography with, "Yes, but . . ."

He could have done better. Could have gone after the big stories. Could have made the big saves. Could have seen the big issues. Could have painted the big pictures.

The symphony that played in his head was one of chaos, self-doubts, and impending fears. And only he knew it. It was as if someone were playing the Beatles' *White Album* backward in his head. And yet it made perfect sense.

Wasn't that how mental collapse began? With self-doubt?

And then there had been the vision of his father's body in the funeral parlor two days earlier.

Down to a hundred ten pounds because the old man wasn't eating. Down to watching cartoons because he wasn't thinking. Down to raking leaves and not recognizing his son because he was walking around but wasn't alive anymore.

Then, mercifully it seemed, one day he just stopped breathing. Living canceled due to lack of interest.

Bill Cochrane, father and son, bore the same name. Did they bear the same cross, share the same eventual fate?

The Big Question. He kept wondering. It wouldn't go away.

What is your worst fear? Death? No. Something worse than death. Something that had already happened.

What is your worst fear?

A living death. A descent into insanity. His father's fate. Hearing voices that weren't there. Seeing people long dead. Feeling forces that didn't exist. Delusion and dementia so stark and tack-sharp that it became a reality.

An inexorable descent into a private insanity. A fate that called Cochrane's name?

"Mr. Cochrane? Mr. Cochrane?"

In the airport, Bill Cochrane opened his eyes.

The short woman with bad skin was in front of him, talking kindly to him. Her airline uniform made her look like a space ranger. Everything in the world was surreal at this hour.

"Sir?" she asked again.

"Sorry," he said. As usual, he kept every emotion hidden far out of everyone's view. "Yes?"

"We've arranged to move you to USAir," she said. "They have a flight to Cincinnati in twenty minutes. You can transfer to D.C. You'll be going around the storms in the area and could be in Washington in a few hours."

"How many is 'a few'?"

She answered without consulting a time chart. "You'd get in around five A.M. at Washington International," she said. "Otherwise, you'd probably need to stay at the airport hotel here overnight."

He sighed. "Thank you," he said. "I'll take it."

She gave him the gate location and he thanked her a second time. He boarded the USAir flight twenty minutes later.

He took a window seat. Within a few minutes, they taxied to a runway. In another few minutes, he was where he wanted to be—within the roar that lifted successfully into the black of the sky.

Then, as the aircraft climbed, he turned his face toward the window and ten years of grief and frustration welled up inside him.

As the plane successfully gained altitude, bucking mildly from the turbulence in the Michigan night, his cheeks were as damp as the windows outside his aircraft, streaked with water as they were.

But no one beyond Bill Cochrane himself noticed. His row was otherwise empty. As usual, Bill Cochrane was on his journey alone.

2

Washington, D.C., is normally a city aswirl with rumors, but rarely more so when the President of the United States lingers between worlds: this one and the next.

On the fifth day of November in the year 2003, almost three years to the day after being elected, George Farley, the seventy-two-year-old President of the United States received a clean bill of health from his physician, Dr. Ivan Katzman.

Farley, Dr. Katzman said, was extraordinarily vigorous for a man of his age, had all his mental capabilities, and all things considered was in one hell of a great shape. The doctor even used those words at an afternoon press conference, informally briefing the media after the President's annual checkup.

The President's health was of no small significance in the first years of the new millennium, for the United States was badly in need of leadership, even the crusty tart-tongued presumptive sort provided by stout gray-haired George Farley.

It was a time when the old political cycles were resurfacing in America. The first years of the Two Thousands were a continuation of the late 1990s, which in turn were a revisiting of the 1930s and 1960s. The rich had grown richer since the 1980s and the poor had descended into deeper ruts of poverty. The American middle class was pressed from both sides, their incomes further enriching the financial elite and their tax money subsidizing the poor. Waves of illegal immigration had pressed everyone into a rotten and unforgiving frame of mind. A third party candidate of the American far right had run for President in 2000. He had finished third behind Farley and the candidate of the other traditional party. But he had won twenty million votes and carried four states.

The arts and media teamed with protest, anarchy, and threatened revolution, which further angered the middle class. Universities were disrupted by protests and civil disobedience. Cities which had undergone renaissances in the 1970s and 1980s now had broken bitter downtowns, centers of commerce having turned into epicenters of crime, drug addiction, and frustration, much of which had spilled to once-safe suburbs. A new wave of bank failures had crested in 2001, but had hit the Northeast particularly hard, destroying housing prices and the job market. And one financial writer for the *Wall Street Journal* had noted that it was hypothetically possible to walk from Washington, D.C., to the Bronx "and never leave the slums."

Hypothetically. No one would have dared to try it. The great fortunes of the day were being made in security systems and self-defense products.

An American looking abroad found little reason for cheer, either. The Economic Community in Europe had collapsed in 1999 owing to matters of agriculture, currency, and general historical distrust by each country of its neighbor. The fighting in the former Yugoslavia was in its thirteenth year. Civil wars in Greece and Turkey were in their second and third years respectively, but these were tiny compared with the potential for civil war in China and almost every country south of Texas.

One day after successfully passing his physical examination, President Farley was in the midst of a meeting with his Secretary of State David Richmond at two-fifteen in the afternoon. This was the sixth day of November.

The President and the Secretary were alone in the Oval Office at the White House, nearing the end of a talk about the continuing agreements to the Camp David accords of 1995. The President's attention seemed to drift from what his Secretary was saying. Instead, he gazed out the window of his office and his eyes—which Secretary Richmond was watching—seemed to settle upon something.

A person perhaps, it seemed, on the south lawn of the White House.

"Who *is* that woman and *why* is she on my lawn?" Farley grumbled.

The President, who had been married for thirty-eight years but didn't really work at it, was prone to such remarks of tourists in what he considered his home and office.

Women—young women in particular—distracted him easily. He missed his days as a Senator when he could make casual seductions from the various secretarial pools around the capital. But then the President suddenly lost his attention for a second time and uttered a phrase which would be remembered for several weeks.

"You know, David," he said to his Secretary of State, "I've got the God-*damned*est *fucking* headache." A moment later, according to Secretary Richmond, the President slowly slumped forward onto his antique desk. His head hit the desk hard and he lost consciousness. So much for the previous day's medical report.

Dr. Katzman was the first medical practitioner on the scene. His immediate analysis was that the President had suffered a massive heart attack. Or a stroke. Or maybe even both at once. The initial symptoms were confusing and contradictory.

The White House press corps was kept at a safe distance while a team of Secret Service agents, suddenly at the point of hyperactivity, rushed the President to the helicopter on the landing pad. The chopper air-evacuated George Farley to Bethesda Naval Hospital, where he would take up residence in a VIP suite at the medical facility's lavish Katherine Duffy Pavilion.

No more than five minutes passed between the moment that President Farley's skull connected with his desk and the moment that the helicopter lifted off. The press had the major part of the story within another two minutes. The broadcast networks and the cable outlets were on the air immediately. The press would never, however, have the full story.

One member of the press corps, Cindy Rowlands of NBC News, always came to work with both a chip on her shoulder and a pair of small green binoculars. The binoculars were purse size in a pink case, Korean with plastic frames so that they'd never set off a metal detector.

Cindy saw the President being loaded on the aircraft on a stretcher. She remarked to the viewing audience—with her enduring penchant for a memorable simile—that his face was "as ashen as a ream of white paper" when he was loaded onto the chopper. Mandy Sullivan of the Associated Press was the first to ask the White House Press spokesman Nathan Thatcher if the President had been breathing when he was placed on the stretcher.

Thatcher, in his usual efforts at doublespeak, said all indications were that, yes, the President had been breathing.

"He either was or he wasn't," said someone at the back of the room. "What do you mean by 'indications'? Can you clarify?"

"He was breathing," Thatcher said.

"Was he breathing with or without assistance?" a UPI woman asked.

"Without," said Thatcher.

"And his heart was beating?" asked Lisa McJeffry of ABC News.

"Yes, it was," Thatcher affirmed.

"That's funny," someone from one of the alternative news services mumbled in the back of the room. "It wasn't beating during his first three years in office."

No one laughed. At least, not audibly.

The President, as the remark indicated, was not universally loved.

Few members of the press corps cared for him. The reporters considered him Reaganesque in a way, a good man at double-talk and with a great Teflon Effect: nothing bad stuck to him. If the scribes could have chosen one noun to describe President Farley, it probably would have been "prick." If they had to choose one adjective, it would have been "tough," although "stubborn" would have drawn some votes. And "devious" would have been given some serious consideration. That the President was a stubborn devious tough prick was common currency among those who covered the White House. But those same journalists would have conceded that those were the very qualities, after all, that it took to bamboozle the public enough to get elected. Those same reporters, however, would also have agreed that, generally speaking, and partisanship aside, the President wasn't doing a bad job.

Not a great job either. But a good job and maybe even a *very* good job. Some of the older members of the press corps recalled that Johnson and Nixon, before getting bogged down in Vietnam and Watergate respectively, hadn't done bad jobs at running the country either. And those two were as personally disagreeable as Farley.

Additionally, only a small segment of the public was enthusiastic about him. Most Americans tolerated him and conceded that since unemployment was low and the country wasn't at war, Farley was as good as anyone. These days, in an age of hypernegativism, that was as ringing an endorsement as any politician received: He's as good as anyone.

Farley had won the nomination of his party not because he was the most popular figure in his party, but because he had paid his party dues for several decades. Once elected, the more liberal press, recalling Washington and Bush before Farley, dubbed him George the Third. When he fell ill, the metaphor seemed particularly apt.

The "Illness of George The Third." That's what the pundits inside the Beltway were calling it. With an ironic snicker.

Farley was, in fact, a seigneurial figure in American politics—though in private he was a cranky, cantankerous man, given to savage sarcasm, cruel humor, and unending, inventive profanity. His foreign policy was clear and conservative. It frequently resulted in triumph following diplomatic gambits. Yet his smile sometimes made him look as if he had just evicted a widow. When he had been younger, as a real estate lawyer in the Midwest, he *had* evicted several widows—a less-than-flattering personal history upon which his opponents had failed to cash in for years.

Thinking back on his career in real estate law, however, the only thing that had made Farley feel bad was that he hadn't been able to evict those widows as quickly as he might have liked, as there had been financial bonuses in it for him. At least that was how he liked to joke about it. The *New York Post* had once reported that Farley had quipped, "I would have evicted their deadbeat husbands, too, but the simple pine coffins weren't in the God-damned living rooms anymore." But the President always denied that line and hoped that no one ever could produce a recording of him saying it.

At Bethesda on November sixth, President Farley lapsed into a brief coma, slipping into out of it within a matter of a quarter hour. His wife broke away from a trip to a women's club of white suburbanites in New Jersey to fly back to the capital. Then, just as the nation was about to get a civics lesson on the Twenty-fifth Amendment to the Constitution—which allows the Vice President to assume the Presidency if the President is temporarily incapacitated—Farley emerged from his coma.

"I want all my work brought to this fucking hospital," was the first thing he said, surly and self-assured as ever. "What the hell day is this?"

When an aide balked, Farley fired her. The next aide didn't balk. The President's work was brought to Bethesda, as was a steady stream of visitors. A great effort was made to make a public display of a busy, healthy President, even though Farley's energy was low, doctors warned of a relapse, and the IV pole was carefully concealed from cameras. Farley's consciousness would come and go without warning, a tidbit of information carefully kept from the public. And a first-rate medical team had been unable to discern what was wrong with him.

And then there was the matter of Gabriel Lang, the Vice President. An extra Secret Service guard formed around Lang upon the President's collapse.

Lang, the former United States Senator from California, was in an unfortunate position in being the Vice President. It was a role he had never particularly coveted. Lang had coveted the top job—the Presidency—even less. Yet in the general election he had agreed to run. It was almost as if—in a flight of personal whimsy—he had come along for the political hayride.

"I never said I *wanted* to be President," he had frequently told reporters. "I only said I was *willing* to be President."

The Vice President was twenty-three years younger than the President and had been talked into taking a place on the national ticket for a variety of reasons, none of them having to do with his qualifications for high elective office. On this issue, Candidate Farley of Nebraska had been more than frank to party members at the convention.

"There are a lot of people who are well qualified to be President," Farley had told them as he prepared for a tough election. "And Gabriel Lang is not one of them." He paused. "But Gabriel Lang can carry California for us, which greatly enhances his qualifications for the job."

Among the delegates, among the faithful party workers, this passed for unusual candor, even amid the gasps. But there was as much truth in the remark as there was cynicism. Keeping California from the opposing party was a way of winning the White House. California's block of forty-five electoral college votes was immense, representing a swing of ninety votes. The mathematical realties of this were even more crucial in the three-way race that the Farley-Lang ticket had won.

And Lang brought a certain youth and freshness to the national ticket, even in an off-beat way. The freshness and unpredictability of Lang served as a counterpoint to the Waspy dourness of Farley. He was also visibly younger, angularly featured, and with thick brown hair. Again, they complemented each other, though never did they compliment each other.

When Lang had announced in 1992 that he was divorcing his first wife, Farley, then also a U.S. Senator, commented, "It's no wonder. The poor woman is probably tired of John Tesh concerts as a substitute for sex." And when Farley won the party's nomination, Lang cited the victory as "democracy in action." The remark was not meant as an accolade.

Farley had never cared much for Lang. And Lang had never cared much for Farley. A dislike of each other was the only subject they had ever agreed upon until they ran together on a national ticket. It was a marriage made not in Heaven but in an old-fashioned political back room. The Washington press corps also reveled in keeping the antagonisms at a brisk boil.

Lang had always been quirky, a Baptist by birth who had dabbled in Zen Buddhism as a young adult. He looked young. Pushing fifty, he was trim and his hair hadn't yet begun to gray. He had been married, and was now divorced, and many women thought him sexy, which he was.

Sort of.

In public, he seemed cool but in person he was often as jittery as a dozen scared cats. And he took great pains to play a now-you-see-me-now-you-don't charade with the press and the electorate. He never seemed to want to let anyone know him too well.

Some things were clear: Gabe Lang had been born in Minnesota, the son of teachers, raised in Southern California and educated at a name-brand private secondary school in the East. He had earned a Harvard diploma in 1971. His parents had urged him to study finance and instead he had studied Eastern religions.

Vietnam? Like most middle-class white boys of his generation, he had missed the experience—suspiciously some said. He had been 4F. The doctors of his draft board said he had a bad knee, which was at the time commonly known as the Joe Namath exemption, though Lang hadn't played pro football with his 4F gimpy knee. He had instead played touch football on the lawns of Charlottesville, Virginia, while he eased casually through the University of Virginia School of Law with a genteel B average.

"Gabriel Lang is a mixed bag of inconsistent neoconservative, neoliberal claptrap, New Age half-witticisms, and a bad sinus condition," wrote one *Chicago Tribune* columnist on the subject of the Vice President. The remark about the sinus condition reflected upon Lang's occasionally squeaky voice, which another commentator once called similar to a "recalcitrant garden gate shifting in a breeze." Millions of Americans didn't see that as too far from the truth, even people who didn't have recalcitrant garden gates, or even gardens at all.

Sometimes intentionally, sometimes inadvertently, Lang went to great lengths to sabotage a consistent public image. He was given sometimes to shocking flights of demagoguery in left-wing ideology, the occasional remark that could be construed as anti-Semitic, and as a divorcee, was frequently spotted around Washington after dark with secretaries half his age.

"It's well known: He picks them up at the local Chuck E. Cheese," another Senate colleague once said. Yet just when people thought they had him pegged as a "new-style liberal," he would take a conservative, almost austere position on some public issue, sometimes even to the right of the President, and outflank everyone. His biggest political asset was being different and unpredictable. Some people loved him for it. Being different and unpredictable was also his greatest liability. Other people hated him for it.

And then there was the "Mercury in retro" remark.

Once a major piece of labor legislation went down the tubes in the Senate. On the same day, a trade treaty with Canada fell apart at the eleventh hour. In an impromptu discussion with a half-dozen reporters at The Four Seasons bar in Washington, Lang explained the dual failures of both.

"The planet Mercury is in retrograde this month," said the Vice President of the United States.

Reporters pulled out their pads and their recorders. But Lang did not shy away.

"What?" asked Lisa McJeffry of CBS News, America's loveliest and leggiest White House correspondent.

"Mercury is in retrograde," Lang explained. "When Mercury is withdrawing from the earth's gravitational pull, it's a bad time to try to complete any negotiations or treaties. Nothing will be accomplished. Have to wait an extra month. An extra month."

"When would be a better time for such negotiations?" Lisa pressed.

Lang shrugged and responded as if the answer were easy. A slam dunk.

"Obviously, Lisa," he said, "when Mercury starts to move toward the earth again. Toward earth again." For emphasis, Lang loved to repeat himself, which only made him sound flakier.

Lang's remarks appeared in most daily papers and were repeated on the broadcast and cable networks the next day. And yet the remarks of this caliber never seemed to hurt Lang politically. Among his hardcore constituents, such ramblings only seemed to turn the public on. And then, sure enough, when Mercury did start to approach the earth again in late summer, all of the pending legislation that had been stalled eventually did pass.

"See?" Lang then asked the press. "See?"

Later that same year, the first for Lang as Vice President, the public learned that Lang had given fruitcake at Christmas to a number of friends.

One former Democratic President commented that the gift was "perfectly appropriate and predictable, coming from Gabriel Lang." The former President then earned more bad press than Lang ever had for any of his comments.

And then there was the comment that President Farley himself made about Lang.

"If anything ever happens to me, in terms of health," Farley once said at a convocation of party members, "the Secret Service is under very, very specific orders. They are to shoot Gabriel Lang immediately."

The remark eventually leaked to the public via *The Village Voice* in New York, and President Farley saw fit to send his Vice President a note of apology. The note alternated from sentence to sentence between subservience and flat-out insincerity. The note, and the remark that prompted it, only exacerbated the feelings between the two men. Lang then gave the note, as a historical document, to Greenpeace to have it auctioned during a Save the Seals fund raiser.

The remark also found new play in the press when Farley took ill. Farley would be damned, he said, if he would relinquish his office to a "political lightweight" for whom he held "so little" respect.

"Actually," Farley told some of the senior members of the Washington press corps. "I shouldn't say 'so little.' I have *no* respect for Gabe Lang."

Conversely, Lang looked with increasing interest upon invoking the Twenty-fifth Amendment just to tweak his boss and show he was now up to the job. The Presidency also would offer him a pulpit for his New Age mysticism as well as strike terror into the stock market.

And so it went in the third autumn of the first term of America's Forty-third President. A situation of total lack of predictability with the new millennium beginning with—in light of the President's sudden and inexplicable medical situation—not one person in the nation having any clue as to who would be leading the country within the next two days.

After all, some of the most talented medical experts in Washington had beaten a trail to Bethesda to examine the President's charts. And not one among them had any clear picture or explanation for what was wrong with him. The President would slip in and out of light comas almost at random times. He'd be lucid one moment, unconsciousness the next. These little absences would last anywhere from five minutes to five hours. And the men who surrounded the President closely guarded the truth of his condition from the public, though various stories managed to leak out of the Duffy Pavilion.

"This is a situation," remarked political commentator Helen Boners on *The NBC Morning News* two days after the President's initial hospitalization, "that could go on forever. But can't be allowed to."

"At what point *should* we notify the Vice President and at what point *should* we invoke the Twenty-fifth Amendment?" asked Secretary of State David Richmond, number two in the line of succession.

"I'll tell you when you can fucking invoke it, David!" President Farley roared during one of his lucid moments. "You can fucking invoke the fucking Twenty-fifth and make Gabe Lang leader of the Western world when my vital signs are gone, when they shove cotton up my ass, and when they roll me out of here on a gurney!"

The Secretary of State was duly chastised. And most of the President's advisors, knowing that they would be gone in an instant in a Lang Presidency, concurred with the President. No news about the comas would be confirmed.

And so it went, late in the year 2003. The executive branch of the government of the United States had never been bigger or costlier to the millions of taxpayers who were tired of paying for it. Never had some efficiency in government been more sorely needed.

And never, owing to the President's potential for incapacity and the Vice President's potential for fruitiness, had it teetered so closely to nonexistence.

One such taxpayer was a transplanted New Yorker named Carl Einhorn, currently a resident of a quiet Atlanta suburb which, in previous generations had won notoriety, if not fame, for the breadth of its Ku Klux Klan rallies.

Einhorn was a mathematician by trade, a short, stocky ferret-faced man of forty-five who had taught in the public school systems of New York City and Atlanta for a combined twenty-four years, before being fired from each.

Carl Einhorn had always known his numbers, from Pythagoras to Mandelbrot. Born in the Bronx not far from the Grand Concourse, he had graduated from the Bronx High School of Science at sixteen and had his bachelor's degree in math from City College of New York at nineteen. During those same teens, his whole world continued to be numbers.

He never went out on a single date, rarely went to a movie, never saw any theater, hated rock and roll and most other music, didn't follow sports, and didn't own a television. Having little else to do, and working on patterns of maladjustment that would last a lifetime, he obtained his doctorate from the State University of New York at Stony Brook by the day he turned twenty-one. Not surprisingly, his doctoral thesis had a quirkiness to it: *Mirror Asymmetry in Time Reversed Worlds.*

College years—including the postgraduate ones—for Einhorn had not been a time to hone his social skills, for by that time he had none to hone. Nor were the times of his first teaching jobs. Interpersonal relations were a lifelong disaster. The better he got to know someone, the more difficulty he had relating. As a graduate student, he taught one course called *Indiscreet Quantities and the Patterns of Chaos* and another called *Chaos Theory and the Science of Wholeness.* In the latter course, he was eventually relieved of his instructor's duties, however, when he gave all five of his students an F, and all five had taken their protest to the dean.

Numbers never betrayed him, but people frequently did. Numbers couldn't lie or be inconsistent. People could. Equations couldn't hurt him, but on the average Carl Einhorn got mugged once a year by another member of the human race. There was truth, orderliness, and predictability in mathematical calculations and none in society. Which didn't mean he didn't have a few other interests.

He loved to read computer magazines, for example, and he was eventually able to design some fairly advanced software that other math teachers found superior to the material on the market. The only other stuff he liked to read was Nietzsche, Kant, and Ayn Rand. He also read the comic *Doonesbury* from time to time, and was fascinated by it because he couldn't figure out what it was making fun of.

He had never dated in either high school or college. Once when he was twenty-two, and one other time when he was thirty, he had gone to prostitutes. He had managed to have sex successfully—sort of—but he had found the experiences humiliating. Aside from those two incidents, Einhorn had never had any partner other than himself. Sex was just one of many things that would inevitably be wrecked by the involvement of another person.

In his home in Georgia, a one-bedroom apartment a few blocks away from a major league Civil War monument, he lived quietly. He had no close friends. When he wanted to express an opinion, he'd send a letter. Sometimes, in a frenzy he would send letters he didn't even remember writing. Most of the times, he would write to a newspaper. The majority of his letters were heavily sarcastic and too strident to be printed.

But when a newspaper didn't print his opinions, Carl Einhorn would stop buying that paper and read it instead at the library, thus depriving the publication of the extra unit of circulation. Letters were his way of fighting back at the outside world. He sent them in every direction, remembering carefully which ones to sign, which ones to leave—ominously—unsigned, and which ones to close with a sly pseudonym.

The mail was one dandy weapon. One good unsigned piece of paper could accomplish more—get under someone's skin better, in other words—than fifty polite phone calls.

He also had a terrible temper, which usually was provoked when he became frustrated. Any time that an orderly logical process of events was thwarted by human beings, Einhorn could quickly find himself in a rage.

Such frustrations were common—if not the norm—in public school administration. Hence his temper frequently led to fiery profane arguments with coworkers, students, and administrators. This tendency grew worse as Einhorn hit his thirties.

Hence, his firing in New York in 1987, when he shoved the vice superintendent of the city board of education, whom he considered his academic inferior. He hadn't been. His final personnel records in New York included the phrase, "might consider seeking psychiatric counseling." Two former students, both of whom were from Haiti, claimed the man was "a demon," and their observations actually landed in his personnel file, too. But there was never any follow-up, either to the psychiatric counseling or the casually alleged demonology.

Hence, another firing in Atlanta in November of the year 2000 when he slapped a female coworker on her breasts. At a hearing, he claimed she had been belittling him. Witnesses testified that she hadn't been. In truth, what had really bothered him in the latter incident was the fact that the woman reminded him of the second whore he had been with. She had belittled him, too.

Carl Einhorn's apartment was sparsely furnished, obsessively clean and fastidiously neat. In his bedroom closet, for example, his six pairs of shoes were lined up against each other, pair by pair, neatly shined, heels together in perfect order. He bought a suit every three years and his four current suits hung on the left side of the same closet, from left to right, according to age, the newest suit being in the middle where it would be a shorter distance for him to reach.

In the middle of the same closet hung a dozen white shirts and six light blue ones. There also were four short-sleeved blue shirts for the summer as well as four white ones. These hung on the far right. Next to them were eight different pairs of slacks. It bothered him when there was an odd number of anything in the closet. If he were to wear something during the day, he laundered it at night, pressed it, and put it back before retiring. He could not bear to face the new day with an odd number of things hanging.

Four suits. Twenty-six shirts and six pairs of pants.

Einhorn loved that arrangement. Four times twenty-six times six equaled six hundred twenty-four.

Six twenty-four.

He had been born on June twenty-fourth, so there was a meaningful personal geometry to that number. He also liked numbers like 624 which formed their own equation:

$$6 - 2 = 4, \text{ or}$$
$$6 = 2 + 4$$

Einhorn liked it when the daily details of living revealed little concrete truths like that. He also loved it when sixes went wild. Six was his favorite number. He once went out to eat at an expensive joint called The Top of the Sixes in New York City just to get six of their matchbooks.

There was another shirt that he owned. This one was pale yellow. His mother had purchased it at Macy's in Garden City four years earlier and had mailed it to him. He had never worn it but had lied—lied to his mother!—and said he had. The yellow shirt was alone on the top shelf of his closet, the only object occupying that space.

In the back of the closet was a stack of pornographic magazines. On top of the magazines was a gun. These were his two vices. When he took out his collection of skin mags, which he did every evening, he liked to take out the gun, also. He always kept it loaded. When he amused himself with his porn, he liked to keep the weapon close by.

He swore that if anyone ever broke in on him and caught him while he had his pornography out, he would shoot him. Or her.

This was no idle fear. When he was eighteen, which was also divisible by six, his mother had walked into his room unannounced and caught him whacking off over a Maidenform bra advertisement. Whenever he ran through the scenario of someone catching him with his filth, the intruder was always a woman. That was just the way his mind worked. To Carl Einhorn, this fantasy was as logical as anything else.

His spat with the local power company bore a similar logic. He was convinced that he was being overcharged by greedy bureaucrats who had fixed his rates. So Einhorn bought candles by the bulk in a local building supply depot and used them instead of electricity for lighting. Like depriving the newspaper publishers of their extra three dollars per week, he felt he had nicked the avaricious bastards who supplied electricity for their extra forty bucks a month. He calculated that he spent twenty-five dollars per month on candles, so was ahead by a hundred and eighty dollars per year.

So much the better.

So much the greater was his victory. And one hundred eighty was also neatly divisible by six squared.

Sometime in the late 1990s, Einhorn also developed an interest in the powers and possibilities of the mind. He began reading treatises on hypnotism and mental powers. He began playing memory games. He considered himself to have a rare and magnificent intellect, so he wondered what the limits might be to his own brain power.

He heard that there had been a book named *Carrie* about a girl who could do things like start fires, close doors, and kill people through the power of her mind. Telepathy, the skill was called. He found a copy of the book at the library and read it. He knew the book was fiction and that the story had been invented by the writer. So aside from its interesting premise, the book was not to be taken seriously.

But he wondered if such a thing were possible. If telepathy were possible, he theorized, the skill would be limited to certain people with majestic but concrete minds. It would be limited to men—definitely only *men*—he reasoned, because women were not as gifted in the mental skills that mattered. So the book *Carrie* was inaccurate on that point, too.

As the months passed in the late 1990s, Einhorn became more reclusive. Then when he no longer had classes to teach, he had little reason to associate with most people. That served him just fine and kept him out of fights. He had a small pension from the New York

City school system—part of the terms of his dismissal—and had a monthly income from some savings. And he picked up a few hundred dollars a month via the local computer store which sold his software.

His isolation helped him come to certain conclusions. First, he figured, the candlelight in his apartment helped him think. The light reacted better with his brain and let him focus more readily on whatever he was doing. He now got his pornography out only by candlelight each night, for example, and was enjoying that experience more than ever. And second, after several months of searching for things to try to do with his telepathy experiments, he hit upon just the challenge.

Why not, he asked himself, start right up there at the top?

Why not, he asked himself, see if he could manipulate the health of the American President?

He had never liked George Farley much. The man didn't seem to be very logical or mathematical. Who cared about him? And so on the sixth of November, Carl Einhorn had himself a little ceremony in his own apartment.

He lit every candle in the place and used them to create a mini-Stonehenge arrangement in the middle of his living room floor.

He sat at the middle of the circle, facing Washington, lotus position, with his hands at his knees, palms outstretched and unfolded.

His pistol was in front of him, in case anyone smashed past the three locks on his apartment door and walked in on him. All six cylinders were loaded.

He closed his eyes and concentrated on the President's health. He spent about an hour on this. He threw his thoughts so hard in the direction of Washington that he broke a sweat. Tears flowed from his eyes.

Then, when some of the candles began to flicker down and burn out, he brought his event to a close. But not before putting out two of the candles just by staring at them real hard.

That evening at eleven o'clock he turned on the radio and heard that the President had been inexplicably hospitalized suddenly that afternoon. No one, the commentator said, knew exactly what was wrong. All that was known was that the President had collapsed, had been taken to the hospital, and was apparently resting comfortably.

Carl Einhorn let out a whoop of joy. He danced around his room with the prissy clumsiness of a pudgy middle-aged man. This type of power was the type of thing that few people could ever imagine! And he had finally—*finally!*—isolated a potent quality that made him different from all other people in the world.

God damn it! he raged to himself. He had always *known* that he was special! This damned well proved it!

A line of an advertising jingle from his youth flashed before him.

Awake! Come alive!
You're in the Pepsi generation!

Little neo-epiphanies frequently jumped into the forefront of his mind like that. Little truths for the ages, courtesy of Madison Avenue, all of them floating aimlessly through his head like little video billboards. Occasionally his mind's eye would settle upon one on another.

Here came a second:

Luckies taste better!
Cleaner, Fresher, Smoother!

Sometimes he would even chirp these aloud, either to himself or to whomever he was speaking at the time.

There was Willie the Penguin, for example. The nicotine-addled Kool Cigarette bird. Probably dead of cancer by now, himself, if a Polar Bear hadn't eaten him. But who the fuck cared, Carl Einhorn raged.

Come up,
Come UP,
Come all the way UP
To Kool!

Carl Einhorn tucked his loaded gun in his belt, carefully wore a long coat so the weapon would elude detection, and drove to the Varsity in Atlanta for a late-night orgy of chili dogs, onion rings, ice cream, and orange freezes. He came home again shortly after midnight, got out his collection of stroke books, and—amid another array of candles—had a fantasy orgy with the most beautiful women therein.

What kind of man reads *Playboy?*

The type of man who can manipulate the President's health with the powers of his mind! That's who!

When he went to bed at 4 A.M., he was very content with himself. His life had finally taken on a clear direction. From here on, he would manipulate George Farley's health at will.

There would be no stopping him now. It was all very clear and immensely logical.

3

For Bill Cochrane, the youngest and longest suffering of the four press attachés employed by Vice President Gabriel Lang, the first week of November marked the end of one part of his life and the beginning of another.

His home was a modern town house in Alexandria, Virginia, and it had in the last few days been pulled apart physically and emotionally. Not only had his father died, but so had his two-year relationship with a well-known woman in Washington. Their affair had been coming apart at the seams for several months. In the final weeks of October, it had unraveled completely and she had taken her cue to leave.

Under other circumstances, it might have been he who had left. Their mutual home had not been the place of passion and romanticism that it had once been. But his name was on the lease, so she—Lisa McJeffry, the rising young reporter for ABC News—had been the one to pack up things and leave.

Not that there was a lot to move. Clothing. A few small pieces of furniture, antiques that Lisa had brought with her from Philadelphia. A couple of artworks that she and Bill had acquired together but which meant more to her than to him.

Nonetheless, she also took with her a piece of his heart. In her absence, he felt as if he had been hit with a tiny cardiac arrest, the type where the one afflicted part of the heart is never the same again. So it was with Lisa's absence.

She was doing well. Maybe too well for the health of their relationship. When she had moved in with Bill two years earlier—actually, twenty-two months, nineteen days ago, to be exact, he had figured in an odd moment—Lisa McJeffry had been a fresh transfer from Philadelphia to Washington. She had done on-air at WPVI in Philadelphia and, then at age twenty-nine, with a degree in cinema from UCLA, always had a bit of aspiring show biz about her.

But she had also been tall and blond—still was, in fact—a striking, pretty five-ten, taller in heels if she cared to be. She was the type of woman who turned heads when she came into a room. The geniuses at network programming gave her a few shots in Washington and she was an immediate success.

She was assigned to cover Congress for ABC. Then the network bigshots moved her to the White House. Good ratings and good work followed wherever she went. So she stayed on the White House beat, the most conspicuous ABC reporter there since the artfully obnoxious Sam Donaldson, but much easier on the eye—if not the ear—than Donaldson. She had MTV looks and a CNN head. That gave her a job at ABC.

The backbiters said that she would never have been anywhere without her dazzling looks. But that was to confuse the issue. Her looks got her noticed; her brains got her the rest of the way. Like her other namesake on television, Lisa Simpson, she was the smartest person on any scene.

Lisa McJeffry and Bill Cochrane had first noticed each other at one of those 6 P.M. political cocktail parties for which Washington was so notorious. The type where everyone arrives on time or slightly early, then leaves en masse to catch the dinner party at seven-thirty with all the same players. Then Bill and Lisa had formally met at a function at the Smithsonian for the Paraguayan ambassador. Bill had chatted her up, made her laugh, and told some irreverent stories about newspaper work and his duties for the Vice President. She had listened "off the record" and hadn't minded.

There was a physical chemistry that clicked between them, more than any philosophical thing. They both knew that right from the start. She was vaguely left leaning, but surprisingly apolitical for a woman in the capital. His politics were somewhere in the middle of the American spectrum, an attribute which enabled him to work for almost anyone.

Even Gabe Lang.

Nor did their personalities particularly match. He was even-tempered and patient. When angry, he would simmer and control it. Her moods were mercurial, her patience usually frayed, and her off-screen propensity for shouting had the potential to become a Washington legend. Earlier in her career, in electronic journalism at WPVI in Philadelphia, she'd gone off half-cocked a couple of times, filing stories that had more anger than substance. It had nearly sunk her career. Now she held those instincts in check. "Older," at thirty, she was also wiser.

But her directness was already the stuff of legends. Of this, Cochrane knew firsthand. He'd been chatting her up the second time they had seen each other, which was five days after that first party at the Smithsonian.

He had been beating around the bush about asking her out. She liked him. But she knew he was intimidated as many men were by her smart good looks.

"Listen," she finally said. "I like you. You like me. Let's just go back to my place and get in bed."

He blinked. "You never even asked me if I was married or not," he said.

"I said 'my place,' didn't I? So it wouldn't have mattered much, would it?"

"You move fast, don't you?"

"I try to."

He was still assessing, trying to comprehend his good luck. Cochrane was six feet tall, trim and not bad looking. But it wasn't every day that he might leave a party with the most attractive woman in the room.

"Not interested?" she asked.

"Very interested," he'd finally said. "Can I get you your coat?"

"Hate coats. Don't have one," she said. "Coats only slow you down when you want to get somewhere else."

"Like in bed with someone you just met?"

"That's an example of what I mean, yes." She smiled. Oh, what a smile.

They went back to her place and she opened a bottle of champagne that she kept in her refrigerator for just such purposes.

"Sometimes," she announced to him, setting a tone, as she sat down on the sofa in her living room, "I just enjoy forgetting about everything and fucking like an alley cat."

"No objection," Bill Cochrane answered.

Then the physical chemistry kicked in between them. Fortunately this was a Friday, because neither would have been much good at work the next day. They swapped the best sex either had ever had.

Both of them. Best ever.

She had moved in with him four weeks later and—Washington being Washington—they both had the good sense not to tell any of their friends, lest idle tongues wag and lest there be accusations of conflict of influence. He was on the Vice President's staff, after all, and she was a reporter. Then they had had seven wonderful months of one-on-one debauchery. After that, perhaps inevitably, things began to cool. It was about this time, too, that the network powers started to advance Lisa on the media food chain.

And then there were the career comparisons. She had moved quickly since coming to Washington. He had stayed in one place. He gave out controlled pieces of news. She liked to dig stuff up. He liked a carefully controlled situation. She loved chaos, particularly if she could help cause it. He liked a neat orderly story. She loved grease and dirt.

Much to his disadvantage, he also liked to need her. She liked to be independent. Finally, the relationship proved to be a curse to her. It created tensions for her at work and further tensions when she came home. She knew how she could end it. It would be brutal, but it would work.

She had a quick, spontaneous, and widely known affair with a member of the cabinet, a man twenty years her senior who was known for charming and bedding—completely without emotion or attachment—some of the best-looking women in Washington.

The affair, and the cuckolding nature of it, torpedoed whatever was left of the domestic relationship between Bill Cochrane and Lisa Mc-Jeffry. So out she moved, first into a hotel, then quickly into a vacant condo at the Watergate complex. The crashing and burning of their relationship left him hurt, wounded, and overworked. It left him as a thirty-seven-year-old man "on the edge," his career not exactly where he wanted it and his personal life nowhere near its original objectives, either.

But it had left Lisa farther on the way up the Washington and network ladder.

"Headed for even bigger things," it was said of her. And meanwhile, he still did press handouts. Occasionally, he knew, there would be times when he would be giving them to her. He would keep his eyes straight ahead, he told himself, and ignore the fact that everyone in the press room knew the situation. Washington loved a good rumor, particularly if it involved fornication. And "headed for bigger things," was also a barb in his direction. Meaning, she could do better than a fourth string press attaché for the flaky Vice President. Lisa was cabinet level, if not Presidential level. It was written all over her. She was a lethal combination of brains and female sexuality, meaning there was nowhere in official Washington where she couldn't go—one way or another.

All of this brought things to a sullen November seventh. Cochrane was alone in the home he had shared with Lisa. He was still missing her presence and even noticing the empty spots in various rooms, from where she had taken certain furnishings.

This particular evening, he was consoling himself with sipping some coffee and toying with some oil paints. He was an amateur painter whose ambitions—as they frequently did—overreached his abilities. But still he tried, mixing colors passionately, studying composition ardently and putting image to canvas with relentless dedication.

He had created a small studio for himself on the top floor of his town house, an airy sunlit loft area that other men might have used as a study or a computer room. The east wall was covered with cork and the cork was covered with photographs. Therein an irony. Captured in photograph was the same likeness that had just departed the house.

Lisa.

On an easel sat a half-finished portrait, one of the woman who had just left him. Periodically he studied it, wondering what to do with it, not entirely wanting to finish it, not yet ready to scrap it, yet not willing either to set it aside and take up another subject.

What to do? He was clueless.

He sipped coffee and hoped inspiration would come from somewhere.

It didn't. And he was still in his studio when the telephone rang at a few minutes after 7 P.M.

Cochrane looked at the phone in his studio and did not immediately pick up.

He had worked a double shift the previous day trying to keep the Vice President out of trouble on a remark he had made about legally documented domestic workers not really deserving to be eligible for Social Security. The day's work had culminated in a nighttime television appearance and the associated paperwork in issuing press releases. It had kept him on-duty until 3 A.M. and had earned him a midweek day off, his first day off of any sort in two weeks. He wished that he had had an option key on his laptop which, when punched, would begin with the phrase, "What the Vice President MEANT was . . ."

Cochrane wasn't due at his office until eight the next morning. So when the phone rang, he growled. He was within his rights to be catching up on some sleep or tending to a few items of personal administration: paying a few bills or writing short letters to friends who lived out West. He considered letting his answering machine do the dirty work. But deep down, owing to a perverse dedication to his job, he felt that answering machines were cowardly. So on the fourth ring, he grabbed the phone.

"Bill Cochrane," he mumbled into the handset. His voice was striking in its lack of enthusiasm. He hoped the caller was a friend, a female acquaintance preferably, desiring his company for dinner. A single man could always hope.

Cochrane's own voice also echoed in his ear. These were the first words he had spoken since waking from an uncharacteristic afternoon snooze two hours earlier and—to his own thinking—his pipes sounded rusty. Almost creaking and elderly for a relatively young man of thirty-seven.

So he cleared his throat immediately after speaking and said his name more forcefully a second time. Then he listened.

The call genuinely surprised him.

It did not come from anyone with whom he worked—there were the four press spokesmen with the Vice President, two men and two women, plus an ever-changing number of administrative aides—and he was the least senior of the four attachés. And unhappily, the call was not from a female friend seeking companionship for the evening.

Rather, this call came directly from the Vice President, circumventing the usual protocol. Cochrane was mildly shaken to receive it since the Vice President—Captain Quirk, as Beltway insiders called him—was in everyone's thoughts. For a private, guarded man, the Vice President was about to lose what was left of his privacy.

"I was wondering, William," Vice President Lang said. "Can you stop over here right away?" It was not so much a request as a command. The Vice President was just one brain clot, one aneurysm, away from becoming President.

"Of course," Cochrane fumbled. "What's going on?"

"I'm at home," Lang said, continuing but not really answering. "How soon could you be here?"

Home did not mean the Vice Presidential Mansion near Rock Creek Park. Home meant the cluttered, rambling Federal-style town house that Gabe Lang kept over in Georgetown.

Lang gave Cochrane a respectful hesitation in response. The hesitation told Cochrane that sooner would be better than later.

"The thing is, William," Lang said, "I want you to see before anybody comes by and changes things. See, something is happening here. I mean, it will wait but it won't wait. But you'll need to see it."

The only further elaboration Lang made was to indicate that there was some sort of special assignment available that might take Cochrane out of Washington. Such missions could go in almost any direction, comprise almost any assignment, and could be either Heaven or Hell. But to Cochrane, who had flirted with resignation recently and had had about enough of the capital, any such talk had its allure.

"I'll leave the proper pass with the Secret Service," Lang said. "They're all over me, you know. On me like a cheap suit. Couldn't even go to the damned outhouse without them. But they'll let you in. You know where the entrance is, so don't worry."

"I'll be there in half an hour," Cochrane said. He put down the telephone and muttered to himself.

Cochrane rubbed his tired eyes.

If it hadn't been this call from Lang, there would have been something else. There was never a moment's peace in this world for a conscientious press attaché, never a time when a man could grab a few minutes to himself in the evening and enjoy it without interruption.

Cochrane found a piece of take-out lasagna from two days previously. He placed it in his microwave for a minute to put some fire— or at least some heat—back into it.

He dined standing up, gathering his briefcase as he intermittently ate the warmed-over pasta and quaffed a diet soda. When he finished, he threw the soda can into a recycling bag and shoved the plate into the dishwasher, where it would keep company with the utensils of the previous two days. He fed some soap into the washer, and turned it on. It splashed and gurgled to life.

Then the telephone rang again. Cochrane had hit his personal daily double. It was the Vice President for a second time.

"It's an *occult* threat to our nation, you know," Lang said, starting off the call. "This threat to Farley. It's actually a threat to *me*, too, as well as the whole damned country."

Cochrane blinked. "Excuse me," he said.

"An occult threat," the Vice President said. "Don't you know what that means? It's coming from another world."

"Another world?"

"That's my feeling," said the Vice President of the United States.

Cochrane drew a long breath and took the measure both of the moment and his employer. He was so sick of this type of nonsense. What sort of blithering idiot had he agreed to work for, he asked himself for the hundredth time in the last hundred days. He had come to Washington to take part in the government, hope to see some serious work, maybe even a little piece of history up close . . . And now?

Not to mention the crazy wacko factor. It was not enough that Cochrane had been helpless to assist his father in a descent into lunacy. Now, the irony of ironies, he worked for someone who had a scrambled head and the entire country thought it was some sort of joke.

"I'm afraid I've never been much of a fan of that stuff," Cochrane answered. "The occult. If that's what you're calling it."

Cochrane heard the Vice President sigh.

"I really don't give it much credibility," Cochrane continued. "Though I know it does have its"—the press attaché chose his wording delicately here—"proponents," he said.

"Yes. Of course, William," Lang said, his tone turning slightly playful. "You're one of the fifty million loyal Americans who think I'm a flake. Or nuts. Secretly or not so secretly. Well, so be it. But the big difference between you and the other fifty million is that you work for me."

"I haven't forgotten."

"So. Well, then. On your way over," said Gabriel Lang, hardly acknowledging that their first conversation had ever ended, "buy a deck of fresh playing cards."

"*Playing* cards?" Cochrane asked.

"Don't open them. Just bring them, okay? I'm going to show you that there's nothing to laugh at here, nothing to make light of."

"I'm hearing this right?" asked Cochrane.

"Get a full deck," the Vice President said.

Cochrane was about to ask what other kind of deck might be for sale. But he skipped the question, fearing the response.

He dressed for his meeting. Just before leaving his home, he studied himself in a mirror. There were still lines beneath his eyes, but they were more from fatigue today than sadness. The pain of his father's death, or at least the pain from the shock, had receded just a little. He was glad.

Moments later, he was downstairs in his garage. He nodded a hello to Mr. Trahn, the quiet overqualified—Trahn had a university degree in engineering from Saigon, it was said—superintendent of the co-ops.

Cochrane got into his car, turned over the ignition, and the engine sprang to life.

A quarter hour later, Cochrane was in his car heading north from Virginia into the capital. The night was clear and within a few minutes the distant landmarks of the city came into view. Washington Monument. Jefferson Memorial. The White House. The floodlit white dome of the Capitol. Many windows were bright. The government was working late.

There was something that used to thrill him about this scene, its conjuring of raw power blended with noble democratic ideals. It had been just such a sense of excitement that had caused him to leave his newspaper career to come to Washington. But much of that excitement had turned to disillusionment over the previous years, working first for a Senator, then for the Vice President. Cochrane was frequently reminded of another friend of his who had worked as a sportswriter and had brought to his job a lifelong love for baseball.

The friend had brought the affection to the job, all right, but after dealing with professional athletes for two years he had developed a deep cynicism and lost his joy for the game. Something parallel had happened to Bill Cochrane with Washington and the government. The better Cochrane personally knew the people who wielded power—and the more he saw the way they wielded it—the less he liked of the whole procedure.

Perhaps, he thought to himself, as his car crossed the Key Bridge from Arlington and as he drove in the direction of Georgetown, a special assignment wouldn't be so bad if it took him out of town. Maybe that was what he needed. A minisabbatical, of sorts. To think about where he was in life, why his most recent relationship with a woman had failed, why he wasn't reporting hard news, what his future might hold.

It might be a better idea than resignation, no matter how queer the pitch from Gabe Lang.

He brooded about it as he crossed the bridge. And he found himself arriving at a conclusion quickly.

All right, he decided, refining his reaction from only half an hour earlier, he would consider anything reasonable for which his government would want to pay him. He would keep an open mind on this special assignment and listen carefully to what the Vice President had to say. Who the hell knew, he reasoned, when an affliction—and surely the Vice President was an affliction—could turn out to be a blessing?

Once across the bridge and into the District, Bill Cochrane stopped at a 7-Eleven. He found a deck of playing cards and purchased them. The usual Bicycle brand cards with blue patterned backs. Lisa had attempted several times to teach him how to play bridge. He had stopped in this same store several times for fresh decks on his way to one place or another.

There were always memories, he told himself, when relationships had just ended. Even a deck of cards could bring back many. Then his line of thought shifted. He wondered how many other press attachés before him had procured stranger items than a deck of fresh cards to keep a Vice President—soon perhaps to be the leader of the Western world—happy.

Then Cochrane was back in his car again. And a strange feeling came over him, almost as if it had entered the car with the playing cards. For years before coming to Washington, he had labored as a reporter on midsized newspapers on opposite sides of the United States. First, there had been six years on the *Springfield Eagle* in Massachusetts, then four years on the *Sacramento Guardian* in central California.

It had been on this tour of duty that he had first met Gabriel Lang while the latter was a United States Senator. In a way, Cochrane had liked Lang, admired his irrepressibility and his freewheeling approach to both his life and his job. As a result, Cochrane gave Lang favorable coverage while still being fair and honest.

Lang at the time had been an easy target for much of the press in his home state and had thus favored Cochrane with certain interviews and scoops. While never completely losing his independence or integrity as a reporter—in his own highly critical assessment, anyway—Cochrane had brought along a relationship bordering on a friendship with Lang.

Very quietly, Lang even threw a big-time favor in Cochrane's direction, giving a demonstration that Lang could also play power politics in his home state. Cochrane had run a story in his newspaper stating that a trucking concern named McDaniel & Polini had been kept in business by a cocaine ring working out of Oakland. Cocaine profits were filtered through the trucking concern, then fed back to the dealers. The concern's owners, Mr. McDaniel and Mr. Polini, according to the article, received fifty grand a year apiece to use their fleet as a four-wheel laundry.

Mr. McDaniel and Mr. Polini did not enjoy seeing their names in the paper in this context. Fact was, Cochrane had the story right, but the methodology of it wrong. The conduit was not the trucking company, but rather a series of warehouses that the two owned. McDaniel and Polini threatened suit for libel and might have won. But Gabe Lang, getting wind of the events, used the California State Police to slip further volumes of previously confidential information to Cochrane. This installment of information was so damning that McDaniel and Polini abandoned their assets in the Bay area and took flight for Costa Rica at once.

No lawsuit. And for that matter, no big expensive trial for the taxpayers of California. Cochrane got to file the exclusive scoop on the flight of McDaniel and Polini, too. The older-and-wiser reporter came out of the sewer smelling just fine.

Thus when Lang went to Washington and needed to staff his own office of media relations, the Vice President offered Cochrane a job. Thirty-three at the time, looking for something new, attracted by the lure of the nation's capital and assessing this as a once-in-a-lifetime opportunity, Cochrane took the post.

Not that Washington was foreign to him.

His grandfather, the first William Cochrane, had served in the Federal Bureau of Investigation during the Roosevelt administration and, in a quirky, largely unknown bit of World War Two arcania, had once thwarted the intentions of a Nazi assassin who came narrowly close to planting a bomb on Roosevelt's private yacht in 1944. That same grandfather had married an Englishwoman and had subsequently taught at Harvard into the early 1980s.

Cochrane's own father, William Cochrane II, had entered the foreign service and put in a decade—a third of it spent at the State Department in Washington—before himself taking a lecturer's position in math and political systems at Amherst College. His father's mind had been so sharp when it was well, Cochrane remembered, that it was doubly horrifying when the man became mentally ill, never to recover.

From his grandfather, Bill Cochrane liked to think he had acquired his genes as an investigator and from his father his instincts about Washington and government. So it hardly came as a surprise when he gravitated to journalism while in college. Nor had it been much of a stretch when, not too long after graduation, he had landed his first job as a political reporter in Massachusetts.

The switch to California had come in 1989 when a wanderlust had overtaken him, when an earlier serious romance had turned sour, and when the bottom dropped out of his nerves and he suffered an emotional meltdown. Sacramento had an opening, Cochrane took it, and sought to redefine his life in the West. With the irony that is always contained by such things, the move west—in that it led him back to Washington—only brought him back East with a vengeance.

Yet even as a Vice Presidential press attaché, Bill Cochrane still liked to think that he still had a bit of the reporter in his blood—his sobering terminated relationship with the network superstar Lisa, notwithstanding. Cochrane saw himself as an independent, enterprising, imaginative soul who could survive by the seat of his pants and sniff out news or a hidden story the way a wild boar rooted out truffles. If he didn't have the stellar brains and female wiles of a Lisa McJeffry, he kept reminding himself, nonetheless he was a solid guy. An oak of his generation. And sometimes steady defeated flash and innate speed when the race was at a longer distance.

He was also not just a good writer. He was an excellent listener, a guy who always knew how to go into a situation with sharp elbows and a patient if occasionally cynical "show me" attitude. But he never forgot that a reporter was no better than his energy, his instincts, and his sources.

"We don't print the truth," the editor of the *Washington Post* had once remarked a generation earlier, during the reign of Richard the First. "We print what people tell us." That lesson had never been lost upon Bill Cochrane.

To get information, he was always willing to talk to the "ordinary" people who surrounded all news stories, the day-to-day working Americans—shop owners, cab drivers, doormen, teachers, beauticians, cops, firemen—who reported faithfully to the same job each day. These people, Cochrane knew, observed things. They often noted what was different from one day to the next. Cochrane would talk to these people. And he would listen carefully to what they told him, no matter how extraordinary. Getting the full story, he knew, was a blend of discounting no possibility, but working hard to be convinced.

Sometimes instincts told him he was on to something. There was nothing scientific or tactile about the feeling. It was just an extra sense, he liked to think. And inexplicably he felt some of those old instincts and feelings kicking in right now as he drove into the District of Columbia.

Something strange was imminent. That was the reading his senses gave him. If asked, if pressed, he could point to nothing other than his instincts. Then again, there were few things he trusted quite as much.

Cochrane's headlights hit the pavement and then swept the sidewalk on a turn in Georgetown. The street was dark. For a moment there was a woman in the streetlights and then she was in the lights from his head lamps, a flickering fleeting image. He found a phrase, an idea, floating into his head.

"Now what the hell is *she* doing *there?*" he found himself thinking.

He noted the irony and smiled at it. The last lucid comment President Farley had made, apparently of a female tourist on the White House lawn, were exactly those words. The quote had made the rounds of Washington gossip and eventually been published in the *Washington Post*. The Secret Service had even checked into the comment and had come away convinced that there *had* been a group of tourists on the lawn.

Cochrane chewed on the thought.

His eyes left the woman on the sidewalk. He scanned the road ahead—a taxi had stopped in an awkward position—and then Cochrane looked again to find the woman. But she was gone. Or at least, he couldn't find her. And the event was so unremarkable really that he thought nothing of it. Cochrane continued on Thirtieth Street and a few minutes later he was down the block from the Vice President's house.

A D.C. cop approached him first, then two Secret Service men, walkie-talkies in their hands, earplugs keeping their brains from leaking out the right sides of their respective heads, and funny little round medallions glittering in their lapels. To the cynical side of Cochrane's mind, they were M.C.U. guys, all the way: Midwest Catholic University. Probably had four varsity football letters between the two of them. And—again to the cynical side of Cochrane's mind—they were probably geniuses at creating spreadsheets or computer printouts of parade routes. But they probably couldn't read the danger on an inner-city street or spot the fix in a good clean game of Three Card

Monte. But here it barely mattered. And fortunately one of the SS men recognized Cochrane.

"It's okay. 'Starbeam' is expecting him," one of the SS men said to the other.

Starbeam: The Vice President's code name among those to whom the protection of his life had been entrusted. "Fruitcake" had been considered too obvious. The dislike of the Service for the Vice President was also too obvious. But at least they were Equal Objectivity Employees: They disliked President Farley and most of the cabinet just as much.

Starbeam. What was funny about it, Cochrane grudgingly admitted to himself, was that it rather fit.

Then, moments later, on this cold November night, Cochrane was ushered into the Vice President's lair. There was a final delay of twenty minutes and then Cochrane was taken in to see the Veep himself. All five feet seven inches of him, all one hundred sixty pounds of national leadership.

Vice President Gabriel Lang stood from a leather chair and smiled weakly at Cochrane. Lang was a bundle of nerves this evening, a man strewn with strange anxieties and a few alien feelings that, for the first time, Cochrane himself couldn't even read.

And once again, Bill Cochrane had a vague premonition, one that he could not shake or understand. It clung uncomfortably to him until it became unbanishable and almost caused goose bumps to crawl across him.

An image took shape in his mind, formed and spun apart, then clung to the outside of him like a wet leaf against his flesh. He would remember the feeling and never question his premonitions again. For in retrospect, Bill Cochrane would know that when he had entered the Vice President's home, he had for the first time passed within the presence of something large and ominous that he did not understand. An extra something that was there but which he could not see.

He would later also recall the horror of what would follow over the days and weeks ahead. And he would for an infinite number of times analyze the chain of events that would burst like flares around his very life. The events that had now—with this meeting—officially begun.

He thought of ex-girlfriend Lisa, at large somewhere else in the city, recording events from a position much closer to the heart of the action. Once again, he cursed his own fate and his own failures, and not for the first time, felt his life to be very much on the edge of something.

But he didn't know what.

Gabe Lang looked up.

"Thanks for coming, William," Lang said softly. "This has been one hell of a week for me." He paused. "Did I ever mention an old pal of mine from Harvard named Tommy Cassatt?"

Cochrane searched the recesses of his memory and found nothing.

"I don't think so," he answered.

"Very dear friend. Fine man. We roomed together in Lowell House. Tommy, me, and one other fellow named Ralph Forsythe." He paused. "Tommy died suddenly two days ago." He shook his head. "Just plain dropped dead, apparently."

"I'm sorry to hear that," Cochrane said.

"You get to this age, William. Fifty-two," Lang said reflectively. "That's what I am now. Half a century in age, plus a deuce. You don't think of yourself as old but the fact is you start suddenly losing friends."

Cochrane nodded with understanding.

"That's why they call the age the 'fearful fifties,' " Lang said. "You start realizing you could check into the next dimension at almost any moment."

Lang managed a weak smile. Cochrane reciprocated. "I suppose any age can be fearful," Cochrane said, trying not to sound as if he were parrying inquiries at a press briefing.

"And with all this shit going on in Washington," Lang said sourly, "I can't even get away to go to Tommy Cassatt's funeral. It's up in Westchester County. New York. Scarsdale. Or Larchmont. Or both. All I know is it's an hour or two away and I can't even get there."

Lang was rambling, visibly upset, which Cochrane knew. If this had been in front of outsiders, Cochrane would have taken steps to stop it. But here he listened and let it continue.

"I can't tell you how bad I feel about this. The death and not being able to go. Tommy was a first-class stand-up friend."

Gabe Lang shook his head ruefully. Then his expression changed and he looked carefully at the taller but younger man.

"I just remembered," Lang said. "You're just back from your father's funeral, aren't you?"

"I am."

"I'm sorry. My condolences."

"Thank you."

"Your mother . . . ?" Lang inquired.

"Died several years ago, also," Cochrane said. "Thank you for asking."

"Sorry once again."

Cochrane nodded courteously, still with sincere sympathy for the Vice President. It was clear that, to a certain degree, the Vice President just wanted a friendly, noncritical ear, one he could both fill and trust.

"Know what a procedure it is for me to even walk across the God-damned *street* these days with decrepit old Farley being half a vegetable over in Bethesda? Used to be I could walk places in this town and no one would even take notice. Or people would just smirk behind my back. Now it's a federal case if I want some air."

Cochrane found a chair and sat down. He said something indulgent about the President's illness—the Illness of George the Third—and mentioned how everyone was overworked, highly stressed, and on edge over the future.

"You always have the right word, William, don't you?" Lang said. "You should have been a member of the Vatican diplomatic corps instead of wasting yourself here as my junior press attaché."

"I'm not complaining," Cochrane said.

"No. Of course you're not," Vice President Lang said.

A moment of uneasy silence passed between them.

"Imagine all this," Lang finally said with a distant touch of self-effacement. "Here I thought the Vice-Presidential duties were breaking ties in the Senate *and* going to funerals. Turns out," he added wryly, "I have fewer duties than even *I* thought.

"Well, if you're ready," Lang said. "I'll tell you why you're here."

For some reason it flitted through Cochrane's mind that, yes, he was a single guy again with Lisa gone and he had no domestic pulls or obligations. So he considered himself as ready as he might ever be at his age.

He told the Vice President exactly that, then settled back in his chair and waited. In no way could he ever have imagined what he was about to hear.

4

Bill Cochrane had known Gabriel Lang for ten years. Now, after working for him for three years, he barely knew him any better than before. In some ways, Cochrane sensed, he knew him even less. Like the smile of the Cheshire cat, the inner truths of Gabriel Lang sometimes receded as one approached them.

"Hope you have some time, William," Lang finally said, not so much to put his attaché at ease as to put himself. The Vice President's tone shifted. Even if he was forcing himself, he was managing to sound a little sunnier.

"We're going to have," he promised his attaché, "a considerable talk right now. Ready, William?"

"Ready."

William. Lang was the only one who called Cochrane by the name on his birth certificate. It was a residue of Cochrane's days in California with the *Sacramento Guardian* when he had signed all his articles William Cochrane. Just hearing his Christian name spoken aloud reminded Cochrane that Vice President Lang had more idiosyncrasies than there were days in the year.

But Cochrane sat.

"Ready to do some traveling?" Lang asked. "Some traveling?"

"How soon? And to where?"

"Right away and I don't know," Lang answered. He steepled his fingers slightly, then twitched them again. His eyes held Cochrane's. "I'm going to send you in a couple of directions and it will be your decision as to where to go first. How's that sound?"

"Logical so far," Cochrane answered.

"Good," Lang said. "Good." He ran a hand across his face for a moment. "You're here because I trust you, Bill," he said. "And I can trust you with things that other people might not be as respectful of. I want you to know that and I want you to know how high a value I place upon that."

"Thank you," Cochrane answered.

Lang paused, hesitated almost, then forged ahead.

"I had a hell of a dream the other night," Lang said. "In it, I became President." He nodded. "President."

"Was the dream before or after President Farley—?"

"One day before George Farley slumped over his damned desk," Lang said. "Can you imagine that? Can you imagine what I was thinking when I got the news that the President was ill?" He paused. "In my dream I even saw George slump forward. Then the next day it damned well happens. Damned well happens."

Cochrane answered with his eyes and watched the Vice President.

"Lincoln had a dream in the White House," Lang continued, a contemplative tone taking hold of him. "It was even reported in the newspaper. Lincoln dreamed he was walking through the White House and everyone was crying. He entered the main rotunda and saw a body on a catafalque. He asked why everyone was crying in the White House and a woman pointed. 'The President's been shot,' she said. Then Lincoln saw himself lying in state. In state."

Cochrane was familiar with the Washington lore. But he let Lang speak. "Well, I had a dream, too. I dreamed I became President. And you know what, Bill. I found the dream frightening. I mean, the way the President is lingering between life and death. Know what I mean?"

"I know," Cochrane answered.

"I'm barely able to go to sleep," Lang continued. "I'm actually afraid that I'll have the dream again, or the next chapter of it, and wake up to find those Secret Service creeps surrounding my bed."

"I understand," Bill Cochrane found himself saying.

Lang's eyes were distant for a second or two, then returned from their voyage and found Cochrane. "The trouble is, it's going to happen," Lang said softly.

"What's going to happen?"

"George Farley will die. And I'll become President."

"How do you know?"

"It's fated." Lang was in dead earnest. *"Fated!"*

"Fated how?"

"It's been decided in another world," Lang said. "You might say, it's in the cards."

Cochrane didn't get it.

"The cards," repeated the Vice President. "That's what I'm talking about." He paused. Then, "Did you bring them?" he asked.

For a moment Cochrane didn't know what Gabriel Lang was asking. Nor did he follow the labored train of thought.

"Did you *bring* them?" Lang repeated. "The cards. I need to show you something."

Abruptly, Cochrane understood.

"Remember what I asked you to buy?"

Bill Cochrane nodded. He reached into his pocket and withdrew a small red, white, and blue box containing a deck of playing cards. The package was fresh and crisp, unopened.

"This?" Cochrane asked.

"That," Lang answered. Lang extended his hand. The palm was wet, the fingers twitching slightly. Cochrane's eyes then alighted on another sitting on a table close by. They were slightly askew. Lang had obviously been playing with the other deck prior to phoning.

"Now I'm going to show you something," Gabriel Lang said. "You'll find this hard to believe, I suppose. But seeing, well, you know? Seeing is proof, isn't it?"

"Except sometimes in Washington," Cochrane answered, making a much-needed joke of it.

But Lang almost missed the attempt at humor, and even when he got it, he managed only the flimsiest of smiles. With jittery, overanxious fingers he opened the box of cards, then stopped short. A second thought had crossed his mind.

"No," Lang said. "No. *You* do it, Bill. Much better if you do it. Okay? Open them."

Puzzled, Bill Cochrane obeyed. He carefully removed the cellophane and, following the Vice President's instructions, opened the deck. They were in order of suits.

"Now mix them up," Lang said.

Cochrane mixed the cards, shuffling them several times, breaking the deck, cutting it, then shuffling again. A Vegas dealer could have done it more effectively, but Bill got the job done.

Lang moved to a table and sat down. Bill Cochrane sat across from him.

"Now deal me a hand," the Vice President said. "As if we were about to play poker, just the two of us," he said. "Deal."

"As long as I've known you, I've never known you to play cards," Bill Cochrane said.

"I don't. Except when I'm alone. You'll see why," Lang said.

Bill Cochrane dealt five cards apiece. Lang looked nervously at the hand before him.

"You've given me at least one red queen," he said.

"What?"

"Queen of hearts. Or Queen of diamonds. One of the two is in my hand. I can count on it."

Bill Cochrane felt his brow furrow. "Fresh deck. You never touched the cards. This is a good trick if it works," he said.

"It's not a trick," the Vice President said evenly. "It's a curse."

Cochrane was used to such remarks from Lang. He let this one pass. Then, "Watch this," said Lang.

He reached to the five cards before him. He spread them out so none touched the other. He stared at them for a moment, then reached down and turned over the one second from the left.

Queen of diamonds.

Bill Cochrane felt something funny at the base of his scalp. Something like the touch of some icy fingers tickling him. And there was something in his ear almost like a subliminal whisper.

He settled himself.

"That's *very* good," he answered. "I won't ask you how you did it. Just tell me what the point is."

"It's a curse," Lang said again. "And the President is going to die. That means I get the job I never wanted."

"I'm not following this," Cochrane answered.

"I'm cursed," Lang said a third time.

"Tell me what you're saying. This is no longer funny."

"It never was, Bill," Lang said. "And I'm not kidding."

"If you're not kidding," Bill Cochrane said, "please explain it to me."

"As I said, it's nothing that can find its way into print, Bill," Lang said. "You've got to promise me that. *No one* can know exactly what I'm going to ask you to do for me."

Cochrane was at first reluctant. He paused for a moment, then said "Okay."

"Take the cards back, assemble them again, and pack them into a deck," the Vice President asked.

Bill Cochrane did as he was requested. The deck suddenly felt very warm, as if the deck had been sitting in a window somewhere, or on a radiator, soaking up heat. He mixed them in his hands.

"Shuffle them real good," Lang said.

Bill Cochrane shuffled them three, four, five times. Then, to make sure, a sixth.

"Now lay them flat on the desk," said Lang. "Go ahead. Spread them out."

Cochrane put his palm to them and spread the cards around on the desk in no particular order. Lang watched him and watched the cards. Bill Cochrane saw the sweat forming on the Vice President's forehead.

Lang closed his eyes, then reached to the pile of playing cards. He drew one quickly and flipped it over without looking at it.

It lay face up.

"It's another red queen, isn't it?" he asked.

It was. Queen of diamonds.

"Yes. Very good. So?"

Lang closed his eyes tightly—Cochrane could see the tensions in the Vice President's facial muscles as he did so—and kept his head facing away from the deck.

Lang's hand foraged through the other fifty-one cards. He flipped over another one.

"Queen of hearts," the Vice President said.

Bill Cochrane felt a cold ripple wash through him as he looked at the card. If this was a trick, it was very good. If it was something more than a card trick, it was downright scary.

Cochrane was silent, momentarily unwilling to answer, unable to assess what was happening. There was something about this which began to acquire disturbing overtones. It already felt like more than a conjuring trick.

"Isn't it?" the Vice President asked a second time. "It's the other red queen."

"Queen of hearts," Bill Cochrane confirmed.

The Vice President turned to face him. "Now assemble the deck again," he said. "Even it up and hold it in your hands."

Cochrane did.

"Now shuffle," Lang requested.

Cochrane shuffled.

"Again."

Cochrane shuffled twice more, very thoroughly each time.

"Now offer me two cards," Lang said.

Cochrane mixed the cards once again, then fanned them out. Keeping them tightly in his hands.

The Vice President, barely looking at them, leaned forward and picked two. He turned them over.

Queen of hearts. Queen of diamonds.

"Want to see it again?" Lang asked. The man was sweating profusely now.

Cochrane repeated, carefully guarding the cards, examining them to make sure they weren't marked, either by a coded design or by touch.

"We'll make it even more interesting," Lang finally said when Cochrane was ready to offer the cards again. "*You* pick out four, would you please, William?"

Cochrane separated four cards from the rest of the deck.

"Put them on the table," Lang suggested.

Cochrane did. Lang never touched the cards.

"Now pick your two," the Vice President said. "What remains will be mine. Mine."

Slowly Cochrane turned over two of the four cards. As if to mock the incarnadine ladies:

Two of clubs. Trey of spades.

Cochrane raised his eyes.

"You can bet your life on what's waiting for me," Lang said. And for a heartbeat or two, Cochrane wasn't quite sure exactly how the Vice President had meant that. But all four eyes in the room remained upon the two unturned cards.

"Should I turn them or you?" Bill Cochrane asked.

"Does it matter?" Lang answered.

He reached forward quickly, grabbed the cards at once, and turned them face up.

The two ladies were back. The queens. Hearts and diamonds. Cochrane felt a surge in his chest.

"I don't get it," he said.

"I always get a red queen," Lang answered. "And I will until this curse is lifted."

"*What* curse?" Bill Cochrane asked again.

"There's a curse on me," Lang said. "A *curse!*"

Despite what he had seen, Cochrane couldn't help himself. "Come on," he said. "Give me a break."

"Don't believe?"

"No."

The Vice President pursed his lips for a moment. He visibly tensed and the lines in his face seemed more severe than a moment earlier. "All right," he finally said. "Take the whole deck, including the jokers, and spread the cards on the table. I won't even watch you."

Lang made a point of standing up and walking across the room. He went to a window and pulled away the curtain, looking down upon a busy Georgetown Street, curious passersby and his bodyguards.

"Got them spread?" Lang asked.

Cochrane did. "They're spread," he answered.

"Take fifty-two cards," Lang instructed. "Look at each as you pick them up. Then discard each by dropping it on the floor. I'll pay you a thousand dollars for each red queen you can get."

Cochrane began. He drew one card after another. Six after eight. King after jack. Nine after ace.

No red queen.

Thirty cards. Then forty. Then the forty-ninth and fiftieth.

Four cards remained facedown.

"Pick two for yourself, two for me," said Lang. "Don't turn them over."

Cochrane pulled two cards toward himself. He left the other two untouched. Lang walked over to the table.

"Now make a final decision," said Lang. "One which I have no way of affecting. Do you keep your cards or hand them to me. Do I take the ones you're holding or the two on the table?"

"Would it matter?" Cochrane asked.

The Vice President shook his head. "No," he answered. "I'll get the same no matter what you do."

Cochrane started to look at his pair. Then he stopped. On impulse, he pushed his two cards together and handed them to Gabriel Lang.

For a long couple of seconds, Lang said nothing.

Then, "Turn over yours," Lang said.

Cochrane reached to the table and turned over two cards. Once again, it was as if an unseen hand was mocking them.

Cochrane turned over two jokers.

Lang showed the two cards in his hand. The two red queens.

When Lang set them down on the table and Cochrane picked them up again, they were almost hot to the touch. Lang's hands, he guessed, must have been smoking.

"Jesus," said Cochrane.

"Yeah. Jesus," Lang answered. "I only wish it *were* Jesus. At least I could talk to the Jesuits over at Georgetown."

"I don't understand this," Cochrane said.

"Think I do?"

"I was hoping—"

"This is why you're here, Bill," Lang said. He sat down again and faced the younger man, something in his eyes asking for help.

"But what's this about?" Cochrane asked again.

Lang shook his head. A smile crossed his lips. "I have no idea," he said. "I wonder if you could contact a psychic and find out for me."

Cochrane blinked disbelievingly, then realized that Gabriel Lang was very serious.

"That's why you're here," Lang repeated. "I couldn't have shown this to anyone else. Anyone else—everyone else who works for me— will think I'm crazy. But I know you won't. And I know I'm not crazy."

"A *psychic?*"

Lang reached to a pad of paper by his desk. "One psychic in particular," Lang said, as if this were a normal order or state. "A specific woman. Used to call herself Lady Elizabeth. Elizabeth Vaughn. I knew her many years ago when I was in high school. I'm going to give you an address in Massachusetts."

To Cochrane's dismay, Lang wrote down a name and a last-known address. He said it went back twenty-some years.

"She was very good," Lang said, continuing. "Really knew what she was doing. The cabala. Clairvoyance. Demonology." He paused, matter-of-factly again, the potential leader of the Western world. "On one and possibly two occasions, she even contacted the dead for me. Acted as a medium, would you believe. She really knew her way around the black arts, this one."

"What am I supposed to do?" Cochrane asked.

"Lady Elizabeth can see into souls," Lang said routinely. "Maybe she can see into yours and mine. Or the President's." He paused. "Maybe she can give us an idea what's happening around here, no?"

Lang finished writing and looked up thoughtfully. Cochrane felt a sinking sensation. Suddenly this all seemed very small, very petty, New Age mysticism, blended with old-fashioned superstition and a heavy dose of Eternal Crackpot sprinkled throughout.

He sighed. Lang made no notice. To Cochrane, it was all unbelievable, this entire meeting. It was, until he thought back for a moment on all the red ladies he had witnessed.

Lang started writing again.

"I'm also going to give you a name within the Secret Service," he said. "Mr. Martin Kane. He's not an agent or one of those gunslingers that stands around outside my door. The fellow's a record keeper over at the Treasury Annex."

Lang paused again, as if to think things through. The pause was a long one, almost as if Lang were wrestling with something inside himself.

"Fellow's a decent sort," he then continued, still speaking of Martin Kane. "He's got a list of people who have threatened the President. Not just the political soreheads. But people who think they can throw hexes and curses. There's something about some other psychic up in Rhode Island. I want you to check it out and report to me. I don't want the Secret Service touching it because they won't take it seriously. Oh, and you're to see Mr. Kane first. Then report back to me. Do the psychic thing second. Lady Elizabeth. I don't even know if you'll even be able to find her. But if you can, that's when you travel. I want you to see her in person. Over the telephone won't do the trick."

Lang wrote down Martin Kane's name and office phone number. He handed the sheet of paper to Cochrane. The Palmer method handwriting of the Vice President's youth had oozed into a middle-aged scrawl. But otherwise, the penmanship was clear. Clearer than the assignment, which remained murky.

Cochrane looked back to his employer. There was both fear and charm in Vice President Lang's eyes.

"All right?" Lang finally asked.

There was an uneasy moment that passed between the two men. Then Cochrane folded and accepted the piece of paper. With it came the mission. An antechamber to possible political oblivion, Cochrane reasoned. And if the newspapers ever caught wind of this . . . ?

"All right," Cochrane said.

"Take these damned playing cards, too," Lang added. "I've seen enough of them."

Cochrane put the paper into his inside jacket pocket. He set the new deck of playing cards back into his attaché case. He looked back up at Gabriel Lang, who was standing before him and looking very grave.

"I know you don't believe any of this, William," Lang said. "I know you think this is flaky stuff. In some senses, that's why I'm asking you to do this. You're the most hardheaded, realistic, and concrete of any of the people I trust. That's why I need you to do this for me."

Cochrane said nothing.

"The threat is real," Lang said again. "And it does not come from this world."

Cochrane looked his employer in the eye.

"Right," was all he could bring himself to say. Then he turned and left the Vice President in his quarters.

Three minutes later, so quickly that he had still not put any sort of supposed logic to all the events that had transpired, he was back out on the street walking to his car.

It was a balmy night in the District. And the events that had transpired were so strange that as he now left the Vice President, he wondered if the evening as he currently remembered it had even taken place.

Then a few minutes later, in his car as he headed back to Virginia, a delayed sense of anger started to settle in.

"Sheer lack of intellectual courage," he told himself. "Easy to call it civility or politeness, the fact is it's intellectual slovenliness!"

He found himself chastising himself aloud in his car. Lang was a crackpot, unfit for any high office, much less the one he held. What in God's name was wrong with the American public that they could elect such a man to the Senate, then to the Vice Presidency?

"A God-damned *fruitcake* with all this occult stuff!" Cochrane ranted in the car. But he cursed himself more than he cursed his boss.

Why hadn't he graduated from the middle-sized papers in Springfield and Sacramento and gone on to join the staffs at the big-time big-city journals in Washington, New York, Chicago, or Los Angeles? Other men reported the news; he spoon-fed handouts and protected a nut Vice President.

Even Lisa, with her hair, her legs, and her background in film, did hard news. He was a glorified copy boy. God, he hated it.

And it was all so much in his character, Cochrane again told himself angrily. Not in the stars as Cassius or Gabe Lang might have suggested. If he had any sort of integrity left, he'd resign, he told himself. Rather than go on some half-wit wild-goose chase. And then there was the whole Looney Tune aspect to Gabe Lang's request:

At what point did it stop being California Quaint and take an actual step into certifiable nuttiness, the type of irrationality that had put the last William Cochrane in a mental hospital? The type of craziness—the type of side trip from reality—that Bill Cochrane deeply feared in his future?

For all these reasons he knew he should avoid such an inquiry on behalf of the Vice President.

But he also knew that the sun would rise the next morning and he would at least embark on the initial steps of the task that Gabe Lang had laid before him.

Even a resignation took two weeks. He was not a praying man, having lost his religion many years earlier. But in this highly extreme case, he said a little agnostic prayer for the recovery of George Farley.

George The Third. May the Illness of George The Third conclude quickly, Cochrane thought to himself as he parked in the garage of his town house in Alexandria. "May the old prick be back in good and nasty mean-spirited health as soon as possible.

"For the good of the FUCK-ing nation!" he exploded aloud as he slammed the door shut to his car. "May the mean old Farley BASS-tard return SAFE-ly and FUCK-ing swiftly," he raged, "to the FRIG-ging White FUCKING House!"

"My thoughts also," came a soft calm voice from behind him.

Cochrane whirled and saw Mr. Trahn again, the superintendent of the building. Trahn gave him a thin cryptic smile, as usual.

The men stared at each other for a moment, Cochrane getting over his shock, Trahn trying to avoid embarrassing a tenant. When the awkwardness passed, they shared a laugh.

Then Cochrane went back upstairs.

Later that evening, before going to bed, Bill Cochrane took out the set of playing cards again. He pushed the deck flat and spread the cards like an accordion.

For several minutes he stared at them, hardly daring to proceed.

Then he drew, looking for a red queen.

He turned up a six of clubs.

He tried again.

Five of hearts.

He tried a third time.

Four of spades.

He put the deck together again, shuffled, and cut the cards. He drew five, looking for the red ladies.

Now the deck almost started to tease him. Two black kings. Then two black jacks.

He felt a little tingle within him, like a man at a Oujia board when the point gathers a life of its own and starts to move.

"You screwing with me?" he asked the deck, speaking aloud.

There was no motion or sound in the room.

But he then drew three aces in a row.

"Shit," he said to no one he could see. "You *are* fucking with me."

When he drew the fourth ace on the next cut, he was so startled that he dropped the cards.

He stared at them. He shook his head and didn't understand. Over and over again, he replayed the scene from Gabriel Lang's town house. Looking for a clue. Looking for some understanding.

If Lang had been putting him on, if this had been a trick of some sort, it was a damned good one. In a surge of courage, Cochrane turned the deck over and looked for the red queens. He found them grouped together—like a pair of sisters—in the middle of the deck, one next to the other.

Almost clinging.

The cryptic little silent smiles curling the corners to the two queens' mouths.

"God damn," Cochrane mumbled to himself. He suddenly did not like this.

He looked at the queens again for a moment, then examined the backs of the cards for a final time. There was no marking that suggested a reading. Nor had Lang been looking at the deck when he drew his queens.

Bill Cochrane set down the deck and went into the bathroom, immersed in thought, now trying to distance himself from his new assignment.

He showered, brushed his teeth, and prepared for bed. For a few minutes he turned on the *CBS Evening News.* He loved to watch Lisa McJeffry and was disappointed when Lisa, his favorite correspondent, didn't have a spot that night. Further, there was little other than a rehash of the day's medical events pertaining to President Farley. One naval surgeon voiced the opinion that the President's illness behaved so unpredictably that there almost seemed like an unseen force affecting it. The doctor had said this with a smile, however.

Next, there were stories on strokes. Then there was a general assessment of the events of the previous week in Washington, events that suggested that anyone's guess was as good as anyone else's when the Twenty-fifth Amendment would have to take effect.

Some scholars said soon. Some said later. Bill Cochrane turned off the television.

He walked past the playing cards again. He stopped and looked at the deck. No, they hadn't been touched. They were exactly where he had left them.

He experienced a funny feeling. It was as if a voice somewhere were telling him to turn over a card or two.

So he reached slowly to the deck and turned over the top card, expecting a red queen.

Six of hearts.

He turned over another.

Two of spades.

He laughed slightly to himself.

He thumbed his way through the deck and found the two red sisters exactly where he had left them, keeping each other company in the middle of the deck. And they were bracketed by the jokers, something he hadn't noticed before.

Again he sighed.

"Shows you what an imagination can do," he said to himself.

He climbed into bed and turned off his light, wondering why he was wasting his life and his time doing special assignments for a superstitious maniac like Gabriel Lang.

But he was unable to sleep.

The room was completely dark, which was the way he had always liked his sleeping quarters. He normally found the darkness soothing and comforting. Nothing had ever scared him about it, even as a child.

Tonight, however, he couldn't help thinking about the decks of cards in the next room. They seemed to share the darkness with him. It was as if they were intruding on it.

He couldn't get the cards out of his mind.

He clicked the light on and rose.

He went to the next room and picked up the cards, finding them exactly where he had left them.

He took them to the fireplace in his living room. He opened the flue. He lit a match and kindled a newspaper with some small twigs. When the flames came up high enough, he fed the cards into the fire, one by one. He fed them facedown. He didn't care to see any queens.

It took several minutes. Eventually, he had incinerated all the cards.

He watched the fire die.

And he felt silly.

But a few minutes later, returned to the comforting darkness, he was able to sleep.

Several hundred miles to the south, Carl Einhorn was not able to sleep.

This stuff about casting a spell on President Farley was the greatest thing since sliced bread! Einhorn arranged the candles in his small apartment the same way almost every day. And he poured out his venomous thoughts toward Farley.

And then he would flip on the radio at night, or read the newspaper in the library the next day. And when he read about the results of the spell he'd placed on the President, he could barely believe it himself.

Carl Einhorn even had a brother in Los Angeles, a snotty little psychiatrist who catered to movie stars, who would have to be impressed. His brother had never forgiven him for being born. As Carl considered things this evening, his headshrinking brother was looming as the next victim of Carl's brain waves. But first George Farley had to be dealt with.

Einhorn had always known that immense power had lurked within his skull. Why else could he have traveled through academia so quickly? And why, for that matter, did all of his enemies—who seemed to be everywhere—want to see him humiliated so quickly?

The two prostitutes he had had sex with, for example. The incompetent teachers and half-wit school administrators he had fought with, for another example. The doltish students who had resisted—successfully in most cases—his efforts to educate them. And how about those two Haitian girls who used to whisper behind his back and call him "a demon," even going to the lengths of writing their intemperate thoughts to the New York City Board of Education?

Well, maybe those Haitians knew a thing or two after all! And wouldn't they all be sorry! Eventually, he told himself, his telepathic powers would be revealed and it would be known how he had altered the course of history by bewitching President Farley.

Now, Einhorn wasn't quite sure whether "bewitchment"was the proper word. Oh, he was casting a spell on the crotchety old chief executive. No doubt about that. But it wasn't really witchcraft that he was doing. It was just—as Nietzsche would have written—a matter of superior intellect over an inferior one.

Then an unsettling thought fell over him.

Somehow he would have to let the world *know* that it was he, Carl Einhorn of the Bronx, New York, who was responsible for the President's sudden ill health.

He would have to be careful about this, because this new psychic power of his would make him a lot of new enemies. So he would also have to carry his gun more often. People would probably want to come to kill him, he realized with a shudder one night, and he would have to defend himself.

Then another series of thoughts was upon him, one that picked him up and made him very gleeful.

He, Carl Einhorn, had all of Washington, and for that matter, much of the world, abuzz. He really should announce that he was instrumental in this. But he should do it anonymously at first so that the world didn't bother him, much less try to harm him.

And further, since this was going to be a glorious segment in his life, he should go to Washington and witness all of this firsthand.

A rush of euphoria was upon him when he thought of this. He could drive to the capital in a day and *just watch* all those fools running around and going crazy over something that he, Carl, was controlling from within his head.

"Hey, Carl! Fantastic idea!" he said aloud.

He congratulated himself. The next day, he used the morning to conclude the work on his newest software program, then spent the day planning for his trip, cleaning and closing his apartment, and packing his car.

> Mr. Clean gets rid of dirt and grime,
>   And grease in just a minute,

Mr. Clean will clean your whole house
And everything that's in it.

Einhorn would leave the next morning. And this would be, without question, the thrill of his lifetime. He would be, he mused as he sang aloud, like Mr. Clean, the powerful household agent, cleaning America's soiled fabric.

5

What is that infernal pounding? What is that banging? What is that incessant disturbing racket suddenly above me after all these years of a rich black silence?

Why am I suddenly conscious?

Awake?

Why can I suddenly see with a clarity that borders on hyperrealism?

Granted: my physical body has now been dead for thirty-one years. It lies somewhere unattended, unknown and unloved, turning to dust, turning to soil. The blackness of spirit and action that surrounded my earthly demise now also possesses my remains. I have attained a certain nothingness over the years.

Almost.

Not that time is in any way important. For me, time ceased to exist along with my heartbeat, just as it will for you. Can you imagine a universe in which time and space no longer play a part? What about light and dark? There is neither where I am. There is a sense of order, but none that you would recognize. I'm not even sure you would recognize me if you saw me now.

But then, you never knew me when I was in the physical world. So why would you know me now?

Does anyone know my name anymore? Does anyone care who I am? Or where I am? Or who I was? How I died? Or why I cannot pass on to another realm? If I came back to speak to my parents—both still living—for a single hour, would I know what to say to them?

Probably not. But this will change soon. Everyone will soon know everything about me. Everyone will be talking.

I had a life. I loved my life. I wanted to live it and live it well. I was on the path to living my life when it was taken from me. I wanted to have a loving partner, and from that union I wanted to have sons and daughters. I wanted to enjoy the exchange of love with another human being as well as with my own progeny. Of all this I was robbed! My existence on earth was truncated in the April of my allotted years.

In many ways I was very ordinary. Height, weight, coloring, and overall appearance. I was not the type of person who made those of the opposite sex notice me, much less stop dead in their tracks. I liked to play tennis and basketball. I enjoyed academics. I went to a lot of movies, watched some television, and had two loving parents. I had one sister who is still alive.

There was only one thing that set me apart, made me extraordinary: I dreamed of being a writer. I dreamed of being one of the greatest storytellers who ever lived.

I wanted to sit alone before a typewriter or a pad of yellow lined paper with a pencil in my hand. I desired to concoct grand stories that would have entertained millions. I would have worked in an isolated cabin on winter nights near a fire, perhaps with a cognac or a warm herbal tea. Or I would have written on a screen porch in the summertime, my only light from a candle or the fireflies on an evening in the mountains.

I would have conjured up vast flights of a fevered imagination, tales of romance and of passion, heroes and villains, princesses and demons, refined ladies and scurrilous gentlemen, noble deeds and reprehensible acts. These would have been my players and I might have assembled them into stories and epics which will now remain untold for eternity.

So, too, would I have assaulted the traditional formats of the novel, announcing precociously in my early years that these conventions were no longer relevant to the world in which I was living. I might have begun my stories in their middle, then forged ahead boldly, working not just forward but also backward.

I would have been very modern. And yet in a sneaky way I would have been very traditional, almost mendacious—announcing that no man or woman could truly write a good novel these days. "How can you have heroes in literature," I would ask, "if there are no heroes in the world? How can you have individuals when individuality is a dated concept?" But then—behind my back, sort of, by slight of my writing hand, sort of, when no one was expecting it, sort of—I would have—voilà!—produced a great great book.

I had, I like to think, at least one great book buried within me. Maybe two.

But I never wrote a chapter of any of the novels that I had in my mind, either the great ones or the ones that would precede or come after my great works.

I never wrote anything.

Well, never other than in university.

I obtained top grades for some stories I wrote and my professors swore to me I had immense talent. They asked me how I had learned to form the rhythms of my sentences. They inquired about my use of language and I told them—without laughing—that refining language was as easy as punching a hole in the sky.

They didn't know what I meant by this, but they were academicians. So they didn't press further. And they also asked me repeatedly, with only the affected solemnity of tenured English professors, "Where do you get your stories? How do you make them up so convincingly?"

They all asked me this. Every one of them.

And I said to each one of them, again without even a smile, "All stories are true. Especially those of mine that you have been reading."

Then they would again look at me strangely, not knowing what else to do.

"You should continue to write," they would mumble. "You are very talented for someone so young. You should continue to create and refine your stories, though they do not fit into any traditional mold."

I know this sounds strange, but I sometimes wonder if they knew I was going to die.

So I never put pencil to paper professionally, or finger to typewriter, in the real world. My future was robbed from me. I would never be permitted to transform a ream of five hundred sheets of clean white paper into a great book.

The world's loss. My loss.

My death interfered.

As I said, my death arrived in the April of my years. And my May, June, and July were to have been so beautiful! Even my November would have been precious, golden and warm. I was in love with someone and that someone was in love with me.

Sometimes my thoughts spiral and I no longer know what I think I once knew. But I know I was in love and I know I never saw my lover alive again. Make that two lives ruined.

And I did not choose to die.

Please remember that.

Death was the last thing I wanted. The farthest thing ever from my imagination. Death was something that found me. Quite by horrible ac-

cident, I suppose. Or quite by malice. By a wall of human stupidity, an evil prank turned very dark and tragic, with its worst turns yet to come even today.

I am listening to that racket again. Disturbing me in my involuntary resting place. I must find out what that noise might be.

I am not forgiving by nature. I never was. I am not sure forgiveness exists in the afterlife, but I am sure than none inhabits my spirit. I was denied a life, a life I wanted. A life I deserved to live. I remain very angry. Very unsettled. It is not that I have trouble resting, it is that I do not wish to rest. Certainly not in that dark place where I am.

For many souls, the burden of life is as heavy as a mountain. Death can be a liberation—as light as a feather borne upon a spring breeze. I wish it could have been that way for me. Then maybe I could rest now.

But I can't.

Who am I? Who am I? Who am I?

I cannot remember the sound of my own name. I think that I could remember it a very short time ago, but once again I have trouble with time. I only know that I liked the sound of my name when I said it. Or when I heard it. When it danced across my lover's lips and breath.

Is my voice reaching you? Do my thoughts have a coherence in your world? Or am I only a gust of wind rattling on your windowpane?

Can you see me? Can you hear me?

I am the thing that flits at the periphery of your consciousness, the slight movement at the corner of your eye, which, when you turn to face it, is gone. Sometimes I am standing right next to you, as close to you as the breath you exhale, but you cannot usually see me.

Sometimes you feel me nearby. On rare occasions—when I let you— you may catch a glimpse of me, even though even then you do not wish to believe what your eyes are telling you. At those times, you deny me, also.

Qua, qua, qua. Do nonsense sounds make any more or less sense than anything else?

I am what I am and I know what I am by what I see in your face. The living—people like you—are my mirrors. But unlike a metallic reflection, you are not capable of holding my image for very long. Your capacity for attention is the same as your capacity for human justice: very short.

Therefore, I must provoke you. To craft the only stories that are left to me, I must come among you. I must wail and weep until my cries are heard, though no human could wipe away my tears of bitterness.

Yet my anguish will be heard. You will mourn my passing. You will know of the dehumanization and degradation and abject terror and loneliness that marked my end. And I will show you the chasm of blackness that rests beneath you everywhere.

Think of the worst thing you have ever done in your life. Think of your deeds coming back to avenge themselves upon you decades later when you thought they had all dispersed themselves, when you were certain they had dissolved into an unmarked dirt crypt.

I am angry. I am sad. I am roused to fury by this sudden cacophony of hammering and banging upon my tomb. And my fury has no limit.

I have a capacity for evil which will defy human measurement.

And I will unfold my singular story in the only way that has been left to me.

6

In the chilly cellar of his new home in Massachusetts, Richard Levin set down the tools with which he was working. He had no idea that he was about to find religion as he hunkered stolidly into middle age.

He walked to the steps that led upstairs from the cellar to the first floor. He thought he had heard a woman's footfall, and in particular a voice, upstairs. The house remained only partially furnished and every little sound frequently gave birth to a litter of small echoes.

"Honey?" he yelled.

No answer in response, other than those tiny ricochets of sound. Funny how one's ears could play tricks on their owners in these old houses. Rich Levin, just past his forty-second birthday, could have *sworn* that he had heard something.

But when he had called upstairs in response, no one had answered. Then, thinking about it a second time, he had thought he had heard a sharp voice, such as that of a woman calling out his name. A voice that sounded like that of his wife, Barbara.

So he set down his hammer, leaving it upright by standing it on its head, and walked upstairs. Barbara's Jeep Laredo was not in the driveway and the doors of the house were still locked. Levin glanced through the living room window and did see some activity across the street at the neighbor's house.

The Maloneys.

Catherine and her two daughters. Well, so much for hearing things. There was the source of at least one female voice, if not three. For a moment, Richard Levin watched the Maloneys—*mère et filles*—unload groceries from their van. Then he ran his hand through the thinning hair on his head and walked back downstairs. The hammer was at the base of the steps exactly where he had left it, though an unseen hand had tipped it over.

This was a bright crisp Saturday afternoon in November, temperature outside near fifty. The kind of late fall day that sometimes gives the illusion to Massachusetts residents that winter might not be too severe, though invariably any New England winter will have its lethal edge. Yet Richard Levin did not mind being busy in the basement. He and his family had just closed their purchase of this home in September. Ownership was something the whole family still wore proudly, like a badge.

The home might have been new to Richard and Barbara Levin and their twenty-two-year-old daughter, Lindsay, but it was not new to itself. It was, actually, quite old, as are many homes in eastern Massachusetts.

The main structure was from the 1750s, or so the local architects, historians, and real estate people said. It might have been built originally in a different location, but probably not far from where it was now.

It was a half-house actually, the original structure having survived only in part over the centuries. Yet what there was of it was quite cozy, centering upon an enormous living room with a massive fireplace with a baking oven on one side. The walls consisted of some of the original plaster—horse hair mixed into it to hold it steadily for more than two centuries—and a large adjoining area that formed a dining chamber. Two rooms upstairs—directly over the living room and dining room—created small cozy bedrooms to which the Levin daughter had been assigned. The rest of the house, again according to town records, had been added in two stages.

One extra room, a den, had been added to the old structure on the main floor in 1910, as had been two extra rooms on the second floor. Plumbing had been extended to the upper floor of the house during a general renovation in the 1950s, and a new modern kitchen had gone in at the same time. The previous owners had apparently kept the premises in good order, modernizing when necessary and not allowing any part of the property to drift into disrepair. It had come onto the market when the previous couple decided to retire and move to North Carolina, and the Levins—having been working with a broker for several months—quickly made the purchase.

To the Levins, the house was the realization of a dream. Richard was a partner in a small ad agency in Boston and Barbara was an administrator at a suburban hospital in Wareham. While living in a rental apartment in Boston, they had also been house hunting for years. And now they had finally found this small, quirky treasure in the town of Hillsborough, which was ten miles north of Salem. Richard's commute to Boston each day took an hour fifteen, which was a small price to pay to escape Boston traffic, Boston crime, Boston taxes, and the Boston school districts.

Levin paused a moment to stand in the den on the ground floor of the house. He had wonderful plans for this room. There was an old pot-bellied stove with a rickety stovepipe in here. One wall was book shelves and another wall could be. He stood still and

Books, yes! I've always loved books.

tried to envision the future.

Richard Levin loved books, as did Barbara and Lindsay. This room could be the family library for the next twenty years, he reasoned fondly. And once he fixed up the old stove—the body of the stove was fine, but the old tin chimney pipe which led up through a crawl space was suspect—a pile of wood could provide all the warmth he needed on a winter night.

Pleased with that thought, Levin went back down to the basement. But when he was there, he was suddenly aware of an intense stillness, one that seemed to surround him. It almost bothered him. He found himself humming to himself just to hear a voice.

Then he had a better idea.

From one of the many unopened boxes in the basement—placed there ever so deftly by the Seven Santini Brothers—he pulled a table radio that had stood on top of his office bookcase in the old apartment. The radio, a Sony from the 1970s, had been packed away with a bevy of scorecards and programs from Fenway Park and the old Boston Garden.

He found an outlet and set the radio on one of the small windowsills up high on the cellar wall. He clicked the radio on and was thrilled to welcome the Saturday afternoon opera into the basement of his home.

Fortunately, the opera was bright and uplifting. Live from Lincoln Center in New York: *The Marriage of Figaro*. Mozart was most welcome this afternoon, whereas Wagner or Moussorgsky would not have been.

Levin went back to his task, examining the makeshift walls that some previous owner had used to divide the basement. It was hard to imagine what some people were thinking, he pondered, when they did things to their homes. Oh, well. At least it wouldn't be difficult to undo some of the things that had happened so many years ago.

There was one wall which was nothing more than a plasterboard partition that had formed a storage area. If the plasterboard were taken out, the room would be four feet wider. So why not get it out of there?

Richard set down his tools in the middle of the floor.

He walked from one wall to another, picturing how this chamber could become a playroom. He examined the wall that separated this from the open section on the other side.

Then, with enormous glee, his picked up a second, heavier hammer. There was nothing supportive about the wall. It was nothing more than a weak room divider. A tacky one, at that.

He drew back his hammer, swung, and punched a hole through it. When he hit it a second time, a huge section gave way. A third swing knocked out even a larger piece.

He was starting to enjoy this now. Blasting away with his implements of destruction. He followed with blow after blow, taking the wall down in a matter of minutes.

As he punched it down, he heard the voice again and reflected anew at how the sound of the Maloneys across the street filtered so oddly into his home, even over the strains of *Figaro*.

But the Maloney house was an antique, too, and as Levin went about his task of deconstruction, he wondered whether the ancient architects of these homes had figured such sound control into their equations.

Two hundred years ago, Richard theorized, one didn't wish to be isolated from one's neighbors.

One never knew when one would need help, even when absolutely alone and enjoying working in one's own home.

Then a second thought flitted across his mind as he knocked down the final bits of plasterboard. Maybe one sometimes needed help *particularly* when working at home alone.

In case of an accident, Levin presumed, continuing that line of thought. No one would want to die a lonely death in one's home simply because one couldn't call out for help.

Then Levin shook his head and chased the thoughts away. Distantly, from Manhattan's West Sixties, the roguish Figaro, the impetuous barber of Seville, was predictably making an ass one more time of the blustering Count Almaviva. Judging by the reaction of the crowd at the Met, audiences were loving it on this Saturday as much as hundreds of others.

Immersed in his work, Levin no longer felt alone in his basement. Quite to the contrary, when he took down a second partition, he was swinging the hammer so dexterously that it was almost as if something were guiding his hand.

7

B ill Cochrane completed his sixth hour at a table in the Ongoing Investigations annex of the United States Secret Service and felt—not for the first time—as if a veil of spiritual exhaustion were slowly descending upon him.

The office was on C Street, N.W. It was harshly lit with long over-head fluorescent lights and located half a block from the U.S. Treasury Building, where the Secret Service kept their headquarters. Cochrane wore two security clearance badges around his neck. And he felt like a jerk.

He wasn't just investigating current threats to the President or Vice President. He was investigating threats that were seen as completely crazy, yet serious. Not imminent, but significant enough to be taken seriously, also.

In this section were housed the so-called "Catch-22s" of threats to the President. Letter writers who were obviously deranged, so they perhaps need not be taken seriously. Yet if they were deranged enough, they were just crazy enough to try to harm the President.

The nation, after all, had a rich history of big-time wackos stepping up to the spotlight and altering the course of history: John Wilkes Booth murdered Abraham Lincoln, and Charles Guiteau shot President Garfield. Leon Czolgosz put a fatal few rounds into President McKinley. In modern times, the names were even more familiar. Lee Oswald, Sara Jane Moore, Squeaky Fromme, and David Hinkley. Not one of them dealing with a full deck.

Then there were the assassinations of Huey Long, Robert F.

Kennedy, Mayor Cermak of Chicago in 1933 as he sat next to President-elect Franklin Roosevelt, Martin Luther King, and George Lincoln Rockwell. George Wallace was shot while campaigning in 1972 and President Truman narrowly escaped being murdered as he entered Blair House in 1950. And there was a pattern to all of this: Half crazed or fully crazed loners pulled the triggers on firearms in every single case.

A half-crazed loner and a gun, Cochrane noted, were just about the only requirements. Nut cases, in other words, were to be taken seriously.

Somewhere in this room, Cochrane wondered, was there a name, a correspondence, with the next wacko to make the American Political Crackpot Hall of Fame? The first big-time hit of the new millennium? After all these years, a sickness was still on the land. No wonder he found it depressing to be here.

Cochrane waited for his next round of files, wondering among other things, how the country could have bred so many nuts who could threaten the President and Vice President. What was out there in America these days, he wondered. What had *always* been out there? he mused, putting it into an historical context. Why, in the most stable democracy in the world, were there always various subcultures of people who cut their teeth by sending insane letters to Washington?

The modern-day ones were a mixed bag, he concluded. Right wing nuts, left wing nuts. Those possessed by chemicals, those possessed by paranormal fixations. The sexually frustrated. The clinically insane. The ones with the delusions of grandeur.

The just-plain-bonkers.

He sighed.

Out there among the general population was everyone's nightmare. Thousands of outright wackos, many of them armed, wandering the cities, suburbs, and small towns of America at the turn of the millennium.

Most were harmless, isolated and mute in their craziness. In a more indulgent, gentler time they might have found grace in a state nuthouse. Yet now they wandered the country. And some of them managed enough occasional mental coherence to land small airplanes at the White House, to stand beyond the White House gates and fire bullets, or—in the case of the more cowardly among them—to plant bombs in nearby mailboxes.

"Crazy people must to be taken seriously," Cochrane repeated to himself, almost as a mantra. He thought of a biography of Teddy Roosevelt he had read as a boy, and how T.R., out of office but campaigning for President as a Bull Moose, was shot in his more-than-ample gut by a madman with a gun. The weapon had been concealed in the bandaged hand of the nut, who was waiting to greet the ex-President.

Just waiting. Just waiting.

Cochrane looked up from the thirty-third file that he had read in its entirety that afternoon, following the twenty from that morning. It was starting to take a certain amount of willpower to keep his hand on this task. Was there anyone out there who was *really* a threat? He wasn't finding anything. Had he overlooked anything? The hardest thing to prove was the nonexistence of something.

Cochrane set aside the thirty-third file. He watched a short, pudgy man with closely cut gray hair and rimless glasses approach his table.

The man's government-issue name tag identified him as Martin Kane. Kane wore a white short-sleeved shirt and a brown print tie and looked like a thousand other Washington functionaries of his generation. Mr. Kane liked to be called Mr. Martin, even by those who had worked here with him since 1963.

"Just the right blend of friendliness and formality, don't you think?" he told Cochrane upon the latter's arrival that morning. "Don't call me Martin. Don't call me Mr. Kane. I'm G-6 Civil Service. Right in the middle of the food chain. So I think 'Mr. Martin' reflects that."

"I couldn't agree with you more," Cochrane said, keeping his tone perfectly sober and starting to understand how Kane had this position, keeper of the mail-in nuttiness.

"Thank you," Kane said.

The G-6 clerk seemed grateful. He also seemed as if he had spent too many years in this same room.

Kane's title was Assistant Reference Librarian, meaning—in this place—he kept track of the "Grade Two" letters of threat that were sent over from Secret Service Headquarters. If this annex was Siberia by Secret Service standards, Mr. Martin Kane was the top trustee of the gulag. He was also Vice President Lang's contact. And worst of all, he was cradling an assortment of new files in his flabby white arms as he approached the worktable where Cochrane had spent the day.

"Here we are, sir," he said breathlessly as he arrived. A thin line of sweat was visible across his brow at the hair line. Kane set half a dozen new files on the table. "I think that's the lot of it," he said. "Everything that matches the description of what you were looking for."

Kane looked at the labels on the files and shook his graying head.

"Don't you wonder what's the matter with all these people?" Cochrane asked. "Mr. Martin?"

The smallest trace of a smile flirted across Kane's lips.

"Matter?" Mr. Kane asked.

"To send this stuff to the White House? Or to the Vice President?"

"Oh, I never wonder about anything in the files, sir," Kane answered. "My job is to find the files and keep them secure. Your job, I presume, is what's *in* them."

Cochrane looked at Martin Kane, then eyed the files. Two of the new files were thick. Four of them were mercifully thin. He lined up all six in front of him.

"I suppose these people get out of their mental hospitals or they stop taking their medicine as outpatients," Kane said by way of a delayed response. "Or they read something and get swept away by it. Who knows?" he asked.

"Who knows?" Cochrane agreed.

"Anyway, these are the final items in your research requests," he continued, looking them over. "Or at least this is what's now available."

"Thank you. I think," Cochrane said.

Martin Kane spoke in a meticulously intense, quasi-hushed voice that he must have learned while picking up his master's degree from George Washington University in library science. Where else could he have learned to talk like that? Where else, Cochrane wondered, could every records clerk in the damned government have learned it?

Cochrane drew a breath and scanned the room as he prepared to examine his final six dossiers. Arbitrarily, he took up a thin one first— it was on top and it was the closest. If anyone had warned him twenty-five years ago, he thought as he opened it, that in the late autumn of Anno Domini 2003 he would find himself sitting in a United States Treasury Department research annex perusing the letters from the insane, he might have wondered where his adult life might have taken such a wrong turn.

He shook his head again and went about his task.

The first file contained letters from an anonymous correspondent believed to be in the Chicago area.

The writer—he was obviously male and had penned three letters in a shaky spidery handwriting on yellow legal paper—contended that President Farley was the reincarnation of Joan of Arc and thus deserved to be burned at the stake.

The writer had decided not to share with anyone else exactly what historical parallels had propelled him to this startling thesis. The writer, in fact, seemed to be remarkably unbothered by the lack of historical parallels. All he had was his conclusion. Cochrane read two letters in the same labored handwriting and passed on to the next oeuvre.

This one came from Rhode Island, or at least had been postmarked there. On this corespondent's agenda was the notion that the President of the United States, by virtue of being a sorcerer, was unfit for the job. Naturally, there were a few utterances about witchcraft and a line about the moon and the stars.

Half moon hex sign is a signel

wrote the correspondent as he wrestled with the complexities of his native language.

> sun and moon together taken as one indicate allegiance
> to devel and covvens of warlocks. This is further
> indecated by Presadent Farley's extensive well knowen
> holdings in Procter and Gambel Company Incorperated
> of Cinncinnatti Ohio which is a well known
> conglomerate of people who practice black sciences.
> P&G products have moon and stars symbel of
> witchcraft on all products to show followers that profits
> go to anti-Christ. President Farllay must die by arrow in
> chest if United states is to be saved from dark forces.
> Gerry Lang is probably practicing warlock, to.

Cochrane scanned through the rest of it, seeking illumination and finding none. There was no signature. Naturally.

He set the file aside and moved to the next. The author of this one claimed to have emerged from a seance in Dublin, Ohio, with a glowing vision of America as a latter-day Canaan, "purged of all sick non-white non-English speaking minorities, rid of Indians, Niggers, Asians, gay lesbians, kikes, other queers and some extreme Cathlics. Finally our shining Ameracan city on the hill."

This went on for fifteen pages, shifting in and out of clarity, tempered with various degrees of racist bile. But as the writer indicated exactly what caliber of bullet he was going to use to assassinate President Farley, the file was taken more seriously than some others. Not that stuff like this didn't arrive every day. But it was the reference to the seance—a reference which was repeated twice per page over the next fifteen pages—which directed the correspondence to this annex.

Cochrane cruised through the whole letter, following the author's lunges in and out of articulation and lucidity. Then Cochrane closed the file and set it aside. It depressed him that there was anyone out there who actually "thought" in such a manner. But from what he could see, it had no bearing on his current assignment. At least he could be thankful of that.

Cochrane picked up the next file. It contained a single letter, postmarked Stone Mountain, Georgia, two weeks earlier.

Sirs,

confided the author, as if ordering from a catalog,

I feel that President George Farley should be shot to death as soon as possible. Farley has betrayed the American dream many times over and is a traitor to his own nation. I shall be stalking him and will be sure that he is set down.

The Unicorn

The author, the self-proclaimed Unicorn, had typed his message on a single sheet of white paper. He had mailed it in a matching plain envelope. Cochrane examined both the stationery and the message carefully. It stood out from the others in that it was grammatical and concise, methodically putting forward an argument. No misspellings. No atrocities of syntax. No nutty racial stuff. And no clue where—or who—out there in the population The Unicorn might be.

Cochrane paused over it a final time. The other thing he noticed was that the author had taken on a pseudonym, albeit an anonymous one. Most of this threatening crap was unsigned. What little insight was this writer betraying by issuing himself a nom de guerre?

Cochrane wondered. Then he wondered further if he were giving the author too much credit. Probably.

He put the file back and moved to the next file before him. When he opened it, it made him blink.

This epistle was a single letter written on lined yellow paper with a pink highlighting marker. Even the handwriting looked frenzied and manic. And the text seemed to scream:

Ho! Lo! Behold! I am Jesus Christ,

wrote this correspondent,

and now that I am thirty-three years old I am preparing to meet my Crucifixion! But I will not go quietly and shamelessly to my True Cross as much work must be done first. And I will do that work, I will! President Farley must died before I can ascend to God Almighty's Heaven in the Sky. Fuck it. I will kill the President with a scythe and the New York-Boston kikes in the communist state department will crucify me for it.

There was a yellow Post-it note which someone in the Secret Service—probably some young agent bored out of his mind—had accidentally left affixed to the letter. Cochrane read it.

Scythe? As long as as we keep Farley away from grain auctions he should be safe from this psycho.

Cochrane did someone in the Secret Service a favor by removing the Post-it before someone else saw it and the handwriting or provenance of the comment could be traced. It would have been just like some supervisor to come down hard on some young agent while paying no attention to the crackpot who had written the threatening letter.

Cochrane placed the dead Post-it in his pocket.

He then read the final file. It bordered on the incomprehensible and had such a loose grip on the English language that Cochrane immediately theorized that its author was a deranged immigrant.

The handwriting was tiny and intense, two dozen letters to the inch on each line. Magnifying glass stuff. The writing paper was scented with something resembling jasmine. The elliptical prose had hints of the Indian subcontinent.

And the note did repeat the refrain that "President Farley must die."

Cochrane examined at the envelope.

This particular note, threatening the President's life, had been mailed from Miami to the Chief Justice of the Supreme Court of the United States. Cochrane looked for some sort of warped logic in that, too, but couldn't find it—as had been the case in the several dozen other messages he had prowled through that day.

A line of doggerel drifted across Cochrane's mind. Hey, man! Statue of Liberty, 2003. Wouldn't this be a tourist attraction:

A big green bikini-clad babe in New York harbor with nose jewelry, holding aloft a tire iron instead of a torch, or maybe just the "Fuck you" upraised center finger:

> Give me your tired, your poor,
> your clinically insane, your
> criminally psychotic yearning
> to continue their crime sprees
> in a more tolerant venue under
> the auspices of a bunch of whorish
> lawyers—

He was getting punchy, he knew. So he pulled himself away from the thought. He sighed again. Sometimes he hated the year he was living in and longed for a time when things weren't really simpler, but somehow seemed that way. At other times, he knew that emotion was a sham and felt, as Lisa once phrased it, "Fuck the good old days."

What he did know was that he had been in this archive too long today. All this stuff was starting to look the same.

So with a sigh of fatigue, he closed the final file and assembled everything he had read. He sighed. He worried that he had missed something. But when he reexamined his goals, he wasn't even sure what he had been seeking. Lang's instructions had been vague. An occult threat to the President. What the hell did that mean?

Cochrane rose and walked to where Martin Kane sat at his desk.

Kane slowly looked up. The light from outside fell upon Kane in a strange way, and for a fleeting few seconds, Kane looked absurdly old. Cochrane felt a strange twinge and felt himself speechless. Then, with a speed that has no measurement in time, the light must have shifted again because the image was gone. Cochrane blinked and Kane looked normal again.

Cochrane returned all the files in his possession and presented his ID. Files had to be checked back in from the same individual as had checked them out.

"Bill Cochrane," Kane said, musing aloud and reading Cochrane's name off his requisition slip. "That's you, is it?"

"That's me," Cochrane answered.

Kane made a dull tapping sound upon the fake wood of his desk. He pursed his lips, then looked up above the frames of his glasses. Two dark brown irises floated on dewy white eyeballs. To Cochrane, Kane's eyes looked like a pair of eggs. Dull and flat. And Cochrane knew that there was a question imminent. Cochrane had learned long ago to sense when a good one was coming.

"Work for Vice President Lang, I see," Kane said with an arch intonation. "My friend Gabriel."

"You know him well?" Cochrane asked.

"Of course I know him well," Kane said. "He sent you to me, didn't he? To check out the Secret Service Lunatic Ward." Martin Kane's nose gave a little snorting sound. "My brother worked for Gabe Lang when Lang was a Senator. They used to go to the same parties."

"I see."

"Seems like a nice man," Kane continued softly. "A little odd, maybe. But decent."

Cochrane offered nothing, choosing instead to wait.

"Did he *really* make that statement?" Kane asked. "The one about Mercury in retro?"

"He made it," Cochrane said.

Kane's soft brown eyes lowered and returned to the work before him. "Good for him," Kane finally declared firmly. "I don't know why everyone thought the idea was so strange," Kane said. "Nothing gets done when Mercury is in retrograde. It's all in the gravitational pull of the stars."

Cochrane said he couldn't have agreed with Kane more. He watched Kane methodically check the files back into the Secret Service archives.

"I wonder if I could ask you something, Mr. Martin," Cochrane began.

"Ask me anything. We'll see if I'll answer."

"Do you examine this stuff when it arrives?" Cochrane asked.

"Unfortunately, I usually do," Kane answered dryly.

"All of it?"

"Just about. Depressing, isn't it?"

"Very," Cochrane said with utmost sympathy. He waited for a moment.

"Why?" Kane asked.

"Well, I was wondering," Cochrane essayed. "If anything comes in that sort of has an *occult* flavor to it, could you give me a call?"

"You don't mean just nutty, do you? Or having an astrological or numerological basis, right?"

"That's correct. I mean demons. Or devils. Or voodoo or Santaria. Occult. Anything that takes that shape."

Martin Kane stared at Cochrane for a moment, just long enough to digest what was unaccountably being asked. Then he pursed his lips and shrugged.

"I can't promise that I'll read every word that passes before me," the government librarian said. "But I'll keep my eyes open. How's that?"

Cochrane said that would be just fine. Then he hurried off to his car.

He returned to his office only long enough that evening to catch up on any incoming requests from foreign media, a territory often delegated to him by Jim Crews, the Vice President's chief press spokesman.

Then Cochrane located the name of Mrs. Elizabeth Vaughn, the psychic recommended to him by the Vice President. He called directory assistance in Lawrence, Massachusetts, and found her. In another few minutes, he had her on the telephone.

Yes, she said, she knew Gabe Lang and she would be more than happy to speak with anyone who worked for him. She was "retired" now, she said, though she did not say from what. And she would be happy to meet Bill Cochrane two days hence if he so desired.

He set a time with her, noted the directions, and called the travel office to book a flight reservation.

When he put down the phone, he once again felt like a damned fool.

That evening in his suite at the Duffy Pavilion at Bethesda Naval Hospital, as Cochrane was completing his travel plans, the President sat down to a cup of tea. Two of his speech writers had just left. His Press Secretary, Michael Thatcher, remained present as did Mitch Michaelson, the President's appointments secretary. Also present, beyond his doorway and down the corridor of the Naval hospital, was the usual phalanx of Secret Service agents. The agents busily and conspicuously manned both the door to President George Farley's suite as well as the corridor outside.

To any observer, the President looked tired. Yet now his age suddenly showed, as if it had been dropped upon him suddenly like a shroud. The stress of his sudden illness had taken its toll too, carving extra lines in his face, whitening hair and slackening skin on his cheeks and jaws. It was as if something terrible and mysterious had happened to him. And in a way, it had.

George Farley's political party had manipulated his image in the press carefully for the past several years. His political spin doctors, as opposed to the medical doctors to be found at Bethesda, liked pictures in the newspaper of a vibrant, healthy man. The George Farley image had been virtually caressed in the media, much like the images of Ronald Reagan had been—Reagan clearing away brush on his ranch, brush that the Secret Service had carted in the night before for the photo ops. Several generations earlier, in a seemingly more innocent time, the other party had carefully managed the public image of Franklin Roosevelt. No photograph of FDR in leg braces or a wheelchair ever appeared in the newspapers during his Presidency.

Yet, unmistakably, the man in the hospital bed in November of 2003 looked old and gaunt, nothing close to his public image. Farley was almost unrecognizable from the daily photographs. Earlier in the day the Secretary of Defense, a former governor of a Western state, had come to Bethesda for a meeting. The Secretary, having believed the optimistic medical reports that had circulated in the media, had been shocked. Farley seemed to have aged a year from when the secretary had seen him last, and ten years from his most recent photographs in the newspaper. The Secretary had left the hospital greatly sobered and had been hard pressed to maintain a cheerful expression to the press corps waiting outside.

This evening, in front of Michaelson and Thatcher, Farley's face seemed to lose concentration toward seven in the evening. Before their eyes, the President's expression glazed over slightly and he rubbed his eyes. He pushed away his cup of tea.

Michaelson, seeing that he had lost the President's attention, stopped talking.

"Frankly, Jim," said Farley, apropos of nothing that they had been discussing, "I'm god-awful tired. I don't know whether I want any meetings tomorrow." George Farley seemed to think about this for a moment as Michaelson and Thatcher kept watch and waited.

"I don't know," he then said. "Better take it day by day. Let's conclude for now. Maybe check with me in the morning."

"All right," Michaelson said, exchanging a glance with Thatcher. "We'll do that."

"I feel like relaxing now," Farley said. "Or maybe even sleeping. I've got this fucking headache again."

That was the cue to rise for both men, which they did.

"Tell me something," George Farley said. "If I had a fucking brain tumor, would anyone tell me?"

Michaelson and Thatcher exchanged a final nervous glance with each other. Then they fumbled over each other seeking to reassure the President.

"Oh, shut up. I was just kidding. I think," Farley snarled. Then Michaelson and Thatcher left the President alone in his hospital suite.

Two minutes later, Dr. Ivan Katzman, the President's personal physician, entered the room. He found the President sitting quietly upright with his eyes closed.

Katzman approached and instinctively placed a hand on the President's wrist to check for a pulse, even though the cardiac monitor showed an ample heartbeat.

There was an acceptable pulse. But the President seemed to be dozing.

Then Katzman realized that George Farley was too quiet. He was alive, but too quiet. He had slipped into another of these light comas, sort of a mininarcolepsy. Just like the day before.

Dr. Katzman broke a sweat and wondered about the thanklessness of his situation. To help conceal the President's ailment was at odds with his own sense of ethics. He also had a sense of country and patriotic responsibility. It should not have been upon him, Katzman thought, that the President's feud with Gabe Lang should dictate a suppression of the truth from the public. And then there was that troubling concept of the Twenty-fifth Amendment. When Farley was out on Cloud Neptune, no one was President.

Seven minutes after 7 P.M. found Dr. Ivan Katzman a deeply troubled health care practitioner with a mysteriously afflicted patient.

Katzman shook his head and sighed. There were some things on heaven and earth, he decided, that were not apparent in medical school, internship, overall philosophy, and thirty years of professional practice. No one else on his team at Bethesda had any further insight into the President's situation, either.

The press release for the evening, however, said nothing of this. Instead, it stated that the President was resting comfortably, had enjoyed a productive day, and was watching television in the evening.

He was even, the reports went, looking forward to a day of appointments on Wednesday.

So once again, as the President lay unconscious, the Vice President was not notified.

The indeterminate nature of George Farley's ailment was hardly settling to the press corps, however. Americans liked quick answers and comprehensible solutions, and the situation with President Farley offered neither. When the press couldn't provide such answers and explanations, they grew surly and contentious, too.

And as a result, sniping had already begun at Dr. Katzman, the bearer of the evil tidings. Among many physicians, following the press coverage of the President's illness, the notion was clear. The nation had a medical mystery on its hands and the case should be turned over to a different medical team.

One headed by a neurologist, perhaps. Or a epidemiologist. There was some suggestion of the symptoms of Paget's disease, theorized some, and hence an endocrinologist should be invited to the party.

In New York that same Tuesday, for example, a team from Columbia-Presbyterian Hospital offered their services. Another team from Baylor Medical in Texas offered theirs. A team of cardiologists from the Mayo Clinic quietly waited. But when Dr. Katzman stayed with his team at Bethesda, augmented only by a few specialists from Walter Reed, the sniping at Katzman broke out from within the medical community and into the open.

So now the competency of the President's medical team had become an issue. One of the more outspoken proponents of this theory was the noted neurologist Dr. Noah Benson of NYU-Bellevue in New York, who had his opportunity to mount an electronic soapbox late Tuesday evening.

The problem, said Dr. Benson on ABC's *Nightline,* was that the

President was getting third-rate medical attention. Any doctor who was any good, said Dr. Benson, would not have spent his career in the Navy. He would have been in a prestigious university hospital. Benson was careful to choose his words well. He definitely said "third-rate." Not even "second-rate."

Once under full throttle, Benson saw little reason to slow down. He even attacked Dr. Katzman's medical school credentials, noting that the President's physician had gone to medical school in Italy.

"It's well known in the medical community," Benson continued, "that foreign medical schools are havens for those who didn't have the mental hardware to win admission to American schools."

"Dr. Benson, I just wish to clarify," Ted Koppel asked. "You're stating outright that Dr. Katzman is an inferior practitioner?"

"What I'm saying, Ted," Dr. Benson said, "is that there are better people available and there are also specialists. So far, the President hasn't seen either."

Privately, Noah Benson referred to Dr. Katzman as "Ivan the Terrible." But somehow he managed to not refer to him as such on the air.

It would be in the national interest, Noah Benson continued, for someone to march into the hospital in Bethesda and replace Dr. Katzman's team with "even some good first-year residents. *Anything* would be an improvement."

When asked to specifically name someone who was an expert in the type of neurological disorders the President seemed to be suffering, and who would be a good choice to examine him, Dr. Benson humbly named himself.

"I am the most renowned expert on neurological disorders in the country," Benson proclaimed, both accurately and without the slightest suggestion of any humility. "Without any question, I, or someone of my standing, should be allowed to consult with Dr. Katzman."

"Consult," in this sense, meant come in and take over the show.

"We're dealing with the incapacitation of an American President, meaning national interests are at stake both at home and abroad. We also could be dealing with the possible implementation of the Twenty-fifth Amendment. At the *very* least, the American public should know what we're facing."

Privately, similar sentiments were echoed a thousand times across the country the next day. When would Dr. Katzman allow others— meaning physicians who were by their own admission more capable, talented, insightful, and prestigious than he—to examine his patient? All over the country, doctors with stellar reputations waited for their call to glory.

It wasn't coming. Not immediately, anyway. And Tuesday, November sixth, turned into Wednesday, November seventh, without further complication.

8

I'm back.
   Or more accurately, I was never really gone.
   You hold this book in your hands and you don't realize that by doing so you have licensed me to communicate with you. These pages exist only in your mind. Take your eyes off them and they cease to be. Close the book, they are gone.
   But close the book and I am still in your mind, aren't I?
   Yes. You see, you have summoned me forth from my grave. I exist because you are thinking about me. That's what the spirit world is like.
   That foolish doctor in Washington! Of course it seems as if there's an external force manipulating the President's health. I'm surprised it took the medicine man so long to figure out something like that. Must have gone to a third-rate medical school, that one. And wouldn't he be horrified to know what's really happening to Mr. Farley?
   Ha! If he knew, would he even believe it? Would he have the nerve to make a statement to explain to the American public that the President's health is being toyed with from the other side of life and death?
   What about you? Can you still hear me? You know I'm here, don't you? Alas, you must believe in me because my thoughts are creeping into your head. In your way, you see me. I am in your mind and yet you cannot envision me completely either.
   Nor do you know why I'm here. You cannot yet know what has so unsettled my spirit that I must wander among you.
   You will know. You will want answers and explanations and you will

have them. And then you will be upset. You will be upset because my existence will rattle the foundations of everything you believe in.

As I said, I wanted to be a writer. I wanted to concoct stories of heroism and romance. This was taken from me. So now I will write a story of horror and terror. You will have to believe it because all such stories are true. A story has its own truth, no matter how wretched. And certainly this one does.

Do you know where I am?

I am in your mind.

But I am also right behind you.

I am that sudden draft that you might feel on the back of your neck. I am that sense of not being alone that you suddenly suffer.

Think hard.

You think you are alone in your room with this book. You are not. Because all stories are true, I am present in your mind.

Thus I am present with you now wherever you are reading this. I am very close. I could press my lips to your cheek and kiss you softly. Or I could protract my fingernails—they are very long because I say they are very long—and scratch your eyes out.

I could blind you. But if I did, you would be seeing me. So would you really be blinded if I had opened your mind to the huge, horrible dark truth that lurks beneath the quotidian world?

You would see without seeing. And I would be your most recurring image.

You shuddered a little. I am getting through to you. In the forefront of your mind, one voice—that of reason—tells you that you are only reading a book. But then there is another voice within you, something darker and deeper inside your mind. It is the voice that tells you that there just could be a man with a machete in your closet or some unfathomably evil creature lurking under your bed.

Care to go check either? Care to think exactly how unspeakable your terror would be if you dropped your hand by the bed some night and felt something grab it?

Or opened up the closet and something big and hairy rushed forward at you?

Or if you were lying in bed an hour from now, just starting to sleep, and felt a firm cold hand on your shoulder, then whirled to look into a ghastly white face with two red eyes inches from yours?

All of this is possible. My soul is in such torment that I can bring such psychological terror upon the living.

Including you.

Specifically you.

As you lie awake tonight, in those final moments before sleep embraces you, it will be my breath you feel on your face.

Oh! I have found a way to manipulate the mental and physical health of the living. By attacking Farley I get at the entire nation and have the pleasure of leading Lang to his ruin at the same time.

What sweet pleasure. What malicious fun.

Ah.

Qua, qua, qua.

I can also read your mind. I know what you are thinking. You are wondering how any spirit can be so malevolent?

Well, you consider what was done to me. You consider how love was wrested from me as well as my life. You consider how the worms for years crawled in and out of my mortal remains until nothing remained but my poor disassembled bones.

No, I was not always this malicious.

But I am now. I will bring death and damnation upon any mortal who crosses my path.

This will indeed be an epic story created by me.

I will write my epic in the sky and I will grind guilty souls into the earth. This will be the masterpiece that was denied to me in my earthly incarnation.

And when you finish with this great fiction of mine, you will also have to confront my reality. For I am the most real of all of the characters in this story. I am the one that will follow you—will be in your head—for months after you finish this story.

By thinking about me, you give me my spiritual reality. I thank you for it. Maybe in gratitude I will prepare a funeral pyre in hell for you.

Do I seem to act in malice?

Well, at least I act with the logic of natural retribution. Much worse was done to me for no reason by men of so-called "upstanding" families and good breeding.

Fine young men all.

Damn them to a hell on earth.

Qua, qua, qua. When you want to blame me for perpetrating evil, I will revert into nonsense and you will never find me again.

Qua, qua, qua. Like that, I mean.

I murdered Tommy Cassatt, you know. Gabriel Lang's friend. In time you'll know why. You'll know why because I will write the story and tell you.

All stories are true, don't forget.

But first, the Levins.

I will toy with the Levins. They, too, deserve it for their transgression.

9

Pudgy little Carl Einhorn wore a dark brown suit with an open collar when he stopped his car at the Hotel Wescott on Connecticut Avenue six blocks from the White House. It was a Sunday afternoon and Einhorn was a man with a self-proclaimed mission.

The Wescott was one of the anonymous midsized hotels that catered to conventions and lobbyists.

On Einhorn's arrival, a husky black doorman politely asked for the keys to his car. Einhorn immediately handed over the keys. The doorman lifted out Einhorn's luggage and whisked the car to the hotel garage.

At the front desk the mathematician produced his single credit card and registered under his own name. For a few moments, he engaged the clerk in conversation about the health of the President, the topic which was upon everyone's lips. The clerk, while admitting that he was not of the same political party as George Farley, expressed his concern.

This clerk was male. He would recall to the police that on sight he didn't like the plump little mathematician. There was something a little too intense about him, though the clerk couldn't place exactly what.

Nonetheless, the clerk handed Einhorn a small plastic card that would function as a room key. Einhorn looked at the card strangely. He had never seen such a thing before as this was the first time in twelve years he had been in a hotel. But he accepted his card and went to his room. He had only one suitcase and he carried it himself.

When he found and entered his room, Number 514, he was pleased with it. It was near a fifth-floor elevator as well as the interior fire escape. Coming and going unnoticed from the hotel would be easy. Not only that, but the numbers 5, 1, 4 had a linear logic to them. He took that as a good sign that his trip to Washington would proceed smoothly and he would go home again without incident.

Again, logic.

Einhorn unpacked methodically. He only planned to stay three days, just long enough to observe his psychic mischief from close range. So he had planned his wardrobe accordingly.

He had three extra shirts and one extra suit, even though he knew he would probably wear the same suit and shirt for all three days. There were six extra pairs of underwear—he would change those twice a day and wash them immediately—and a pair of newly purchased navy blue sneakers, in case he wanted to go out at night. There was also a heavy wool turtleneck, and dark jeans, his only pair. He brought these dark outdoor things in case some enemy was looking for him and in case he would have to hide somewhere.

There wasn't much beside clothing for Carl Einhorn to unpack, but what was there was important. He had brought his laptop computer. There were two dozen candles for casting his continued spell upon President Farley. There was some blank writing paper and some plain envelopes, plus some stamps with flags on them. And he had three books of matches.

He had a newly purchased book on psychic phenomena and a book on black magic which included two interesting chapters on telepathy, so he had brought this book with him, too. He wanted to reread those and see if he would pick up some pointers. And in his suitcase there was also a local street map of Washington. The map had some markings on it in pen.

Einhorn had also brought his pistol. He had heard what a dangerous city Washington was, particularly after dark. So he would take no chances. Better to be judged by twelve strangers than to be buried alone. Then he had two of his favorite porn magazines and a Ping-Pong paddle. That was it. He was traveling light.

Einhorn studied his room for a moment and wondered where to keep his important things, things that were dark "bad boy" secrets that he didn't want anyone else to see. As he had suspected, the hotel room was far from secure.

He went back down to his car and fetched a heavy lock and a bicycle chain from his trunk. He would keep his important things—the porn, the paddle, the candles, the computer, and the gun—in his suitcase. And he would chain the suitcase to something immovable in the room.

Something like a radiator.

But when he looked around the room upon his return from the garage, he saw nothing that was immovable. He grew angry very quickly. He was almost in a rage!

The room was just a box with furniture in it! Now he would have to go up and down the elevator or the stairs with his suitcase if he wanted to lock up his possessions! He would have to do this because the only *safe secure* place would be the trunk of his car.

And going up and down with the suitcase could arouse suspicion. People might think he was ducking out without paying his bill or doing something else funny or unnatural.

Einhorn grew red in the face. He shrieked profanely and nearly had a full-blown tantrum. This was at variance with the way he had planned things!

When he did this—when he got so mad!—Carl Einhorn thought inevitably of his mother. Whenever he would throw fits like this as a boy, she would quickly punish him with a strap, pulling down his pants to make sure the strap found the flesh of his buttocks nice and smartly. She was a big burly German-American woman and she would do this with great gusto and enthusiasm. Many times Carl thought back on these punishments in a bittersweet way.

Often his father spanked him with the same strap, but even harsher physically. Sometimes Einhorn felt like he needed just that type of punishment these days to calm him down—preferably from a female. Sometimes he even *knew* he deserved it, and at those times he would take out his pornography and flagellate himself with the Ping-Pong paddle. That's why those two damned whores had belittled him many years ago. That's what he had asked them to do. They had refused.

But today in Washington, Carl finally controlled himself.

He mumbled abjectly to himself, cursing more quietly now, and managed to settle down. He breathed heavily and thought of his loaded gun.

He considered how if anyone ever walked in on him and saw him in this state, he would probably have to kill that person. Have to, because how could a man with such magnificent mental powers allow there to be a living witness of the weak side of his nature?

Simple logic, once again.

Some people had to die. Einhorn's will to power, he postulated, had already set him apart from the ordinary herd of humanity. As a superior intellect, he would deserve to live at the expense of lesser humans. Nietzsche, again. Or at least Carl Einhorn's interpretation thereof.

But something else helped calm him, also. It was evening, and through his window he could actually see, just as a crescent obscured by a neighboring building, the top part of the dome of the Capitol.

So a wonderful idea was upon him. Why not take a quick drive by the area today?

Case it.

See the U-S-A
In a CHEV-ro-let
America's the greatest land of all!

But don't go too close to the White House or any other seat of government. One never knew how his unseen enemies could inadvertently tangle up the best-laid plans of execution.

Einhorn loaded his gun and placed it in his belt, under his jacket. He took the elevator down to the lobby. He approached the desk so quietly that no one saw him until he was right before the desk. It was a quiet move that he enjoyed. He used to do it to his students and fellow teachers—appearing suddenly beside them with no warning—because he knew it disturbed them. No one was better than Carl Einhorn at mind games, he reminded himself. He had always been excellent at them!

There was a pretty young Asian girl on the desk now, about twenty-one years old. She was visibly startled when the small pudgy man was suddenly in front of her. When she looked up, he was just two feet away from her, staring at her with big open eyes and trying to look down her cleavage as she wrote something in a ledger.

She gasped and collected herself, adjusting her blouse. A name pin above her left breast said that her name was Sue.

Then Einhorn was intentionally rude to her, angrily demanding the return of his car key and complaining loudly that it should never have been taken from him.

The young woman at the desk apologized. He asked if she was the manager and she said no, she was part time and a night student at Georgetown. She said again she was sorry, but Einhorn kept interrupting her and wouldn't accept her apology. Better to keep her on the defensive so she couldn't belittle him. She rattled easily and gave him his key. He could see that he had upset her considerably and was glad. She was the type of pretty girl who would never speak to him when he was a student and a teacher.

When she asked if he wanted to talk to the doorman who had taken his key, he quickly said no. Then he turned and walked down to the hotel garage. No one was there. He found his car and no one paid any attention to him.

He stepped into his car and started it. When he drove out of the garage, the attendant didn't even look up.

Then he was out into the early evening. The sun was completely gone and dusk gripped the city. He drove around the Capitol and passed in front of the White House. He went on his own small sight-seeing tour of the Lincoln Memorial, the Jefferson Memorial, the Ellipse, and several departments of government.

Once a police car stopped right behind him and put its flashing lights on.

Einhorn's heart soared. He wondered how his enemies had found him so quickly. But he shouldn't have been surprised, he thought next, because his enemies were everywhere!

They always had been.

So he pulled his car abruptly to the curb with a jerking, nearly stalling motion. And he reached within his jacket. His sweating hand found the handle of his gun and he started to draw it.

But the police car, lights still flashing, sped past him, paying him no attention. It drove off and was gone in a matter of seconds, presumably in the direction of a more urgent call, a convenience store stick-up, no doubt, punctuating the night in the American capital.

Einhorn felt his heart flutter back down to earth. Those few seconds of excitement were more than he had really bargained for on his first night in Washington. But they did serve as a warning. He would have to be very, very careful. And he would constantly have to be ready to defend himself.

He found a fast-food place that looked safe and went in. He ate two hamburgers, two orders of artery-clogging fries, and a large cola. Then he drove back to the hotel and put his car in the hotel garage without using the doorman.

He walked up the stairs from the garage to the lobby, moving with his usual stealth. He stood near the doorway to the stairs and saw young Sue at the front desk.

She was sitting quietly and writing something. Probably her homework, Einhorn reasoned. And she was probably as unaware of what a great academic intellect he possessed as she was unaware that he was even watching her.

Modess. Because . . .

Fleetingly, it passed through his mind what power he had over her. He could kill her right now and she would never even know what had hit her. His hand played with his gun. Another vision tiptoed through his naughty mind about making the sobbing girl cry and take her clothes off for him.

Carl smiled. He liked power.

Sue never saw him.

But when he heard footsteps approaching the lobby from the outside—more guests checking in—his mood broke. His thoughts shifted. He moved quietly to the elevator.

Still, no one saw him. Oh, he was having a good laugh to himself! He was the most powerful man in Washington, he reasoned, and no one knew it and no one was paying any attention. This could go on forever until he killed the President.

George Farley: six letters in each name.

More perfection.

Carl Einhorn ascended to the fifth floor in the elevator. Then for the rest of the evening, he disappeared into his room and locked his door tightly from within.

10

There are men in their thirties who return to the counties and towns of their childhood and find their youth beckoning them from every direction. Bill Cochrane felt just such a pull as he drove north from Boston on a highway that would have led him—in another time and another season—into the frigid countryside of New Hampshire.

The signs on the highway proclaimed a route that traveled north toward the home of the as yet unseen Elizabeth Vaughn. But it also beckoned both to an uneasy present, an unreadable future, and the bittersweet distant past.

Woburn. Stoneham. Bayardvale. Andover. With the name of each town, for Bill Cochrane, the son of an Amherst professor, the grandson of a Harvard lecturer, a hundred associations came forth with each, associations which lingered in his mind like spirits unable to rest.

The images flashed before him as he drove. And for some reason his adolescence, his teen years, were those that he recalled most vividly. As if conjured up by the road signs, the memories poured forth, first steadily, then as a torrent. They were before him as if suddenly *un*-hidden, as if coming out of the clouds of his memory into a brief and uneasy sunlight.

There were scenes of biting cold winter days playing hockey on unnamed open air rinks and clunky ponds in New England. Wild end-to-end games. Fire wagon hockey, Cochrane playing defense, blocking a frozen puck with a shin covered with only blue denim and a wool sock. On some days he had blocked shots until his shins were criss-crossed with welts, the blood from each fresh aching laceration quickly freezing on his jeans. He came home after each game looking as if he'd been machine gunned across the ankles. And in some ways, he had been.

Then there were hot sticky summers at a Dairy Queen, longingly watching girls in the next car. Beautiful young things in summer dresses or T-shirts and cut-off shorts, unattainable females who would never look back at him as one of those damnable FM radio stations from Boston kept playing Blondie and ABBA. Unattainable, but who eventually married electricians or went to work in banks or supermarkets.

Then there were sharply bright autumn days when Amherst, Massachusetts, Boston College, Boston University, and Harvard football crackled across the competing radio waves, each with a distinctive sound, and, having sympathies with all those institutions, he could never decide where to let his affiliation settle: Brainy Amherst, Middle Class UMass, Irish-Holy B.C., working-guy B.U., or self-confident, patrician Harvard.

Thoughts of autumn, particularly in this context of retrospection, also lured him into thinking back on the first girl he had ever loved—physically and emotionally. Her name was Wendy and her father was a civil engineer in Lowell. They had met at a basketball game in the winter of his junior year in high school. He had phoned her relentlessly, and in the following spring, at a time when no parent was home in her house, they had quickly made love in her bedroom, concluding almost exactly as they heard her father's car come into the driveway.

Thinking back on it, that springtime had been one of his better ones. But then there were all the rest of them. Reluctant springtimes, he considered them. Reluctant because the spring thaw had always come late to New England, sometimes as late as May, and Opening Day at Fenway—which he went to once—was usually attended by hearty men and boys in dark parkas and the big Marathon in Boston was run by thin, swift guys and girls in shorts, T-shirts, gloves, and wool caps.

He reached the town of Lawrence on the Merrimack River, carefully laid out by conniving capitalists in the last century. Lawrence was the scene of the great strike of 1912 and the great fire of 1995. The mills were gone and so was much of the economy, gone to cheaper means of production in smaller hotter countries. A few of the old red brick buildings still stood like hulls of old ships, too archaic to sail away, too proud to knock down.

Cochrane's car left the highway. His memory of Lawrence was vague, and once off the exit ramp, he pulled to the side of the road to consult a map.

The address he had for Elizabeth Vaughn was on Trammel Street. As he studied the map, he saw that Trammel was adjacent to something called Benoit Park. Train tracks weren't far away, either.

He checked the scale on the map and saw that he was within two miles. He checked his watch. He was right on time and hoped that Elizabeth Vaughn would be home.

Another five minutes of driving time took him across the train tracks and led him past a quiet freight depot. When he took a final turn toward Trammel Street, he found that his route brought him past a mobile home settlement which proved to be Benoit Park. Outside his car the temperature was in the forties, but several families had laundry out to dry.

Trammel Street was a modest little route, a settlement of small neat homes across from the trailer park. It was dreary under today's gray sky, but Cochrane conceded that almost everything was. So he found Number 12 easily and pulled his car to a halt.

For a moment, he saw himself as a much younger man, a reporter on his first paper fourteen years earlier, knocking on strange doors to report on all sorts of stories, from homicides to shop liftings to winners of cheerleading contests to lost-cat stories.

But when he stepped out of the car and looked at Elizabeth Vaughn's house, the old images departed him and he mentally transposed himself into his current assignment.

"The woman is a psychic," he told himself, "and the Vice President of the United States wants to know whether she has any insight into the situation in Washington. That is my assignment and it makes perfect sense. If the Secret Service can keep files on people like this, I can run down a lead for the Vice President."

He grumbled to himself again, cursed his current assignment, and steadied his growing sense of the absurdity of his situation.

"Just how soon will *I* go crazy dealing with things like this?" he asked himself.

Elizabeth Vaughn lived in a small frame house on what looked to be a 100-foot-by-100-foot lot. The house was a dull pink and had a low wire fence around it, the type used to keep children or pets within a yard. A flagstone walkway led to a double gate, the latch of which appeared to be broken when Cochrane tried it. Then he passed through the gate and went resolutely to the door of 12 Trammel

Street. The front porch was still littered with faded remnants of Halloween, including a dead pumpkin.

At the door, he knocked once. When there was no answer, he knocked again. His knuckles hit the door harder the second time, his patience quickly wearing away. There were two small panes of glass on the upper half of the door, with a heavy curtain on the other side. The resident of this home could see out. But he, as yet, could not see in.

Cochrane heard a small commotion on the other side of the door. Then the inner curtain brushed aside slightly and he saw part of a woman's face peer at him from a low position, as if to quickly inspect him.

The curtain quickly dropped back into place, followed almost immediately by the rattle of a chain on the other side of the door.

Then there was a clicking—or unclicking—of locks.

The door opened partly, held on a chain. Back a few feet from it, at a height not much greater than that of the doorknob, was a narrow suspicious face with tense frightened eyes, the same face as had peered out at Cochrane a moment earlier.

"Yes?" she asked suspiciously.

"I'm Bill Cochrane," he said. "I believe we spoke on the telephone."

There was a pause as this registered on her.

"Jesus," she finally said. "Will wonders never cease?" There was a rasp in her voice, as if from too many cigarettes or an unending case of bronchitis.

"I wonder if we could speak?" he asked.

The suspicious brown eyes of Elizabeth Vaughn held Cochrane for a final moment. Then the door pushed almost completely shut again and the woman undid the latch from within.

The door reopened, wide this time. The woman was in a wheelchair.

"Sure," she said. "Come in. If you could close the door behind you, it would help."

The door came wide and Cochrane entered the small house. Mrs. Vaughn had skin the color of mocha ice cream and two large brown eyes. Her hair was short and frizzy, gray sprinkled with black. She was wearing a faded print dress and Cochrane took her to be the offspring of a mixed marriage, if any marriage at all. Certainly a mixed union. She wore one large gold hoop earring and appeared to be in her sixties.

Her home appeared to be in the sixties, also. Furniture and decor that had probably been with her for forty years. And the place was filthy, or at least the living room was. There were newspapers piled on tables, empty bottles, glasses, and cups scattered around the room. There were few pieces of furniture and almost everything was positioned far away from everything else so that the wheelchair could roll with unlimited access. As Cochrane stepped into the room, he could see through the door that led to the kitchen. Plates and cooking utensils were piled high, even in the sink. He had the impression that Elizabeth Vaughn used everything until it ran out, then washed it all at once. Hopefully.

"This is quite something, I have to tell you that," Elizabeth Vaughn said. "Come in and sit down. It's been a long time since Gabe Lang had anything to do with me. I can hardly imagine this."

She asked if Cochrane minded waiting for a moment and he said he didn't. She was just brewing some tea in the kitchen—it was herbal, she said—and wanted to finish.

He said that was no problem but, with one eye upon the hygiene of her kitchen, declined to join her. She wheeled herself to the kitchen where a radio was playing softly—a talk station which sounded as if it were from Boston. The delay, as she puttered wordlessly through her kitchen, gave Cochrane a chance to look around.

Her music system was an old record player. Mrs. Vaughn may have been the world's last holdout for vinyl, but if so, she was an enthusiastic one.

In a library off from the living room, Cochrane came across her university diploma, prominently displayed on the wall—a bachelor's degree from the University of California at Berkeley, 1965. Then in that same room, she also had a massive record collection running along the floor against one wall.

At his feet, down where she could easily reach them, there must have been four hundred 33 LPs, and predictably many of them were from the Jimi Hendrix era. There was a small section at the end containing three albums which she had marked with a divider labeled COMEDY.

Cochrane couldn't resist. He peeked: The Firesign Theater, Barry Manilow, and The Captain and Tenille. Comedy, indeed.

He smiled and set the records back, unobserved.

Then, when Cochrane's eyes lifted from the records and upon her bookcase, he was not surprised to find hundreds of texts on psychology, parapsychology, witchcraft, and various other forms of the supernatural and the so-called paranormal. Juxtaposed against all this was an extensive collection of classic English and American novels, plus a heavy smattering of poetry.

Eclectic stuff. Pound. Elliot. Masefield. Ferlinghetti. There was an original first edition of Alan Ginsburg's *Howl*.

Cochrane opened it and discovered it was signed. He began to read:

I saw the best minds of my generation destroyed by madness . . .

He closed it and put it back. He was fingering an early edition of Robert Frost when he heard her wheelchair set heavily upon the floorboards of the living room. He returned there.

She politely directed Cochrane to the sitting area in the living room. There was a sofa that seemed to be in better condition than anything else in the house, right next to the single lamp in the room which was not yet turned on. The sofa was probably of more recent salvage, Cochrane noted, than anything else in the room. Thus its superior condition.

She again offered Cochrane something to drink, a cold soft drink this time, which he again declined. A few moments of small talk ensued until Cochrane, anxious to get on with things, moved the conversation forward.

"Gabe Lang says you're a psychic."

"Why would he say that?" she asked.

Cochrane shrugged. "He sent me a long way to see you, Mrs. Vaughn. So the Vice President seems to believe it."

"Balderdash," she said.

"Are you?" Cochrane asked.

"Am I what?"

"Psychic?"

She pursed her lips and made a little plaintive gesture. "Used to be," she said. "I had a vision or two in my time." She managed a slight but wary smile. "And still could have one on occasion, I suppose," she said.

"Anything I'd want to know about?" he asked. "These visions?"

"Don't know," she parried. "What interests you?"

Cochrane took a calculated risk. "Well, I work in Washington, as you know, Mrs. Vaughn," he said. "I'm interested in the President's health. And the Vice President's future."

She assessed him for another few seconds, then gave a slight grimace.

"Oh," she said softly. "So that's what it's about, is it?"

"What?" he asked.

"The Washington situation. The President's going to live. The President's going to die." She drummed her fingertips on the arm of her wheelchair. Cochrane's eyes drifted for a moment. On the table before the sofa, just by the television, was a stack of recent mail. On the top was a government check, Social Security, Cochrane guessed, with a Fleet Bank deposit slip clipped to it, already made out. He guessed that a trip out for Mrs. Vaughn was a major event.

"Which is it?" Cochrane finally asked. "What do you foresee?"

"In Washington?"

"Yes."

It was like extracting a tooth. But finally she was ready to give.

"Oh, the President's probably going to die," she said. "Gabe Lang will take office. Something of a Devil's prophecy. A deal with the Devil."

"A deal Gabe made?"

"Sort of," she said.

"Why don't you tell me about it," he said.

She gave a little snort, then became churlish.

"Damned if I'll talk about *that*," she said. "I know what's good for me. I know what's not so good. What's going to happen is going to happen no matter what I say or no matter what you do. So why should you want to know ahead of time?"

He shrugged. "So I might better prepare," he said.

"Ha!" she said. It was a legitimate laugh. "Prepare. Nothing to prepare for other than having Gabe Lang as President. And everyone can prepare for that at once."

From somewhere a large red tomcat appeared, traipsing slowly but proudly through the room, its tail aloft and perpendicular like an exclamation point.

"Ask me something else," she said.

"Gabe said you could see into souls," Cochrane said.

"That's not a question," she snorted, picking up the cat for a moment. Cochrane could hear the muscular beast purr even from six feet away.

"It's not a question," he allowed. "But it's quite an amazing talent. Can you see into souls?"

Her eyes seemed to drift for a moment.

"He said that, did he?" she asked. "He told you I could?"

Cochrane didn't answer. Mrs. Vaughn half snorted and her gaze drifted to something far away for a moment. Then, in half a heartbeat, it was back.

"Yes, he did."

"That Gabriel is such a character," she said. "I think he'd say anything."

"But *can* you?" he pressed again. "Or was Gabe just having some fun with me?"

For a moment, she sipped her tea. There was a heavy silence in the room and Cochrane was aware of the sound of the drizzle on the roof of the house. He once had loved the sound of rain on a rooftop. Today it depressed him.

Mrs. Vaughn, in a small way, must have been reading his thoughts, the ones about depression, because she reached slowly to a lamp by her end table and lit it.

"Dark in here, isn't it?" she asked. "It seems to be bothering you. We could use some light, couldn't we?"

"Can you?" he asked, almost as a non sequitur.

"Can I what? Use some light?"

"No. Read souls," he asked.

Once again, she looked him up and down. There was something in her eyes that perplexed Cochrane. The look was both defiant and defensive at the same time. Then, just as quickly, it changed to something trusting, longing but scared.

"I can sure as shit read yours," she snapped. "And I can read Gabe's. And I could even read the President's. What the hell do you want of me?"

"Then read them."

"I do that professionally," she said softly. Mrs. Vaughn's mood changed almost word-by-word.

He felt a sinking feeling. "I do not believe in this crap," he found himself thinking. "And I do not wish to be part of it." Nor was he in any mood to make nice about it. He felt himself on the verge of a flash of anger. Then, viewing her withered legs in the wheelchair, he gathered himself.

"If you do that professionally," he answered patiently. "I want something for my money."

"Uh-huh," she answered.

It occurred to him that it may have been a long time since she had scored. And in a way he took pity on her. His eyes glanced downward to the mail again and the Social Security check. He could see that the first of the three figures on her deposit slip was a five.

"How much are we talking about?" he asked.

"Twenty-five dollars," she said.

He thought about it for a moment, then reached to his wallet. He pulled out a pair of tens, then, for good measure a third. He placed thirty dollars on the table.

"Look deeply into my soul, Elizabeth," he said. "I'd like to think that I'm getting what I paid for. I'm giving you an extra five for good will. How's that?"

She picked up the money. She was obviously more used to men of a contentious temperament because she appeared as if she half expected him to lunge quickly and grab the money back. But he didn't. Instead, he settled back in his chair.

"I'm keeping this, you know," she said. "You don't get this back."

"I know."

"Good," she said.

"Just make me happy," he said. "Let me leave here knowing something I didn't know to start with."

She pursed her lips. Her lipstick flaked slightly. Her fingers tightened, one hand against the other, and Cochrane—feeling a surge of pity again—saw that the rings she wore were loose. They were nice rings, probably quite expensive, and they were loose on her fingers because in the old days there had been more flesh on her fingers, too.

"The President," she said. "A very strong-willed remarkable man. Machiavellian from time to time. Very political . . ." Her eyes found her client's. She was relating nothing that anyone who bought a newspaper wouldn't know.

"What's wrong with him?" Cochrane asked. "Why is he sick?"

Her hands wrenched the other again.

"I get a bad feeling about it," she said. "Something powerful. Something evil. It has him in his grip."

"His body? His soul?" Cochrane asked.

"Both," she said. "It's impossible to separate body from soul. The soul *defines* the body. A tormented soul afflicts a tormented body."

"So that's what's happening here?"

She thought about it.

"No. No," she said slowly, easing further into her purported clairvoyance. "I see this differently. The President is not a good man. He has harmed many. He is not benevolent in that he is concerned mostly with his own standing in history. But . . ." She hesitated slightly. "That's not the problem here."

"Then what is?"

"Something from outside," she said. "The President has an aura around him. He's afflicted by something from outside his own realm. That's why the doctors are so helpless."

It was like, Cochrane couldn't help thinking, something straight out of a supermarket tabloid. One of the tackier tabloids.

"What about me?" Cochrane asked.

"What about you?"

"I'm right in front of you," he said. "Look into my soul. What do you see?"

Her gaze held him steadily.

"A lot of loneliness. A lot of indecision. A sense that your youth is passing and you haven't done anything important in your life yet. A sense of wanting to have a relationship with a woman but not having succeeded." She paused. "You're not married."

She said all this as a statement as much as a question.

He felt a tiny surge of anxiety. She had been close to the target, after all. Then he dismissed it.

"No," he said. "I'm *not* married. And the fact that I'm not wearing a wedding band could offer you a hint like that."

"Ha. Wedding bands," she scoffed. "What man bothers with one of those anymore? Everything about you offers me that hint," she said.

"Like what, 'everything'?" he asked.

"Your eyes. Your face. There's a certain sadness. A recent sadness. Maybe a romance just ended. Maybe a death."

For a moment he thought of Lisa, then his father.

She squinted. "I also see some deep self-doubts. Some insecurities, some—"

Something within him flashed and his mind uneasily jammed itself back into the present. And into reality. Was she fishing, he wondered, like a daily horoscope in a newspaper? Or had she actually hit something that she had sensed? Just a tiny bit, it bothered him. Any small bit of accuracy made her more difficult to dismiss.

"Did Gabe tip you off?" he asked.

"About what?"

"My personal life."

"You asked me to look into your soul. I just did."

"Uh-huh."

"I haven't spoken to Gabe Lang for years," she said.

"Then why would he have your current address?"

She shrugged. "I'm sure he has his reasons. Ask him. Not me."

"But you're a psychic," he said, thinking he was closing a neat trap. "You should know, shouldn't you?"

"What I know as a psychic comes forth involuntarily," she answered. "I can't *want* to know something, then know it."

"I don't really believe in this stuff, Mrs. Vaughn," he said.

"I know that, too. You're a skeptic. You came in here with a chip on your shoulder."

"I came in with no such thing," he said.

"You came to see me as a psychic. But you don't believe. Well, I can't help that," she said, "but I would call that a chip on your shoulder."

"Gabe tipped you off," he said.

"I haven't spoken to the Vice President since he was in college. Make that twenty-six years. Dates are approximate."

"How did you know him?"

"I was his teacher."

"What?"

"In high school. English."

Which explained the dichotomy of the book collection, Cochrane thought to himself.

"Where was that?" he asked.

"Novato, California. It's above San Fran—"

"I know where it is," he said.

"Taught Gabe in eleventh grade. Well, he was always interested in psychic stuff. It was a time of psychedelia, you remember," she said. "Flower power. Acid. Grass. Speed. Jefferson Airplane. The Dead. Filmore East and Filmore West before Bill Graham's private plane landed on an electrical power line."

"Don't remember the era but I know about it," Cochrane said.

"From VH-1, no doubt," she said acidly. "Well, Gabe was a pretty good student of mine. Got A's. Loved to dabble in ideas. In reading. Read a lot of Vonnegut. *Cat's Cradle* blew him away, if I remember. So did *Slaughterhouse Five*. Ever read that?"

"I think I saw the movie," he said.

"Figures," she said. "Donald Sutherland and Valerie Perrine dancing around nude."

Once again, in a small way, she had read his thoughts. Or at least his associations.

"Anyway, Gabe was impressionable," she said. "I'm not surprised he gets himself fouled up with the media. Those things he says. He was a boy who left himself open to a lot of ideas, no matter how wild or unwieldy."

She was making sense. And becoming more talkative.

"Went off to Harvard. Came back. I ran into him in San Francisco. It must have been 1972. That's when I first sensed something amiss in him. I looked into his soul. I saw the dark forces."

"Like what?" he asked.

It was as if she were on the edge of a threshold but wouldn't step past it. Somewhere, it seemed, there was a line drawn in some distant metaphysical sand.

"I don't know," she said flatly.

"Come on," he said.

"I don't know."

"What you mean, Mrs. Vaughn, is that you won't tell me."

An expression of exasperation and mild disgust overtook her.

"I've traveled a long way," he said gently. "I might not be a believer the way you are, but I have an open mind. I want to hear what you have to say."

"Do you *really?*" she asked.

"Please don't play with me," he said. "Yes. Really."

Expecting more anger or evasion, Bill Cochrane was surprised when Elizabeth Vaughn looked down and frowned. She seemed to be thinking, very deeply.

Then, abruptly, as if reaching some distant psychological threshold herself—and passing it, making a decision as she passed—she clapped once very slightly. She wheeled around in her chair and traveled a few feet across the bare floor. She set herself before her bookcase and appeared to be looking for something.

But she wasn't looking for anything, Cochrane quickly deduced. She was settling herself, preparing herself for what she next had to say.

"I wouldn't go any farther with this if I were you," she said.

"Why?"

"I just wouldn't."

"Mrs. Vaughn. You were a teacher. I came here to learn. I'm an adult. I can make my own decisions. I want to hear what you have to say."

And somewhere in the back of his mind, he realized, a little voice was warning him that maybe—just maybe—this woman had been hitting on things in his personal life with something more than blanket hunches and lucky guesses.

When she spoke again, her face was in a shadow from the shade of the big lamp.

"I think dabbling in the occult can be dangerous," she said. "I was raised as a devout Christian. Were you?"

"Yes," he said. "A Catholic."

"But you've lapsed," she said.

"Millions of us have," he said.

"Of course, of course," she said, speaking slowly. "And it is exactly that sort of spiritual weakening that lets the Devil in."

"Come on," he said again.

"Ah," she continued. "But even then, you would understand. Maybe you would understand this even better than a devout Lutheran, such as myself. The thing is"—she weighed her words carefully now— "by our belief in Christianity we conclude that there is a world beyond this one. We believe in inherent good and inherent evil. I'm psychic. Or at least I believe I am. You may believe me or you may think I'm a fraud. Today, I honestly don't care as long as you leave me the thirty dollars. But you seem to be a good, but troubled, young man. And you're on a collision course with this stuff."

"You're losing me."

"Why did Gabe Lang *really* send you here? You have to tell me the truth right now."

"If I tell you, you can't repeat it," he said. "I don't want to see it turning up in any newspapers."

"Don't make me laugh," she said. "As if any newspaper in the eastern hemisphere would listen to me."

"He occasionally puts forth the opinion," Cochrane said delicately, "that the threat to the President comes from—as he puts it—'another' world. He asked me to investigate. And he asked me to talk to you."

"That *is* the truth, isn't it?" she said. "I recognize the truth when I hear it."

"It's the truth," he answered.

"Something happened to Gabe Lang when he went away to Harvard," she said. "Something happened and I don't know what it was. I don't want to blame the university and I don't want to blame the fact that he did so much reading. But something foreign got into his head. Into his soul, which is what you asked me about."

"You could 'see' this?" Cochrane asked.

"I could see it clearly," Mrs. Vaughn said. "You see, Gabriel started to get into things that I would never dare touch. I feel that I have an insight into other worlds. That's why I'm sometimes psychic. I can see where other people can't. And because of this, I know—I really *know*, Mr. Cochrane—that there are other worlds beyond this one. They're like walking through hidden magical doors. Hard to find, but you can arrive there if you work at it. But then you have to decide if you wish to go through."

She paused.

"Gabriel went through," she said eventually.

"Into what?" Cochrane asked.

She shook her head. "I don't know what you'd call it. I'm not sure that there is an accurate name for it. But people try to invent names: The occult. Black magic. The cabala. It's all the same thing, isn't it? It's the worship of the dark forces beyond our realm of existence. Idolatry of the Devil. Satanism."

Cochrane listened to her and wondered exactly what it was that he thought was off-center. Or right on target.

"And you saw this in his soul?" Cochrane asked.

"Very clearly," she said. "Gabriel Lang's spirit had gone over to some dark forces."

"You really believe that?" he asked.

"Yes, I do."

"You think that the current Vice President of the United States, my employer, is into Devil Worship?"

Mrs. Vaughn sighed.

"See?" she said. "This is where I knew you would misunderstand me. What I'm saying is that when one's own structure of faith wavers, sometimes—*sometimes!*—something else creeps in and takes over. That's when we encounter true evil on this planet, when someone has passed through those hidden doors."

Outside it was dark. There was a clicking sound somewhere and it startled Cochrane. Then he recognized the sound from his youth. Brittle branches rattling together in the cold wind. The sound of bones walking, someone once described it. One of the branches was scraping the roof of Elizabeth Vaughn's home.

"How many of our soldiers in Vietnam do you think were into the worship of the Dark Forces?" she asked.

Cochrane shrugged his shoulders. "Very few."

"Then how do you explain how boys from Missouri and Oregon and South Carolina, good boys from nice American families, could burn villages? Explain My Lai to me in some other terms. Tell me how

Marines and Special Forces soldiers could go around with human ears pinned to their belts, some of the ears from babies."

Cochrane reached. "Battle stress. Lack of discipline. A form of war weariness and battle insanity."

"A few years ago I saw on the TV news," she said next, "this story about these boys who had broken into a home. They'd put live fish from an aquarium into a microwave and turned it on."

Cochrane was silent. He remembered the clip.

"Tell me what possesses young people like that," she challenged. "Tell me that someone with a strong faith in Christianity would do something like that." She barely paused. "You can't tell me that because things like that are done by people with no religion, and it is when religion has slipped away, as I said, that the Devil, or Evil, or whatever you wish to call it, comes in to take its place."

"Mrs. Vaughn . . ."

"Tell me what possesses a man like Charles Manson. Or Richard Speck. Or Ted Bundy."

"An extreme callousness within certain personalities," Cochrane tried. "A lack of a conscience for one reason or another."

" 'For one reason or another'?" she repeated. She snorted a little half-laugh. "You explain it your way," she concluded. "I'll explain it mine." She paused. "What I'm telling you is that I sensed this type of thing with Gabe Lang. I saw evil in his soul. I sensed blood on his hands. This is nothing to laugh at. If something strange is going on in Washington, you should examine Gabriel Lang first."

Cochrane looked at her for several seconds, waiting to see if she would add something. By this point, he no longer had any idea whether Mrs. Vaughn was seriously off-center or totally on the mark.

But she wouldn't add something. She had gathered strength as she spoke. She had the convincing tones of one who believed herself, even if she couldn't completely transfer those beliefs to her guest.

"Thank you for your time," Cochrane said. "I think I should be going."

"I'm sure you should be," she agreed. "Right back to Washington to report what I've said. Right?"

He opened his hands gently. "Right," he said.

"I do hope Gabe will be understanding with me," she said. "I always liked him personally."

"I doubt very much that you'll hear from him," Cochrane said. "Or that you have anything to fear."

"Sure," she said. "Of course." And this time it was Mrs. Vaughn who remained unconvinced.

Cochrane rose from the sofa. The clairvoyant's wheelchair rolled along with him for a few feet as he moved toward her door. He thanked her again, trying to end the visit on an upbeat tone, and told her again that she need not be concerned with this visit or anything they had discussed.

But in terms of conversation, she hurtled right past him.

"A collision course between two worlds," she said. "That's what I'm talking about."

"What?" he asked.

"That's what you're embarked on, Mr. Cochrane," she said.

"I think you warned me once already."

"You're in way over your head on this," she said. "I'll tell you something for free. You'll be a much happier man if you walk away from this right now."

"Thank you," he said.

"Don't cross the line. Don't go through the doors that Gabe Lang passed through."

"I appreciate your concern, Mrs. Vaughn. Honestly, I do. But I can take care of myself."

"Can you?" She said it as a challenge.

Then she told a final story.

"When I was at Berkeley," she said, "studying as an undergraduate, there was something of a miniscandal in the psychology department. The thing was, the free speech campaign came around then. The big student strike. It was early 1965, I think. Mario Savio stuff. So nothing from the psych department made the major media.

"Two psychologists, a husband and wife team, were interested in what they referred to as the paranormal. Or the 'occult.' In particular they were interested in an old nonsectarian cemetery that lay right by their home. There was a particular grave that had caught their attention. The headstone on it read simply 'Wing Hu.' And under the dead man's name was the phrase 'My burning bloody feet.' "

The afternoon outside was dead. It was dark and there was the raw chill of a November New England evening that Cochrane could feel beyond Mrs. Vaughn's front door.

The two Berkeley psychologists, she said, had looked into the death of Wing Hu. From old newspaper accounts, they discovered that he had been a wealthy Chinese seaman, a ship owner who carried on a lucrative trade with the Orient in the 1850s during the first boom years of California.

Someone, however, had had it in for Mr. Hu. The Chinaman had been accused of raping a white woman in 1861. There was no evidence of a legal trial but there was evidence of so-called vigilante justice—an illegal closed trial that took place in a saloon. At this proceeding Hu, in response to allegations that he had walked from his own hotel to the Nob Hill home of his victim, could only recite the line in English, "My burning bloody feet."

The defense the man was trying to make—to the extent that he understood the charges against him—was that on his most recent voyage, his feet had become lacerated and infected first from sunburn, then from walking on a hot salt-strewn deck. And because of this, he contended, it would have been impossible for him to walk from his hotel to assault his victim.

"My burning bloody feet." Everyone in San Francisco in 1861 heard the phrase, the core of Hu's defense.

The vigilantes laughed at him. They convicted him after a ninety-minute trial. Then they hanged him. According to some witnesses years later, the rope was too slick. The noose decapitated him when he dropped from the gallows. The body twisted and writhed—the usual muscle responses when the spinal cord is severed—for several minutes. Then when he was still they quickly buried him in St. Kevin's Cemetery. His wealth was divided evenly among the jurors who had found him guilty, who received half, and the family of the victim, who received the other half, as recompense for Hu's alleged crime.

"Apparently the local sheriff was one of the witnesses," Mrs. Vaughn said. "And he profited from the verdict, too. But about ten years later, the woman who claimed to be the rape victim was dying of scarlet fever. On her death bed, she confessed that her husband had put her up to the allegation against Hu. The Chinaman had been an innocent."

"What's your point?" Cochrane asked Mrs. Vaughn.

"Just this. The husband and wife team figured that in Hu they had a subject who had died an extreme, traumatic death. They were into spiritualism and wanted to summon Wing Hu's spirit. I suppose their intent was to perhaps rebury him in sanctified grounds. But they also wanted to communicate."

"And?"

"They held a ceremony at Hu's graveside. Night after night. They used a local medium, a gypsy woman who was probably a fraud. According to their friends, this went on for a month."

Mrs. Vaughn paused.

"Then the day after the experiment ended, the gypsy woman was found dead in her home. She'd been hanged to death with a rope in her bathroom. It was ruled a suicide. Two weeks later, Mrs. Akalitis died the same way. Her husband, while a suspect in both crimes, fell mute and entered a lunatic asylum. He lived there for twenty years. The only thing he would ever say was, 'I saw him. I saw Hu.' "

Mrs. Vaughn's eyes found Cochrane's.

"Then Dr. Akalitis died by hanging, too. All three people involved eventually died the same way as Hu. Coincidence?"

"Group insanity maybe," said Cochrane. "On a small scale."

"All three, the gypsy, Mrs. Akalitis, and Dr. Akalitis, had their heads severed by their ropes, even though it should have taken at least a twenty-foot drop to do that to a human body. And standing before all three of the bodies were footprints from a small pair of feet. Bloody footprints."

Mrs. Vaughn let her point settle upon her visitor. And even Cochrane, a rational man by nature, felt his flesh crawl. He even felt something morbid come over him.

"That's my whole point," Mrs. Vaughn concluded. "I know there's a supernatural out there. I've sensed it. I know it's there. But look into it? Summon it up? Go past that hidden doorway?" She vehemently shook her head. "I wouldn't dare. And if you're as smart as I think you are, Mr. Bill Cochrane, you won't either."

Recalling all of this in his rental car as he drove back to Boston, Cochrane had the sensation of having seen Mrs. Vaughn that day through the wrong end of a telescope. The closer he had come to her over the course of the day, it seemed, the more she had receded. The more time he spent with her, the less he could figure whether she was on target or off-center. What he did know was that she had profoundly disturbed him. What he did not know was exactly why.

He turned this over in his mind as he drove. Had it been the disquieting tale she had told at the end of their time together? Had it been the dead seriousness with which she had spoken of Gabe Lang's dark side? Was it the overall kookiness and *unusualness* of the woman? Or was it something greater? Or more serious?

After all, for his entire adult life as a reporter he had told himself that he trusted his instincts. His instincts were telling him something here. And he was—yes, he realized—he was trying to *dismiss* what they were saying to him.

"And why am I doing that?" he demanded of himself, whispering aloud in the dark car as he retraced Route 37 from that morning. "Am I afraid to accept what Mrs. Vaughn believes? Am I afraid to alter the basic beliefs I've held all my life about death, dying, and the afterlife? Am I—?

Or are you afraid to approach and pass through one of those doors that Mrs. Vaughn described?

That question came to him from somewhere out of the cold night, clear as a church bell on a cold winter morning. It had come to him in the midst of another thought, almost like a news flash breaking into the midst of a scheduled broadcast.

He waited for another such flash. None was forthcoming. Wherever the first headline had been sent from, he mused to himself, they must have been in short supply.

He thought back to that afternoon, trying to construct some sense out of what Mrs. Vaughn had said.

Of Gabriel Lang: ". . . I saw blood on his hands."

Of Cochrane, her visitor: "A lot of loneliness. A lot of indecision. A sense that your youth is passing and you haven't done anything important in your life yet."

Of life and spirituality in general: "You've lapsed . . . And it is exactly that sort of surface weakening that lets the Devil in."

But what had Mrs. Vaughn been saying? That *any* defense, *any* system of spiritual values would at least provide a fortification that would fight back the evil forces? Satan loves a moral void?

Was *that* it?

How in hell did that make any sense?

He felt himself turn against her as he navigated the traffic on the highway. Who the hell was she kidding? What did she know? What had she given him all day other than a couple of vague lucky guesses?

He neared Boston. He left Interstate 93 and followed signs to return to Logan International Airport. For some reason he thought of Lisa, his superior as a reporter, and wondered how she would have handled the cryptic Mrs. Vaughn. And then his thought spiraled again, back to the religion he had grown up with and how he had lost it.

He thought of the Irish and Italian nuns who'd taught him school as a boy and he thought in particular of one priest, the benevolent foggy Guinness-tippling Father Heller, who had breath that could have been ignited by any stray spark.

He thought of the incense in the churches, the hovering angels, the refracted light through stained glass, the devout old people clutching their beads, the way he'd moved his hand the wrong way the first time he'd ever crossed himself, the endless incomprehensible masses, the cheerful baptisms, the interminable wakes, the painful overwrought funerals and the overall bitterly sorrowful sweetness of the whole Roman Catholic ordeal.

And from there he connected with how, when he passed his sixteenth birthday, much to his mother's horror and his father's knowing indulgent silence, he had rejected the whole damned Catholic boatload of it as so much latter-day superstition and hocus-pocus.

No more Confession. No more "Our Father." No more having to fold his hands in a certain way if the "amen" to a prayer was to succeed. And no more having to negotiate for heavenly joys by bartering away earthly delights.

He'd stopped going to church on Sundays, then he'd stopped going on Easter, and it was only the social occasion of the midnight mass before Christmas—surely not the service itself—that now drew him in once a year.

Well, what was that if not a void?

He caught the last flight back to Washington from Boston.

Alone again in a deserted first-class cabin of an 11 P.M. flight, a pretty stewardess indulged him in much idle conversation along the way. He saw a ring on the third finger of her left hand and felt his spirits tumble again for the day.

Toward 1 A.M. he was back in Virginia and his home.

As soon as he came in the door, he could feel a presence. He knew someone had been there. Then, in his living room, he found a note and an explanation.

Lisa had been by to pick up a few of her things that had remained behind. Cochrane sighed. He wished that she had stayed. But she also acknowledged in the note that there were still a few more things to collect in the future. Did he mind if she came by again, she asked. She would drop off the key when she was finished.

He set down the note. When he reviewed his answering machine, he also learned that she had phoned before coming in. Better not to walk in at the wrong moment, unless one wished to.

The emptiness of his own place set upon him. Lisa's absence had an echo, particularly today. He thought of phoning her but decided it was a bad idea. Then the image recurred of his father raking leaves at the state cracker box, looking up at him vacantly and uncertainly. He cringed and felt his spirits sag even further. Who was really to say whether or not his father had actually been a victim of some bizarre form of witchcraft? It explained more than the shrinks ever had.

He dismissed the notion. He was ashamed of himself for even letting it creep into his head.

Witchcraft! Hah!

Made him think of the wrecked pumpkin on Elizabeth Vaughn's decrepit doorstep. A decaying home sinking into the earth of Massachusetts. Her own private giant wooden coffin, filled with New England charm.

Then another idea shot before him. It found words.

Faith is very much a matter of habit.

He turned the thought over to himself. And then he realized that he hadn't thought that at all. It had been another one of those flashes.

He wondered where they were coming from. He still didn't know.

Seeking solace, he went to his studio, the one by the garage, and examined his oil paints. He felt like painting and putting some emotion into a canvas.

But of whom?

On the walls were the photographic studies he had made of Lisa before she had moved out. A very beautiful woman from every angle. In some ways, he felt it was presumptuous to paint her. How could he ever capture what he felt he had loved?

So her portrait remained unfinished.

Maybe, he thought, someday . . .

A surge hit him in the middle of the stomach and the surge was hunger. He reminded himself that he had hardly eaten all day and he was suddenly all appetite. He made himself a sandwich and knocked it back with some beer.

He went back down and examined the unfinished portrait again and he set a plan for himself.

He would gather his emotions, he decided, and be a mature adult about the severance of their relationship. That was the least he could do. He would put his emotional pain aside, he told himself, and do a highly professional job in completing the portrait. He would do this over the next few weeks, he decided as he finished a second bottle of beer. Then he would let the oils set on the canvas. He would find a good antique frame for the painting—something for $5 in a second-hand store, most likely—and he would mount the work.

He would have this done by midwinter. By January, he told himself. Then he would mount it and send it to her for Valentine's Day in mid-February.

She would be so impressed, he theorized, that she would return to him. Or failing that, at least he would mark himself as a class act among her former lovers.

This was an absolutely perfect idea, he told himself. There was a geometry in this universe for everything.

He climbed back upstairs, showered, and prepared for bed.

Then he turned off all the lights in his home and retreated to the darkness—the soothing comforting darkness—of his bedroom.

And despite all the ideas that were newly buzzing through his head, he slept like a child.

11

Rich Levin walked through the ground floor of his house and drew a breath.

He stood perfectly still and listened. He saw nothing. He felt nothing. But he heard something.

He stood still again and, with a twinge of anxiety, cocked his head. It was 2:30 A.M. and he couldn't sleep. He had had another in a series of repetitive nightmares reflecting strangely upon the safety of his family. And now the sound that perplexed him so much in this house bore an eerie relationship to his bad dream.

He inhaled deeply to calm himself. Upstairs, wife Barbara and daughter Lindsay slept soundly. Nothing was bothering them, and damn it, women were so much more intuitive about danger than men.

So why were his nerves scrambled? Why couldn't *he* sleep? he kept asking himself. Why was he the only one in the house who heard or sensed something strange?

He took a step into the living room.

There, he told himself. This was an ordinary room like any other. Nothing wrong with it, even though it was beginning to give him a creepy feeling. Everything was in his imagination. He moved to the front window and glanced out, looking toward the Maloneys' property once again.

A single outdoor porch light glowed, a little yellow beacon in the late autumn night.

He turned and surveyed the interior of his own house. He drew a breath. Rich Levin was an intensely rational man. He liked to think of himself as creative, but he knew he didn't have a wild imagination.

So he attempted to attack his sleeplessness with a certain rationality.

What, he kept asking himself, was really bothering him?

He froze for a second. He thought he heard a distant tapping sound, almost like fingers on a typewriter. That was strange. Was Lindsay awake, working on some of her graduate work? He walked to the stairs and glanced upward. No, he found, his daughter was in her bedroom, the light off.

And the tapping, or the typing, persisted.

That sound was funny in and of itself. No one typed at a typewriter anymore. Not like they had, say, back in the 1960s when he was in college. Keyboards were all of the computer variety now, and the sound of key whacking paper with an ink ribbon in between was something out of the past. Gone the way of carbon paper, political campaign buttons, and Nehru suits.

He smiled at the thought. One springtime Saturday long ago, a friend of his named Steve had once shelled out eighty bucks for a brown serge Nehru suit at a now-defunct store called Alexander's in New York. The following Monday, the price on the Nehrus, the fashion catastrophe of the decade, dropped to twenty bucks. By Wednesday, the price had dipped to nine ninety-five.

The thought gave him solace, amusing him in retrospect. But a nearby sound catapulted him back into the present.

That typing sound again. Where the hell *was* that damned tapping? It wouldn't stop.

He glanced through the downstairs again and still couldn't locate it. It seemed to move as he looked for it.

He went to the kitchen and retrieved a radio. He brought the radio back to the living room and turned it on. He looked for an all-night talk show from Boston. Sometimes just listening to radio chatter took his mind off other things.

"Damn," he muttered.

Reception in this room *just stank!* He adjusted the radio slightly. He tried to reposition it. The receiver wasn't the newest one in the world. Maybe it just wasn't strong enough to pick up the signals. He turned the radio off again.

The tapping persisted.

Damn it to *hell*, he thought to himself. The clicking sound, the tapping, really *did* sound like fingers on an old typewriter. What in God's name, Rich Levin wondered, was making that sound?

Then he stopped again.

"Now what's *that?*" he asked himself. This was stranger still. And for a moment he was transposed back nearly thirty years to a scent he'd known as a young man.

Perfume. He would recognize it anywhere. It was *Replique*. A girl he had dated while he was at Princeton had worn it. God, that was funny! He hadn't thought of her or encountered that scent for—

Then the fragrance was gone. Oh, now he knew he had imagined that! Barbara didn't wear *Replique*. She wore the more sophisticated *Shalimar*, which frankly he liked better. But it was funny that it had flashed into his mind.

Along with the typing sound.

Then something even stranger happened. Something cold swept through the room. It was almost as if someone—or something invisible—had walked right past him and left an icy air current in his way.

Which brought on another feeling. He knew he was alone. By everything rational Rich Levin knew he was alone.

But he didn't feel alone. He felt as if someone were watching him.

"Just crazy," he muttered to himself. "This is just crazy." But even the echo of his own words bothered him.

He felt it again. The air current. He wasn't sure whether he was imagining it or whether it was the real thing. He couldn't figure where a draft could be coming from. And then the typing sound was louder, as if it were practically in one of the other rooms downstairs.

Suddenly, he was very anxious.

He called softly. "Hello?"

No answer.

"Anyone awake?" his voice asked again. Still no response.

He went to the door to the den. There was a creak somewhere behind him in the hallway. He looked. Nothing. The floor creaked again, right before his eyes. He was looking right at the precise spot that had creaked and he could not see anything.

A shudder was upon him. He was scared. Reason told him not to be, but instincts told him that something was there. Something he couldn't see.

"No," he said softly. "This isn't happening. And I'm not scared."

He decided to prove it to himself. He would reestablish that the house was secure and then he would go back to bed, ignoring everything.

Fear was in his mind, he told himself, and he was the master of his own mind. He would exorcise his own private demons and that would be the end of them.

The next series of events was even stranger.

The human voice—the female voice—that he thought he had heard a few weeks ago was again audible. Or so he thought. It was still faint and in the background of his mind. But he could *hear* it lurking beneath the nighttime silence . . . and that damnable tapping.

Then things changed considerably. The cold draft was gone and so was the scent of perfume. And so was the tapping. It was as if all of those strange nocturnal things misted together and flew away, replaced immediately by something else.

There was now a fluttering thumping sound. And Rich didn't like the feeling of it. Worse, it was demonstrable, this noise. It sounded *live*. Very much present and nonelusive. It came from the den.

"Jesus," he mumbled to himself. "What am I hearing?"

Rich Levin stepped in the direction of the den. There was an "old house" creak in the floorboards. He continued. He approached the door to the den and wondered what was in there in the darkness waiting for him.

Three paces forward. Then a fourth. He continued bravely. Something was there.

He found himself fighting off the instinct to run. From the front hall closet, he pulled a softball bat, something he used once a year at the company picnics.

He asked himself again. What in hell was going on in this house? Why did he hear things and have nightmares? What lay ahead of him in a dark room into which he could not yet see?

The thumping fluttering sound grew louder and more intense. With his heart pounding in his throat, he stepped cautiously to the door of the den. He reached in and his moist palm found the light switch on the wall.

He flipped the light on.

In front of him was an empty room. Suddenly silent.

He scanned quickly, holding the bat in both hands, waiting for something to move.

To rush toward him.

Nothing did.

Then the sound commenced again. And suddenly he understood it. In the chimney pipe of the old stove something was alive. Alive and making a noise.

Rich calmed slightly. The source of the noise became more comprehensible. What was it? A small animal? An aberrant back draft?

He calmed slightly more. But his heart was still kicking like a boot in his chest.

He drew a breath again. He approached to where he was within a few feet of the pipe. Then he reached forward with the bat and tapped it slightly. The noise ceased. The flimsy old pipe wavered and shuddered. Levin tapped it carefully a second time.

The desperation of the sound intensified within the stovepipe. Whatever was in there

—an evil spirit?—

was flapping like a fish out of water.

Levin stood back. He waited. The source of the noise seemed to shift within the pipe. Then, completely inappropriately, he felt that cold draft again. It was all around him. Then he was aware of the perfume again. Or he thought he was.

A sudden, deeply morbid feeling came over him, something he could neither place nor understand. The feeling made him impatient and gave him a sense of dread. He suddenly wanted to end all this and go back upstairs, almost as if his warm bed represented safety— even though it had been a frequent host to nightmares recently.

Impetuously, he held the bat forward. He was still surrounded by the cold. He whacked the pipe. He would drive the intruder either down into the pot belly of the stove or back up the chimney. He'd put an end to this, that's what he would do.

He opened the flue and then rapped a fourth time on the pipe, this time harder than ever.

Too hard.

Everything happened at once. Chaos in the middle of the night.

"Oh, Jesus!" a voice filled the room. A man's voice. His own.

A scream was in Levin's throat as the old metal stovepipe disintegrated from within, rust flying in every direction, metal collapsing as its support dissipated.

Levin recoiled in holy terror as a huge flapping beast screeched and fought its way free from within the pipe. The beast

—an apparition?—

was feathered and had huge eyes, massive wings, and was angry as a wounded bear. It was black as tar from the soot and rust within the stove and it flapped and swatted at the air like an emissary of the devil, loudly screeching again its disapproval of all things in heaven and earth.

In fear, in surprise, in shock, Levin threw himself backward into a line of furniture, the bat raised above his head to save his life if necessary. His heart was no longer in his throat. It was in his mouth. It choked him and tasted like a fistful of copper pennies.

A long frenzied second passed. Then another.

Dazed and black on the floor before Levin was what appeared to be a barn owl, somehow roused from where it must have nested for several winters.

It was breathing as hard as Levin was, and was probably every bit as confused. The owl's beak opened but no shriek came out this time. Its eyes were wide and yellow as a demon's as they rudely appraised the human who had dislodged it from the pipe, perhaps even saving its life.

Its wings were extended, stretched as if to take flight. And all Levin could think of now, as he slowly calmed, was how he could somehow drive the beast from the house before it flapped fifty years' worth of stovepipe soot all over the downstairs.

As Levin's heart settled, high terror had degenerated into low domestic comedy. His nerves still felt as if they were scattered all over the place, though, much like the fragments of old tin all over the floor.

The bird must have been even more dazed than Levin, because it stayed in its place for many seconds. Levin ducked out of the room and shut the door. When he returned a few moments later, he had a broom. And he had also opened wide the back door of the house.

It took several minutes and countless thrusts with the broom. But he successfully expelled the bird. As soon as the owl was out into the night where it belonged, Levin closed the door. The chill that poured in was much like that draft that had surrounded him minutes earlier.

He looked out the back window just seconds after driving the blackened bird outside. He couldn't even find it. The bird—and there had definitely been one, he told himself—had disappeared into the night just that quickly.

Slowly, Levin turned to survey the den. He stood at the door. In one sense he was relieved. All the emotions, all the dark feelings that had disturbed him, the rappings, the would-be voices, the bad dreams, he could

—dig!—

somehow link to the owl's presence in the house. Who knew what kind of vibrations that bird had given off? Well, he figured, at least something was settled.

He cocked his head. No more noises.

He sniffed. No perfume anymore, either. Just rust and, he winced, what must have been a splendid array of bird dung in the old pipe.

He wondered how long the owl had been an unseen tenant in this house. The only thing that disturbed him now was the amount of dirt and damage in the den. With the type of insane reasoning particular to the overtired in the black hours of the morning, he wondered if his homeowner's insurance policy was going to help him with installing a new pipe.

Then logic prevailed. He knew, from many years of practical experience dealing with insurance companies, that there was probably a specific exclusion for a wide range of nocturnal feathered creatures in stovepipes.

No matter. Levin felt better about things. He put the broom to good use again and spent a few minutes sweeping up. He glanced at his watch. It was past 3 A.M. It was going to be a long day at work tomorrow, he told himself. He'd be amping himself up with coffee all day, but dragging nonetheless. Fortunately, as he thought ahead, he had no important meetings.

Then he went upstairs and went back to bed.

The bed was still warm. It comforted him and welcomed him. Barbara seemed restless for a moment. She shifted around as he came into the room, then settled again.

He thought she was sleeping.

"Rich?" she asked groggily.

He answered softly. "Yeah. Everything's okay."

"Were you up?"

"Yes."

"I thought I heard something." Barbara was still half asleep.

"You did. The old stovepipe fell apart in the den."

"Hmmm? It *what?*"

"It fell apart."

"By *itself?*"

He sighed. The dark watches of the night did not lend themselves to tidy explanations, particularly ones involving stovepipes, female voices, and tapping sounds. Or barn owls.

"It's all okay. I'll clean up tomorrow," he answered.

"Okay," she said, after another few seconds. "I was having a dream," she said. Then apparently she drifted away to another one, because she didn't say anything more.

"A dream," he thought to himself. "Yes. That was what had started all this with the owl." A bad dream which had caused him to get up. He wondered how much reality and real emotion somehow filtered itself into the planet of dreams.

The house was very still as Rich pulled the covers around him. It was as if all the bad spirits had been driven out.

Then, on the edge of sleep, another thought came to him, one that offered to put many things in order for him.

It had been some sort of bird noise that had suggested the human voice, he decided, either a scratching of the owl's talons or a low cackling. The tapping sounds also came from mice, he figured. He'd suspected he had some ever since he'd bought the house. This new theory seemed to support his original thesis. And the owl, he concluded, had been lured into the house by both warmth and a supply of hot rodent lunches.

Levin drifted to sleep. The family would get a cat, he decided. Barbara and Lindsay both liked cats, so why not?

As he drifted away, he again felt secure. And everything made sense.

These were not the days and nights of glory for Dr. Ivan Katzman, either. At least Rich Levin had discovered a misdirected barn owl. Ivan Katzman, M.D., the President's physician, hadn't uncovered much other than a torrent of criticism of himself in the press.

"Ivan the Terrible." Even some of his peers were calling him that behind his back. That really hurt.

So, very carefully, he had yielded to public pressure and brought in a specialist, a longtime friend and a peer from the Bethesda staff. The new physician was Dr. Felix Gundarson, who was to examine the President and add a consulting opinion.

Gundarson was a neurologist. He was a soft-spoken unassuming man of fifty-six, graying, Swedish by birth, and with an excellent professional pedigree, having graduated first in his class at the Medical School of the University of Pennsylvania. Marcus Welby with unimpeachable credentials. He was also a means to get the jackals off Dr. Katzman's back. Not only was Gundarson an excellent practitioner, but he knew how to play politics within the medical mafia.

Dr. Gundarson noted in advance that he knew of what may have been a similar case in Baltimore the previous year. That is, he knew of a patient in his seventies who had suffered small sporadic seizures that led to short periods of unconsciousness. In the Baltimore case, high blood pressure had been a contributing factor, as had a circulatory problem and a drug interaction.

Taking this approach, Dr. Gundarson put a surly President through a three-hour morning examination on November 9, much of which repeated tests that Dr. Katzman had done in the previous forty-eight hours. George Farley was not happy. He was, in fact, an impatient, combative, wildly profane and barely cooperative patient.

The neurologist also reexamined George Farley's family history, looking for any parallel events or any conditions that would shed light on the medical mystery. Nothing emerged from the records of any Farley parent, grandparent, or relative. Records were scanned of the Farley children, who were grown. Nothing came forth from that source, either.

The President's blood pressure was excellent for a man of his age—a mellow 126 over a happy 84. His circulation was fine. Another EKG yielded nothing. Farley only reluctantly yielded to a follow-up electroencephalogram, but brain waves on the second test proved to be perfect replications of the first. And once again, the electrical impulses from the brain were normal. If there were anything wrong there, it defied detection. Drug interaction was also ruled out as the President was on no medication. He even had a good diet and reported, with some hesitation, having sex with the First Lady "two or three times" per month. The latter was the one part of the workup that aroused skepticism from the doctors.

So Dr. Gundarson thus arrived at the same conclusion as Dr. Katzman, following a battery of similar tests. President Farley was in perfect health—except for the fact that he kept mysteriously passing out.

In the afternoon, the President kept appointments. He dressed and received leaders of Congress at his hospital suite. He had been in for three days and was tired of it. As he spoke with the Congressmen, Dr. Katzman and Dr. Gundarson conferred in the former's office at Bethesda.

Gundarson's point of reference remained the case in Baltimore, a history which somewhat resembled "petits mals," tiny epileptic seizures which resembled blackouts. The "mals" lasted for short periods, anywhere from a few seconds to an hour. Low blood sugar could occasionally be the culprit with "petits mals" and better regulated blood sugar, plus Conazine, a mild medication, could minimize their occurrence. The perilous aspect of the "mals" for President Farley, however, was that they could serve as a precursor to an onset of a more serious and virulent form of epilepsy that had first been diagnosed in the late 1990s.

" 'Petits mals' can lead to 'grands mals,' " Gundarson reviewed aloud. "Grand mals can trigger a complete physical breakdown which would make the President incapable of continuing his duties."

"Do you think that's what we're looking at here?" Katzman asked.

A common medical conclusion: "No way of knowing," Gundarson answered.

"What finally happened in the Baltimore case?" Katzman finally asked. "Did Conazine control the seizures?"

"Two weeks after the seizures began," Dr. Gundarson explained, "the patient had a massive cardiac arrest and died."

The sentence hung in the air for several seconds.

"I'd call in another heart man," Irv Katzman said, "except every heart specialist here has already looked at the charts. Either formally or informally. There's nothing abnormal."

Dr. Gundarson opened his hands. Elusive diagnoses on patients over age sixty-five were not uncommon, they both knew, even with the billions of dollars spent every year on new research and diagnostic instruments. In almost all such cases, however, there was no public attention on the patient. Physicians had time to work out courses of intervention without being second-guessed daily in the media. Celebrity patients, however, created larger problems. And the President created an enormous one.

Following that line of thought, however, Dr. Gundarson did have the further suggestion that perhaps a specialist in disorders of "older" patients should also have a look at the President, or at least a look at the President's charts.

"Either that," Gundarson said, "or a neuropsychiatrist."

Katzman looked up. "You're kidding. Really?" he asked with sudden curtness.

"Well," Dr. Gundarson said, "we have to conclude that the problem is coming from *somewhere*. If it's not neurological, maybe it's psychiatric. Mental."

"I can't wait to relay that to the President," Katzman said.

"I'd try the first course of action first," Gundarson concluded. Again, the two men found common ground.

The President, meanwhile, spent the afternoon with the Congressional delegation from both parties. There was then a short break, followed by forty-five minutes with speech writers and members of the

White House staff. His daughter came in from Chicago to see him as well.

When Dr. Katzman came back to see the President at five-thirty in the afternoon, the doctor was surprised to find George Farley on his feet and wearing a suit. Even more surprising, there were two White House aides assembling the President's working documents and two more packing his clothing.

Katzman stood perplexed for a moment, then knew the direction things were going.

"What did that Swede figure out? Anything?" President Farley asked. There was a challenge in his tone.

"Dr. Gundarson came to conclusions similar to mine," Dr. Katzman said. He amplified his statement by discussing the possibility of "petit mals," though he was also quick to point out that the two doctors were also talking theory. No definite diagnosis.

Then Dr. Katzman moved the conversation along. "Felix also suggested, and I concur, that we might want to also bring in a geriatrician."

There was a moment of silence in the room. It preceded a fire storm. "A *what?*" the President roared.

The doctor repeated.

George Farley built upon his previous reaction with the vilest torrent of obscenities ever unleashed in the Duffy Pavilion since the days of Lyndon Johnson's annual sygmoidoscopy. No way—or as the President so indelicately phrased it, "no frigging motherfucking cocksucking way"—was he seeing a doctor for old people. He damned well had every intention of running for reelection in 2004, he raged, and didn't feel like having the political liability of having seen a gerontologist in 2003. Despite the fact that he was currently hospitalized, he was not about to allow his health to become a silver platter campaign issue.

"Know something, Katzman? This sucks!" exploded the President of the United States. "I see some doctor for doddering old people, and sure as hell," Farley raged, "the other party will run someone in their God-damned forties. Not to mention what the Neo-Nazis will run against me," he continued, using his usual contemptuous term for his Far Right opponents.

Farley's eyes were sharp as tacks. "What the fuck else did Gundarson suggest?"

"That was our primary consideration," the doctor answered. Katzman didn't even wish to use the word *neuropsychiatrist*.

"Well, good. Then *that's* settled," the President hotly concluded. "And now I'll tell you where we stand. If you and your team can't figure out what's wrong with me, you can monitor me just as well in the White House as here. There's no point of me staying. I have a job to do. I have appointments to keep, asses to kick, and a God-damned election to win in one year. I'm going back to the White House tonight."

"Sir . . . ?"

"You can fly all your damned equipment over to the White House by helicopter. Or rocket packs. Or send it by Galapagos tortoise! See if I fucking care! Your wires, your hoses, your machines. Keep it there on call. But I'm going back to Pennsylvania Avenue. There's no point for me to stay here."

"Of course," was all Dr. Katzman could say. "We'll move the medical staff to the White House and remain on call."

The President turned to three female members of his staff.

"All right. Let's get this done now," he said sweetly. "And we can make the evening news in the East."

The White House staff had already concocted a press release saying that President Farley had passed all tests at Bethesda and was in perfect health. Public appearances would be minimized over the next few days, the report continued, as the President did need some rest.

George Farley left the hospital at 6:03 and perfectly captured the national news audience at 6:32 that evening. He was seen to be cheerful and in good health as he waved to reporters on the White House lawn while stepping from the helicopter.

He didn't falter at all until he was long out of the view of the public and the press, upstairs on the second floor of the White House, in the First Family's residential suite.

There, George Farley had to be helped to his bed. He had another headache, this one worse than any of the ones previous, and retired to bed immediately.

His last words, before drifting out of consciousness, were that he adamantly refused to return to the hospital. That, and something about seeing the image of a playing card.

To be specific, the Queen of diamonds.

Relatively unnoticed, one particular visitor to Washington watched the President's helicopter with more than cursory interest as it descended from low in the sky to the carefully guarded landing pad within the White House enclave.

The visitor was Carl Einhorn, who stood outside the front gates at 1600 Pennsylvania Avenue that evening of George Farley's return. Einhorn had only wanted to take a close look at the White House itself in order to get a sense of the vibrations of the place. The better he could focus on the actual physical location where the President lived, he figured, the more effectively he could send telepathic messages.

Seeing the President's chopper was a real bonus. And from the angle through which the aircraft descended from the sky, Einhorn glimpsed—or thought he glimpsed—the silhouette of the President himself, aloof and impatient as the helicopter neared its destination. But then, of course, the chopper swooped noisily into White House grounds and Einhorn's view was gone.

But nonetheless, he had actually seen him. The object of Einhorn's telepathic assault had come right into view, almost as if by preordination. The pudgy little numbers-rumbler was thrilled!

He stood at the gates with his face close to the ironwork. He peered in. He concentrated with all his might and sent evil, malicious, and hateful thoughts in the direction of Farley. Einhorn concentrated upon this for several minutes. He was distracted only when a Secret Service guard strolled into view, within the grassy area on the other side of the fence.

Einhorn knew immediately that he was under surveillance, even if a casual low-key surveillance. It broke Einhorn's concentration and caused him to withdraw a step or two. And as he reminded himself that he was carrying a weapon—he never left his hotel without it—he decided that the sooner he made himself scarce, the better off he would be.

The Secret Service man was looking right at him. *Right* at him. Surely this was an enemy. Einhorn's gun had never felt so heavily concealed in his belt. It was as if the Secret Service man were mentally frisking him.

The agent was only fifteen feet away, walkie-talkie in hand.

"Nice night," Einhorn said.

"Real nice," the agent grumbled, still watching him.

"Is the President home?" Einhorn asked.

"I wouldn't know, sir. The chopper goes in and out all the time."

"Oh," Einhorn answered.

But yet, he *knew*. He had *seen* the Chief Executive, after all. And he sensed that he had returned.

"Getting late," Einhorn said next. He turned and walked away. He expected trouble from backup guards. But none came.

Back at his hotel thirty minutes later, Carl Einhorn did something terribly unusual. He turned on the television set.

RCA Victor!
His master's voice!

As it happened, Einhorn was too late for the evening's headlines, but he saw on CNN how the President had been airlifted back to the White House. This *proved* to the former math teacher that he could trust his instincts. It even proved to him that his eyes were sharp as thorns, so good that he had seen correctly right into the Presidential helicopter.

Only one thing puzzled him.

On the news, George Farley was reported to be in excellent health and excellent spirits. This didn't jive with the bad karma that Einhorn had hurled in the President's direction from the gates at Pennsylvania Avenue. It bothered him considerably to learn this. He had wished that Farley would collapse upon reentry to his living quarters.

For several minutes he wondered why in hell this hadn't happened. Then he knew.

The press spokesman must have been lying to the public. Of course! That was it! The government was filled with liars and cheats, anyway, so a big-time falsehood about Farley's health wouldn't have been such a stretch.

Farley had probably collapsed much in the manner that Einhorn had wished, he decided. Such was the power of his intellect, he reminded himself. And such was his confidence in the messages he was sending.

Einhorn slept well.

The next morning he dashed off a couple of letters. One went to the White House, admitting that it was he who was controlling the President's mind. The other went to the *Washington Post* making the same assertion.

He didn't sign his real name. He used something playful, instead. Something mocking. Something in the now-you-see-me-now-you-don't mood.

He had a good laugh. He started thinking Presidential.

I like Ike!
All the way with LBJ!
AuH$_2$O in 64.

He went out and mailed both letters.

Everyone is voting for Jack
'Cause he's got what all the rest lack!

Then Carl Einhorn went to a luncheonette in Georgetown for breakfast, devouring a huge portion of fried eggs and bacon with milk and coffee. During his meal it occurred to him that after he snuffed President Farley, Gabriel Lang would ascend to the Presidency.

That was an interesting thought, Einhorn mused. But as far as Lang was concerned, Einhorn had no strong feelings one way or the other.

12

R alph Forsythe felt foolish.
     There he was out for a hike and there he was sitting down.
Of course, the view was splendid, overlooking the Pacific Ocean
in Marin County just above the San Francisco Bay. It was a rare and
glorious afternoon in mid-November, far from his legal practice down
in San Jose. This was the type of afternoon that he often needed to
cleanse and renew his spirit. It had been a long time since he had escaped for such an afternoon, particularly with a woman as beautiful
as the one whom accompanied him this day.

His daughter, Vicki.

Vicki Forsythe was twenty-two years old and a senior at Berkeley.
How her father loved her. How Ralph Forsythe looked forward, more
than anything in the world, to seeing her graduate this coming May.
She was a smart, beautiful young woman. She was Phi Beta Kappa and
on her way to law school, perhaps at nearby Stanford. He wanted her
to go to a law school in California so that she could eventually join
him in his practice.

Forsythe and Forsythe. It was almost, he felt, as good as having a
son. In some ways, it was even better.

Once or twice a year his schedule and hers—the intersection of
downtime from his law practice and a similar window in her academic
schedule—enabled them to go on these long walks among sequoias or
redwoods. They would hike together, finding new trails, seeing new
sights, and talking about life and law and anything else which a father-
daughter confidence could embrace. Then he would like to stop at this
spot and gaze at the ocean. She would go on ahead, take one of the

final high trails that led away from the ocean view and up into the rougher timber. Then she would circle back down to meet him.

Sometimes he worried about such a beautiful girl off by herself. He knew how evil some men could be. He knew too well that even within the kindest and most decent of men—and he considered himself to be among such—there could be a certain amount of . . . of what? . . . of

—badness?—

Well, yes. That term just seemed to come to him, as it had frequently over the years.

Badness. Evil.

Unintentional malfeasance. God knew that everyone did certain things he regretted in life. Often the bad was unintentional, as it had been in Ralph Forsythe's case.

He sat on a bench that had been donated by a conservationist and breathed in the air that came off the ocean. Life could be so demonstrably good sometimes. Like right now.

But a certain sadness had also been upon him recently, the type of sadness that afflicts a man in his fifties when he looks back upon things that he regrets. There were emotions within him—particularly over the last few weeks—that were difficult for him to confront. An old guilt that seemed to come up out of an unmarked grave and bother him.

There were things in his past, one thing in particular, that he would always regret. Something which he would somehow have to make his peace with in the next two decades. He didn't want to take it to his own grave, for example, and he would somehow have to seek grace or forgiveness before he died.

Thank God, he mused, that he was in such good health now. He didn't really have to face this quite yet. He still had time, he reasoned.

He didn't know why he had thought of it so much recently. He didn't know why an old spirit had seemed to walk. But he knew exactly what was bothering him. And he didn't quite know how to make it go away.

For some reason—and deep down he knew the reason—it was much on his mind whenever he saw his daughter. Maybe it was because she was of a similar age as—

As what?

Who ME?

As a certain nasty memory? Of a name lost in his past? One from long ago when he was at Harvard? Sometimes he cringed when he thought of what had happened back then. Sometimes he sat upright in the middle of the night, replaying old events, wondering how they might have sorted themselves out differently.

Then he reminded himself why it had been so much on his mind recently. The death of Tommy Cassatt, one of his two Harvard roommates at Lowell House. It bothered him in particular that Tommy had just dropped dead. Forsythe, a religious man, wondered if Tommy had made his peace with his Maker before he died. He hoped for Tommy's sake that he had.

He inhaled deeply again.

A Pacific breeze caressed him and he felt as if he could not possibly be more comfortable. He gazed over the blue ocean and wished he could see all the way to China.

Ralph Forsythe then looked to his left and saw no one. But he thought he had heard something. So he also looked to his right. There he saw a young woman—in her twenties, maybe—emerging by herself from the same trail that would lead his daughter back to him.

He smiled. He thought it was Vicki.

But when he glanced a second time and could see the clothing that this girl wore, he realized that it wasn't his daughter. Vicki had worn hiking shorts and a sweat shirt. This girl had a Sixties-style peasant dress. Her garb was a bit of a throwback. But it was not all that unusual in northern California, even at this time of year. Some of the kids today looked the way they had looked in 1968.

"The neo-hippie look," he mused, giving it a name. He absently wondered if his daughter was into "free love" the way some of the girls in his generation had been. He liked the way so many girls of his generation had just casually "given it away," as he termed it in his mind. And he hoped to hell his Vicki wasn't behaving in the same manner.

Forsythe turned his attention back to the Pacific Ocean.

He looked at it for several quiet seconds and the girl wandered into his view. Her dress was down to just above her ankles, but her arms were bare. She had very pale skin.

"Probably," Ralph Forsythe said to himself, "a vegetarian." This, too, amused him in a condescending way. How could anyone not eat meat?

The girl walked to the edge of the cliff that rose upon a rocky palisade above the ocean. The wind whipped at her dress and it clung to her. Forsythe watched her and found himself aroused. He smiled. It had been a long, long time since he had sexually enjoyed a woman of that age. About ten years ago, on a trip to New York, he had arranged for an expensive call girl. No harm done, as it turned out. And he had enjoyed it. But he had also felt mildly ashamed of himself.

Just as now.

He was looking at this girl as she leaned against the short wooden fence that separated the promenade from the cliff. She was standing near a broken spot in the fence. He wondered what she was thinking about, staring out at the ocean so long.

He tried to read her thoughts but couldn't.

Forsythe stood.

An urge was upon him. Sometimes, even as a happily married man, even as a successful man of law, and a loving father of a beautiful daughter, he enjoyed the company and conversation—just the company and conversation—of a pretty young woman.

Was there any harm in that?

Certainly not, he reasoned. It was not as if he was trying to put his hand under every skirt that passed, much as he might have liked to.

He stretched, unkinking his legs and back. And he strolled forward to join the young woman in the peasant dress.

He arrived at the fence several feet away from her, carefully avoiding the damaged link of fence. He didn't want to scare her or surprise her, so he tried to make a little noise as he arrived. He coughed.

She didn't turn. Yet somehow he figured that she knew he was there.

The wind swept her hair and she turned toward him. He couldn't quite see her face because her hand was in the way as she brushed her hair from her eyes. It was windy on that precipice. But he saw that she had fleetingly given him a smile, then looked away.

So she knew he was there and he figured she was friendly. He would engage her in conversation and his daughter Vicki would return, find them together, and later affectionately tease him about being an old roué, still flirting with young girls.

Well, so what? Sometimes life was fun like that.

He moved over to her.

"Gorgeous day, isn't it?" he tried.

"It is," she answered.

A chilly wind hit him hard. Something abnormal. It felt like a narrow, intense draft. But the air currents in this area were legendarily unpredictable. Just watching the gulls soar could demonstrate that to any fool upon this hill.

"It's a lovely area," he said. "Great for hiking. Great for sun. Great for just enjoying life."

"I'm sure," she said.

There was an edge to her tone. At the fringe of his consciousness a little voice was warning him about something.

But what?

That she didn't want company? That she thought he was trying to pick her up? He considered retreating. Sometimes women were innately suspicious of male strangers. And sometimes they just wanted to be alone.

So he tried to set things straight, put her at ease.

"I'm not trying to pick you up," he said. "I'm waiting for my daughter, who's your age."

She looked at him sideways. Her face was very pale, almost as if there were something aberrant about her skin. And her facial features were rather homely, even though her body was nicely proportioned. She looked a lot like one of those pale teenage girls who turn up at horror conventions, or spend all their time in their rooms reading Gothic novels.

"I'm just being friendly," he said.

"I don't give a fuck," she answered.

Her response hog-tied him. The mouths on some of these girls today! It was fine if men talked that way to each other. But these days it seemed—

Then she turned toward him. And when her eyes found his and fixed on them, it was almost as if she had locked upon him with some strange ocular radar.

It was the strangest feeling—as if he were hypnotized. As if he had stepped through some unseen doorway. He couldn't pull his gaze away, no matter how hard he tried.

"I'm so glad you're here, Ralph," she said softly and intently. "I've waited for such a long time."

In his mind, he hit a little mogul of disbelief. Then as the recognition factor escalated, the mogul turned into a mountain.

His name? She knew his name?

You're fucking correct I know your name, Ralph!

This was a girl of twenty-two. Who the—?

Someone's daughter? Her eyes held his. He searched for something familiar because he already knew it was there somewhere. He groped for something he had seen somewhere before.

Then something horrible clicked.

Yes, there *was* something agonizingly familiar. But what?

His mind shot into overdrive.

There was something . . . something . . . *something* . . .

Then he had it. And when he had it—when he placed the face and the woman—he felt his heart jump and he felt something akin to his blood flash-freezing in his veins.

His face paled. He was looking at something so twisted and macabre that it could only have risen from a hell beneath the earth. Nothing in his religion, nothing in his past, could ever have prepared him for this moment.

He was staring at an impossibility and the impossibility was staring with pure malice directly back at him.

His jaw was slack with terror. But somehow he found a few syllables.

She began to smile.

"No . . ." he said. "It's not . . . I mean, how could —?"

"But it is," she said softly.

A male voice intruded from the opposite direction.

"Ralph?"

Forsythe's head swiveled toward the invocation of his name. There was Tommy Cassatt. The dead man. Tommy was standing there talking to him, his feet resting on a cloud of nothing just on the other side of the cliff's edge.

"Ralph, be nice to her this time," Tommy warned.

Forsythe answered instinctively.

"No! No! You're dead!" Ralph snapped to his friend.

Tommy Cassatt smiled.

"But I don't deserve to be," he offered plaintively. "None of us do."

Forsythe's head snapped back in the other direction. The girl was still there. He knew who she was. She was dead, too.

His eyes widened as if they would burst. A scream started up from the pit of his stomach. It found its way through his throat, up into his mouth, and out into the open air above the ocean. Another creepy little smile crossed the young woman's white face when she heard it.

It was like music. Like the end to a finely constructed chapter in a long story. And yet there was no one there to appreciate it.

Forsythe's feet were frozen. He made a desperate attempt to flee. But some force was upon him and held him fast. A few more seconds in eternity passed.

Tommy Cassatt vanished. Back to from wherever he had journeyed.

Then next thing—and one of the last things on this earth—that Ralph Forsythe knew was that something hit him that felt as if it had the force of a freight train.

It walloped him so hard that it drove him straight through the rails of the wooden fence, toward the cliff, and far out over it. And it held him aloft for a moment, just long enough to suspend his anguish for a few extra seconds.

Another scream roared up out of his throat. And like the first one, this one went unheard by anyone living.

Ralph Forsythe had the sensation of being decapitated from reality. His feet were in the air and there was nothing but a long lethal plunge underneath him. His scream accompanied him downward.

The last thing he saw as he left the cliff was the smile on the woman's face—a wretched evil smile. Her amusement guided him toward the jagged rocks below. And in the short time he had, it occurred to him that looking up at her was something like looking up from a grave while being buried alive. He would have appreciated the irony were he not so stricken with terror and disbelief.

He fell faster than a hundred miles an hour. He hit the rocks within three seconds. The end was not instantaneous. Death took half a minute of sheer head-to-toe agony. Comprehension of how this could have happened would never come in this world.

Vicki returned two minutes later and missed her father right away. She found the seating area empty where he usually waited. A few minutes later, however, something borne on the wind

Examine the view!

told her to look downward toward the ocean.

When she did, she discovered—two hundred feet below—her father's twisted mangled corpse. Then she let go of a scream that would resound in her own ears for the rest of her life.

Ralph Forsythe may have been silenced forever, but Noah Benson, M.D., would not shut up.

When it came to the President's health, Benson, who had nothing to do with it, felt he had a calling. Or so he explained. His behavior was one of the most intrusive maneuvers in the history of American medicine, but such a detail hardly mattered to Dr. Benson. This *was* to him a calling. Keeping quiet was not something he voluntarily could have done. And the quality of the President's health care *had* become a public issue.

So he called himself another press conference in New York, using a conference room at his plush office at Park Avenue and Seventy-sixth Street. He assembled twenty-eight members of the media and once again analyzed the President's health and how he felt—again—that George Farley was not receiving proper treatment.

There was something big that the President's team of "backwoods naval sawbones" was missing, Dr. Benson insisted. He didn't know what it was, but he sure knew that Drs. Katzman and Gundarson didn't know, either. That much, said Benson, was painfully clear.

"Any fool can see *that,*" he said.

"How might a more accurate diagnosis be obtained?" a reporter asked.

"As I explained last time," Benson said, "I would need to examine the existing records *and* the patient."

"With all due respect, Doctor," another reporter asked, "isn't there something inappropriate about one medical practitioner attempting to impose himself and his opinion upon another practitioner's patient?"

In response to this, a long-suffering but indulgent expression crossed Dr. Benson's face. It was as if he had been waiting for the point to arise again.

"I explained this before and I'll explain it again since certain of you seem to have missed what I said," he said. "I'm not on an ego trip here. My concern is the public interest. I feel ethically and morally compelled to step forward for the good of the country and the welfare of a patient who could conceivably die if he does not receive adequate medical intervention. I," Dr. Benson humbly reminded everyone, "am the best neurologist in the United States."

It was the first time that Benson had ventured quite so far and behaved quite so adversarially in his challenge. The press was all over it.

"Are you saying that the President will die if you don't get to see him?" another reporter asked.

"Any patient faces catastrophic consequences when a serious condition is left without proper medical intervention," Benson said.

"What I'm saying is that I have a staff ready. I have some theories as to what to look for. I have better experience in this field than any other medical doctor in the United States. I and my associates are ready to travel to Washington at the earliest opportunity. In the national interest, I'm hoping that we will be invited."

There was a brief silence as the scribblers scribbled. A hand rose in the rear of the conference room.

"Have you been in touch with the President's medical team?" someone asked.

"I've sent them a fax and a memo," Dr. Benson said. "As yet, I've heard no response."

"Will you call them again if they don't respond?" a female voice asked.

"I'll approach that when and if it happens," Dr. Benson answered. He paused. "My phone is connected, I'm available. I reiterate. At a moment's notice I'm ready to fly to Washington."

Many of the reporters didn't exactly know what to make of Dr. Benson. But respected as he was in epidemiology, he was too big and too noisy to ignore. And he made excellent newspaper copy.

He also made good television. Not only was he on the evening news on two of the three broadcast networks, but he again found his way back on the closing ten minutes—termed by industry insiders as the "ass end"—of *Nightline.*

Thereupon, Dr. Benson repeated much of what he had said during his afternoon press conference. This time, however, Noah Benson made his assertions with even greater smoothness. The afternoon had served as an excellent dress rehearsal. Benson was developing into one of the nation's leading medical experts on TV sound bites as well as infectious diseases.

All he now needed was the country's most famous patient.

13

When the sun rose the next morning, President Farley emerged from his bedroom. He once again had a pounding headache and mentioned it to Drs. Katzman and Gundarson. They gave him empirin with codeine.

By 10 A.M. the President felt well enough to make a public appearance, meeting as a surprise with a delegation of American teachers who were touring the White House. It was a brief appearance and the President made the best of it, shaking hands with the leader of the delegation and getting his picture taken for the evening news.

Farley was careful to smile. He was almost always careful to smile, but these days he was more careful than ever. It had always been his political liability that people felt that he looked grim-faced and ornery without a smile. Sort of like a mortician in need of work. These descriptions were essentially accurate, though Farley could break into a legitimately merry grin when he was informed about any misfortune befalling someone he didn't like.

To get elected President, he had battled the public perception that he was old. And now, looking ahead to his reelection in 2004, he was fighting the notion that he was also infirm. So an appearance as a smiling, energetic President, if only for a few minutes, was a welcome opportunity, particularly today.

Then his advisors got him away from the teachers before he suffered one of his dizzy spells or fainting episodes in public. There was no use overdoing things. He retreated to a working area of the residential apartment in the White House. He dressed casually and would conduct business there for the duration of the day.

That afternoon, the White House published a full list of appointments kept, but most of them were of the "powder puff" variety—easy meetings with nothing of serious substance. Appearances again, as opposed to real meat-and-potatoes issues. But the various scribblings on the Presidential calendar did count as a "nearly full" schedule, even if nothing important transpired. And it did make it seem again that the President was fine.

Which he wasn't. Not completely.

He couldn't be fine if no one knew what was wrong with him, unless nothing was wrong. But that wasn't the case, either, because something obviously *was* wrong. A man didn't just slip in and out of consciousness.

And as the headaches continued, little Carl Einhorn continued to hold his ritualistic "sessions," at the Hotel Wescott, resolutely beaming evil vibes toward 1600 Pennsylvania Avenue. Einhorn was having a deliciously good time with these sessions and was looking to agitate world events further by doing some homework on the Vice President. He had heard that Gabe Lang kept a place in Georgetown, for example, and he wondered whether he'd be able to find it.

Maybe, Einhorn could even find it by telepathy—by just going over to Georgetown and following his blunt little nose.

Deputy Prime Minister Jean Bellocq of Canada was in Washington and called upon President Farley in the late afternoon. Bellocq was under instructions to express the concern and good wishes of his government, which he did. The American Secretary of State, David Richmond, was on hand for the visit.

Farley received the Minister cordially. Afterward, the Deputy Prime Minister and the Secretary of State adjourned to the Secretary's office in the White House. There they could engage in more substantive talks. That evening Farley commented to Richmond that he thought Bellocq looked "particularly shifty, even for a French Canadian."

Richmond agreed, adding that it was his understanding that Bellocq had a Creole grandmother who had emigrated to Montreal from Haiti in the 1940s. Farley was intrigued with this, noting that Bellocq hadn't seemed "entirely white, which figures."

Farley continued by commenting that he'd never cared much for the current Prime Minister of Canada, Richard Montgomery, either, even though the latter was of pure English Protestant stock.

"Even though he's English, he reminds me so much of that smart-ass Trudeau from the 1970s. Know what I mean?"

Richmond knew. Both Trudeau and Montgomery were partially bald and were from the same political party.

He also knew that Farley didn't even much like Canada. The Canadian government was always agitating with what Farley considered to be "petty, insubstantial problems. Mostly trade and tariff bullshit. Things like cod fish filets and beaver pelts."

The neighborly disputes with Canada were small change on the international scale. But an accumulation of them had once caused Farley's political party problems in Maine, New Hampshire, Minnesota, Michigan, and Washington around election time, even though Farley had asked if the Canadians could "hold their water" until after election day. When they hadn't, he threw an Oval Office fit on the telephone to Prime Minister Montgomery. With the problems unsettled, Farley's party lost two U.S. Senators and nine Representatives from the five affected states.

Farley had not forgotten and, with the Canadians in the forefront of his mind, had even ranted profanely about this to Dr. Katzman when he came by at 6 P.M.

Ivan the Terrible nodded indulgently and grinned.

This was a good sign, Ivan Katzman decided, which was why the White House doctor smiled. The President seemed like his old ornery self that evening, an optimistic sign if ever there were one. Maybe, the Conazine was showing some speedy benefits, Katzman reasoned. And even though neither he nor Dr. Gundarson had any better idea of what had ailed the President, at least the Chief Executive had gotten through one day back at work without a collapse or a blackout.

For that, both doctors could be grateful. But they agreed to stay on call and on the premises of the White House till midnight when the President would be safely asleep.

Across town, however, the Vice President was having not as busy a day. The weather had turned sharply colder in Washington and the reduced temperatures outside seemed to have given the Vice President a permanent blush.

Exactly why, Cochrane did not know as he entered the Vice President's office and sat before his boss. Lang was rarely outside. It was someone like Cochrane who wore down the shoe leather, running assignments, or at least beating a path from a car to a library or to an airport or to a long-lost teacher who dabbled—supposedly—in clairvoyance. So how could the weather have affected the wrong man's color?

This was one of many questions that Cochrane did not yet dare ask.

"Ah, William. William, William, William . . ." Gabe Lang said as he leaned back in his chair behind a desk. It was almost as if he were trying to find a range on his press attaché by finding a range on his name.

The Vice President stood up from where he sat behind his desk. He was wearing a pale yellow buttoned down shirt and a regimental tie. His suit was dark but he had removed the jacket. He looked almost professorial today. Almost like a normal person.

And as he stood, he was flanked by a pair of flags, one American, the other from the State of California. Lang kept them both and used them individually or in tandem, depending on how he wanted his picture taken.

"Hello, sir," Cochrane answered.

"Have a seat, will you?" Lang said.

Cochrane was already sitting. Lang sat also.

"This is one hell of a city," Gabe Lang said. "Hell of a city. All anyone talks about is George Farley and his damned fainting spells. His fainting spells. Or whatever they are. I envy you a little being able to get out of here for a few days."

"It was just one day," Cochrane said.

"Was it? Seemed longer. Seemed longer. Maybe because I was waiting too anxiously."

Lang's eyes moved up and down on Cochrane, almost as if they were looking for something specific.

"One day," Cochrane answered. "And I found Elizabeth Vaughn."

"Ah! That's good," Lang answered. "That's very good. Of course, I knew you *would* find her. Now I want to hear every little thing. So let's have it."

There were no pleasantries and nothing as a lead-in. Bill Cochrane went straight into his briefing.

Cochrane began with a report on what he'd found through the Secret Service two days earlier. That was, nothing.

He had carefully read every file that had some bearing on the occult plus every other crackpot document in the annex, he explained. There was nothing there that he could yet put a finger on, he said, that would support Lang's contention of an occult threat to the President.

"Maybe it's a threat to the country. The United States. Or maybe it's a threat directed at me," Lang said in a low voice, listing targets presumably in their order of importance. Exactly why he recognized a need to identify what country he was referring to was something else that Cochrane let pass.

"I'm not even sure who or what the threat is against. I just know it's real," Lang said. "And it comes from another world, William. I know it does. I'll tell you more in a few minutes. Please go on. Go on."

The Vice President rested an elbow on his desk, his hand supporting his chin as he gazed forward at his visitor. His brown eyes were sharp and intense. He was on edge today even more than he had been the last time Cochrane had seen him. Lang's free hand played with a small pile of paper clips that were at the edge of a blotter.

Why was Lang so hyped, Cochrane wondered. The potential pressures of moving into the White House? The love-hate relationship Lang had for the office of President? More antagonisms between Farley and Lang?

Or was there an extra element of looniness about Lang now that there was actually the prospect of him attaining the Presidency? As Cochrane spoke further of what he had found over in the Secret Service gulag, these questions played through the back of his mind as he spoke through the front.

And, God! Cochrane thought. If Lang was ready to crack *here,* how little would it take for him to freak out *after* moving to the White House? The President was suffering seizures and the Vice President was on another planet and Bill Cochrane was trying to pretend that Washington was just plain eighth grade civics as usual. His final thought in that chain settled upon David Richmond, a Wall Street lawyer, a successful business guy from New Jersey, who was the Secretary of State and totally lacking in World View. Third in line of succession and not much better or worse than the first two.

Cochrane shuddered.

What nonsense. If he weren't convinced that most governments in the world functioned with a similar Moron Quotient, he might have been more depressed or alarmed.

"Your friend Martin Kane said he would contact me if anything else interesting came in," Cochrane continued. "So I'm waiting to hear from him."

"Okay. Tell me about Lady Elizabeth," Lang asked.

At this point, Cochrane saw little reason to sugar coat it.

"She said you were going to become President," Cochrane said. There was a beat. A moment passed. Lang never flinched.

"I expected she would," the Vice President said. He thought about it. "Did she say how. Or when?"

"No."

For some reason, Cochrane now hesitated.

"Well, come on, William," Lang said. "Give it to me straight between the eyes. Regale me with the anecdotes. I haven't seen the old witch for two and a half decades. What did she say?"

When the words came, Cochrane was uneasy with them, uneasy because he didn't believe them himself.

"She said there was some sort of Devil's prophecy," he said, deciding suddenly to unload all of it at once. "She said that due to it, this 'prophecy,' you would eventually take office. A 'deal with the Devil' that she believed you had made. She also said there was an aura around George Farley and that his health was being manipulated from the outside."

Lang waited a moment.

"From the outside?" Lang asked. "You mean, like via some psychic force?"

"She gave me the impression that was what she meant," Cochrane answered, to his own shame.

"Uh-huh." Lang pursed his lips for a moment. His free hand found a pencil to fiddle with. The hand that held his chin didn't move. His eyes looked distant.

"Anything else?" he finally asked.

"Yes. She said that she saw something dark in your spirit. Said she saw it many years ago and saw it again now."

"Did she say what might have caused this? An event? An idea?"

"No."

"She didn't say that she had seen, or envisioned, any event in my past. Something I might have, say, done or been witness to?" Lang asked.

"No."

"You're sure?"

"I was there," Cochrane said, his patience fraying. "She wasn't much for explaining things. Only giving impressions. Very general ones, too, I might add."

"Of course," Lang said softly but with easing intensity. "That's what she's like. That's what she's always been like."

The Vice President thought about it and then his mood seemed to change. He leaned back in his chair and a little wave of relaxation seemed to go around the room.

"Well, then?" he asked. "That was it?"

"That was the essence of it," Cochrane said.

Lang rubbed his hands together.

"I know where I stand with Lady Elizabeth then, don't I?" Lang asked.

Cochrane said nothing, only watched his superior.

"To the extent that it's important, that's good. Very good," said Lang. "Of course"—he wrung his hands for half an instant as he spoke—"most people think she's a nut, so why should I pay her any attention? Correct?"

"I was wondering the same," Cochrane said.

Lang forced a smile. "Just a little superstition of my own," he said. "We all have them, you know. Superstitions. One way or another. Like not walking under a ladder. Or always putting your shoes on in the same order. Or not opening a letter for a short while in case there's bad news in it. Know what I mean?"

"I know what you mean."

"What are yours, William?"

"What?"

"Your superstitions?"

Cochrane thought about it. And in the back of his mind the scenario of writing a letter of resignation began to unravel again. This was all so preposterous that he wondered what he was doing taking part in it. It depressed him.

"I don't have any," Cochrane said.

Lang laughed. "We all have some."

"Then I'm not aware of mine," Cochrane answered.

"That's a better answer," Lang said. He smiled. "You're telling me you've never crossed your fingers or carried a rabbit's foot or a lucky penny or hung a horse shoe in your home?"

"Not as an adult."

Cochrane wondered where the Veep was taking this.

"A completely rational man, eh, William?" Lang pressed. "Nothing funny or cloudy going on in William Cochrane's fine head, is that right?"

For a moment, Cochrane thought Lang was—of all things!—ridiculing him for his hard-eyed rationality. A little flash of anger surged through him. But Cochrane stayed within himself for a moment longer.

"I try to judge anything put before me on the body of its visible evidence," Cochrane said, again shamed to even have to explain such matters. And he could hear a certain terseness creeping into his own tone. He tried to temper it. In the back of his mind, the resignation letter was now doing handsprings.

"Well, that's good. That's good," Lang said, again seeming to change directions. It was as if there were an emotional breeze in the room and it buffeted Lang around at its own gentle will.

"After all," the Vice President continued, "that's why I hired you, didn't I? To be my hardheaded realist. Right?"

Cochrane said he could live with that analysis of his employment.

Then Lang rose from behind his desk. He turned slightly and pressed a hand to his chin. He stared out the window for a moment at the city of Washington, then turned back to his attaché.

"Shit," Lang said. He turned fully. "William, I want to ask you something important," Lang said. "Even though I *know* the damned answer, I want to ask. We talked about a Devil's prophecy," he said, seeking to make a small joke of it, "now I'll be the Devil's Advocate. All right?"

Cochrane shrugged. "Go ahead," he said.

"I want to know if you believe in ghosts."

Cochrane felt his heart beat once. Normal rhythm. What was surprising was the blatancy of Lang's question. It was right out there in the open where anyone could shoot at the screwball nature of it.

Cochrane sighed.

"Well?" Lang pressed.

"Is there a right or wrong answer to this?" he parried.

"The honest answer is the right answer, William. The honest answer." He paused half a heartbeat. "Well? I don't have all eternity, even though I wished I did. Do you believe in the existence of ghosts? Departed spirits?"

Cochrane waited for a moment. A creepy feeling was upon him, but he managed to chase it away.

"No," he answered.

"Why not?"

"Never seen one, for one thing," Cochrane answered, parrying carefully.

"Ever seen God?"

"No."

"Then what's the difference?"

"Not much," Cochrane said. "I have my doubts there, too."

Lang laughed. "Ah! Agnostic? Atheist?"

"Agnostic," Cochrane conceded. "A lapsed Catholic, but—"

"No longer 'practicing'?" the Veep asked.

"I've had enough practice," Cochrane said. "Now I'm lapsed."

"In other words, you just don't believe in spirits. Holy or otherwise," Lang said.

And again in the back of his mind, Cochrane realized that this conversation had a funny echo of the one he had had with Elizabeth Vaughn. A lapse in faith which created a void, into which evil—or something—was free to enter.

"No. I don't," Cochrane answered.

Lang laughed again. "Well, if you're an agnostic on God Almighty and Jesus Christ, then maybe you could be an agnostic on the ghosts, too," Lang said.

"Why?"

"I'd just like you to keep an open mind," Lang said. "A few moments ago you said something concise and intelligent about examining visible evidence. I liked that. I liked that. Think you could do that in any direction I sent you?"

Cochrane said he could.

"Then that's fine," Lang said. "That's all I'm asking."

Lang let a long, long pause hang in the air. When he began again, his mood had darkened.

"I'm just sick about something that's recently happened, William. Sick," he announced.

Cochrane waited.

"I lost my other Harvard roommate two days ago," Gabriel Lang said.

"Lost?"

"Died," said Lang, who was clearly distressed and uneasy with the topic. "Very suddenly again. Some sort of hiking accident. Or it appeared to be an accident. Or"—he shook his head—"or something. God knows what."

"You're kidding," was all Cochrane could immediately say.

"Wish I were," Lang said. "But I'm not. First, Tommy Cassatt and now, Ralph Forsythe."

"Two old friends in the space of what? Ten days?"

"Eight," said Lang.

"I'm sorry," Cochrane found himself saying. "That's terrible. I really do sympathize."

"I'd like you to be more than sympathetic," Lang said ruminatively. "I'd like you to see if there was any . . ." Lang searched for the word.

"Pattern? Link?" Cochrane asked.

"Yes. Would you?"

"Just curious," Cochrane answered. "Why don't you ask the FBI?"

"Would you if you were me?" Lang asked petulantly. "It would be all over the papers in twenty-four hours if I spelled out exactly my concerns. Same as your trip to Lady Elizabeth."

Lang then amplified a bit.

The Vice President *had* asked a friend at the FBI, an agent named John Gleaves, to put together a brief profile on his two departed classmates.

"I told them it was bedside reading," Lang said. "I wanted to know a little about my friends' lives so that I could drop a lengthy note to the widows and half-orphans. That sort of claptrap. I didn't state my real purpose for the reasons just discussed."

Cochrane supposed that the Vice President was correct on that point.

"I'm told the files will be complete in another day or so. I'd like you to have a look."

Cochrane nodded. "All right," he said. "And then what's this mean next? More travel?"

"More travel," Lang affirmed.

"I don't mind," Cochrane said.

And in the back of his mind yet another thought had emerged. These may have been mortalities, these two former roommates. But at least there was probably a logic to them. Which is more than could be said for what Cochrane was witnessing close up.

And besides, he further reasoned, a couple more trips might do him good. So he said he'd do the investigation. Lang gave him the proper addresses, plus the phone number of John Gleaves, the contact at J. Edgar Hoover's old boys' club.

"I knew once again," Lang said in closing, "that I could count on you, William. See, a hard-eyed realist such as yourself is what I have to have on this case. A realist. I can't have a dreamer. I need someone stable. Someone stable."

Back out on the street in Georgetown fifteen minutes later,

Cochrane was still trying to put a cohesive form to his latest conversation with Gabriel Lang.

Despite his youth, Cochrane was spiritually from the old-style generation of newsmen and press attachés who felt that the idea of coincidence did not exist. If something happened with an apparent pattern, then there *was* an apparent pattern. And it was up to the investigator to determine what that pattern was.

But initially, as he turned over the events in his mind, Cochrane found himself lifted slightly. It was as if the specter of two sudden midlife deaths, coincidental though they may conceivably have been, were what had thrown Lang into a funk.

They were the reasons why, Cochrane theorized, the Vice President had seemed particularly spacey.

He sighed and went to his car, hardly noticing a pudgy little man who was standing across the street from the Vice President's residence, and who turned away quickly and fled when Cochrane looked twice in his direction.

Ivan the Terrible was lousy at squash, also.

Or at least that was one of the many thoughts that was going sourly through Dr. Katzman's mind as he stepped off the squash court in the basement of the White House.

It was 10 P.M. that same evening. The day hadn't been all that great. And yet, Dr. Katzman felt good.

Katzman sensed that he was starting to get a few breaks in the press. He also felt that the President's health seemed to have stabilized— for that day, at least.

Katzman sat on a bench in the small locker room that adjoined the Presidential swimming pool. He sipped a Diet Pepsi. Dr. Felix Gundarson, fresh from beating Katzman 15–9 and 15–7, sat down next to him. The game had allowed the two doctors to remain on the premises of the White House but catch some exercise also. It was a good deal all around.

And yet the same thing bothered both of them. Dr. Noah Benson, suddenly the country's best-known medical busybody, kept sending faxes from New York and making waves in the press. It was just a matter of time until Dr. Benson graduated from *Nightline* and turned up on *Larry King Live*. Or *Oprah*.

"I wish," said Ivan Katzman with a rare dose of candor mixed with sentiment, "that the son of a bitch would just go away. Or better, get hit by a truck."

Felix Gundarson, the icy Swede, had been giving some angry thought to the same subject. And he had come to an altogether different conclusion.

"There's another way to look at it, of course, Ivan," Gundarson answered.

"What might that be?"

"Benson is grandstanding," Felix Gundarson said. "He's well known for that. The best way to put someone like that in his place would be to call his bluff."

Dr. Katzman got the message. But he wasn't yet convinced.

"What are you talking about? Allowing him to see the President?"

"Perhaps. Or maybe just the President's charts."

"Risky," said Katzman.

"Maybe less risky than you think."

"We call Noah Benson and his team down here and we're conceding that we're stumped," Katzman answered.

"If President Farley is not having 'petits mals,' we *are* stumped," Gundarson said. "All the more reason to cover ourselves by doing the extra consultation."

"I'm not following," Dr. Katzman said.

"Noah Benson said he was ready to put a team together and get here immediately. It would surely take him two or three days. Then another day or two to gain access to the President and offer a diagnosis. I say, we put Noah Benson on the spot. He wants the hot seat, let him have it. If he finds something further that we've missed, we concur. If he doesn't find anything further, he's been shown up as the loudmouth that he is. Meanwhile, we're covered in that we solicited a further opinion from an expert in epidemiology."

Ivan Katzman started to think about it. The idea was quickly growing upon him. And he knew that if there were a part of medical practice at which Gundarson excelled aside from neurology, it was politics.

"You have a point," Katzman said.

Gundarson looked at his watch. It was 10:15 P.M.

"He said he was available for a call at *any* hour, didn't he?" Gundarson asked.

"I didn't listen exactly. But I think that's what he said."

Gundarson smiled and raised an eyebrow. "I watched him carefully. It's exactly what he said."

"So?"

"So clear it immediately with the President. Then call Dr. Benson at 2 A.M.," Felix Gundarson advised. "You'll get his answering service. Leave the message. Then leak to the press that Benson's been invited to consult. The reporters in New York will be all over him before he's even out of bed tomorrow morning."

Katzman looked to his friend and set aside his soft drink. He pondered the point and found paths of both reason and mischief within it. For the first time in several days he allowed himself a long wide smile.

He began to undress for a shower. He tossed his empty soda can toward a trash basket. It missed.

"In which course in med school did you learn tricks like that?" Katzman asked.

"Ethics," Gundarson said. "One practitioner has no right to intrude on another's patient. If he does, he deserves to have his ass kicked."

Once again, Katzman and Gundarson concurred in their diagnosis.

14

It was the middle of a cold night, and Barbara Levin was in that elusive land midway between wakefulness and sleep.

She rolled fitfully in her bed. She tossed. The night outside her home was quiet. The last thing she had seen when she had looked out the window was a clear beautiful sky, plus the Christmas tree and decorations that the Maloneys had put on their property across the street. They even had a big porcine Santa Claus on their roof top near the chimney. Santa looked like Burl Ives.

Barbara had always loved this time of year. Nice and cold. Crackling with energy. Inside her new home, it was cozy. The holidays were coming and she had a beautiful family.

So why was sleep elusive? She was safe in her house, wasn't she? Her husband was next to her. But a husband and a home were physical protections within the tangible world. And what was bothering her was coming from somewhere else.

A nightmare.

Every parent's worst nightmare. Her only child dead.

Worse, Barbara had the sense that she had had the same dream the previous night! Yes, damn it! That was it! She was hurtling through the same mental horror every night.

And here it came yet again, pounding through her like an unwelcome wave.

It was a vision.

An image. A horrible one was coming together in her subconscious mind, and she didn't like it. She knew it was going to be unsettling. Frightening. She knew it even before the image took over her.

She rolled over again in bed.

She could almost hear herself thinking. Barbara had seen Lindsay in her coffin, a beautiful girl—the loveliest and most beautiful daughter in creation—dead in a long white satin dress.

Sort of like a bridal gown.

"Oh, God," Barbara thought with a tremor. Her eyes were open in the darkness of her bedroom. It was a 3 A.M. world and not a pleasant one.

Buried alive!

"Now where did *that* come from?" she wondered. That thought, that little phrase, was so clear that it sounded like a human voice. Something—someone—was whispering evil in her ear in the middle of the night.

A dead woman's lips are pressed close to your ears, Barbara Levin.

Was this a nether world inside her head? Or another world somewhere else?

"Where *are* these thoughts coming from?" Barbara asked herself.

Whispering to you,
I'm
whispering to you.

Barbara was so deeply upset that she sat up in her bed, half expecting something to move in the darkness.

Ah! Wonderful! You can sense me!
You know I'm here! Well, that's fine
because I'm dead and I know you're
here, too!

"Go away!" Barbara said in a dry, croaking nighttime voice. "Leave me alone! Go!"

She tried to settle back into the warmth and comfort of her bed. But she wasn't able.

Again, the voice was so clear that it sounded like a pair of lips near her ear. Horrible nearby whispers in the dark. Whatever spiritual creatures inhabit the night and the land of half-sane half-rational dreams, they seemed to be here.

Very close by.

A blast of cold air hit her. Cold as a frozen lake in the Berkshires. Cold as a granite mausoleum on a winter morning.

Fuck you!
Dead daughter!
Barbara Levin!
Fuck you!

Barbara's eyes were wide now. A line of sweat, thin little beads, were across her brow. Her vision settled into the darkness of the room and, oh, my *God!*

She thought something moved.

"Jesus!" she thought, sitting up now in stark terror. "Something *is* moving! There *is* someone in here!"

Her heart hit a beat that felt like a firecracker. The fear in her mouth tasted like a rusty knife.

"Rich!" she yelled. "Rich!"

Her hand punched at the lamp on the night table beside her. She fumbled with the switch.

His voice: "What the—?"

Her husband emerged quickly from deep sleep, sitting upright. Baffled. Confused.

Scared.

Searching the room.

Wondering—

Barbara found a grip on the light switch and put it on. The room flooded with a rude, stark, intrusive unwelcome seventy-five middle-of-the-night watts.

Everything was still.

"Honey . . . ?" Richard said, looking around quickly, wondering anew what was happening. "What's the matter?"

She looked around the room. There was nothing there except all the familiar objects. The usual dressers, the drawn shades. The clothing her husband had left out. Everything where it had been left when the Levins had crawled into bed at 11 P.M.

He reached to her.

"Barb . . . ?" he asked.

She exhaled a long breath. Her heart still felt like a fish flapping in her chest. As her fear subsided, she felt silly.

"I'm sorry," she said.

"Nightmare?" he asked.

"Yes. A nightmare."

He put an arm around her.

"Want to talk it out?" he asked.

She shook her head. She didn't want to. It was too terrible.

He held her more closely. She had a feeling that he understood very well. He sympathized. That helped her immensely. The fear was still within her, a little menacing blue pilot light that wouldn't extinguish.

"If you change your mind," he said, "wake me up."

She nodded and kissed him.

"All right," she said.

He settled back into their bed. "Leave the light on if it helps you, honey," he said. "I'll fall asleep no matter what."

"All right," she said again.

Barbara Levin sat in bed for several minutes without moving. There had been something about that dream, that vision, that disturbed her more than anything similar that she had previously experienced.

It was as if that particular nightmare—that particular horror—had had her name on it.

Several minutes passed as she tried to relax. Then, with another of those inexplicable cold drafts, another thought came to her. It was accusatory and personal, like an unwelcome footstep elsewhere in the house:

*It does have your name
on it, Barbara.*

She shuddered. She trembled.

What was happening? Was she reading her own thoughts? Carrying on some psychotic dialogue with herself? Or was this—she wondered yet again—originating from somewhere else?

Yes. It is.

"Yes, *what?*" she whispered aloud.

No answer was forthcoming. But she had the worst damned feeling that there was a presence in the room. Something that she couldn't see. And something that she deeply feared.

She experienced a shake so abrupt and violent that she thought it would raise Rich again. But he was starting to breathe evenly and deeply in the cadences and rhythms of sleep.

—Sleep! Death's substitute!—

Barbara told herself she was being silly. She tried to wheel all of the artillery of her rational mind into place to dismiss these night terrors. She looked around again and saw nothing out of the ordinary.

She practiced deep breathing. The deep breathing reminded her of the exercises from when she was pregnant. And that in turn made her think of her nightmare again. But eventually she settled back onto her pillow and tried to relax.

Now she tried to hear that voice again to see if it would come to her. It wouldn't. She breathed a little better, thinking she had dismissed it. In any case, it wasn't there.

Or she couldn't hear it.

She closed her eyes, then opened them for a moment.

She was still safe. Secure. Rich was snoring lightly. Normally that might have bothered her. Tonight it reassured her.

She left the light on. And she closed her eyes for another grasp at sleep.

It did not come easily but eventually it came. And it was not peaceful.

This time, she even felt the terror coming. The sensation reminded her of a lakefront cottage her parents had had in the Catskills when she was a little girl. The lake was many miles long and on hot summer afternoons she could see storm clouds rolling in, coming toward her, presaged by an extreme drop in the afternoon temperature.

Well, hell. She had felt a cold draft again right when she'd started to enter this realm of sleep. So why not storm clouds, too?

The storm—the dream—approached stealthily until she experienced the sensation of tumbling. She knew she was drifting downward into the scarier nether regions of sleep.

Tumbling, tumbling.

Free falling through reality.

Or into another reality.

Faster and faster . . .

And then she was shocked. She felt herself twist in her bed, but her eyes were locked shut. She knew this was a dream. But she couldn't escape it.

"Oh, God!" she thought.
She knew:

Hey!
It's the same dream, Barb.
Welcome back!

She was at a funeral again. She was under a clear azure sky. Lindsay was all dressed up to be buried.
"Good-bye, Mom," said Lindsay's corpse.
"Good-bye, Lindsay," said her mother.
Open coffin. Plenty of conversation between the dead and the living.
Barbara's daughter was in a favorite dress, and she was lifeless. Gradually, in Barbara Levin's dream, people came into view around her and everyone was crying. These were people she loved. Her family. Her mother and father.
Her grandparents were there, both of whom had died years earlier.
"Hello, Barb. Grampa and I came back just for Lindsay's funeral," her grandmother said.
Barbara shook in her bed. So nice of her grandparents to make the trip.
"From where?" Barbara wondered.

From the other side of life,

the voice whispered.
Someone laughed.
Three strange young men—looked like college boys from the late 1960s—turned and walked away.
So what, that someone's daughter was dead?
Everyone else was devastated.
Everyone else was crying because their lovely Lindsay was lying perfectly still and lifeless in the coffin, hands folded across her chest. Rich stood by, looking as if he had expected something like this. In her dream, Barbara again felt herself twist in bed, fighting the sheets and the pillows and wanting to cry out.
But she couldn't.
She wanted badly to escape this vision.

Not just a nightmare, Barbara.
Remember! It's also the future.

In the dream, she couldn't move, and she couldn't move in her bed, either. And she realized that she was looking at herself estranged from her own body. She was at Lindsay's funeral, and suddenly she was seeing it through the eyes of others.

Then there was something else.

Her head turned quickly away from her daughter's coffin. Then she looked back. Barbara's eyes opened and went wide. Bright as headlights, windows on a soul in torment.

Lindsay was gone. She wasn't in the burial box anymore. Didn't want a funeral. Or couldn't bring herself to be buried here.

"So she's alive?" Barbara begged.

No . . .

"Then where's Lindsay?" Barbara asked. "Where is my daughter?" She searched.

Gone!

"Where?"

See how it feels!

Suddenly everything was dark around Barbara. It was as if night had fallen out of the sky in the middle of the dream afternoon. She was in a dark place. And Lindsay was standing before her, but fading.

"No! Lindsay, come back!"

Barbara was speaking aloud in her sleep. She was reaching out for the girl she had brought into the world through a difficult pregnancy and a painful delivery—

—the girl who had been created from her own flesh—

Barbara kept reaching. Lindsay kept fading.

"Mother, help me! I'm too young to die!"

Lindsay sank into the earth, calling out for her father also. Barbara was reaching, mother's and daughter's hands trembling and grasping for each other . . . but Lindsay finally slipping screaming into the ground.

An unmarked grave.

And the final horror, as Lindsay's pretty face convulsed with fear, as Barbara watched helplessly, still trying to pull her back.

Lindsay's beautiful face contorted into something feral and horrible and then

—then? what then?—

became a different young woman completely. And she sank beneath the level of the earth and disappeared.

There was another cry of terror in the throat of Lindsay's mother. But Barbara opened her eyes first. She caught the scream before it escaped.

The dream was over. Barbara was lying in her dark bedroom, Rich asleep beside her. She felt a thumping sound and knew it was her heart.

In the stillness of the night, she waited for several minutes. She was so shaken that she was afraid to move. Finally, she rose from the bed. She felt that she had to leave her bedroom just to escape this atmosphere.

She went to the bathroom first. Then she quietly put on a light in the second-floor hallway. She found her way downstairs and turned on a light in the living room.

She sat down on the sofa. She was very conscious of the quiet of the night that surrounded her.

And then in the stillness, somewhere in the house, came a soft noise. The sound of a tapping. The sound of—what was it, she wondered—almost the sound of something enclosed somewhere and which wanted to escape.

Tap, tap, tap.

Barbara was highly apprehensive.

What now? What was *this?*

A strand of Beatrice Potter rose from a distant memory to greet her.

Tap tap, Tap tap it
Who's there?
A tiny rabbit

The nursery rhyme mocked her, its innocence juxtaposed with her terror.

She was distressed out of her mind, stricken by a nightmare and hearing strange noises in an old house.

The tapping continued, like some wicked bird with talons hacking its heels against a roof.

Or, or, or like a typewriter, she suddenly realized.

Tap, tap, tap.

That's just what it was like. Tapping on a typewriter.

Then it stopped completely. And it was replaced by heavy footsteps.

Her heart jumped again.

A human voice. Male. Questioning. Concerned.

"Barbara?" it asked.

She let go a long sigh of relief. It was Rich's voice.

"I'm downstairs," she said.

Rich stood in the upstairs hallway, looking down. He turned on a hall light. Then he slowly came downstairs. Barbara was still sitting on the sofa in the living room, looking at him.

"You okay?" he asked.

This time, she didn't answer.

"It's silly," she said. "I'm having a lot of trouble sleeping."

"Something bothering you?" he asked. "Or was it a bad dream?"

"Both," she said.

He sat down next to her and put his hand on hers. At times like this, she thought, he was as fine a husband as a woman deserved. Many men would have laughed at her and told her she was silly.

Then a vision flashed in front of her.

They were at the cemetery. Rich and she.

It was a replay.

Their daughter was being lowered into the ground. Then that vision dissolved in a flash and the even worse one was in front of her, of Lindsay's face turning into another girl's and sinking into the earth.

She trembled again.

Her husband squeezed her hand hard. He gently put his hand on her jaw and shook her.

"Hey!" he said. "Hey! Come back! What is it? What do you see?"

He guided her back into reality.

"A nightmare," she said. "And it won't stop. It follows me. I've had it several times. Right now," she complained. "I know I'm awake, but I keep seeing pieces of it flashing in front of me."

"And it's about Lindsay, isn't it?" he asked. "In the nightmare Lindsay has died and we're at her funeral."

A special terror rolled through her. "How did you know?" she asked.

"Do you remember several days ago?" he asked. "You woke up and found me downstairs? At the kitchen table in the middle of the night?"

"I remember."

"And you asked me not to lie to you if something was wrong. And I swore to you it was office stuff."

She waited. Then, "I remember," she said.

She was pale now. So was her husband.

"I was having the same dream," Rich said softly. "Lindsay was dead. And we were at her funeral."

Barbara Levin felt another deep surge of fear. It didn't flow through her or wash over her. It ripped through her. At the same time, she felt something cold pass beside her, as if someone had opened a window to the winter.

The coldness seemed to circle her. It danced around her and then it vanished. Rich felt it, too.

Her husband sighed and took her hand.

"Barb," he said slowly. "I think there's something in this house. A presence that I don't understand and I don't like. It doesn't want us here and it's going to try to hurt us if we stay."

She looked at Rich's eyes and saw a fear in them that she had never seen there before. She wondered if it reflected her own. She decided that it did.

Then she looked away.

"This is crazy," she said. "We don't believe in such things."

"Don't we?" he asked.

"I don't know," she said after too long a pause.

"What are we going to do?" he asked, almost rhetorically. His arm wrapped itself around his wife. He held her tightly.

She shook her head.

Neither would admit it to the other, but both waited to see if anything would move in the living room, whether the tapping would recommence, or whether that strange whispering would start again.

Nothing did.

"The first thing we do is get some sleep," he finally said, trying again to take the lead and show some strength. He spoke bravely. "This is our home now and we're going to stay till we decide to leave."

"You're right," Barbara said softly.

"We'll leave lights on if it helps," Rich continued. "But I have a job to go to tomorrow and I need some rest."

They rose together and walked up the stairs. Whatever was plaguing them, it seemed to have been dispersed for the night. Seemed to.

Barbara returned to bed. The bedroom was very still. She and Rich turned off the light and settled in to sleep. They were conscious of each other's proximity. Rich managed to sleep first, then Barbara, out of fatigue, started to drift away second.

The journey was peaceful this time, almost completely undisturbed. The only thing that unnerved her was the matter of the lights in the room.

She realized that she had left the bedside light on after being awakened from a nightmare the first time that evening. The light had been off when he woke the second time. And Rich had told her that he had turned the light on to find her gone.

"So who turned it off?" she wondered as she approached sleep toward 4 A.M. "Who?"

She had a hunch.

You're right. I'm here.
It was I,

came the response.

But unnerving as this was, the message didn't rouse her this time. Sleep fell upon her. It was like shutting a door, with Barbara inside.

Or as she considered it the next day, like being sealed into a long wooden box with the lid being closed. But at least it wasn't forever.

Dr. Noah Benson arrived in Washington on a Monday evening. Drs. Katzman and Gundarson invited Benson to come to Bethesda where the President's charts could be examined in a clinical location. Benson balked, arguing that the agreement he felt he had before leaving New York allowed him to visit the White House.

"Charts first," Dr. Katzman insisted. "Then you are invited to see the President at the White House *only if* he still wants to see you."

Grudgingly, since Benson was already in Washington, he agreed. A driver arranged by the White House took Dr. Benson and two other physicians, who had accompanied him from New York, to Maryland.

Benson borrowed an office from a Bethesda surgeon whom he knew from medical school. He spent an hour with the charts. What he saw in that initial hour troubled and confused him. So he spent another hour prowling through the President's health records and then did some computer data searches on suspected ailments. Finally, there were a pair of telephone conferences to peers in New York.

At the end of that time, he picked up the telephone and called Drs. Katzman and Gundarson, who were at the White House. Katzman apologized and announced that the call was being recorded.

"Standard security," Katzman said. Dr. Felix Gundarson picked up an extension in the same office and also came on the line.

"I've never heard of such a thing," Benson said after a hesitant pause.

"New with this administration," Gundarson said. "What can we do? This is a conversation involving the health of the President of the United States, so we can't bend these rules."

"When do I get to see the patient?" Dr. Benson finally asked.

Dr. Gundarson took over the conversation at this point.

"First, what was your impression of the charts and history?" Gundarson inquired.

"It's difficult to tell whether the history was even done properly."

"You mean you're again questioning the competence of the current medical team?" Gundarson asked.

"Don't play games, Doctor," said Benson.

"We are simply trying to understand what you're saying."

"I've learned to trust only the histories I've done myself."

"But this is an unusual circumstance. So assuming it *was* done properly?" Gundarson asked.

Dr. Benson sighed.

"Assuming it *was* done properly," the New York epidemiologist said, "it's difficult to see what's wrong with George Farley. For a man of seventy-two, he would appear to be in excellent health."

"Then you can't find anything?" Gundarson asked, closing the door on the trap.

"I would need to examine the President personally," Dr. Benson said again. "Whatever is afflicting him is not apparent within the data I've been provided."

"Then where would it be coming from?"

"From something not contained within these charts."

"These are complete physical workups," Gundarson said. "How could—?"

Dr. Benson's voice began to tighten with anger. "Complete physical, yes," he said. "But there's been no psychiatric evaluation, for example."

"The President would refuse any audience with a psychiatrist. You know that."

"I'm merely making a point, Dr. Gundarson. I flew down here with two other physicians to try to assist with a diagnosis. I expected to be able to—"

"None of the three of you could find anything in the charts? Is that what you're saying?" Gundarson inquired.

Dr. Benson fell very quiet. For several angry seconds he did not say anything.

"Are you there, Doctor?" Gundarson finally asked.

"When will I be able to examine the President?" Noah Benson asked tersely.

"Well, unfortunately we're not going to be able to let you do that, after all," Gundarson said.

"What?"

"We just saw the President," Ivan Katzman chipped in indulgently. "We spoke with him at length on several subjects. And I mentioned that you had come to Washington and were looking at his charts from the perspective of an epidemiologist."

"And?"

"And personal medical access to the President is decided by the President himself," Dr. Gundarson said, playing the final part of his hand. "Or by the First Lady, other than in an emergency. There is no emergency right now and President Farley is comfortable with his current medical team. I might add that we have the complete confidence of Mrs. Farley, as well."

On his end of the phone, three hundred miles from his home office, Dr. Benson's face glowed a bright red. His two associates, sitting nearby, listening to the call on speaker hookups, understood the trap, also.

"President Farley has no desire to *see* any other practitioner at this time," Dr. Gundarson said. "We do appreciate your input, however. And we're really terribly sorry if we've inconvenienced you."

On his end of the line, Dr. Katzman smirked to Dr. Gundarson. On the other end, Dr. Benson struggled to remain cool.

"You could have sent the charts by courier," Dr. Benson said. "If you were going to pull a stunt like this, there was no need for us to come down here."

"I understand that," Felix Gundarson said. "And you should have understood that, also. You volunteered publicly to come at your own expense and risk. As it happens, the President is feeling much better and has no desire to have another exhausting examination."

"Wait till he collapses!" Benson snapped.

"You just said yourself that he appears to be in fine health," Felix Gundarson answered.

It was at that moment that Benson realized how badly he had been snookered. He set down the telephone and filled the air with a majestic arrangement of profanities that stunned even his two medical peers.

The next morning, Dr. Benson took the early shuttle from Dulles International Airport back to LaGuardia. He was back in his office by 9 A.M.

Toward noon the press caught up with him and began to phone his office. In a prepared statement that his nurse wrote and faxed to anyone in the media who inquired, Dr. Benson had little to say. He did acknowledge, however, that he had examined the Presidential charts but had not been allowed access to the patient. As medical records were confidential, unless released by the patient, he did not feel he could comment publicly. Or at least that was his position.

Inwardly, he seethed.

A reporter named Jack Ferrara of *Newsday* phoned Dr. Benson's office at 3 P.M. Benson took Ferrara's call. It was then that Noah Benson learned that Drs. Katzman and Gundarson had issued a statement that afternoon suggesting that Dr. Benson had found nothing within the President's history that would suggest any diagnosis other than theirs.

"Is that accurate?" Jack Ferrara asked.

That successfully ticked Dr. Benson. If he couldn't shed light on the medical situation in Washington, surely he could shed some heat.

"It's accurate. But it's not complete," Benson said.

"Could you expand on that?" Ferrara asked.

Noah Benson said he could.

He began by suggesting that the charts hadn't been drawn properly and that a less than stellar medical team at Bethesda may have missed something big.

"But I have no way of *knowing* that, having not seen the President myself," Benson hedged.

"Did you feel that the team in Washington, in the end, was not interested in cooperating with you?"

Benson was tempted, but declined comment on that point. He chose instead to stay with his talents as an epidemiologist.

"I just have my instincts as a physician," he said, "that something isn't adding up in this case."

When asked repeatedly if he had seen anything dangerous or life-threatening in the President's charts, he said that, no, there hadn't been anything.

"But that doesn't mean that something big hasn't been *missed*," he insisted again. "Look. The two hardest things in the world to prove are that something exists that you can't see or that something doesn't exist at all."

"What does that mean?" the reporter asked.

Dr. Benson, fully exasperated, was now in full flight. "It means I have a theory that the team in Washington is fanning on something big. Just because they can't see it, doesn't mean it's not there."

"What sort of 'something big'?"

Benson paused and concluded offhandedly. "I don't know," he said. "Maybe the President is being manipulated by some exterior psychic force that we don't understand. Now, that would account for everything. Maybe this is a line of diagnosis that his team in Washington should explore."

He meant it as a joke, a sample of his well-known gift for sarcasm. But two hours later, the comment was widely quoted in the media. None of the national news broadcasts or cablecasts carried it, however. Which made things worse.

The suggestion thus became an innuendo and the innuendo became rumor. Because of that, it received wider circulation than if it had been identified as a facetious remark from the beginning. And thus the suggestion took on a life and reality of its own.

15

A t 7 A.M. on the morning after his most recent meeting with Vice President Lang, Bill Cochrane woke up with a dull ringing in his left ear. There was no rational reason he should have awakened with a ringing in his left ear, but he woke up in that condition anyway.

Cochrane showered, figuring the ringing would go away. It didn't. He made some toast and coffee, then sat down in his kitchen and opened the *Washington Post* that had been delivered to his door.

He scanned the headlines, making an unhappy assessment of the state of the world, the nation, and the capital.

Right-wing Russian nationalists had almost completed their takeover of their parliament and their nation. In keeping with a long nontradition of civil rights in Russia, they had managed to undo all of the reforms of the Gorbachev-Yeltsin era. Their leaders spoke longingly of the days when Mother Russia held Eastern Europe in subservience and when a leader with "big shoulders"—which was meant to evoke that shining Marxist light of the twentieth century, Josef Stalin—had led the nation into the modern era. Everyone seemed to have forgotten about Siberian labor camps or the ten million Russians who had been executed during the regime of Uncle Joe. Selective amnesia was always a charmingly Russian talent.

Added into the international equation were the continuing problems the Russians were having along their southern borders with Moslem nationalists. United Nations troops—including twenty thousand Americans—had been in the area in great numbers since 1998. Once again, the region was tense and looked as if it was set to explode. One catastrophic "incident" could bring several hundred young

American men and women home in boxes just before Christmas. The lights would be glowing late in the Capitol on such a night.

Cochrane shuddered and searched, as he frequently did, for some perspective on events.

As a college senior when the Berlin wall had come down, Cochrane had read this hare-brained but pervasive theory about "the end of history," a thesis that all conflict was at an end in the course of world affairs. The theory lasted about six months, of course, and accomplished nothing other than selling a lot of books and magazines. History always continued, and so did human conflict.

Russian-American relations had collapsed precipitously since the turn of the millennium. In an odd echo of a war of almost a hundred years earlier, diplomatic missions had nearly been recalled when Japanese, Chinese, Russian, and American fishing fleets had battled over tuna territory in the South Pacific, the Sea of Japan, and the China Sea. With the world's food supply dwindling on an overpopulated planet, the fishing issue was no small matter. President Farley was scheduled for a meeting with Japanese and Russian heads of state in January to address the worldwide hunger crisis. A separate meeting was on the agenda in February with the Chinese. It was hoped that this issue as well as several others could be moved to a less incendiary stage.

Nationally, there were some nervous signs in the financial community. Pre-Christmas sales in November of 2003 were not as strong as economists had hoped, giving rise to some theorists' predictions that the first sharp recession of the new century was lurking just beyond New Year's Day. All that was needed were sluggish sales at Christmas. The stock market, which had looked strong as recently as two weeks earlier, had dipped unexpectedly by three hundred points the previous week. Helping it slide, an article in *Business Week* had explored the reasons behind the severe recessions of 1804 and 1905.

All this passed before Cochrane's eyes, while his ear kept ringing. It was as if he were keyed in on a persistent autoalarm several blocks away. But his other ear was fine. It reminded him of the ringing in his ear that had plagued him in the week after his mother died in 1988, a ringing that came and went mysteriously but which doctors had ultimately attributed to trauma and emotion.

And crying.

Where was the trauma and emotion here? His father's death? Wrenching as that was, there had been relatively few tears. He had been filled with sorrow, but emotionally ready for the moment. His father had more effectively died the day he had entered the mental hospital ten years earlier.

He didn't care for his current job, but that was nothing new. He didn't like the assignment of trying to find some parapsychological reason for the Veep's nuttiness or the Illness of George the Third, but he was used to unpalatable tasks also. When he really thought hard about the ringing, and tried to remember when he first was aware of it, he thought of the last evening that he had seen Gabe Lang. Cochrane had felt the ringing in his ear when he had gotten into his car to leave.

Right then! That was it! That evening! What had been unique about that moment?

Nothing, he concluded after some thought. He wondered, in addition to the emotional spin, whether going out into the cold after being in the Veep's overheated home had had an effect. But he knew he was now searching for things.

Was the ringing one of those things that just *happen* as a man grows older? Maybe, he decided.

But more importantly, Cochrane had also finally come to a pair of other ugly conclusions: the Vice President was unsuited to be President and the passionless self-aggrandizing President was barely suited to be a member of the human race. But these opinions were just the conventional wisdom that he had only recently come to share with everyone else within the Beltway. So he was slow. This wasn't the stuff that emotional distress was about.

So what was bothering him. Why was his ear ringing?

His job? He would chuck that eventually. His loss of any spiritual values, as suggested by Lady Elizabeth and her ersatz fortune-telling parlor in Massachusetts? Well, that bothered him, too. He had thought about her and her theories quite a bit since he had visited her. But the loss of religion was surely nothing new either.

So what *was* it that was gnawing at him from within? What *was* it that made him anxious in the morning and jittery during the day and restless at night? Whatever it was, it was recent. Much like that creeping feeling that something significant was just set to happen, but hadn't quite shown itself yet. That feeling that he had endured the first night he had visited the Vice President and been confronted by this whole "occult" theory against the President.

What was it?

Death? Depression? Anxiety about his future?

Or was it Lisa and his loss of her?

Her departure. Her defection.

The way she dumped him and moved out.

He was still in love with her, he reasoned, and—fuck religion, he irreverently thought to himself—*this* was the big something missing from his life.

She had agreed to have dinner with him that evening, an event which caused him to put off his travel plans to see the Cassatt and Forsythe families for an extra day. Could that have triggered some inner tensions that resulted in a dull ringing sound in one ear?

He doubted it. But he was ready to entertain the notion anyway.

But in terms of tears and emotion, which *really* might have caused such a ringing, he felt he had been largely drained as a much younger man. There were few tears left and not all that much passion or emotion. So he theorized that he must have gotten some water in his ear from the previous day's shower and the water had formed a tiny blockage. Or maybe there was a tiny infection that would run its course if he ignored it for a few days. Funny how resilient the human anatomy could be one day, he reasoned, and how fragile the next.

That thought led him directly into the next part of the front page. The President's health, he realized, was an unseen participant in each story.

There were several major international meetings coming up at the beginning of 2004. But there was now open speculation in the foreign press that President Farley would be unfit to travel. The speculation had subsequently bred similar discussions domestically. And the nervousness over the economy had equally been intensified by the question of Farley's health. The financial community liked when Farley dealt with international politics: affairs of state allowed Farley to be Presidential, meaning high-minded and disreputable at the same time.

The prospect of Gabriel Lang taking over the government did nothing positive for the financial community. Big business and Lang had long been adversarial.

Once, while a Senator from California, Lang had let fly a remark about "the problem of American business is the all-holy sacrosanct profit motive. Maybe there should be some other higher goal for American business, a public service factor, perhaps. Social incentives. Social incentives."

When Gabriel Lang spoke, Wall Street cringed. Cringed.

Lang had also made a remark detailing how the owners of American sports franchises should be divested of their teams and paid par value dating from 1994.

"Then the franchises should be restructured as municipal trusts and frozen into their current cities for ninety-nine years," Lang had explained. "Ninety-nine years." Never mind Mercury in retrograde. Lang's frequent statements on business and corporate responsibility were enough to have most Harvard and Wharton MBAs bolting upright in their beds at night.

There was another article on the front page about the President's health and another one about three more members of the opposing political party ready to declare themselves as candidates for President. Lurking beneath this was the feeling that George Farley was medically unfit to serve another full term. Farley was the only popular figure within his party. The occasional comas or "mals" or headaches, or whatever they were, were having a deep rippling effect now throughout domestic and world politics. The previous day, Farley had had to cancel two meetings during the afternoon, which was not exactly a show of health and vigor.

Cochrane finished his coffee and toast.

He flipped to the editorial pages, but there was no escape from the key subject matter of the day. The lead editorial asked the question of whether the public was being told the truth about the President's illness or whether the medical and political team around the President was "stonewalling the truth."

Cochrane smiled at the old Watergate term of thirty years earlier. But he wondered the same thing as well.

When he flipped back into the national news section, there was even more. The Chief Justice of the United States Supreme Court, Ruth Bader Ginsburg, had stated that the intent of the Twenty-fifth Amendment, Section 4, was to protect the nation from even a short-term incapacitation of the President. Should one of the President's comas or blackouts or whatever-they-were last for more than a day, the Chief Justice said, the Vice President and members of the cabinet were duty bound under law to submit to Congress their written declaration that the President was unfit to continue in office.

Under that procedure, the Chief Justice affirmed, Gabe Lang would become Acting President until President Farley resubmitted a document stating that he was again fit to assume his office.

There it was. The future, if Farley's blackouts continued. Either an invocation of the Twenty-fifth Amendment or a Constitutional crisis for not invoking it.

Cochrane closed the news section. The whole damned country was suddenly adrift, he suddenly realized. When he scanned back through the previous day's news, he also noticed that President Farley hadn't even been seen in public for two days.

Highly unusual.

No meetings. No public appearances.

Where was he? In a coma? Too sick to appear? What *was* going on over at the White House? Why *had* the President's doctors refused to allow any other physician to see him?

Had the President really refused? That was believable. Or had the circle around the President drawn in tighter and was it warding off outsiders to maintain control of the government?

As a good former reporter, he wondered.

Even the comment that the windy Dr. Noah Benson had made had a certain currency now. "A powerful exterior force." Benson's remark may not have launched a thousand ships, but it had busied thousands of journalistic keyboards.

Cochrane wondered what significance to hang on the remark. But then the ringing in his ear seemed to intensify slightly and he was distracted. Besides, he had to get to work. There would be a day of controlled and tempered mendacity before him, he knew, as the press badgered him with questions about Gabe Lang's ability to take over the Presidency. Cochrane would need all of his wits about him to put the proper spin on things. It was his job to help give off the misimpression that Gabriel Lang was every bit up to the job.

Which, of course, Cochrane knew he wasn't.

He placed the newspaper back on the table, where he would find it again that evening.

"Situation in the world normal again," he said to himself. "All fucked up."

What was new, he mused to himself a few minutes later as he drove to work, was that as a well-spoken male thirty-seven-year-old college graduate, he got to play a part in the fucking-up.

"God," Cochrane muttered to himself. He hated this and looked forward to the day when he could get out. But aside from his distaste for what he was doing, his day at work would proceed uneventfully.

16

The first thing everyone noticed about Lisa McJeffry, whether meeting her for the first time or the one hundredth, was that she was tall, blond, and beautiful. But she was also smart enough to have been a Phi Beta Kappa, and—in the opinion of some—wore her trademark skirts too short all over Washington. But no one seemed to complain, especially at her network. Lisa made ratings soar. She drew attention to everything she did.

One of the national Sunday supplements did an article on her when she first started at ABC. The article referred to her as "The New American Woman—Smart, Sexy and Articulate," and generally concluded that if she was the New American Woman, any New American Men were very lucky. The article played upon her education in California and her background in filmmaking, hammering home the point that she had been media-savvy from the day she'd escaped celluloid academia and joined the workforce.

The other networks were currently stumbling over themselves to find clones. But there weren't any. There were only substitutes and wannabes, women who were sort of great, but not *as* great. The sign-off line, "I'm Lisa McJeffry, ABC News at The White House," was worth two rating points each night. Unlike all other correspondents, she was shown full screen, head to toe. And why not?

Cochrane arrived at their table first, ten minutes early at a small but trendy bistro called Alan H's in Georgetown, two blocks from the Vice President's lair. The restaurant was smart, packed, and noisy. The proprietor was Alan H, himself, a brilliant Southern lawyer—an Atlantan and an Emory law school graduate—who had made a fortune doing international taxes in Brussels but who had also learned big-time Belgian cooking in his off-hours from the ledgers and tax volumes. Now Alan H—the man and the restaurant—combined new-style Belgian cuisine with old-style Southern cooking and was packing in media and government types night after night.

Alan H, a burly dark-haired man with an easy smile, presided from the end of the bar where he mainlined Coke Classic. The Real Thing, none of the frivolous Diet stuff. His arm was slung across the shoulders of a tall dark-haired Italian woman half his age. She was a fixture at the place, an Italian contessa with long legs and silky hair. She manifested no interest in anyone in the house other than the genial proprietor. There were perks to this trendy restaurant business and she was one. Meanwhile, a few feet away, Cochrane nursed a more powerful drink, a neat J&B, and watched for Lisa.

Cochrane knew she would make a grand entrance. She always did, sometimes without even meaning to, but often with every intention.

When she arrived and when the maitre d' led her to their table, he watched her partly with pride—because she was coming to his table—and partly with bittersweet affection—because they had been lovers until recently. The only male heads she failed to turn when she entered belonged to men who were visually challenged. And the decibel level in the restaurant dropped like the barometric pressure at the approach of a storm.

Watching her, Cochrane shared a view of millions of other American men. There were no substitutes. There was only Lisa. The original. Seeing her again instantly made him miss her more.

"Hi," he said as she arrived at his table.

"Hello, Billy," she said. That was always what she had called him, in good times or foul, in passion or in anger.

Billy. He still liked the sound of it, particularly from her. In one motion she leaned forward slightly so that he could rise and kiss her on the cheek and then she slid effortlessly into her seat, an attaché case at her side which she placed on the floor, carefully positioned against the wall.

"How's stuff?" she asked. That was always her line, too. At the end of a day or in the early morning or late at night. Before breakfast or after sex or both.

How's stuff?

"Stuff is fine," he answered.

He gave her a smile. He hadn't seen her for ten days, other than on the tube. For an elusive moment, it seemed like old times and he liked the glow of it, even though the high lasted only for a few seconds.

"Stuff is real fine," he said, looking at her and lying a little. Stuff wasn't fine at all, which they both knew. Stuff could have stood some serious improvement, at least for him. But that was the simplest, best, and least controversial answer that served the moment.

Stuff. It was the type of word that Gabe Lang would have used.

Stuff. Stuff between Bill and Lisa was anything from the baseball scores to whether the sex had been good to how the day at work had gone.

He sipped his drink and looked at her. She had recently been his woman and wasn't anymore and he hoped that at this dinner they could discuss the future, not the past.

There was the usual small talk, five to ten minutes of it. A waiter appeared, announced the specials, and they ordered.

"So how are things with Gabriel Lang?" Lisa finally asked of her former lover. "Situation normal?"

"This is off the record," he said. "Right? This is Bill to Lisa, not unnamed press spokesman to Lisa McJeffry, ABC News."

She smiled her fifty thousand–kilowatt smile. "It's Billy to Lisa," she said. "I'll keep this between me and my closest twenty million viewers."

She winked. The waiter arrived with their wine. A fine Italian Barolo. The waiter opened it. Cochrane tasted it and gave a nod. The waiter poured for both.

"Lang's being his usual space cadet," he said. "He's all strung out about there being some occult threat to him and to the President and, I think, to the United States as well. That's if I understand him right, which I don't always do."

"Occult?" she said softly. She rolled her blue eyes.

"You heard me." He kept his voice low. Like Soviet Russia, the walls sometimes had ears in even the fanciest District of Columbia eateries.

"Any truth to it?" she asked without cracking a smile.

He gave her a grimace, then a smirk. "What the hell do you think?"

"I think I'd keep an open mind and investigate everything before I dismissed anything," Lisa answered quietly and seriously.

"Funny you should say that," he said. "Because that's what I'm stuck doing."

He then told the story of visiting Lady Elizabeth. Then there were the two red queens who seemed to sing and dance when Lang played cards with them. And finally there were the details of his travel plans over the next few days, focusing on the two Harvard ex-roommates—Cassatt and Forsythe—who had suddenly dropped dead on different coasts. Natural causes on each drop, and he was to study some FBI reports before he went on his journey.

"Our paranormal Vice President wants to know if there's a connection among all of it," Cochrane shrugged. "An occult connection, at that. And that's my job these days." He paused. "My 'stuff.' Not as glamorous as yours, is it?"

Expecting Lisa to share his cynicism and grudging amusement, Cochrane was surprised at her reaction. Lisa looked downward thoughtfully, as if to focus mentally on something far away.

She seemed to still be thinking a moment later when she looked up again. She found his eyes and her mood had changed. And Cochrane realized he had missed something significant in her original reaction.

"I personally find all that occult stuff intimidating," she said.

He blinked twice. "What?" he said.

"You heard me. I think it's dangerous territory. I'd treat it with respect."

He smiled and thought at first she was joking. An image of his father flashed before him, his father when he first became ill, hearing voices and seeing things. Then he flashed back to the present. And knowing her, he quickly reassessed. He lost his smile.

"What are you saying to me?" he asked.

"As I said, I wouldn't dismiss anything," she reiterated.

"Lisa. He's talking *nut* stuff. Gabe Lang is one incapacitating blackout away from the Presidency and he's talking about spirits and ghosts."

"Yes. I know," she said sweetly. "I follow."

"Doesn't that strike you as a little fruity for the future leader of the world's oldest and finest democracy?"

"Maybe not," she answered. "I wouldn't dismiss *anything,*" she insisted. "Not until you check everything with an open mind. That's the last time I'll tell you."

He sighed.

"Ever had an experience with anything in the occult?" she asked. "No."

"Well, it will change your mind very quickly when you do."

" 'When' I do? You're not even going to say 'if' I do?"

"No," she said. "Because eventually you will. I promise you. As we get older, sometimes we start to realize there are things in this world that defy explanations. They're all around us if we keep our eyes open."

He sighed again. "Californians. . . ." he teased, not so gently. "First, Gabe Lang. Then his Lady Soothsayer, the Vaughn woman. And now you, Lisa."

"Yes, and Charles Manson before me, right?" she shot back with characteristic all-purpose sarcasm.

"And William Randolph Hearst before that," he said, making a joke of it. "The original 'Rosebud.' "

But she and her mood were undeterred.

"Billy," she said. "Listen to me carefully because I'll only tell you about this once, okay?"

"Okay," he said, inclining forward, two elbows gently on the edge of the table. At the nearby bar, Alan. He was joined by yet another beautiful woman.

"I used to feel the same way you did," Lisa began. "Then my sister Dee Dee moved into an old house in Pasadena, California, about four years ago. You *met* Dee Dee and her husband about a year ago. Remember?"

He remembered. She went on.

"For the first year they lived there, Dee Dee and her husband were certain that they heard a baby crying somewhere within their home. It really bothered them because they were trying to conceive a child, and Dee Dee couldn't get pregnant."

Cochrane noticed a U.S. Senator and his girlfriend who were entering the restaurant. They drew little attention, though the proprietor nimbly left his position at the bar to safeguard the Senator and his squeeze to a top table.

Then Cochrane's eyes flashed back to Lisa.

"Well, I visited the house myself several times when I was on assignment in Tinseltown," she continued. "I constantly heard the same noise. It *was* a baby crying, Billy. And it seemed to come from the second upstairs bedroom. But it would stop whenever we entered that room. It got to be very scary. It gave us the *creeps*. Middle of the afternoon. Middle of the night. You'd hear the crying and not be able to tune it out. It was a *horrible* frightening crying. It was like a child pleading for its mother, begging for help in a desperate situation."

She paused for a moment as she recalled.

"Sometimes it was unbelievably loud," she said after a breath. "Inconsolable crying. Then you'd not be able to stand the sound of it anymore. You'd go in that second bedroom and the crying would stop. Right away! Just like that. Like a radio being turned off. Or a door being slammed shut. It was as if this invisible baby, or whatever it was, could *see* you. Like it *knew* you were coming."

She paused to take a sip of wine.

"We couldn't find any other source of the crying," Lisa said, "and no neighboring house had small children."

Cochrane listened as a waiter arrived with their meal. Lisa knew enough to stop until the waiter had gone. Then her soft succinct voice continued.

"Well, one time I was there for several days. I also kept having the impression that a thought was trying to form within my head. A foreign thought from somewhere else. But I couldn't quite read it. And when I mentioned this to Dee Dee, she said she felt the identical thing. Then we identified the thought at exactly the same time. 'The name of the child is—.' Something, some force, was trying to tell us the child's name, the child we were hearing. Suddenly we both felt we had it. But neither of us would say it aloud. So we both wrote down the name without revealing it to each other. When we compared, the name we had both written was 'Timothy.' "

Their food sat untouched in front of them. A few seconds passed. Cochrane had never heard any parallel story from Lisa ever before.

"And?" Bill finally asked.

"The next day, Dee Dee and I were at the Gelsons in Burbank," Lisa concluded softly. "We ran into the man who had previously owned the house. A Mr. Pendleton. I remember his name. Same as the Marine base in San Diego. Dee Dee inquired about the noise. The crying. Mr. Pendleton looked as if we'd kicked him in the stomach. He got angry. 'Don't ever mention that to me again!' he said. 'Our first child was murdered in that house. Suffocated by a drunken drug-addicted baby-sitter one night in the second bedroom. That's why we sold the place. Too many memories. If you hear anything else, don't tell me about it. And if this was a joke, it's not in very good taste.' "

Cochrane fingered his fork.

"Before he walked away, we asked Mr. Pendleton his late son's name. He turned around and shouted at us. I'll never forget. 'Timothy!' he said. 'Timothy! Now leave me alone.' "

Cochrane gave a small defensive shrug.

"That still doesn't mean there was a ghost," he said. "There could have been something funny going on in everyone's subconscious."

"Yeah? Sure," Lisa answered. "Want to explain it in 'subconscious' terms for me? Because it makes more sense as a story about a lost spirit."

"And if you were covering it for ABC, that's the handle you'd put on it?"

"I would."

"And ABC would let you on the air with it?"

"Are you kidding? I'm hotter than a cheap pistol right now, Billy. They'll let me on the air with anything."

There was a lingering silence between them. He didn't know whether to hate her or envy her for her youth, looks, and self-confidence. He tried hard not to do either.

"Oh, hell," he finally breathed, breaking the awkward silence. He picked up his fork and knife and so did she. They both began to eat. "Just when I'm looking for a rational evening, even you turn on me."

"Sorry," she said. "But that's the way I see it." She knew he was kidding, at least a little.

"Everyone's got a ghost story for me these days," he said. "Everyone's trying to make a believer out of me."

"Billy," Lisa said. "I'm a journalist. You may work for the Vice President, but at heart, so are you. A journalist. You examine facts as you see them. I don't know about your occult case with Gabe Lang. But to be in that house in Pasadena, to hear the crying, to *see* this happening, was to learn how to believe. That's all I'm telling you. Some days your reporter's cynicism will see you through the bullshit within an official version of something. And on other days, you have to learn how to believe."

For several minutes they then ate in silence.

To some degree, Cochrane had the sense of sleepwalking, of gliding through his movements and not being genuinely focused on what was before him. But as a pleasant meal passed, Lisa, sensing his unease and concern, managed to push the conversation to more approachable matters.

Cochrane's better humor eventually returned.

Over coffee, he reminded her that there was still a valise and a few other things of hers at his home. She would be welcome to come pick things up whenever she wished. She still had a key and he was not in the mood to ask for it back.

"When you come by next time, try to do it when I'm home, however," he said. "There's something I want to show you."

"Is it a 'nice' something or a 'not nice' something?" she asked.

"It's a nice something, I think. But the sooner you see it, the better."

She looked at her watch. It was only nine-fifteen. "Now would work just fine for me," she said.

She knew the route as well as he did, but followed his car from Georgetown. She drove a Mercedes convertible. The little two-seat roadster. It fit her as if it had been tailored. A twenty-five-minute drive took them back to Alexandria and her former home.

He led her directly to his studio, his skylit workplace that was still adorned with her unfinished portrait, complete with all the photo studies on the wall.

For several seconds she stood before the canvas. He had worked some of the background, which was red and pale blue, two colors she liked, and had sketched the shape of her head and the flow of her hair.

The details, of course, the facial characteristics that would make it a portrait of Lisa McJeffry and no one else, were not there yet.

"My major work of the twenty-first century," he said with affection. "And my model has deserted me."

She looked at the easel and the photographs on the wall. Then she looked at him. "I'm flattered," Lisa said softly. "Really I am."

"But not surprised," he said. "You knew I was painting you."

"I knew," she said. "I'd forgotten, but yes, I knew."

"How is it going with your other boyfriends?" he asked.

"What's that mean?" she asked.

"Anything serious? Anyone you love?"

She gave him a strange look and he noticed how beautiful she was in person, particularly juxtaposed against snapshots and a canvas that still hadn't acquired its soul.

"Love," she said. "Relationships don't work for me. And who the hell loves anyone anymore?"

He was opening his mouth to tell her he loved her, or had loved her, and could again. But she could feel it coming and raised a hand, one finger to his lips.

"Trying to talk me into coming back, are you?" she asked.

He nodded.

"Don't," she said. "Please? We've had all these discussions. It was difficult enough to move out."

"Then maybe at least you'll sit for the painting," he said after a moment. "Maybe you'd come back long enough to let me finish."

"You have photographs," she said.

"There's nothing like the original," he said. "Please?"

She looked into his eyes and then at the pictures on the wall. This and the half-concocted canvas in the easel.

"How much time would we be talking about?" she asked.

"A few hours here and there. I need certain angles. A specific look in your eyes. We could arrange the time at your leisure," he said. "If you don't have leisure, we could create some."

She nodded.

"Still missing me, huh?" she asked.

"Yes," he answered. He took her hand. There was a moment between them.

"I'm sorry," she said. "I wish you weren't."

"I wish I weren't also."

Then the telephone rang.

"Jesus," he mumbled to himself. "Fantastic timing."

She pulled her hand away and exhaled a long breath, the earmarks of a relationship that could never find time to rekindle itself, one that doused its own flames. He left the room and went downstairs to the telephone in the bedroom.

Cochrane picked up the phone and found himself talking to Martin Kane again at the Secret Service annex for mental patient messages.

"Am I calling you at a bad time?" Kane asked.

"Would it matter?" Cochrane asked.

Mr. Kane missed the sarcasm. "No, probably not," he said, taking the question literally. "But I think you'd better come over. This evening."

"What's going on?" Cochrane asked.

In Lisa's direction, he thought he heard the sound of footsteps, hers on the stairs. Then he felt he was imagining it and wasn't sure at all.

"Well, you asked me if I noticed anything, you know, in the 'occult' mode," Kane said. "You asked me to call you."

This occult thing would not leave Cochrane alone. "Yes?" he asked.

"And I also noticed what the doctor in New York said the other day. You know. That line about 'an exterior psychic force'?"

Out of a sense of duty, Cochrane's ears perked. Out of sense of mortification, his spirits sank just as readily. Out of sense of sanity, he felt like fleeing.

"So what about it?" Cochrane asked.

"We have a letter from one of our previous correspondents. One of the people you read already. It's another written threat."

"And why is it so important and urgent that you'd call me now at home?" Cochrane asked.

He listened in Lisa's direction. It was quiet. Then there was the sound of a door closing downstairs and, distantly, the sound of her car's engine turning over. And Cochrane was thinking that yes, this phone call had fouled everything, and yes, she's gone again. God damn Martin Kane to hell, God damn this whole occult project to hell again, and for that matter, God damn the ringing in his ear that had kicked in again within the last few seconds!

"There's this letter that fits your request perfectly," Kane said. "A man making psychic threats against the President. It's a textbook case of exactly what you were asking about."

"What's his name?"

"It has a pseudonym."

"What's different about it? And what's so urgent?"

"Well," Mr. Kane said, "it wasn't mailed from the usual location. This one was postmarked right in Washington. See, as the President has been falling into these little lapses of consciousness, this man has moved closer. And he claims he's manipulating the President's health."

Cochrane breathed a long dispirited sigh.

How was he to check out Lang's two dead classmates and a local kook at the same time? He felt that aura of tension around him increase again. He felt as if he had had sixteen cups of coffee since midafternoon.

"I'll be over in the morning, first thing," he said.

"Not tonight?"

"Not tonight." He couldn't have faced it that night.

"Secret Service has a team coming over in the morning, too," Kane said. "You might want to look before they do. They take material away and don't return it."

"I'm sure they do," Cochrane said.

"They say they'll bring it back, but they don't," Kane ranted.

"Uh-huh."

In the distance, the car engine that he thought was Lisa's grew distant.

"The man calls himself 'The Unicorn,' " Mr. Kane concluded. "That's the pseudonym. Cute, huh? A mythical beast as a correspondent."

"Couldn't be cuter," Cochrane said. And he set down the phone.

He walked back to his studio and knew exactly what to expect. When he came to the empty room he had a difficult time deciding what was worse.

His job? His life? The loss of Lisa? Or this Mickey Mouse nonsense with crackpot assassins and occult threats?

Or this beastly low sickened feeling that seemed to possess him?

Or were they all part of the same thing, the same manifestation? He didn't know.

He did know, however, that he cursed Martin Kane's timing. Next time, he swore, the phone could ring till hell froze over.

Lisa had left him a short note. She didn't want to get back with him, she wrote. The intimate part of their relationship was over, she reminded him, and if they were to continue to see each other, it would be as friends. Or not at all. And flattered though she was, she felt that another woman should eventually grace his portrait. She was gone and had taken her final valise.

The relationship was over. Period. But she would always have a certain love for him. Or so she had written.

He folded the note and drew a breath. He told himself that he was no worse off than he had been earlier in the day. Things were just more official now. More settled as much as she was concerned.

So he could think in terms of his future, not resurrecting something from the past that never could rise again. And he could also think about her damnable ghost story, which was already lurking in the back of his mind.

He went downstairs and hit a bottle of brandy for the first time in months, his sense of moderation about to embark on a dangerous slide. Two or three long gulps of the stuff made him feel better and worse.

But better yet, it made him feel sleepy.

So he was drinking a little. Why the hell not, he thought to himself. As a young reporter, he'd hit the bars and the bottles quite hard. In its day, the drinking boozing life had quite agreed with him. So why not go for an encore performance? Thirty-seven wasn't exactly ancient. Why should he quietly let the final years of his youth slip away without a little hollering?

If this were a crutch, it was a damned handy one. A few good hard drinks and the whole world would look rosier.

He didn't know when he took his last drink and he never knew quite why he could never find his bed that night.

What he did know was that he woke up the next morning with a genuine buzz in his head. Upstairs, something had knocked the easel over as well as the canvas that he had planned for Lisa's portrait.

He assumed that he had crashed around drunk, which scared him a little, since all the doors were locked, and since he had found himself conked out on the living room sofa.

He staggered to the bathroom and blasted himself with the shower, first cold, then hot. He drank a cup of coffee and took two caffeine tablets. When his blood started to tingle, he felt he was ready for the day.

Then he took a second look at his watch and realized that he must have broken it, because it wasn't moving. It wasn't eight o'clock as he'd thought, but nine-thirty.

He was late for work.

Martin Kane's rancid claustrophobic annex lay ahead in wait. He hoped that Secret Service types with their big pious Irish faces hadn't beaten him to The Unicorn's latest message.

So he was quickly out the door and into his car. Much like many other men of his generation, he was off for the day, hating his job, hating his life, and hating the task that lay before him.

He was already behind the eight ball for the morning. And his ear, he noticed, was still ringing like a horrid little demon.

17

Bill Cochrane sat down at a research table in the Secret Service annex. Martin Kane stood before him with a file folder. Wearing gloves, Kane lifted a one-page document out of the folder and placed it before Cochrane.

Cochrane looked at it.

It was a single sheet of white paper, handwritten. It was difficult to mistake the belligerence and arrogance of the author.

> Greetings, morons!

it began.

> Forty-four is a mystical number. Forty-four is magical. Divisible by 2, 4 & 11. And Gabriel Lang will be the 44th President of the United States. Why? Because it must be so. I am controlling the health of George Farley through brain waves and cosmopological vitriol. I have laid eyes on the man in person (Farley) as he flew through the skies above me and will lay him into a grave by thinking fatal thoughts of him. He will perish. I will kill him. The President must die, die, die, so that the peasants of America can come to understand the power of my mind and my intellect.
>
> Attention, Morons!
>
> I AM the threat to the President that comes from somewhere else.

I AM the superior intellect who can unbalance the
equation of this world. I am laughing at you who read
this because you cannot know who I am even though I
am under your stupid fucking nose.
I AM The Unicorn.

Cochrane sighed. Assorted planks of insanity seemed to be building a corral around him.

"What's troubling to the Treasury Department is that the postmark
has moved that much closer," Kane explained, showing Cochrane the
envelope. "See?'

Kane provided the original "Unicorn" file. The first letters had
borne the postmark of Stone Mountain, Georgia, as Cochrane recalled. But this one had a Washington, D.C., postmark from two days
earlier. There had also been one on the middle that had explained how
"the death of George Farley would fit into a philosophy of the universe as an ordered whole." Then there was another paragraph, un-
linked to the first, talking about some mathematical concept called
"grue."

"Rather remarkable, isn't it?" Cochrane said lightly. "No misspellings. A cogent thought development within its own field of insanity. Well educated and well spoken. And probably clinically nuts."

He paused, trying to shun off the parallels within his own family
history.

"Mm," Kane hummed slightly.

"It *is* a little troubling that the man is right here in Washington,"
Cochrane said. "I wonder what he means in this reference to having
'seen' the President 'in the skies.' I wonder if he's stalking Farley. Or
watching the White House. Or is the reference to astrology?" He
thought for another moment. "Logic within illogic, but how do you
latch on to it?"

Kane had no better insight than Cochrane. "Don't know," the
archivist muttered.

"Cosmopological vitriol," Cochrane repeated next. "That's a new
one on me, too. Does anything that distinctive turn up in any other
mail?"

"None that I've seen," Kane said.

"Anything else from Stone Mountain either?"

"No. I've already checked. This guy is highly distinctive, to say the
least."

"And I also notice that the first threat antedates the President's first seizure," Cochrane said, examining the first correspondence. "What do we make of that?"

Again, Kane shrugged. "Coincidence?" he asked.

"I hate that word," Cochrane answered.

Cochrane thought about it and paused. In the back of his mind he began to run through the quasi-prophesies of Elizabeth Vaughn in Massachusetts, who also saw something bizarre from the "outside" being imposed on the President and Vice President. But he was unable to assimilate anything.

Unable, he then wondered, or fighting against his instincts?

After a moment, Martin Kane spoke again,

"As I said," Kane continued with a troubled tone and expression, "this all fits into the occult thing you were talking about. It makes reference to 'controlling' the President's health. It's exactly the type of thing you asked me to call you about."

"Indeed it is," Cochrane said, looking up from an examination of the text, the paper, and even the ink used by the printer. "It's also possibly the ramblings of someone who's a complete lunatic."

"Absolutely the case," Kane said. "But this whole annex has been built and financed and given a reason to exist by the ramblings of madmen." Kane paused. "I owe my job and my pension to hundreds of insane people around the country," he added with mordant sarcasm.

Then he allowed himself the slightest trace of a smile, the first one Cochrane had ever seen from him.

"You have a point there, too, Mr. Martin," Cochrane said, returning Kane's comment in a matching tone. "But then I suspect you're far from the only federal employee in this town who can make that claim. And from what I've seen out on the streets of this country, you've got plenty of job security."

After a moment, the joke succeeded with Kane. He almost smiled broadly.

"How seriously is the department taking this guy?" Cochrane asked.

"Based on the fact that he started threatening the President in Georgia and now is doing it here in the District, *fairly* seriously. Every agent has received a 'Unicorn' bulletin, for example."

"And maybe then a unicorn tapestry on retirement," Cochrane suggested, seeking to amuse again.

"What do you mean?" Kane asked, failing to understand.

"Never mind," Cochrane said. "Not important."

Cochrane took a final look at the material, hoping that a second examination would alert him to something that he might have missed on the first go-through.

Nothing emerged, however. And he left the annex knowing little more than he had when he had entered.

Nothing emerged in a reading room at the FBI later in the day either. Agents had prepared brief profiles on the lives and deaths of Thomas Cassatt and Ralph Forsythe, both of Gabriel Lang's Harvard class.

Both men died suddenly within a few days of each other, one of an apparent accident, the other of a heart condition. Both men died in their early fifties when they could have had many more productive years. Both men left families and both had been poised in their professions on ladders that were still extended upward.

One man had lived in Westchester County, New York, the other in Marin County, California. One man left a son. The other man left a daughter. Each man had been married once. Both had been popular and respected. The funerals had been attended by scores of friends. If there were a tint of scandal or aberrant behavior, Cochrane couldn't see it.

He closed the FBI files. The ringing in his ear had subsided a little, then kicked up acutely while reading the notes on Cassatt and Forsythe. Cochrane began to try to link everything with patterns of cause and effect.

"These men died at approximately the same time, because . . . because of what?" he asked himself.

"My ear is ringing because of . . . because of what?" he pondered.

He sat for a moment, then returned both files to the Bureau librarian.

As he walked from the FBI building, an old history lesson was upon him, one with a modern parable.

John Adams and Thomas Jefferson, the second and third Presidents of the United States, each fell ill and died on July 4, 1826, several hundred miles away from each other. Their lives ended exactly a half century almost to the minute from the time they had signed the Declaration of Independence in 1776.

Had this happened in modern times, Cochrane reasoned, conspiracy theorists would have written books, filled newspapers, flooded the Internet, and been all over television and movie screens. The controversy would have continued for generations. Added into the mix was the fact that the fifth President, James Monroe, also died on July 4, five years after Adams and Jefferson.

Moral?

Cochrane asked himself.

Sometimes, he concluded, a coincidence is nothing more than a coincidence. And working the notion backward as he walked to his car, he wondered anew about the advent of The Unicorn's threats, arriving as they had two days before the President's first seizure.

Just a coincidence, he told himself.

But if he fully believed that, why was Cochrane still thinking about it? Why couldn't he dismiss it? It haunted him the same way the incident did with the Vice President and the playing cards, the bizarre way in which Gabriel Lang had continually drawn red queens.

Somehow, Cochrane had come to a realization that something *was* wrong somewhere. Something *was* off. Reality *was* askew. But damned if he could figure out where or what.

Approaching his car in the section of the FBI garage for guest parking, Cochrane was startled.

Something small, quick, and unexpected moved between cars. Then Cochrane settled down almost as quickly as he'd been alarmed. He recognized the creature as a cat.

It may have been black and it might have crossed his path. There was a time when he wouldn't even have given a second thought to such an event.

Today, however, it bothered him. But he attributed his anxiety to his old newspaperman's instincts about something being amiss more than to actual superstition.

He just wished he could put his finger on *something*.

That same afternoon, George Farley had yet another opportunity to try to look Presidential and healthy. The occasion was a meeting with members of the Federal Reserve Board at the White House.

Economic meetings were the type of convocation that normally made Farley snooze. He would show up, shake the proper hands, and express complete confidence in his Secretary of the Treasury and the economists who actually attempted to run the nation's financial interests.

He would have his picture taken at the head of the table and, in the manner of Lyndon Johnson, excuse himself after a quarter hour.

Essentially, he disliked and distrusted economists and their theories. A hot air balloon, Farley had once pointed out to them, was also an example of inflation, as well as an apt analogy for a lot of unproven monetary theory. The economists had not been keen on the President's analogy.

Then, on one other occasion early in his Presidency when the economists couldn't come to an agreement over interest rates, Farley locked the door to their suite. He kept it locked for six hours and refused to release them until they had an agreement *that day*. The method was in keeping with Farley's approach to politics. No subtlety, no charm, but highly effective.

Today was a little different. Still plagued by headaches, still feeling woozy, the President had managed to last through a one-hour meeting with the Prime Minister of Thailand in the late morning. Then, on a roll, he had met his Federal Reserve Board economists in the afternoon.

These were two good photo ops, particularly the second one, since the first just showed Farley seated in a chair near a visiting Asian whom most Americans would not recognize. The second—at a round-table economic discussion—actually depicted him working, even if he wasn't. So he was willing to put in more time, lest it appear as if he had departed the meeting early for health reasons.

The press was invited in to take a look. Twenty-four of the reporters who were normally on the White House beat came in. When the President stood to leave, impromptu questions flew in his direction, most having to do with how the President felt.

"Fine. Fine. Just fine," Farley repeated over and over. "Couldn't be better."

Other questions brought up the issue of Presidential incapacity and the invocation of the Twenty-fifth Amendment.

"It's not even being discussed in the White House. I feel great," Farley answered.

Roger Kendall of the Fox Network was close enough to ask a follow-up question.

"Are you happy with the meeting with the Fed board, Mr. President?"

Farley knew Kendall and his network and didn't like either of them. It had been his habit for years to give them responses that the network couldn't use.

"I'm as happy, Roger," George Farley said, "as a pig rolling in shit. Put that on your ten o'clock update."

Lisa McJeffry of ABC News, as was her special skill, was one of the few reporters who could get close enough to launch a specific question. Typically, her question was hot-wired enough to a draw printable response.

"Mr. President?" she asked. "At this point, with potentially serious health considerations, would you even *want* a second term?"

Farley turned toward her with a glare.

"Yes, I'd want a second one, Lisa," a testy George Farley barked back, "and I'd also sure as hell like a *first* term."

A moment later, following the flash of anger, Farley's eyes glazed. Some witnesses said that the President was at the point of sudden collapse. Videotape of the incident showed that the arm of Howard Jermyn, the White House Chief of Staff, was quickly extended to support the President. And the tape—replayed scores of times on national television—definitely showed the buckling of at least one First Leg. It strongly suggested that the President would have fallen without support. It was not the first time, the joke circulated in D.C. watering holes later that evening, that Lisa McJeffry had knocked a male politician off his feet.

Thirty minutes after the incident, however, George Farley's press spokesman said that the President had "slipped" on a recently "over-waxed" floor. Despite what millions had observed, there had been no serious problem.

"Where is the President now?" asked Bret O'Hara of the *New York Times*.

"He's in his private residence," Thatcher said. "Working."

"Isn't that highly unusual?" someone from the rear shouted.

"Not necessarily," Thatcher said. But everyone in the room knew it was.

"Why isn't the President keeping his final two appointments of the day?" Peter Ferrara of the *Wall Street Journal* asked.

"The other appointments," Thatcher said, "were canceled by those who held the appointments, not the President."

The briefing lasted ten minutes, went around in circles, and convinced no one. Quietly also, the President's staff began to lighten the appointment schedule for the remainder of the week.

Two hours later, the British Prime Minister also phoned to express concern. But, as Reuters reported late the same day, was told that George Farley was unavailable to take the call.

The *New York Daily News*, above the photo of the buckling Chief Executive leg, the next morning, would trumpet the question:

US GOV'MENT
ON VERGE OF
COLLAPSE?

Millions of other Americans would ask the same question, as would the heads of government in all foreign capitals. It was a question that was not going to go away.

18

I am incensed!
  Men are such swine. They nurse and care for the guilty, those people who have inflicted grievous pain upon the innocent. And yet how much do they sympathize for the victim?

None at all.

Their memories are like errant shooting stars. A brief flare, glowing brightly, then gone into oblivion.

I have been in a grave for thirty-one years. Does anyone remember me? Does anyone care? Look sometime at a monument to the young dead of World War One. Does anyone recognize these names anymore? Is the spelling of their names any different from scrambled letters?

I am crying out for justice and they see me as evil. There is a tremendous irony about the murderers among the living. They look like everyone else. They are your neighbors. Your friends. Your leaders.

My grave is very cold. It is in a cold unfriendly place and I do not like it. I would cry if I could. Won't someone move my physical remains? Won't someone reach down their hands with the grace of human kindness and elevate my body to a place where it might allow my soul to rest?

Does no one hear my cry?

Worldly death is not what you would think it to be. There is a quality about it that defies human comprehension. There are dimensions to it that cannot be charted on any map comprehensible to the living. In a way, I am not navigating in the proper direction myself. That is because I am so angry.

Who is this man named William Cochrane? How dare he look upon Tommy Cassatt and Ralph Forsythe with sympathy? Would you murder a bride on her wedding night? I am going to visit their families and watch them in their grief.

In my dimension, there is no past, present, or future. There is just one sense of time. What has already happened is exactly the same as what will happen. Events circle upon themselves. Take a strong enough beam of light, guide it across the ocean, and eventually it will circle the earth and bend back upon itself. So where does it begin or end?

Where I am, events are like that. Past suffering is present suffering is future suffering is past suffering.

Need I say more? More say I need?

Am I in your head? I want to be in your head. When you close the book, I will still be in your head.

Think of me in the darkness. The invisible hand that you are about to feel settle on your shoulder is mine.

I am more than words on a piece of paper. I am talking to you from beyond the grave.

I am still constructing my story. And I wish to be more than a narrator. In the loneliness of my living death I type, type, type

—*tap, tap, tap*—

whenever I see fit, whenever I feel the need to add a chapter.

There have been deaths in addition to mine. There will be more. My story will be on a grand canvas. The heroes will become villains and me, the villain, the hero. The President will die and the President will live.

I will be a poor woman's Tolstoy.

Did you ever hear of those "near-death" experiences where the living "die," experience a sense of weightlessness and white lights? Where they are "out of body" and see themselves from above? Then they experience a tunnel and they see people they knew long ago?

Then they return?

That is somewhat what it has been like for me, though my return has taken more than three decades. And I have returned for my body, not in it.

The amusing thing is this: When the living mind ponders death, it cannot ponder anything other than something living. That's why granite statues stand as absurd sentries in cemeteries. That's why, when a living soul encounters a disembodied soul, the living must conjure a human form to contain it.

And they see a ghost.

This will be part of my story.

The Levins have almost begun to comprehend.

This man Cochrane, who so readily protects the heinously guilty, will be made to understand.

Another absurdity. Another delicious irony:

The Levins, because they know I'm there, because they hear me writing my story, have acquired a cat.

I love cats.

Carl Einhorn loaded his gun again and placed it in his belt, under his jacket. Also within his jacket he placed his next letter to the President. The letter—sealed, stamped, and ready to be mailed—explained that he, The Unicorn, was one all-powerful Individual, able to bend other people's wills with his mind. It was he, The Unicorn, who was making the President drop like a wounded duck.

Don't fuck with The Unicorn,

he wrote.

Don't mess with The Intellect That controls the
President's Health . . .

Einhorn took the elevator down to the lobby of the Hotel Wescott. It was 7 P.M. and the lobby was surprisingly quiet. He approached the desk, furtively hoping that the pretty young Asian girl, Sue, would be there.

She wasn't. There were two young men. Einhorn took them to be gay and didn't want to talk to them. He looked in the opposite direction as he passed the desk then went down to the hotel garage. He found his car. He climbed into it and started it. A minute later, he was back out onto the street.

Once again, he drove toward Pennsylvania Avenue. He drove around the Capitol and passed in front of the White House, slowing to glare into the President's official residence. At the same time, he had an eye open for a mailbox. Mailing his latest epistle from the enemy doorstep would show them how powerful he was, Einhorn reasoned. But he couldn't find a postal box.

He circled the White House grounds for half an hour, always slowing to look in. It was he, Carl Einhorn, who had caused Farley to come up ill the previous day. Obviously, Carl's head games were finding their mark. They seemed even more direct when he was able to glare directly into Farley's home. It was just as clear to Einhorn that being able to *see* the President as he rode in his helicopter had helped aim Einhorn's thoughts.

Einhorn went on his sightseeing tour again. The Capitol Building. The big monuments. Still no mailbox. Then he circled back to the White House. He wanted to set out on foot, press his small plump-but-powerful face to the White House gate, and beam his mental vitriol in the direction of George Farley.

He cruised past the White House three more times. There was nowhere to park for several blocks. The lack of parking infuriated him. And he sure wasn't going to hike five blocks in Washington at night, even with his handgun.

So on his sixth pass in front of the White House, he pulled his car to an abrupt halt at the curb in front of the Presidential grounds. He put his flashers on and reached under his jacket. His sweating hand found the stock of his pistol. He adjusted the weapon carefully and lodged it securely in his belt.

Then he stepped out of the car. He walked to the front gates and stared beyond. The sturdy white building was bathed in light. On the roof, the flag was still flying with a spotlight upon it. From somewhere nearby, Einhorn smelled burning tobacco.

Where there's a man,
There's a Marlboro!

Einhorn ignored the smell of the idiotic smokers and went directly to the iron gates. He pressed his face against the metal, and held the bars on each side of his head.

He stared and concentrated. "Die, George Farley. Die," he said.

A moment or so later, Einhorn was aware of movement within the White House grounds. Two of the nuisance security people were within ten feet of him in the shadow of the front guardhouse. They had been exchanging quiet conversation and pausing for a good hard cancerous smoke. But they'd stopped to watch Einhorn.

They had also heard him. Carl could tell.

"Fuck!" Carl Einhorn whispered.

The guards dropped their cigarettes and crushed the butts with their shoes. One of them slowly moved toward Einhorn, quiet as an eel in dark water. The one in the back mumbled something into a walkie-talkie.

Carl could still smell smoke. He could remember when television viewers were encouraged to commit slow deaths through nicotine and carbon monoxide poisoning:

You get a lot to like with a Marlboro;
Filter, Flavor, Flip-Top Box!

Einhorn tried to tell himself something funny to calm down.

"Yeah, sure." He spoke maniacally aloud. "The filter and the flavor is the cigar butts and and the fucking flippy fuckety-fuck 'flip-top box' will be the cough-cough-coffin they put you in. Flip-top box comes in bronze or pine, bronze being the color of your lungs after heavy smoking, pine being the dumbassed hardness of your brain for puffety-puffety puffing in the first place."

But then, Einhorn felt his little mathematical heart flutter anew and could not concentrate on anything funny. Too much excitement again! Was this the moment he would have to defend himself? The Secret Service dudes were positioned in front of him.

He reached to the side of his jacket where the pistol was concealed. He patted it down.

"Can I help you with something, sir?" the nearer Secret Service agent asked.

Nietzsche. Superior intellect. Time to act. It comes to all strong men:

"It's me who's making the President sick," Einhorn declared. "Eventually, I'm going to kill him."

It was all very logical.

The agent moved nearer.

"Is that right?" the agent asked.

"That's right, you fuckety-fuckety-fuckhead," Einhorn said, withdrawing toward his car.

"Just stay right there, sir," the lead agent said. "And keep your hands where we can see them."

Hands?

Hands of time.

Turn back the hands of time . . .

Hands across the water. . . .

Hands Christian Anderson.

Einhorn's mental circuits jammed and went even more haywire than usual.

He panicked. He patted his gun again. Then there was quick movement within the gate. Carl turned toward his car and saw that it was already blocked by two huge men in dark raincoats.

The enemy!

Einhorn made a move to the left and a move to the right, quick but clumsy. He reached under his jacket. If he showed them the weapon, he reasoned, it would scare them and—

Something the size of an Atlanta Falcons lineman hit Einhorn from the side. It sent him sprawling to his right, hitting the concrete hard with two hundred and fifty pounds of muscle landing hard on top of him.

The little man's entire body convulsed from the impact. Einhorn had trouble breathing. The wind was knocked out of him and it seemed to him that his arms had been yanked out of their sockets as they were pulled behind his back. And he had hit the sidewalk so hard that he felt as if he had fallen out of a second-story window.

He felt metal click into place on both wrists and knew he had been handcuffed. He kicked and screamed. He filled the pleasant Washington evening with profanities and, for some reason, first thought of his mother, then thought of the beautiful Asian girl who he wanted so badly from the lobby of the Wescott Hotel.

He kept wishing the Asian girl would come upstairs and spank him. The way his mother used to. With a paddle.

Then he felt himself being violated by these brutish men.

Hands were all over him. Reaching in, pulling away his weapon. Grabbing into a pocket, pulling out his next letter threatening the President before he could mail it. (Waste of a forty-eight-cent stamp!) Probing his pockets and grabbing all over his body to see what else was concealed.

Exploring his balls. Patting down his ass.

He heard walkie-talkies crackle over his head and, as he cursed, felt the weight of a strong man's foot on the back of his neck, holding him in place.

He cursed again. Then the Secret Service told him that if he didn't shut up, they'd knock out every tooth in his mouth. Einhorn happened to know that he had twenty-six teeth. He used them to eat and wanted to keep them. So he fell silent.

As if in one motion, he was hoisted up by the armpits and seemingly seconds later he was in the back of an unmarked police van. It was all unreal. His enemies had been there waiting for him and had successfully attacked and captured him.

Nietzsche would have been ashamed of him. He had failed to act! Obscene thoughts came to him.

"God is dead."
—Nietzsche

"Nietzsche is dead."
—God

Two agents climbed into the van with Einhorn. The door slammed and the van started to move. His body was still aching from the hit he had taken, and the joints of his arms throbbed from the way he had been trussed into handcuffs. Another set of shackles had been snapped across his ankles. If he wanted to "run," he realized, he would have to hop away like a penguin.

Worse, the two agents were sitting across from him in the back of the van, glaring at him with hatred.

As the van bounced through the Washington night toward who-knew-what destination, Einhorn had nothing to say.

His letter would explain who he was and why he was there. And the rest of the world could deal with that.

Rich Levin and daughter Lindsay still liked the idea of having a feline in their family. So they went to the Massachusetts ASPCA that same weekend in search of a cat.

They settled upon a big black and white tom and named him Sam, after Rich's boss at work. Sam was long haired and regal in bearing. There may have been some Persian, it was observed, in his family history.

As a mouser, Sam was very good. But he also aspired to greatness.

He nailed two unsuspecting rodents in his first day on the job. Loose in the attic, he nailed two more his next night. The Levins would find him in the morning, not far from his prey, content with himself and furling and unfurling his tail slowly, awaiting some large gesture of appreciation from his owners.

It was when the Levins tried to put him in the basement that Sam balked at his new job description. When they tried to carry the cat down the cellar steps, he would scratch and squirm and leap from their arms. Sam, it was clear, wanted nothing to do with the basement.

"You might find your biggest and fattest mousies down there," Lindsay said to Sam, attempting to reason with him. But the cat was having none of that, turning away from Lindsay's careful line of reason. And even though the death toll of mice rose in the Levins' house—which was a positive accomplishment, no matter what—the tapping didn't cease.

The tapping.

The typing.

Rich, Barb, and Lindsay Levin almost called it by each term interchangeably.

The tapping and the typing. Same mysterious thing. And it continued to unnerve them, as did a few other things. The presence in their house, it seemed, liked to make itself known.

The Levins frequently kept newspapers and twigs near the hearth to start fires on cold nights. Frequently, they would come downstairs in the morning and find several pages from the newspapers crumpled up and scattered around the living room. No one had been downstairs all night.

At first, Sam took the rap on the newspaper mystery. Then, without being read his rights, with no recourse to a jury, Sam got incarcerated in the kitchen as the family slept. And the newspaper blitz continued. So Sam was off the hook, pardoned by the Levins. But no reasonable alternative explanation presented itself. And no other suspect emerged.

Similarly, there was the mystery of the books in the bookcase.

Sometimes the Levins would find books that had been pulled off the shelves overnight and placed on the sofa. Some of them had been left open, as if someone had been reading them and put them down suddenly when he or she heard someone approach.

Barbara Levin tried to figure a method to where they had been left open or whether the titles meant something. She got a little chill when she realized that most of the books disturbed were titles that would appeal to a female reader. But the books in question also came from her section of the shelf. So the topics and authors might not have mattered.

The only method she could find was to the music. .

The Levins still kept their music collection in the downstairs den. It included many old vinyl albums. Sometimes certain albums had been pulled from the cases overnight or when no one was at home.

Once, most disconcertingly, Barbara came home in the afternoon and found the original Broadway sound track of *Hair* playing softly in the den. The presence, or whatever it was, seemed to be partial to music of that era. It was always stuff from the mid-1960s, the focal point of Richard Levin's collection.

"Little poltergeist tricks, that's what they are," Barbara's friend Hazel Brubaker, told her with a laugh. Hazel lived in Wareham and was a new friend. She was a jovial warmhearted woman in her fifties who was trying to talk Barbara Levin into getting a real estate broker's license.

Hazel knew the area, having been in hundreds of buildings and having heard almost as many stories.

"What's happening in your home is harmless," Hazel said. "It happens in these old houses. I wouldn't worry."

"You don't live with it," Barbara answered.

"No. But I used to. We lived in a house in Chatham in the 1950s. Was built by a man named Caleb Stephens, a fisherman in the 1850s. Used to see him walking around the lawn at dusk every couple of years. Couldn't mistake him. Wore one of those old winter mackintoshes and one of those old sword fisherman's hats with the tucked-up brim."

"I'm not laughing, Hazel," Barbara said.

"You don't have to laugh, dear. I'm not joking."

"It's driving me crazy. I'm afraid to go into my own home."

"Don't be silly. It's probably a benign presence," Hazel said, as if this sort of thing were routine. "Is it a man or a woman?"

"Is what a man or a woman?"

"Why, the spirit, of course. Your ghost."

"I've never thought much about it."

"Maybe you should. He or she probably just wants to be sure that you're taking care of everything."

"We are," Barbara said without enthusiasm.

"Then tell it. It's probably a poor worried soul and needs to be comforted. People live with these things all the time. Pay no more attention to it than a ticking clock or a squeaking gate."

"A clock or a gate can be fixed."

"So can a ghost if you treat it right. Be kind. Be understanding."

Suddenly Hazel, a pious little suburban lady, member of the DAR, sounded like a crackpot.

But Barbara had to admit, if she hadn't initiated the conversation, if she hadn't lived through the occurrences in her home herself, she could have more easily dismissed Hazel.

What happened next, however, was not quite as easy to live with, though it did answer one of Hazel's questions.

Barbara and Rich were lying in bed around midnight on a Friday night. Lindsay was out on a date. The nightmares auguring Lindsay's death had stopped, but their parental concern had not. Twelve-thirty came, and so did quarter to one.

The Levins heard a girl's voice downstairs. It was Lindsay, they reasoned, though she must have come in so quietly that they hadn't heard her open or close the door. And obviously it was Sam she was speaking to. Unless a friend had stepped indoors with her.

They heard her puttering around downstairs for several minutes, then listened to her footsteps climb the steps. Rich started to drift back to sleep. But Barbara was awake and cross.

"Lindsay?" Barbara called.

A moment later, the figure of a girl appeared in the bedroom doorway, silhouetted by the hall light.

"I'll talk to you tomorrow, dear," Barbara said. "But you need to be more considerate. If you're going to be that late, you should phone us."

Rich opened his eyes, saw the girl, then closed his eyes again.

Barbara rolled over. But she could see the figure of the girl standing in the doorway for several seconds, staring at her. Then the girl moaned in displeasure, angrily turned, and marched noisily down the hall.

Seconds later the door to Lindsay's room slammed. Hard.

The next morning, Barbara spoke with her daughter, asking why she had been so rude.

Lindsay expressed surprise. "Rude how, Mom?" she asked.

"Last night when you came in so late."

"Oh," she answered. Then she explained.

Her date's car had been hit by another driver, she said, and she hadn't come home till 2 A.M. She didn't want to wake her parents up with a phone call that late, she continued, and they had both been sleeping soundly when she came in. So she had tiptoed in and gone quietly to bed.

"You mean *one* A.M., don't you, dear?" her mother asked. "And you slammed your door."

"No. Two A.M. Definitely two A.M. And I closed it as quietly as I could."

"You stood in our bedroom doorway and didn't even answer when I spoke to you," Barbara said.

"I never came to your doorway."

"I saw you."

"Mom. You're imagining things."

Barbara's heart started to kick. "I know a girl was standing at our doorway watching us," she said.

"Well, it wasn't *me,*" Lindsay said.

Barbara Levin was so distressed that she checked to see if there had been a police report for the accident. There had been. For 1:10 A.M. And Lindsay's date's father vouched for the kids' account of the late evening.

In thinking back over the incident, both Rich and Barbara Levin recalled a strange darkness around the female figure that they had seen at their bedroom doorway, and the unusual way that they had not been able to see the female figure's face. The silhouette had seemed strange, they remembered, and it was impossible to recreate when they tried to resurrect it by standing there with the same lights on.

It was only then, with some reluctance, they fully admitted to themselves that they had a ghost.

A young female ghost.

They kept waiting to see her again.

In the hallway. In the bedroom at night.

Standing behind the next door to be opened.

Almost anywhere. Several times they thought they sensed her. But they couldn't be sure.

One night, without having previously mentioned the subject, Rich was sitting in the downstairs living room.

"I wonder what her name is," he said aloud, staring into the fireplace. He didn't even explain whom he was referring to.

"Juliet," Barbara said, almost involuntarily. "The girl's name is Juliet."

They both raised their eyes and looked at each other. It was as if the question had been inserted into one mind and the answer into the other, both having come from somewhere else. It was as if someone else had keyed the conversation and had wanted the name out in the open.

"Juliet, huh?" Rich said with an ironic appreciation of sixties lore. "Perfect. Our own 'Juliet of the Spirits.' Imagine that."

Rich and Barbara Levin both managed a small laugh. It was the first time either had cracked even the slightest smile over the subject.

But the funny thing was, in retrospect, the moment provided a turning point. As unpredictably as the poltergeist activity had begun, it suddenly stopped after Juliet's name was spoken aloud.

No more messed up newspapers.

No more books out of the bookcase.

No moldy-oldie thirty-three RPM albums pulled from their cases.

Nothing.

Even the newest member of the Levin family, Sam the Cat, acted differently.

Sam, however, seemed to know a few secret feline things about the paranormal. For the first day or two after the "sighting," Sam would skulk around the house, walking low and carefully, giving new and demonstrable meaning to the term "pussy foot." Sam would stay close to walls and keep his own company by sitting under chairs or small tables, his tail to the wall so that he had the unobscured view of whatever room he was in.

A couple of times, in full view of the Levins, the cat believed he saw something. He would get to his feet and get his back up like a Halloween version of a scared cat. Genuinely frightened, he would lower his ears and hiss at something specific which the Levins could not see.

Once, in response to a creak in a floorboard, Sam did all this and then fled the room. The Levins were equally convinced that something was there as that unwelcome cold draft ripped through the room, too. Though they never admitted it to anyone else, the whole family left the house that night and slept in a motel. When they came back the next day, they were as frightened as Sam.

But Sam, conversely, had settled down. After the name Juliet was spoken aloud, an uneventful week went by. No apparition, no noises. There was a faint typing sound

—tap, tap
tap
tap tap tap—

once. It was almost as if the spirit wanted to say, "Hello, don't worry, I'm still here, but do not be scared."

Nothing more happened. Anxiously, the Levins settled into a routine, cautious but optimistic. The feeling of siege had lifted like a curtain. Maybe they had won their home back. The nightmare about Lindsay's death was never far from their minds. But they didn't live each day in fear either.

And neither did Sam.

The cat patrolled the house with vigor now as Thanksgiving approached. He would even, the Levins were surprised to realize, allow himself to be carried into the basement.

The fact was, Sam was now often anxious to go down there. It was as if there were something there he liked. It wasn't mice, because he never caught any downstairs. But the lure must have been highly attractive because whenever the door to the cellar opened just a crack, Sam would slip down the steps and disappear.

"First Sam hated the basement. Now he loves it," Barbara observed. "What's going on?"

Rich hunched his shoulders. Again, he blurted out a thought. "Maybe he's got an invisible friend down there," he said.

Rich's reference was to his own childhood, and how children make up invisible friends. But in the spiritual context, his remark gained a richer meaning.

Once again, the Levins just looked at each other.

"No, I don't think so," Rich said eventually. "I don't think Juliet's down there. In fact," he said. "I think she's gone."

The funny thing was, the final irony was that they almost

—almost!—

missed her.

For one hour that evening, Bill Cochrane sat before Vice President Lang in Lang's Georgetown home. Slowly, Cochrane recounted the preliminary details of the deaths of Lang's former Harvard roommates, Tommy Cassatt and Ralph Forsythe.

Lang listened intently and occasionally interrupted to ask a question. But the parallels of their sudden deaths were difficult to come by, and a pattern was reluctant to emerge, other than the previous details of the lives the men had lived. Their deaths illuminated nothing.

Lang had already decided that Cochrane was to travel to try to find out more. With some hesitation, Cochrane agreed. With the President's most recent falling fit, Washington was a strange place to be. The city was both overanxious and paralyzed at once. Everything was happening and nothing was happening.

"If I move to the White House, William," Lang said gravely, "I'll have to use most of the President's press people until I can goad them into resigning. But you'll go over there with me, if you want to. I'll find a place for you."

"Thank you," Cochrane said. He still remained uncertain whether such a move was something that he wanted. But he supposed it was.

Toward 8:30 P.M., Lang's private telephone line rang. Both Lang and Cochrane were startled. Calls on this line were either Presidential or had to do with security.

Lang went to the phone and answered it. For several seconds he listened. Then some deep tension lifted from his face and he broke into a smile.

"I think that's fantastic," he said. "I think this is what we've been hoping for."

He looked at Cochrane as he spoke and Cochrane was unable to discern the subject matter. For a moment, horrible as it seemed, he thought he was watching Lang's reaction to news of Farley's death.

Then reason prevailed.

"Well, William Cochrane is here right now," Lang said eventually. "You can speak with him. I think William should go over and have a look."

Lang motioned that Cochrane was to come to the phone. Cochrane rose and crossed the room.

"It's Martin Kane at the Secret Service annex," Lang said. "The department has made an arrest."

Cochrane took the phone and Martin Kane—Mr. Martin—was all over himself with the details.

Apparently agents had come in an hour earlier and wanted to read through the kook files. They had made a bust outside the White House that evening, a small belligerent man with a gun.

"When they took him into a holding cell across the street," Kane said, "they did a search on him. Found a letter threatening the President."

"How's this tie to us?" Cochrane asked.

"The man seemed to think he was threatening the President through psychic waves or something," Kane said. "That's what the Secret Service agent told me. Went through our files. The man had a history of writing letters. We had some of them."

"Which ones?" Cochrane asked.

"Unicorn," Kane said. "Remember? We just got another from him. Postmarked—"

Cochrane let his mind unzip for a moment and try to ferret its way through all the babble that had transpired in the last few days.

"I remember it," he said. "Postmarked right here. Two or three days ago."

"I'll tell you something else," Kane said.

Cochrane waited.

"The suspect's been signing his name 'Unicorn.' And his real name is apparently 'Einhorn.' Unicorn. Einhorn. Get it?"

Cochrane groaned. He got it.

When he put down the phone, Lang said he would make the proper arrangements with the Secret Service. The Vice President wanted Cochrane to go over to New York Avenue and take a look at the suspect before the FBI buried him so deeply that no one had access to him again.

"I have a friend over there at the Treasury Department," Lang said. "A man named Winston Lassiter. Know him from California. Talk to this little Unicorn man and find out if he's been sending out the bad karma. I'd like to know. I really need to know."

"I'll take care of it right away," Cochrane said.

Lang grinned from ear to ear. Cochrane, in departing, hadn't seen the Vice President so pleased in several weeks.

20

The police annex on New York Avenue was a small brick edifice which seemed to owe more to the Civil War than to any advanced theories of criminology. It was nestled without marking in between two larger government buildings on New York Avenue. It was one of those typical capital contradictions, a building that had outlived its usefulness but was still, on occasion, useful.

Hence it existed, passed by and ignored every day by thousands of tourists and taxpayers who were ignorant of it but nonetheless paid for its upkeep every year.

In the open marble lobby, Cochrane presented his government credentials, a security pass signed by Lang which was matched by a faxed-in pass from Winston Lassiter, Gabe Lang's friend in the Treasury Department.

A D.C. police officer was at the front desk. He was a thick, graying man in full District police uniform, including sidearm. His name tag said he was Sergeant Sandirsky.

"You want Room 4," he said evenly. "I'm supposed to inform you also that the suspect has been read his rights and has refused an attorney. The arrest concerns the White House and possible federal charges, so the room's wired."

"Wired?" Cochrane asked, surprised.

"Everything's being recorded."

"Does the suspect know that?"

"Do we care?" Sandirsky asked.

The two passes allowed Cochrane to be buzzed past the front

lobby and through a steel door. That, in turn, sent him down a long depressing brick corridor toward another door.

The building still had the stink and atmosphere of a military guardhouse, which was what it had been in the 1860s, protecting Lincoln's White House from possible Confederate agents and soldiers. The walls were painted deep green, and the only windows were high with bars. No prisoner stayed here very long, so the security was basic and fundamental. And dated.

Cochrane arrived at the door that led to Room 4.

There was a guard in a chair outside the door. He was a fat, balding man with a walkie-talkie across his lap and he knew that Cochrane was coming. The guard was reading a newspaper and barely looked up. Then, as if with great effort, he stood, turned, and unlocked the door from the outside.

Cochrane came into the room. His eyes settled immediately upon Carl Einhorn.

The small mathematician was seated silently at a plain round wooden table. He was wearing a white shirt and what appeared to be dark suit pants. Einhorn's hands were folded before him, his wrists manacled. Cochrane could also see that the man's feet were chained and his shoes had been taken from him, as had all objects from his pockets. A Secret Service agent sat across from him.

From years of working a reporter's beat, Cochrane felt his mind flip into an immediate assessment of the arrested individual in front of him. He saw Carl Einhorn as an ornery incensed little porcupine of a man, indignant but also frightened. He didn't look like much of a threat, but Sirhan Sirhan and Squeaky Fromme probably hadn't either.

Einhorn did, however, immediately impress Cochrane as a certifiable lunatic. And yet, Cochrane approached the little man with a lingering sense of hesitancy, unreality, and even fear. Cochrane felt that he was face to face with exactly the type of insanity that had gripped his father. He knew it could be seductive. Contagious. A voice within him told him not to get so close.

Like a child expecting to be punished, Einhorn looked up at the new arrival, wondering what this new visit would bring. His soft but intense brown eyes found Cochrane's. His gaze settled there to return Cochrane's.

Their eyes locked. Cochrane felt a surge of revulsion. Couldn't anyone else see that the little man's eyes burned with a hideous intelligence, a dark cunning.

Almost a mind-warping malevolence.

"No," Cochrane said to himself. "I will resist this. I don't believe what is in front of me. This is a lunatic and nothing more, as if that is not enough."

"So they sent *you* over, did they?" Einhorn said to the new arrival. "Well, you don't scare me."

"You know me?" Cochrane asked guardedly, exchanging a glance with the Secret Service agent.

"No," yawned Einhorn. "But you don't scare me anyway."

The Secret Service guard was a big ramrod-straight blond man named Dick Bradley. Einhorn's gaze darted away from Cochrane only when Bradley spoke.

"I don't know why he'd talk to you," Agent Bradley muttered. "He hasn't said much to anyone else, other than gibberish. I want some coffee. Mind if I take a walk? He's unarmed and shackled to the table."

"I don't mind," Cochrane said.

Bradley rose from the chair where he'd spent the last two hours. Cochrane had seen the Bradley type more times than he could count. A starchy conservative kid, laden with muscles and overanxious. Without a suit, a gun, an ID, and a lapel button, Bradley, who looked to be about twenty-five years old, would have been mistaken for any other big dumb white kid.

Watching a nut prisoner like this was a sewer detail, Cochrane knew. Without asking, Cochrane assumed that the arresting agents were somewhere filling out forms congratulating themselves for their efficiency and already bucking for promotion to duty *inside* the White House instead of patrolling the perimeter. Bradley most likely got yanked out from behind a desk somewhere and was told to sit here and make sure little Carl kept breathing. And now Bradley was trying to show how butch he was.

"He's also a crazy little asshole," Bradley said.

Einhorn stuck his tongue out.

"Shanty Mick cocksucking bastard," The Unicorn taunted. Einhorn expected to be hit. Bradley thought better of it, particularly in front of an audience. "Go get your coffee, Potato Face. Hope you figure out how to hold the mug."

"I reckon the federal marshals to be here in another ten minutes or so," Bradley said evenly. "I don't know what sort of chat you think you're going to have with this little idiot. But you've only got ten minutes."

"I understand," said Cochrane. "Did the D.C. police do an initial questioning?"

"Yes. So did our people. He's an uncooperative little fart. You'd think he'd want to help himself, looking at all that prison time."

"It took four of these dumb Secret Service motherfuckers to wrestle me to the sidewalk," Einhorn bragged.

Bradley grimaced.

"He could have been subdued with a fly swatter," Bradley said, giving his own color to the events. And Cochrane had to admit that the line was a pretty good one coming from a young agent like Bradley. He had probably heard it somewhere else.

Bradley took a final contemptuous look at Einhorn and couldn't resist. He leaned over him. Einhorn closed his eyes and cringed. Bradley took the tiny mathematician's ear in his hand and twisted it till Einhorn yelped.

"Fuck! He's killing me!" Einhorn screamed. "He's fucking killing me!"

Cochrane watched without saying anything.

Bradley grinned and quickly released the prisoner's ear. The Secret Service man held an expression on his face that suggested that he was about to say something further. Then, recalling that the room was wired, he decided to say nothing.

Bradley left the room.

Cochrane sat down. He was already sweating.

"Hello, Carl," Cochrane said.

Einhorn looked at him blankly.

"Fucking Mick bastard tried to fucking *mutilate* me! Did you see that?"

"No, I didn't. I must have missed it," Cochrane answered calmly.

"Figures!"

"You're fine, Carl."

"I'm in extreme pain. You're all in this together."

"My name is Bill Cochrane, Carl. I'm not a policeman. I'm a press aide," he said. "A spokesman. A public relations writer sometimes. I work for Vice President Lang."

"Fuck you up the ass, Bill Cochrane!" Mr. Carl Einhorn said by way of warm greeting. "Fuck you *hard* up the ass. Fuck you up the ass with a broken Coke bottle. How's that?"

Einhorn grinned.

Then, "Remember, kids," Einhorn said, "You can tell Wonder

Bread on your grocer's shelf by the red, yellow, and blue balloons on the wrapper."

Cochrane almost had to suppress an ironic smile. There was a certain hopeless charm in dealing with the overtly deranged. He then noticed that Einhorn cringed slightly when Cochrane raised a hand to reach for a pencil.

"Expecting me to hit you, too?" Cochrane asked evenly.

"Why not? Everyone else hits me. Secret Service would have liked to beat me to death."

"Do you understand why they're upset with you, Carl?"

Einhorn was silent. He chose not to turn the heat of his ample charm upon his latest visitor.

"It's their job to protect the President," Cochrane said. "You had a gun outside the White House. And you've been writing letters."

Einhorn looked away.

There was a puffiness beside his small nose. Every few seconds he raised his manacled hands to press a Kleenex to his face. His nose kept running and Cochrane assumed that some of the heavier-handed types in the Secret Service probably had given Einhorn a little hosing.

"I know a bit about you, Carl," Cochrane said. "The Secret Service told me that you're a mathematician. You used to teach school in New York and Atlanta. And now you write computer programs."

"How do they know all that? Someone writing a book?"

"They took your wallet. Wallet contains ID. ID contains Social Security number. From that things get pieced together quickly."

"Fuck!" said Carl Einhorn. "Fuckety fuck. You know something? That is *il*-legal! SocSec number not supposed to be used as a national ID. Law. Nineteen fucking thirty-three. 'Hey, Mabel! Black Label'!"

"I'm told they took a hotel room card from you, too," Cochrane continued. "My guess is that someone's over there right now looking through your things."

"They won't find much."

"Probably not. But I know even more about you."

Einhorn's eyes narrowed. "How?"

"I've read your letters. The Unicorn. That's you, Carl."

A long pause. Then, "So?"

"I'm not like the others, Carl. I'm impressed." Cochrane, as a former reporter, always liked to offer a first-class bluff when he needed one. "Can you really cast spells?" he asked.

Einhorn looked away. "Don't shit me. You don't believe that I can do that."

"Now how would you know what I believe?"

"I can see inside your head."

"Then you should be able to see that I believe you."

"I can do a lot of things with my mind. My mind is stronger than anyone else's. So I can do a lot of things."

"Did you put a spell on the President?" Cochrane asked.

Einhorn was quiet.

"It's not me who wants to know. It's the Vice President. He believes you might have done that."

"Maybe I did," Einhorn allowed.

"You said you did. In your letters."

"If I said so, it must *be* so."

"That's what I was thinking."

"They're going to execute me for it, aren't they?"

"I don't think so, Carl. No jury would think that any man would be capable of a spell. So how could they convict you?" He paused. "Why don't you tell me your secrets while Agent Bradley is away for coffee?"

Einhorn looked at him. It was not, Cochrane realized, a completely rational look.

"Balzac drank over fifty cups of coffee a day and died of caffeine poisoning," Einhorn said.

"That's interesting. You don't like coffee?"

"No."

"Do you like Balzac?"

"He was all right. I prefer Prozac."

"What have you read by Balzac?"

"Would you know titles?"

"Try me."

"*Père Goriot?*"

"I liked that book," said Cochrane. "I read it in translation in college."

"The translation calls it—"

"*Old Goriot,*" said Cochrane.

"That translation misses the point," Einhorn complained. "Should be *Father Goriot.* Part of the point of the book is the beleaguered old man's relationship with his bitchy-witchy daughters."

"And you read it in French? I'm impressed. I could never learn a language."

"My mind is superior to yours."

"I'm sure it is."

"I taught myself French when I was a senior in high school. Did all four years in two terms."

"Very commendable."

"Yes, it was. But no one commended me. Instead, they made fun of me."

"I'm sorry. They shouldn't have done that."

"Do what?"

"Made fun of you for being smart."

Einhorn looked at Cochrane for two seconds, which seemed much longer. Einhorn had a way of pinning him with his eyes. Cochrane felt the surge of revulsion again.

"Now you're making fun of me," Einhorn said.

"Don't judge me by what anyone else has done to you, Carl. I respect intelligence."

"Hrrph. 'Double your pleasure, double your fun' . . ." Einhorn sang softly, croaking off-key.

A certain childish anally-retentive aspect of the would-be assassin's nature was emerging right before Cochrane's eyes. Increasingly, he had the impression of dealing with an emotional eight-year-old. And then there was Carl Einhorn's intellect. Einhorn's mind was so left-sided that Cochrane wondered why the little man didn't tip over.

Einhorn finished his brief concert. ". . . with double good, double good, Doublemint gum."

"Where did you go to high school, Carl?"

"Bronx High School of Science. New York."

"Follow the Yankees?"

"I hate baseball. Sixty feet six inches. The six inches makes no sense, though three hundred sixty feet around the bases does."

"I'm surprised you don't like it. Baseball can be very mathematical, as you just noted."

"Sixty feet, plus the length of Abner Doublemint's penis," said Einhorn. "That's where the extra dicklength came from."

"Then you *do* follow baseball?" Cochrane asked.

"Why should I care if other people win or lose? Those numbers mean nothing. Do the players on a team worry about me? No. So why should I care about them?"

"A lot of people enjoy sports."

"Baseball is for idiots. So is football."

"Chess is considered a sport. Do you play chess?"

"P-K-Four to you, too."

"What about playing cards?"

"What about them?"

"Do the red queens mean anything to you? Queen of diamonds. Queen of hearts?"

"Red queens. Staten Island fairies. All the same."

Cochrane suppressed a sigh. He was starting to understand why the Secret Service did without the formality and just started pounding the infuriating Einhorn right away.

"What did *Père Goriot* mean to you?" Cochrane finally asked.

"The book?"

"Yes."

"Don't trust women. They take advantage of you. All they want is your money and your semen. The man Goriot was led into ruin by his daughters. Bitches."

"So you don't like women? From that book?"

"Didn't like them anyway," Einhorn said boldly. "Except to fuck."

"Do you have a girlfriend?"

Einhorn didn't answer. The question made him pause for a moment. Then he regathered.

"Did you know," Einhorn asked, "that the word 'vanilla' comes from the Spanish word for 'vagina'? Vanilla is so named because of the elongated shape of the pod which has a slit in it?"

"That's fascinating, Carl. But I want to talk to you about the spell you put on the President."

"Chocolate is often used as an aphrodisiac also," Einhorn said without wavering.

"Carl, the President collapsed the other day. That's what I want to discuss with you."

Einhorn folded his arms. "I have nothing to say."

"Did you do it?"

"I might have."

"You did, didn't you?" Cochrane said. Cochrane's ear began to ring louder again.

"I'm not saying," Einhorn answered.

"Why did you do it?"

"To show that I could."

"Show who?"

"The world."

"How did you do it?"

Einhorn looked directly at Cochrane, nuttiness dancing in his eyes. "With my magnificent mind," he said.

"You put a 'spell' on the President? Would that be the right term for it?" Cochrane asked. "A spell."

"You could call it that. For a spell."

"What would you call it?"

"A telepathic curse. Lethal karma."

Cochrane let half a second pass as he digested this. "Would you consider removing this 'telepathic curse'?" Cochrane asked.

"No. I'm not going to do that."

"Why should I?"

"Might be a good idea if you would," Cochrane said.

"Yeah?" Einhorn snorted. "Why?"

"To prove that you can control the spell," Cochrane said.

"I refuse," said Einhorn.

"That's not very helpful. If you remove it and wish the President well, maybe we will all forget about it."

"Forget about what?"

"The spell. See, something strange is going on here, Carl. You arrived in front of the White House with a gun."

"It was for my protection."

"I'm sure," said Cochrane. "But you were talking about hurting the President."

"With a spell. Not a gun. I could make him die with my mind."

"Did you tell the Secret Service that?"

"No. But here's what I'll do. Get me a female Secret Service agent. I want to smell her vagina. Then I'll tell my secrets."

"I can't understand why you were fired from your teaching jobs, Carl."

"Really?"

"No."

"Well, fuck you, too. There is no spell. All the police want to talk about is the gun."

"That's how they think. Why did you have the gun?"

"For my protection. On the street."

"You can't protect yourself on the street with a telepathic curse?" Cochrane inquired.

Einhorn, flapping within the loose net of his own illogic, retreated. "Lipstick was invented by prostitutes in ancient Egypt. It was their way of advertising that they would do oral sex on a man for pay."

"Carl, I want to talk about the spell you placed on the President," Cochrane said.

"Hrrph," Einhorn answered. Then his expression changed slightly. "So why are you different?"

"Different how?"

"Different from the Secret Service people who come in here to beat me up and talk about the gun."

"I work with the press, Carl. I'm not a policeman."

Einhorn looked at him for a moment, then slid back into a belligerent stance.

"I wouldn't believe you no matter what you told me," Einhorn said. "People lie to me all the time. Math makes sense. No exceptions to any rules. It's neat and ordered. For some reason, some were just born with the secret decoder ring for people. I didn't get mine."

"I'll decode for you, Carl."

Einhorn grunted.

"But we've only got about five more minutes."

"Flying fuck," said Einhorn. "And . . . ? Do you know why the number eight two eight is so important in numerology?"

"Carl," Cochrane pressed, "have you ever heard of anyone named Ralph Forsythe?"

"What if I have?"

"What about Tommy Cassatt?"

"Fuck you." He stared at Cochrane. "Dead men."

Hairs prickled on the back of Cochrane's neck. "Why did you say that?"

"Are they dead? Ha! Lucky guess!"

"Carl, I wouldn't take an uncooperative position if I were you," Cochrane said, his patience starting to fray. "I'm the one person in here who might have an interest in going easy on you."

Einhorn looked sullen but relented a little. "Why is that?" he asked.

"Because no one is angry at you for putting a spell on the President. People are angry because you wrote letters and made threats. And because you had a gun in front of the White House."

Einhorn brooded on it.

"Ever fired that gun?" Cochrane asked.

"Sure."

"Secret Service says it was pristine. Never been fired."

"They lie."

"What did you shoot?"

"Uoy kcuf," Einhorn said.

"Does that mean you're going backwards? Changing your mind? You now want to cooperate?" Cochrane asked.

Einhorn turned away.

"Ever *heard* of Tommy Cassatt or Ralph Forsythe?" Cochrane tried again.

"Sure."

"Who are they?"

"You just mentioned them. And they're dead."

"Did you have anything to do with their deaths?"

"Why should I tell you?"

"Because you're in a lot of trouble."

"I know who they are but I won't tell," Einhorn said. "And I know why they're dead."

"Why?"

"They stopped breathing."

Einhorn began to giggle. It was enough to convince Cochrane that Einhorn didn't know anything. But a further thought was upon Cochrane. He reached into his pocket and pulled out a fresh deck of cards.

Einhorn eyed the deck. "What's this?" Einhorn asked.

"A deck of standard playing cards. Ever play?"

"Cards bore me."

"Normally me, too," said Cochrane.

He spread them on the table, facedown. He picked two and turned them up. Two of clubs. Six of diamonds.

He tried again. Four of hearts. King of spades.

He silently played the game a third time as Einhorn watched in apparent interest, but confusion.

Three of spades. Seven of diamonds.

"What are you trying to do?" Einhorn asked.

"Draw the two red queens," Cochrane answered.

"In two draws?" Einhorn asked.

"Yes."

A pause. Then, "Your chances of doing that are fifty-two times fifty-one, or one in two thousand six hundred fifty-two," Einhorn said. He paused again. "Unless there are jokers in the deck. Are there jokers in that deck?"

"Yes, there are, Carl."

"You didn't tell me that!" The Unicorn snapped. "That means the odds are, let me see, seven point nine one percent higher. Or one in twenty-eight hundred fucking sixty-two."

"What would you say if I told you that I knew someone who could do it every time?"

"I'd say you were full of shit," Einhorn said, his Bronx intonation emerging. "Twice in a row, the odds against would be two thousand six hundred fifty-two squared."

"What would that be?"

Einhorn thought for a moment.

"Approximately," suggested Cochrane.

"One in seven million." He conjured it through. "One in seven million, three hundred thousand fourteen."

"Fairly remote."

"That's right."

"Unless some other factor is at work," Cochrane suggested.

"Like?"

"Telepathy," said Cochrane.

Einhorn's eyes froze on the cards.

"If you can make the President fall ill, surely you could make a pair of playing cards come forth, Carl. Ever tried?"

"No. I wouldn't want to."

"If you can do it," said Cochrane, "I'll take you out of here."

"What?"

To his shame, Cochrane lied again.

"If you can make the red queens come forth consistently from this deck, I'll walk you out of here. I'll set you free."

Einhorn stared at him. Enhancing the bluff, Cochrane held up his car keys and jangled them.

"You're lying," said Einhorn.

"You have to trust someone, Carl," Cochrane said. "I'm at least willing to believe in the powers of your mind. Now, can you make the two red queens come forth?"

"Maybe."

"Let's try."

Cochrane squared the deck again, shuffled it, and spread the cards facedown on the table. He watched Einhorn watching the cards and watching him. The little man's eyes darted back and forth.

"Remember, Carl. This is your ticket out of here."

"Uh-huh."

Cochrane saw a thin line of perspiration form on Einhorn's fore-head, just along the hair line. Cochrane kept his eyes on his suspect.

"Now," Cochrane said. "Draw the red queens."

Einhorn studied the deck. Then his plump fingers drifted above the cards. With an awkward quickness, his hands landed on two. He turned them over.

Strangely, Einhorn drew two one-eyed jacks.

Cochrane thought about it.

"Too bad," Cochrane said. "I'll give you another shot."

He integrated the two drawn cards back into the deck. Then he asked his suspect to draw again. Einhorn tried.

Six of clubs. Six of diamonds.

"You keep drawing pairs. But the wrong pairs."

Einhorn shrugged. His voice taunted. "Coincidence."

Cochrane did not appreciate the recurrence of that word.

Then they tried a third time, a fourth, and a fifth. The cards came up with a funny logic: odd even, red black.

But Einhorn couldn't find either red queen, much less both in one drawn pair. After his sixth failure, he leaned back.

"Can't do it?" Cochrane asked. "Even with your freedom at stake?"

"This is dumb!" Einhorn snapped. "It's a trap. Some sort of fix."

Cochrane opened his own hands in a helpless gesture.

"Maybe, Carl," he said. "But I now have trouble thinking you could cast a spell on President Farley. You can't even draw cards, can you?"

"Put 'em together and what've you got, fuckety-fuckety you," Einhorn chirped. Then he glared at the cards as Dick Bradley reen-tered the room. With Bradley came two federal marshals to transport the suspect to a more secure facility.

"Time to go," one of the marshals said.

Bradley produced a key and undid the chain that held Einhorn's ankles to the table.

"Already?" Einhorn asked.

"None too soon," Bradley said.

Einhorn looked at the two marshals and suddenly started to scream. When they informed him that they had contacted his mother in Florida, he screamed even louder. For a moment he looked im-ploringly at Cochrane, as if to seek help. Then his eyes changed as quickly as an image on a television screen.

Mad eyes gleamed. Then, as Cochrane first stiffened, then recoiled in horror, Einhorn's eyes went soul-dead and Cochrane saw the final vacant empty look that his father had borne during the shuffling zombie period of his final years.

Cochrane sat there numb. Had he really seen that? Or had it been a horrible mirage?

"COCK-suckers!" Einhorn howled.

He screamed so loudly that Cochrane recoiled again. Then he started to resist the marshals. He swung his chained hands and his shackled feet. He somehow managed to turn over the table.

The marshals were huge men with massive arms and shoulders. But Einhorn, filled with the strength of the insane, gave them trouble. He landed a blow to the nose of one marshal. Blood poured forth. He brought a knee up toward the groin of the other marshal and hurt the man. It wasn't until Bradley, the Secret Service agent, yoked Einhorn's neck with a powerful arm that the law enforcement officers gained control.

Cochrane watched with incredulity. But then, just as abruptly, the fight went out of Einhorn. Moments later, Cochrane saw why. The first marshal had shoved a syringe into the little man's right arm. Einhorn still resisted, but his strength was evaporating with his consciousness. Bradley was able to back off and let the marshals have their man.

Cochrane, soaked with sweat, continued to sit still. He watched the prisoner being pulled from the room. During the powwow with The Unicorn, the ringing in Cochrane's ear had grown so progressively worse that now it almost hurt physically—a barometer, perhaps, of his anxiety level. The latter was now soaring.

And within Cochrane, a debate raged. Einhorn had disturbed him greatly. And there was no rational reason why.

"What did you think?" Bradley finally asked.

"Just as you said in your introduction," Cochrane said. "He's a crazy little fart."

Down the hall, they could hear Einhorn braying softly, then there was a heavy clank of the metal door and the little man's voice mercifully disappeared.

Cochrane stood.

"But as a threat? Psychic or otherwise? I don't think so. Bonkers, sure. But I doubt if he even knew how to fire the gun. And he can't even control himself with his own mind."

"You don't believe that, uh, telepathy stuff?" Bradley asked.

Cochrane looked at the young agent in surprise. "He discussed that with you, too?" Cochrane asked.

"Not with me. But I overheard some talking. With you. With the other officers. And there's been all that stuff in the papers about the threat to the President coming from another realm. Or another world. Or whatever it is." He shrugged. "I was just wondering if there was anything to it."

Cochrane felt something scary. "Come on. How could there be?" he asked. An excellent bluff.

Bradley seemed to withdraw quickly from the notion. "I don't know how there could be," he said. "I was just wondering what *you* thought."

"You think I'd have some special insight?"

"I didn't know," Bradley said defensively. "Maybe. Maybe not. I'm just asking."

It was then that Cochrane realized: Bradley had paused in his pursuit of coffee and had been standing somewhere in the building where the room recording was being monitored. He was standing somewhere and listening in. That, and Einhorn had spooked him, too.

"I think Einhorn's a harmless nut case," Cochrane repeated, as much for Bradley as for the unseen listeners. "In terms of the real world, though, I don't think Carl Einhorn could organize a cat fight in a sack, much less hurt George Farley."

Bradley thought about Cochrane's analysis for a moment, his face showing confusion. Then he hunched his shoulders.

"That's pretty much my impression, too," Bradley said. "Just about exactly."

"I'm sure it is," Cochrane said. "I'm sure it is."

As he left the room, Cochrane wondered if the young agent could read the fear on Cochrane's face, as easily as he could read it on Bradley's.

21

That evening at home, in the painting loft of his town house, Bill Cochrane stood before the incomplete portrait of Lisa McJeffry and wondered what to do. The canvas was unsatisfying. He had set out to capture her, brush stroke by carefully considered brush stroke, hoping to catch her beauty or at least her spirit. Instead she had left him. Could he still paint her, he wondered, with the affection that he had once held? Or would his sense of loss permeate the painting?

He wondered for several minutes. He looked at some of his oil paints, which lay in tubes on a side table.

Flesh tones for Lisa? Exactly which? Again and again he considered what to do. Should he use a red base or a blue? Should the look in her eye be affectionate or filled with challenge and defiance?

Which Lisa did he want on the canvas?

If any.

He sighed in frustration. Without her physically in front of him, he despaired of being able to capture her with any accuracy.

Of course, he realized the irony: He had failed to win her heart. So how could he expect to capture her soul?

He set the project aside again for the evening—untouched for the day—and went to his living room. He read for a while and then watched the 11 o'clock news.

Still nothing from the White House. No one had seen the President all day. There were military decisions to be made in the Mideast and North Africa, and executive decisions to be made on Capitol Hill. But the American government seemed to be on autopilot. Most ominous, however, was a rumor that Cochrane had caught before leaving work: two bills that the President should have signed that day were still unsigned. And while they were minor bills there had been signing ceremonies scheduled. The scuttlebutt around town was that the President was too ill—too mysteriously ill—to even get to his desk, much less partake in a ceremony. Strangely, the inactivity at the White House had turned into the new norm. While speculation was rampant as to how long it would last, to some degree the capital and the public had accepted it.

But for how long, Cochrane wondered. A few days? Two weeks? No longer, he was sure.

The television sports caught Cochrane's attention. The Boston Red Sox, Cochrane's team, had engineered a significant trade with the National League champion Arizona Diamondbacks. The Sox were once again determined to bring a championship to the New Fenway Park, a crowning achievement in Neo-Throwback Baseball Architecture.

New Fenway had opened in Revere in 1999 on the site of the old Northgate Shopping Center, complete with a Citgo sign beyond the left field wall. The team had a new playground, but the franchise had now been without a World Championship for eighty-five years. And counting. As recently as the World Series of 2001, the Red Sox had staged their own Space Odyssey, blowing a four-run lead in the ninth inning of the seventh game, making champions anew of the resurgent New York Mets.

Cochrane flicked off the television and went to bed. At one point the ringing in his ear dulled to a level where he thought it had finally vanished. But then he was conscious of it again. As he drifted off to sleep, he made a mental note to call a doctor if the ringing persisted for another two days. And he tried to remember when it had first started. Somehow he associated it with the advent of Carl Einhorn, the little mythical one-horned beast himself. Even as he approached sleep, Cochrane couldn't displace the little psycho from his mind. Einhorn was like a mental virus that had somehow found its way into Cochrane's system.

On the brink of sleep, his body spasmed, one of those quick muscle movements that sometimes presages sleep. Then he settled again.

As Cochrane finally drifted toward dreamland, he was even more aware how much the little mathematician had upset him, a perverse diminutive presence to cast a shadow on all other events.

An occult threat to the President . . . a threat to the President from another world . . . a little man of numbers who could control things with his mind . . .

> *It's as credible as anything else,*

a little voice whispered to him.

Cochrane opened his eyes for a moment as those words formed within his brain. He held the thought. Then he closed his eyes again. Finally, around midnight, Cochrane was asleep.

But not to stay.

Three hours later, something startled him.

Cochrane found himself lying in bed, bathed in sweat, his eyes wide open in a dark room. Oh, this hour of the night, he told himself. Any man could go mad at this hour. Go mad and never come back! This was the time when a man's rationality could tiptoe past the brink!

> *Good!*

"Who said that?" he wondered.

> *Welcome! You are past the*
> *brink. You will see things*
> *differently now!*

He sat up in bed. "Who the hell . . . ? What the hell . . . ?" he started to say. Something muffled him. Almost felt like an invisible finger pressed to his lips. He should be quiet.

He blinked at his clock. It was 3:30 A.M. and he had the distinct impression that he was not alone.

There wasn't anything specific he was aware of. No noise. No disruption. No motions in his bedroom.

But he could feel something. A sense. It was as if the barometric pressure had plunged suddenly in advance of a storm. His home *felt* different.

> *Why?*

He almost answered that question aloud.

Why? He didn't know why.

Then he sniffed at the air. He caught a slight suggestion of perfume. What the hell was *that* all about? He sat up in his bed. Was there a woman present? Had some female friend let herself in? If so, he didn't recognize the fragrance.

Replique

"What?" he mumbled aloud.

Replique. Come see . . .

"What?" he said again.

This time, no response. He turned on the room light and looked around. The bedroom was still. But his fears were galloping. His anxiety was expanding and growing like Mickey's broom in *Fantasia*.

"Sure," he told himself. "I'm imagining this."

But he also knew that he wasn't alone. Once again, he had that reporter's unerring sense, that instinct that—once developed—will follow so many men to their grave.

Or to another grave.

He climbed out of bed. He knew he should have been even more frightened, but wasn't. He knew he should have had a sense of foreboding, and did.

He left his bedroom. He stood in the hallway on the second floor of his home. He looked at the stairwell that led downstairs into the darkness of his living room. And he knew he had no choice now but to follow his instincts.

He stood at the top of the stairs and slowly started downward. He knew something was waiting for him.

Someone.

But he didn't know who.

Replique.

The scent was ever stronger as he descended the stairs.

Smelled nice. But it was combined with a mustiness. And a cold draft that he couldn't place.

There are always the firsts in every man's life. The first time one experiences an emotion or an act that carries an overwhelming intensity, the emotional impact is greater than it will ever be again.

The first love, found.

The birth of the first child.

The first death in the family.

The first professional success.

The first love, lost.

The first time a man sees a ghost.

Not *thinks* he sees. Not feels he *might* have seen.

But *really sees!*

He reached the bottom of the stairs. Two more steps and he was in his living room.

He stopped cold, too stunned to do anything but gaze upon what his eyes had found. There was a woman in the living room. And from the first second that he laid eyes upon her, Cochrane knew that she was someone who was not living.

He wanted to think of her as something that was not real. Or unreal. But he couldn't. He couldn't because when his eyes settled upon her they attached to her. Although she was something from a plane that he had never encountered before, he knew she was there.

Right in front of him.

It was a moment that was made up of more than he could comprehend. He was looking at a disembodied spirit and he knew it.

He should have been terrified. And in one part of his mind, he was. But another part of his mind was in open revolt against the first. And this second part settled him. Something told him not to run or scream or turn away. Afterward, he would decide that she had sent him this message, that it would be all right to stay.

The room was shadowy, not completely dark. The only light flowed in from the outside. It came from the moonlight and the reflected illuminations of street lamps. It cut swatches of brightness across the chamber. And—he later figured as he was thinking back—there was light from *her.* From the ghostly woman. Or maybe it just seemed that way because she was shimmering.

He slowly reached for the light switch, his eyes never swerving from the female form. But instantly he was aware of the fact that she was gently shaking her head.

No . . . Please don't . . .

He was not to put the light on. Natural light was all that was needed. And he obeyed. He was suddenly dreadfully frightened that she would be gone if he lit the room. Gone or—worse—angry. Already he was mesmerized by her.

He wanted to know who she was. Instinct once again, a triumph of intellect over fear.

Her face was not pretty. It was plain.

Homely, with heavy overtones of sadness and tragedy.

But the visage was also filled with contradictions: While it was a young face, it was also ageless and timeless, intensely pretty in almost a mythic way. She was sinister, yet enticing. Worldly, yet ethereal. Emphatically feminine, yet androgynous. Reassuring, yet threatening.

He knew time was passing, but he also knew it was standing still. And he could only think of her in terms of such contradictions and analogies. He felt as if he were taking a secure well-trodden path through the jungle. But he now had stepped from the sunlit familiar route and was in some strange exotic place.

He knew he was lost in this plane.

He knew the longer he stayed here, the less the chance of ever returning. The familiar and the secure were tumbling into the past, along with every notion or belief he had ever held about life or death.

But he was so fascinated that he didn't care. He knew he didn't dare *be* lost. But that was exactly what he wanted to be.

Her eyes were incandescent. They were eyes unlike any he had ever seen before. And now the entire room was their color, which was a light grayish blue.

He spoke softly. "Hello," he said.

She didn't mouth an answer. But an answer came to him from somewhere. It was like the whispered *"Why?"* a few moments earlier. Somehow, it had gone from her and was in his head.

"Hello," she replied.

"Who are you?"

She only smiled. Then, with barely any movement, she was seated at the dining table. For a second it made him doubt the reality of what was in front of him, because one second he was looking at her standing and the next moment she was sitting.

No transition. One place one instant, another the next. He never saw her move. And he found himself thinking, "So that is what it must be like after one is dead. One moves from one place to another but doesn't transverse the space in between. Neat."

"Sit down. Join me," she conveyed.

He did. He pulled back the chair and sat down across from her. Already, she was more important than any other woman who had ever been in his life.

"Yes, I'm dead," she said, as if to read his thoughts. He could hear her voice. It was sweet and very feminine.

"I know you are," he answered. "You're a ghost."

Her eyes glimmered.

"There aren't really such things," she said. *"I was living. I am living no longer. But you still see my spirit."*

"That's a ghost," he said. "You are a ghost."

"I'm not a ghost, but I am a ghost," she said. *"That's how it is after you're dead."*

He was aware of a smile on her face. He could not take his eyes off her. In his mind, there was another canvas, and brush stroke by brush stroke, her face was painting itself upon it. He could picture the paintbrush moving but no hand was upon it.

Then, distantly, there was the sound of a young woman laughing.

"Me. That's me laughing," she seemed to say. *"I've been dead for thirty-one years. It feels so good to laugh again."*

Then he saw something on the table. It gave him a shock. Not a shock like an electrical shock, but a shock like an emotional reaction. In between them was what appeared to be the deck of cards that he distinctly remembered having fed into the fire several nights ago.

The deck of cards. And she was going to deal them.

"I burned those the other day," he said.

"It doesn't matter," she answered.

"To me it does."

But she ignored him. *"I'm here to warn you,"* she said. *"Our fates have intersected. You cannot escape me now until you put me to rest. Does that interest you?"*

"Interest me?" He didn't understand.

"Our fates have intersected," she said again. *"You haven't come to find me and yet you have come to find me. Are you able to understand?"*

"No."

More contradiction.

"Of course. Good," she said. *"If you understood, you would not have to discover."*

"I don't understand!" he said again. "Help me understand." He could feel himself very wet now, starting to sweat again. Almost starting to shake.

His eyes lifted from her for a moment. They found the mirror across the room. He saw himself seated at the table alone. No one else there. No ghost. No woman. He flicked his eyes back and she was in front of him, just as she had been.

Then there was her laughter again, and he quickly became frightened.

"Tap, tap, tap," she said, making an accompanying sound. *"I'm tapping, I'm typing, I'm making a wonderful story."*

"Is it a true story?"

"All stories are true," she answered.

He looked at the table. Her pale opaque hands looked like cold white marble. They resembled a sculpture in a Sicilian garden. Lifeless. Yet they were moving.

Her long female fingers flicked with the edges of the playing cards, making that clicking, tapping sound. It had an echo resonant of an old Olympia portable typewriter that he had owned as a boy. His father had used a similar typewriter years earlier.

"Before he went nuts," he found himself thinking. "Same way I'm going nuts."

"Never seen a spirit before?" she asked.

"No."

She laughed. *"You may never again."*

"Why do I see yours?" he asked.

"Because I allow you to see me. And because you are a good man. And you want to discover the truth."

"Which truth?"

Her laughter rang sharply in his ears. *"All truth,"* she said. *"All."*

There was a pause. It may have lasted many, many minutes, he realized later. He had the sense that some part of her spirit was circling him. He had that sense because he kept feeling something sweep past him in the shadows. Suddenly he had the knowledge that a spirit could dissemble. Some parts of it could be before him, the other parts could travel.

Then, *"I want your hands,"* she said.

He held out both wrists. She took his hands.

He jumped. The touch of her lifeless flesh was like a block of ice. But he was not able to resist her. She pulled his hands onto the playing cards and settled them. Then she withdrew her own hands.

He looked at her.

She smiled.

For a fleeting moment, she was realer than ever before. She was no longer shimmering, but very substantial. Almost as real as living flesh.

Almost as if there were a real live woman sitting across from him. He was aware of the perfume again, plus the cold.

"What do I do?" he asked. "What do I do now?"

"Follow," she said.

"Follow what?"

"My story," she said. *"Follow my story."*

"I don't understand."

Another smile. For a split second, she was more beautiful than any woman he had ever seen in his life.

"You will," she said. *"At the end of the story, you will understand."*

He wanted to ask more questions. He wanted to know when he would understand. And why. And even though she was still in front of him, he wanted to know when she would reappear.

But somehow he felt himself frozen, his soul hanging out by itself on some spiritual clothesline. And he couldn't speak.

He wasn't aware of turning away from her, but he was aware of staring out the window of his living room. And as he became conscious of what he was watching through the window, he had the notion that he had been looking in that direction for a long time.

Several minutes. Maybe as long as an hour.

His eyes shot back into the living room. The seat at the table across from his was still drawn out.

But the woman—the ghost—was gone.

He spoke aloud.

"Where are you?"

There was no answer. He had not really expected one.

His gaze shot to the window again.

Beyond the window, the sky above Virginia was lightening. He again had the impression of having been in that position for a long time, unmoving. Frozen in time while time itself traveled, he supposed. His eyes found the red digital glow of the clock face on his VCR. He saw it was 4:45 A.M. An hour and a quarter of his life had been rolled up into a little ball and thrown into eternity.

He wondered if the little ball were bouncing around somewhere.

His hands were wet. His fingers were still upon the playing cards. He looked at the dissembled deck and wondered by what terrifying warp in reality could cards that he had burned two weeks earlier now be back in his hands.

And above everything, he knew that his life would never again be the same.

Not his physical life.

Not his spiritual life.

Not his mental life.

Since becoming an adult and falling away from religion, he had always believed that death was the end of existence.

Now what did he believe? What, Mrs. Elizabeth Vaughn might have asked him at this moment, would he allow to fill the void in his consciousness? He could almost hear her voice asking that question.

Rationality?

A belief in the supernatural?

Eastern mysticism?

Superstition?

Insanity?

A vehement denial that this ghost had even appeared?

All of the above?

He played with that idea for a moment. But as the room filled with the light of dawn, his eyes kept settling upon the playing cards. Just as this spectral woman seemed to have returned from the dead, so had the deck.

Playing cards. Her calling cards. Was he imagining something there?

He cut the deck and turned one card face up.

Queen of diamonds.

He stared at it.

He cut the deck again and drew another card, knowing in advance what he would get, but dreading it at the same time.

A surge of fear coursed through him.

Queen of hearts.

He left the cards face up and stared at them in almost a dreamlike state. Later, he wasn't sure whether he had fallen into a trance or whether he had fallen asleep with his eyes open. All he knew was that there was now a shrill jangling in his home, in addition to the interminable ringing in his ear.

This time it was the telephone.

He didn't even know when the phone had first sounded. He shook his head as if coming out of deep sleep. He pulled his hands away from the turned-up red queens on the table. He went to the phone.

At the same time, he noticed the time. It was now six-fifteen. He had passed one hell of a scary night.

He answered the phone. He found himself speaking to a sourtempered man whom he knew: Lieutenant John Appleton of the White House Secret Service.

"Hope you've had a good night's sleep," Appleton said.

"I haven't."

"I couldn't frigging care less. Get over to the White House."

"What's going on?"

"In another hour you're going to become a Presidential press attaché." Appleton said. "Now move your ass."

"What?"

"It's all over the news, you jerk. Put a TV or radio on. Farley's been in a goddamn coma since yesterday morning. The Chief Justice is on her way over to the White House now. Twenty-fifth Amendment, Cochrane. Your man Lang is going to take the oath of office in fifty-five minutes."

"Oh, Jesus," said Cochrane.

"My reaction, too," Appleton grumbled. "God help this country. It's going to be the United States in retrograde now, not just frigging Mercury."

Cochrane slowly set down the phone. He stared at his living room. The chamber was empty as a broken dream.

He went to his kitchen and quickly made some coffee. He felt as if his brain were coming apart at the seams. And once again, he wondered if that—incipient dementia—was one of the only things he was correct about these days.

A few minutes later he was out in his car, driving through a Washington morning that was sharply colder than the ones that had preceded it. There was frost everywhere, even in northern Virginia, and for the first time there was a real suggestion of winter.

Traffic was heavier than normal. Automobiles were everywhere. Cochrane looked at all the other drivers and knew that everyone else knew that there would be a change in the American government that day. And no one had any idea what it would mean, either domestically or internationally.

Cars. Drivers.

A line of commercial doggerel came to him from nowhere, the type of thing that little Dr. Einhorn would have chirped, echoing a string of rural highway billboards years ago:

> Rip a fender off your car,
> Send it in for a half-pound jar.
> —Burma Shave

Cochrane cursed the little maniac for the way he had sneakily permeated Cochrane's head without Cochrane even knowing. He hoped he never saw the little twerp again.

More crap, *à la façon de l'Unicorne:*

> Send to us 500 jars,
> We'll send you on a trip to Mars.
> —Myanmar Shave

"Shut up, Carl," Cochrane said aloud in his car. "Shut up with the Burma Fucking Shave."

Cochrane was having one hairy morning. He almost thought he could hear Einhorn laughing, wherever the Secret Service had him ratted away.

Cochrane settled himself. He crossed the Potomac at the Arlington Bridge. No more messages from other worlds.

As he drove, prowling around in the back of his mind was a complicated new problem, one presumably linked to everything else.

He had seen a ghost. For the first time in his life he had *really seen a ghost!* He hated to admit it, but the existence of such a thing then opened up the possibility of almost anything else that the human mind could imagine.

An occult threat to the President? To the country?

Why not?

Sure! Einhorn really *was* manipulating the President, Cochrane told himself. Mercury in retrograde really did affect the earth, Mrs. Vaughn could see into people's souls, Lisa's sister Dee Dee had a child spirit in her attic, and red queens could waltz at will out of any deck of cards if the dealer just bore the proper curse.

In this context, everything now made sense.

Even Lincoln—sober, staid, Emancipation-Proclamation Honest Abe—past whose Monument Cochrane now drove by eerie coincidence on this frost-bitten morning—had claimed to have encountered his own ghost in the White House in the days before John Wilkes Booth murdered him. Just as Gabe Lang had explained a few weeks earlier. The story had a bizarre resonance now with Lang in the White House and an unidentified female specter haunting Cochrane.

Damned right! Anything was possible!

And Cochrane did not know one person in official Washington whom he could possibly tell.

PART
TWO

22

At an historic but hastily convened ceremony in the Oval Office of the White House, Gabe Lang raised his right hand and repeated after Chief Justice Ginsburg.

"I, Gabriel Lang . . ."

"I, Gabriel Lang . . ."

". . . do solemnly swear . . ."

". . . do solemnly swear . . ."

". . . that I will faithfully execute the office of President of the United States . . ."

Standing against a wall at the east side of the crowded executive office, Bill Cochrane watched the proceedings with disbelief. He had been in Washington for the swearing in of George Farley as well as Lang's swearing in as Vice President. On a cold January day nearly three years ago he had watched both events from forty yards away, cold and shivering on the makeshift steel seating of a temporary pavilion. But there had been a naturalness to that setting, as natural as those grainy old television clips of Kennedy standing in front of an aging Earl Warren, or Johnson aboard Air Force One raising his hand as a disbelieving Jackie Kennedy looked on, or some twenty years earlier, when an absurdly young-looking Bill Clinton took the oath on a surprisingly balmy January day. And Mrs. Clinton had worn that strange blue dress.

All of that had been expected. All had been part of a logical flow of events, even the changes in office caused by assassination. But now Gabriel Lang, every fruity inch of him, was taking the oath as something that had never before happened in American history and might never again in the lifetime of anyone present.

Acting President.

With Farley in a coma that defied medical comprehension, Gabe Lang would serve until Farley could rise from his hospital bed, put forth a fresh string of profanities, and demand his job back. Right now, Farley was out as cold as a kayoed boxer, lying again in the Duffy Pavilion, lost somewhere in a dream world between consciousness and reality.

And the problems of state now fell to Gabe Lang. Already the political pundits were wishing him well, and simultaneously questioning his capacity for the job.

Cochrane's eyes played across the room. Lisa McJeffry, looking beautiful even though she had thrown herself together as abruptly as everyone else that morning, stood with the other White House correspondents. She glanced Cochrane's way for half a second. She acknowledged him and the events with a rueful half smile. Then her eyes drifted back to near-President Lang.

The invocation of the Twenty-fifth Amendment, mused Cochrane. Twice before, elements of the Twenty-fifth had kicked into effect, he recalled, but one had to go back three decades.

Once in 1973, Gerald Ford had been appointed to fill the office abandoned by the notoriously corrupt Spiro Agnew. And then the same procedure had been invoked again in 1975 when Ford had succeeded to the Presidency following Richard Nixon's abdication to California. Good trick by Ford, Cochrane thought, his mind wandering, having attained the White House having never won an election outside of Grand Rapids, Michigan. When Ford moved up, that Man of the People, Nelson Rockefeller, became Vice President.

Nixon. Agnew. Ford. Rockefeller. Lang.

A litany of former Vice Presidents, some who made it to the next office, some who did not. And the two who did couldn't stay there. The government was stable, Cochrane concluded, but the electorate was ever-fickle. He wondered how long Lang's honeymoon would last. Or for that matter, how long his Presidency would last. Farley could come out of his coma and start screaming at any minute, throwing an extra spin on the proceedings of that morning.

But over in Maryland, Farley wasn't moving, much less saying anything.

". . . so help me, God," concluded Justice Ginsburg.

". . . so help me, God," repeated Gabe Lang. "So help me, God," he tacked on a second time.

Gabriel Lang lowered his hand. He was now Acting President of the United States.

"There," he said, congratulating himself since no one else bothered. "That's done. That's done."

Justice Ginsburg offered her hand as soon as someone relieved her of the Bible. Cochrane would remember afterward that the only one in the room smiling was Gabe Lang.

Later in the morning, Lang went to considerable efforts to—as he termed it privately—"steady the nation and convince them that I'm not a space cadet."

He made some brief remarks in a televised address, and Cochrane was not the only one to comment privately that Wall Street was lucky that this was a Saturday. The stock market was closed. The sight of Gabe Lang sitting in the Oval Office was enough to send a huge flight of capital to gold and drive the Swiss franc to a one-to-one exchange rate with the dollar. Hopefully things might calm down by Monday.

In the afternoon, Lang met members of what was now his cabinet, all of whom made a show of sitting around a table and having a friendly chat. Most of the cabinet disliked Lang intensely. Private meetings were scheduled for the next week.

In the very late afternoon, Lang met with the members of his Vice Presidential staff who were to make the transition to the White House, at least temporarily. With these workers, whom he'd known longer, Lang increasingly dropped his new Acting President facade. He seemed more and more like Gabe Lang, as opposed to a President of the United States. It was almost as if one persona emerged as the other waned.

Toward 6 P.M., Cochrane found himself alone in the Oval Office with Lang.

"I was wondering," Cochrane eventually broached, "would you still like me to continue looking into the deaths of your two classmates?"

"What do you have so far?"

"Same as we spoke last time."

"And what was that again, William?"

"Nothing extraordinary."

The Acting President made a thoughtful gesture, followed closely by a grimacing one.

"What do you think, William?" Lang asked.

"I'd like to finish what I started," Cochrane said, "even if it means travel."

"That's fine," said Lang. "Arrange it with the Travel Office. It goes on White House Budget now, rather than VP/Staff."

"I'll arrange it myself," Cochrane said. He paused. "There's one other thing, too."

"What's that?"

"The man with the gun who was arrested outside the White House gates last week. I'd like continued access to him."

Lang frowned. "Whatever for?"

Cochrane shrugged. His ear rang like a little siren. "Can we call it 'instinct'? A feeling?"

"Call it anything you want," said Lang, who was always in touch with his own feelings. "Arrange it through John Appleton. John Appleton. He's head of White House Secret Service."

"I know him," Cochrane said.

"He likes me," Lang said.

Cochrane, recalling Appleton's actual comments, said nothing.

"A lot of these people in this building think I'm a breath of fresh air after George Farley," Lang continued. "Maybe one of them put George in a coma, ever thought of that?"

It was intended as a joke but even Lang knew it had failed. Cochrane managed a weak smile to at least acknowledge the attempt. "No, I hadn't," Cochrane eventually said.

"Well, don't bother chasing down that angle," Lang said. "You know eventually, they'll do all these tests and things on Farley and find a blood clot or discover he was mean to his mother and this is God's revenge or something. Then they'll have their explanation as to what's wrong with him. What's wrong with him."

Cochrane listened, amazed at how Lang could sound so coherent in front of reporters and the public, then let his Starbeam side show when he dropped his guard.

"Could be an extreme planetary thing, too," the Acting President said. "Everybody makes fun of that. Wouldn't dare suggest it in public, God knows. Problem is those damned astrologers in the tabloids are a bunch of charlatans. Charlatans. Don't know what they're doing. Need to have a good workup on the star angle sometime for Farley. Might accomplish more than his doctor, Ivan the Terrible."

By this point, Cochrane had fallen cautiously silent. He feared that Lang was proposing to have Cochrane smuggle a serious star gazer into the White House, the first since the Ron and Nancy era.

Lang rambled forward. "You know when I was growing up, my dad had one of those Presidential plates. Know what they are?"

Off hand, Cochrane did not know. "No," he said.

"Oh, sure you do. You see them in antique stores, the better ones. And I used to see them advertised in *Parade* Magazine. They were these plates that you hang on the wall. Got the pictures of all the American Presidents on them, plus the years we served. Usually the guy who's in office is in the center, which is sort of my point. I wonder if somewhere someone's breaking into a mold today to push Farley down to the lower rim of a plate and get me in the center. You know, with the year 2003 underneath?"

"Don't know," Cochrane said, feeling a response was needed.

"Well, I don't know either. Could be a collector's item. A collector's item. Strange little historical footnote." He paused. "If I serve more than a month, I've got William Henry Harrison beat, I know that much."

Cochrane nodded.

"There's just one final thing," Lang finally said.

Cochrane waited.

"I'd like to be called Mr. President now," Lang said. "Could you put out a release to the staff and to the reporters? It's not that I'm on the ego voyage or anything, but there's a certain respect for the office, isn't there, that should be shown?"

"I'll write up a memo before I leave," Cochrane said.

"I knew I could count on you," Lang said. "Thank you, William. That's all. That's all."

Cochrane had difficulty with the sentence that allowed him out the door. "Thank you, Mr. President," he said.

Before leaving the White House, he stopped at the Travel Office and made arrangements for the next day. He would go to New York first, then California, not even knowing what answers he was seeking.

Yet on his way home, an event occurred of massively disturbing proportions. Driving southbound on the Washington Memorial Parkway in Virginia, Cochrane was moving at about sixty miles an hour when he saw a quirk in the headlights on a vehicle in the opposite lane heading northbound.

The driver of the other vehicle, a battered old van, apparently lost control of the wheel. The vehicle hit the center divider and careened wildly. The car left the roadway and tumbled toward Cochrane's lane.

Cochrane saw it all the way. The head-on collision would take his life. He hit his own brakes as hard as he could and swerved wildly to his right, somehow evading the hurtling, burning metal and glass while it flew directly toward him.

He would forever again see the vehicle in slow motion as it bounced, evaded other cars, and seemed to be searching him out. But its momentum didn't carry it far enough. It spun to a halt in the middle of the parkway while Cochrane's own car skidded to a stop, inches away from the other vehicle.

For one moment arrested in eternity, Cochrane stared at what was before him. On the driver's side of the van was a man with a monstrous face, bearded like a devil, mouth open in a scream, matted with blood, eyes burning.

A vision from hell. Fire engulfed the man.

All Cochrane could think of was getting his own car out of the way, before he was killed by a rear-end collision. He managed to evade other swerving cars again and went to the side of the road.

He had a fire extinguisher in his trunk. Perhaps if he moved quickly enough—

But he was already too late. With a roar, the crashed vehicle burst completely into flames. It would be fifteen minutes before a fire truck could even arrive.

Bill Cochrane reentered his home that evening, confused and frustrated by his work, and shaken by the death he had witnessed on the parkway. He went to his den and set down on his desk the files on Tommy Cassatt, Ralph Forsythe, and for good measure, one on Carl Einhorn that the White House had duplicated for him.

He wandered to his kitchen and made himself a sandwich. He took food back to his den along with a bottle of beer. He sat down at his desk and tried to calm himself.

With a remote control, he turned on the small television that sat in his bookcase.

He slowly settled down as he ate and channel-surfed. For one of the first times in his life, he had had enough of politics. Enough about the Twenty-fifth Amendment. Enough about the President's illness and enough about whether Gabe Lang was up for the job.

He kept flicking the remote. Bull's eye. Hockey. The Washington Capitals were playing the Philadelphia Flyers. Perfect. Lindros on his way to another sixty-goal season. White guys beating up on each other with no political significance whatsoever. Who said there was no such thing as quality television?

Television: A mischievous little tirade came to him from out of the past. Must have been from when he was a teenager:

ABC—Anything But Culture

CBS—The Commie Broadcasting System

NBC—Nothing But Crap

FOX—Films Originally X-rated

He smiled for a moment.

Seeing the ghost the other day had turned his brain inside out, it seemed. In some ways, it had been a liberating experience. After all, now that he knew ghosts existed, well, hell . . . he could entertain any line of thought.

Couldn't he?

Thoughts seemed to cascade forth from the past sometimes. He wondered where she was.

He groaned. Cochrane leaned back at his desk and kept a highly critical eye upon the TV screen. Somehow the National Hockey League of the new millennium seemed to be leaving him behind.

He took a long gulp of his beer. He devoured his sandwich. He thought about the travel arrangements he'd made to leave for New York the next day. He wondered if Washington could possibly survive without him.

The city, not the team.

Maybe, neither could.

Ah, it was silly time, Cochrane knew. He had been maxed out on work and his mind was freewheeling in strange directions.

He couldn't tolerate the Capitals anymore. He clicked off the television and wondered why his mind was wandering in so many strange directions.

He had a bizarre feeling. Was it overwork? His association with Gabe Lang? The concept of the occult acting upon the so-called normal world? Or was it the lingering consequences of seeing a ghost?

"Hey, Ghost! Where are you?" he shouted.

He listened to an echo bounce quickly around his home. Then he laughed aloud.

Something made him think of his father. Cochrane grinned. Maybe the old man hadn't been so nuts after all, he reflected. Maybe he had heard voices and seen people that *were* there. Maybe there was something wrong with everyone else who *couldn't* see those things.

Cochrane looked around him.

Anyone there? Anyone *else* there, he wondered.

"Hello?" he said aloud. "How's stuff, Lady Ghost?"

No response. He laughed again.

Sometimes over the course of the last day, it seemed like he was never alone, as if there were an invisible presence near him at all times. A female presence, he liked to think. His right ear continued to ring. It was as if there were an alarm sounding somewhere and only he could hear it.

An alarm. Signifying what? Danger? The crossing of a threshold. Alarm.

The Strawberry Alarm Clock

"Oh, yeah, right," he concluded, finishing the beer. "That's it. Psychedelia, as Mrs. Vaughn would have me believe it."

Then he sighed. A wave of rationality gripped him for a change.

Must be overwork, he told himself. It had to be! These past weeks following his father's death there were too damned many questions leading nowhere. Too many things that meant everything and meant nothing. He looked at the impenetrable files that sat on his desk like small flat manila gauntlets.

Another line of commercial doggerel came to him:

> Brylcream, a little dab'll do ya,
> Brylcream, you'll look so debonair,
> Brylcream, a little dab'll do ya . . .
> You fuck 'em with their feet up in the air!

"Jesus!" he thought ruefully. A lurid revisionist commercial brain wave from The Unicorn? When was he going to get that little runt out of his head?

Brylcream, of all things! The original greasy kid stuff.
Then, as if in response,

Use, Vitalis! For a healthier, more natural look!
Rub it in your girlfriend's pubic hair!

"Shut the hell up, Carl!" he snapped aloud. His own words echoed in the empty town house. And he shuddered. What sign of madness was this?

The first? The last?

And did he really think little Carl Einhorn could hear him? Did he really think the elfin Unicorn was sending him messages?

Then his mood subdued and turned from anger to glumness, though he didn't know why. He had another sense of foreboding, one that he couldn't quite grasp. He wished he didn't have to make the trips to California and New York to investigate the deaths of Ralph Forsythe and Tommy Cassatt. He felt like an actor before a curtain is about to go up, but he didn't know his lines, much less the role, much less the theme of the dramatic piece.

He felt adrift. The original "dazed and confused." Where the hell was he heading with all of this? What did he hope to prove? His mood seemed to be on a minute-to-minute roller coaster ride.

Would his discoveries propel Gabe Lang from the White House or onward to a great Presidency? Would Lang serve nine more years or nine more hours?

And yet a certain notion clung to Cochrane like a wet shirt heavy with sweat. The notion was that there was some sort of shadowy logic to everything that was happening and that somehow he was destined to put a name or an explanation to it. It was as if there was an unseen watcher somewhere, or a control, or a master plan, or some sort of order within the chaos, something he rarely saw but only felt.

His whole body seemed to tingle with the intensity of it.

Out of thin air, he grabbed another metaphor, one which presented an inquiry.

"If I were walking through the jungle and I came to a door," he asked himself aloud, "just a door upon its own frame, and it seemed to open upon nothing other than a wide open other side . . . ?"

He thought about the wording of the question that he posed to himself.

". . . would I walk through the door or around it?"

He knew he would walk through it. Just in case it offered something special. Just in case there were something to it that he couldn't otherwise see.

". . . would I choose to go insane or would I opt for remaining rational?"

Somewhere in his town house there was the slight rustle of a windowpane. But there was no wind outside.

He looked in the general direction of the noise but saw nothing.

"Which doesn't mean nothing's there," he said aloud. "Right?"

No answer within the town house.

He wondered about the name of the female ghost whom he had seen. He decided, retroactively, that she was pretty, not homely. He wanted to know again what it was that he would need to discover, and why she had sought him out.

Was there a special way, he wondered, that he could summon her? He thought the two of them should have a nice chat.

After another beer, he closed the downstairs of his house. The last thing he saw as he rose to the bedroom was the deck of playing cards sitting on the table in his living room.

"My own little superstition," he said. "I will leave them right where they are in hopes that they bring back my new girlfriend."

Toward midnight, he turned out his room lights and lay in the comforting darkness. For several minutes he lay in bed waiting for something to happen. At one point, from the corner of his eye, he thought he sensed something move in the room.

He felt his heart beat and his flesh tingle again.

He waited to feel an invisible body to sink onto the edge of his mattress, the feeling of someone sitting down.

Very badly, he *wanted* the ghost to return. He wondered what need she must have been filling in his life.

The absence of religion? The absence of a lover?

The answer to a mystery?

But she didn't appear. Instead, he was revisited by images of the crash on the Memorial Parkway on his way home.

He kept seeing the tortured face of the man who was burning alive within the vehicle. And he kept hearing Carl Einhorn's threats about Cochrane dying in an accident.

Worse, as he thought back, he had a strange sense of the steering wheel in his own car. It was as if he had had to battle it to evade that accident.

It was as if there had been another force—another hand? telepathic vitriol?—on the wheel.

"Lunatic stuff," he warned himself as he tried to drift off. "This is absolutely lunatic stuff!"

Eventually, he slept, though it was fitful. Which was not good, because the next day he would begin his travels.

23

Cochrane flew from Washington the next morning to Westchester County Airport, twenty miles northwest of New York City. At the airport, he rented a car and drove to the home of the late Thomas Cassatt.

Patty Cassatt, the widow, received him at a split-level suburban home in Larchmont. She was a very pretty woman in a snug black sweater and a red plaid skirt. The latter she wore short, Cochrane noticed immediately, maybe theoretically too short for a woman in mourning. But Cochrane equally had to concede that she was very pretty, and why shouldn't a woman in her late thirties want to look attractive? And did the tight black sweater, he wondered, betray her conflicting emotions on the loss of her spouse?

But she was an outwardly gracious woman, well spoken, thin, well educated, and with long brown hair. She had beautiful high cheekbones and Cochrane remembered that Lang had told him that "Patty and Tommy" had apparently been having some troubles in their marriage. Lang once had openly speculated that Cassatt, always a bit of a stuffy old goat in Lang's opinion—even when Cassatt was younger—had bitten off too much when he married a woman twelve years his junior.

"Can't keep up with her," Lang had explained. "Physically. If you know what I mean." ·

Cochrane knew.

Then there had once been a rumor about Patty and a ski instructor at Aspen on one of the Cassatts' many separate vacations. Tommy had spent much of their thirteen-year marriage putting on weight, while his wife had spent much of it keeping in shape. Cochrane had a notion, based on what he saw, and based on the few clues that Gabe Lang had let drop, that their marriage had turned into a relationship that no longer had any harmony, other than the home they shared and the children they raised.

Cochrane had seen this so many times, where couples had lost calmness in each other's company and where even the most quotidian of conversations could take strange, rambling, sometimes inflammatory directions. It saddened him to see it again, having as it did an echo of his own relationship with the departed Lisa.

All of this came back to Cochrane as he sat before Patty Cassatt and all of this meant nothing, other than the fact that she looked like a woman for whom an affair would be easy, whether it had been or not. And involuntarily, Cochrane wondered whether Patty had been having an affair at the time of her husband's death, and now was dealing with her guilt in her own defensive way.

He began by conveying the grief and condolences of Gabriel Lang, her late husband's onetime roommate at Harvard and currently—for who knew how long?—President of the United States.

She nodded and accepted this, speaking in small general terms, never saying anything wrong or inappropriate, but without much emotion one way or another. A few minutes into his visit, Patty offered Cochrane a cigarette from a small silver case. Cochrane declined, and then, apart from lighting the little cancer stick, she held it in her hand and let it burn, never smoking it.

Carolina incense. Presumably it would ward off evil thoughts.

She discussed the circumstances of her husband's death without much hesitation, like a story about a trip to the supermarket. She had been away, she said. She worked part time as a buyer at a woman's clothing store in Greenwich, she explained, and this enabled her to get around the country on buying trips. On one such trip recently, her husband had apparently had a stroke. It was a weekend, she recalled, and he had been alone in the house at the time while she had been in Colorado. He had collapsed on the stairs, she recounted, fell backward, and hit his head. There had been an autopsy and even the doctors weren't sure whether he died from a blood clot to the brain or the blow to the head when he fell over.

"And you know what?" Patty asked without passion. "It doesn't matter. Gone is gone."

"As I said," Cochrane repeated. "I'm very sorry."

"I wish he had stayed in better physical shape," she said. "Just generally. I think we could have lived a better life that way. Both of us."

"But you were still close, you and your husband?"

"Why are you asking me that? Of course we were," she answered.

"Sorry if it sounded like a question," he said. "It was meant as a statement."

"Oh. Yes. Of course," Patty said.

"And you know the Forsythes. Out in the San Francisco area?"

"I know them."

"Incredible coincidence about two Harvard roommates dying so close together," Cochrane said. "There couldn't possibly be anything about it that doesn't meet the eye, could there?"

"Are you suggesting something?" she asked. The cigarette, which she held somewhat like a pea shooter, almost took the plunge into her mouth at that point. Instead, the smoke started to irritate her eyes and she snuffed the entire reed.

"Not at all. The President simply wanted me to ask. That's all."

"It's a fucking stupid-assed question," Patty Cassatt said politely. "You can tell the President I said so. Quote me."

"I know he'll enjoy your choice of terminology," Cochrane said.

"Yeah. I know he will." She paused. The first glimmer of a smile crossed her face. "Gabe Lang is a skunk," she continued. "I know that's why he's done so well in politics. He propositioned me once at a party about five years ago. In Manhattan. A fund raiser. He was out to raise more than funds that night. Seemed to think I'd think it was some sort of honor to sleep with a Senator. As if it's a difficult accomplishment. I've known a lot of politicians. That's why I don't vote. Can't stand them."

"If you don't mind my asking, did your husband know?"

"About Gabe coming on to me?"

"Yes."

"He just laughed when I told him about it. He said I had to expect that type of thing. Should have been flattered, he said. I was supposed to take it as some sort of flattery that he thought I'd be a quick lay?" She paused. "I think Gabe cleared it with Tom before he hit on me."

"Why would he do that?"

"You're a man," she answered. "Maybe you can explain it to me."

"I can't."

She looked at her visitor carefully. "Aren't you going to ask if I accepted?" she inquired.

"Nope."

"Are you curious?"

"Not enough to ask. And it's not what I came here to discuss."

She smiled. "Then you'll never know," Patty Cassatt said.

Cochrane shrugged. "I could ask the President," he said, half facetiously.

"As if you could believe anything he said," she countered with annoyance.

The phone rang. Patty picked up a portable phone that was near her. Cochrane sat tight and waited for her to finish, which she did quickly. Obviously, whoever was on the line, she did not wish to speak in front of him.

"I'll call you back," she said.

The call ended. A few minutes later, so did her audience with her visitor.

Cochrane flew back to Washington that same afternoon. His reading on the flight was again the file on Carl Einhorn. Einhorn had been moved to a federal psychiatric center in Washington while the government decided what to do with him. Was he a small-time local nut or bigger game, best left to a federal prosecutor? While such weighty matters of state were decided, doctors at Elm Hill Hospital were trying to decide whether Einhorn was competent to understand any charges against him, state or federal.

When he arrived at home that evening, Cochrane went through the messages on his answering machine and listened to the evening news at the same time. As was often the case, the news and the messages sometimes overlapped. Acting President Lang had mentioned something about teaching astrology in the public schools on an experimental basis, and most of his press staff had spent the day trying to downplay the remark, only to be undercut that same evening when Lang, out for a walk in Georgetown, said that he had "meant what I said. Exactly what I said."

Cochrane sighed. He was pleased to have been out of town that day. He wondered how long this could last. Three new doctors had been added to the President's team in Bethesda, but all were under the direction of Ivan Katzman. The press releases from the hospital were filled with bold optimistic statements, but the bottom line was that George Farley was still ill—repeatedly slipping in and out of consciousness. And the doctors still didn't know what was wrong with him. All of which made Cochrane again think of the crazy little Unicorn.

Nonetheless, Cochrane slept well that night. He spent the next morning at his office, but did not see the President. In the afternoon he flew to San Francisco, stayed over at a glittering new hotel at the Embarcadero, and on the next afternoon drove north to Marin County where he would visit with Mary Forsythe, the second of two newly widowed women. Mary had agreed to receive him toward four in the afternoon. Cochrane was anxious to keep the appointment and get past it.

He met Ralph Forsythe's newly made widow at her home, which was in Marin county. Cochrane reached his destination by driving over roads he remembered from when he was a Californian himself. In some ways, he was again retracing steps of his earlier years. It seemed sometimes that life continued to run in concentric circles, none ever escaping the same center.

The Forsythe home was a big expensive Victorian, with a high porch and a roof that lifted above several surrounding tree tops. It was a lush piece of property, the prize awarded to a man who had sold his soul to his law practice but—on this plane of existence anyway— may have received a pretty fair price.

Cochrane entered the property via a long gravel driveway which brought him up to a front entrance. As he stepped from his car and was greeted by the fresh air, he heard all around him the restless ticking of wet leaves. Showers had played peekaboo with Marin County for the last two days, and the most recent rain had ended an hour earlier.

But now the sun was apparent and Cochrane found himself reaching for a pair of sunglasses. He never put them on because Mary Forsythe, the recent window, emerged from the front door of her home and immediately greeted her visitor.

She was a small pretty woman with short black hair, dressed more conservatively than Patty Cassatt. Exactly what one expected. Around Mary Forsythe, as well as her beautiful home, there was an air of sadness prevailing over the air of wealth.

She led her visitor through the first floor of her home, and Cochrane spotted the familiar things that were endemic to a long successful marriage. An upright piano, littered with musical scores. An oil portrait of their daughter which Cochrane could see was professionally done. A blend of antiques from the East Coast, combined with a few more curious items from Asia. Booty and souvenirs from trips, Cochrane guessed. There was a wedding picture in a silver frame on a side table in the living room. It was ajar and Cochrane wondered if Mary Forsythe had been looking at it when Cochrane had pulled into her driveway.

She led him to a sitting area on a back patio. The flagstone were still wet from the rain and so was the outdoor furniture. Another woman appeared, a larger slightly older version of Mary. The other woman was introduced as Susan Miller, Mary's sister. Susan lived down in Encino outside of Los Angeles and was married to a man who arranged banking services for motion picture makers. Susan was staying with her sister indefinitely following the recent tragedy. The invocation of Ralph's death gave Cochrane the opportunity to express his sympathy.

"Thank you," said Mary Forsythe. Her sister took a sitting position not too far behind her on a damp lawn chair.

Cochrane, former reporter, professional press attaché, found himself reaching for the convenient phrases and thoughts.

"I think I mentioned on the phone," Cochrane said, "I've worked for Gabe Lang for several years. Gabe, the Vice President, the Acting President, is greatly saddened by your loss. He considered it his loss."

"Thank you," she said again. "I received a handwritten note from him just yesterday."

Now Mary Forsythe found it her place to don sunglasses.

"They kept in touch over the years. But I'm told politicians do things like that."

"I know how distressed Gabriel is personally," Cochrane said, "even in the midst of all that's happening in Washington."

Mary Forsythe seemed to soften slightly. "I do appreciate that," she said. "I'm sorry if I'm seeming cold. This has all been like a nightmare. My emotions are completely spent. The funeral was only two days ago."

"I know you're aware," Cochrane said, "the Cassatt family suffered a similar tragedy."

"Yes, I know."

"Do you communicate with them?"

"Patty Cassatt called me when she heard about Ralph," Mary said. "We couldn't believe it. We had known each other for so long. We'd both become widows so close together."

"And at such an early time in their lives," Susan Miller added from behind.

"Do you think there's any method to that?" Cochrane asked.

"What? A link?"

"Yes."

"How could there be?"

"I don't know," Cochrane said.

"Is that what he sent you here to ask? All across the country to ask me *that?*"

"My primary reason to visit is to convey my concern and sympathy," Cochrane said, retreating again. "And naturally, President Lang wanted to know as much about your loss as possible. Or whether he could do anything for you."

Once again, she softened. She shook her head and managed a brave smile. "There isn't anything," she said. "No link. No insight. No special"—she searched for the proper word—"no special 'New Age' meaning or anything."

She paused. Cochrane waited because he knew she was working her way to saying something more.

"The only special link was what existed between those three men in their lifetimes," Mary said. "There was always something. Some shared experience. Some bond I could never get through to. I asked about it many times. Maybe it was something a wife can't understand."

Cochrane thought about it. His eyes moved to Susan Miller for a moment. He had the impression that Mary's sister had plenty of opinions, not all of them positive. But today she was keeping them to herself. Or at least between sisters.

"May I ask you the most difficult question of all?" Cochrane asked.

"Go ahead."

"What do you think happened to Ralph on that cliff?" Cochrane asked.

She looked at him. Steel gaze behind the dark frames. "Oh. I see," she said primly. "This is the 'Jumped, fell, or pushed?' question, isn't it?"

"Yes."

"There is no reason he would have jumped," she said. "That's all I'm going to say."

Cochrane nodded. They spoke in small talk for several more minutes.

"I won't take any more of your time," Cochrane eventually said. "President Lang asked me, however, to say a prayer at Ralph's graveside. I wonder if you can direct me?"

"Saint Anselm's Cemetery," Susan Miller chimed in. "I can take care of that. I have a map."

"Thank you."

"It's not far from here," the widow added. "I think you'll find it very easily."

Both women rose. The meeting was over.

As Mary Forsythe had promised, Saint Anselm's Cemetery was just a few minutes away. A caretaker was hanging around the gates, anxious to lock them for the night. Cochrane had fifteen minutes to find inspiration among a brigade of tombstones. Or at least near Ralph Forsythe's.

Cochrane walked into the cemetery and tried to remember the directions Susan Miller had given. Was it Plot B, Row 16, South Quadrant, or Plot 16, Row C?

His memory seemed askew. But it barely mattered because when he looked up, in the shadows by the rear wall of the graveyard, he saw that he had help.

Standing way back in the cemetery, about sixty yards distant, a woman in an old-fashioned printed peasant skirt stood facing the entrance of the cemetery.

His gaze settled upon her immediately and he knew just as quickly that she was the ghost he had seen in his apartment. Cochrane stopped short, although he was entirely surprised to see her. He had sensed her presence so much on this trip.

"Getting brazen as hell," he said to himself. "Appearing in the light of day like this." After a moment, he waved to her.

The distant woman raised a hand and waved toward Cochrane. A friendly wave, not one of beckoning. Then she pointed toward Ralph Forsythe's grave. He started to walk in the direction she indicated. Then he took his eyes off the figure and turned to the caretaker.

"See that woman back there?" he asked.

"What woman?" the caretaker answered.

"*That* one," Cochrane asked again, motioning with his head. He looked back to make sure she wasn't playing poltergeist tricks on him by disappearing. But he could see her.

"What one?" the caretaker asked again. "I don't see nobody."

Cochrane turned his head and looked again where the figure was. He could see her clearly. Even from this distance, he could see her smile.

The caretaker looked at him curiously. "You been in the sun too long?" he asked. "We're the only people in the yard."

Cochrane sighed. "That's what you think," he said. "One of the things I've learned recently: There are people all around us."

"Huh?"

"Spirits. They're there."

Cochrane received another long look from the custodian.

"I see things that you can't," Cochrane added.

"Right," the man finally said. "Look. Finish what you got to do. Then we close. Okay?"

"Okay," Cochrane said.

The caretaker was not a happy man. He looked for a final time in the direction that Cochrane had indicated. His bemusement turned to an impatient scowl. He clanked a set of chains which he wanted to put on the main gate: a reminder to the day's final visitor that closing time was imminent.

Moments later, Cochrane found himself crossing the thick grassy turf of the graveyard, walking directly toward Ralph Forsythe's plot.

The cemetery was a peaceful place, much nicer than the crowded oppressive human dumping ground where his father had been buried. This was Cochrane's second trip to a cemetery within a month, and he wasn't happy about it. At least, he rationalized, this second trip packed less of an emotional wallop than the first.

As if by instinct, he arrived at Ralph Forsythe's grave. He stared downward. Forsythe had been alive a month earlier. Now where was he, Cochrane wondered. Oh, his *body* was here. But where was his animus? His spirit?

Cochrane raised his eyes. He knew he wasn't alone at the grave site. He saw something shimmer near him, then worked up the nerve to look directly at it.

The ghost of the young woman was a few feet away from him. As Cochrane looked closer, he saw that she was in deep sorrow. He thought he saw tears, but wasn't sure. Cochrane found more courage and stared at her. She must have felt his eyes upon her, because her gaze found his in return. She faded to nothing after a minute. Cochrane then turned and left the graveyard.

Before heading back to the airport, he also went to the hiking trail where Ralph Forsythe had his fatal accident. The section of broken fence had been repaired. There were extra signs of caution in the area now, and Cochrane also noticed that a park ranger was stationed in the area, making sure there were no copycat reruns.

Cochrane stood where Forsythe had stood. He gazed out over the Pacific Ocean. There was a haze but the day was sunny. He took in the view that Forsythe must have taken before he died.

Cochrane again knew he was not alone. He spoke aloud.

"Why did you push him?" he asked.

He couldn't see her but he heard her answer.

"He did something hideous to me," she said.

"Hideous how?"

"No," she answered. *"It's too much to even describe. You must learn for yourself."*

"And Tommy Cassatt?" he asked.

"The same."

At the periphery of his vision, he sensed her. He was aware of a female body near him. Not substantial. As shimmering as the breeze in from the ocean.

"So you killed him, too?" Cochrane asked.

"Yes."

"Why don't you push me over the cliff?" Cochrane asked.

"Why would I?"

"Why not?" He paused. "Maybe I'd like to be pushed."

"I have nothing against you."

"Then there's a reason why you've done this?"

"Of course."

"What is it? Tell me what."

She faded. *"No,"* she said.

He looked in her direction. She was completely gone. Then from the other side, he felt something touch his shoulder. He turned back.

His father was standing next to him. Smiling. Younger. Healthy. Cochrane recoiled in shock.

"There is nothing to fear from death," his father said. "But it's not your time yet. You have much to do."

"I'm losing my mind," Cochrane said.

"You're gaining it," his father answered. "You've learned to see things that most people can't."

"Is it a blessing or a curse?"

"What would you like it to be?"

Cochrane couldn't answer. "Where's Mother?" he finally asked.

"We're together. We're happy. She's well."

"Promise?"

"There are no promises because there are no permanences."

"What?"

"Are you thinking about stepping off the cliff?" his father asked.

In truth, Cochrane was feeling a strong pull.

But, "No. I don't think so," he answered.

"You'd have to be crazy." The elder William Cochrane laughed. "It's not your time yet, son."

Someone behind Cochrane yelled. "Hey!" The voice was quick and sharp, like a bark. The elder Cochrane disappeared.

Cochrane turned. The park ranger was walking briskly toward him, not pleased with how Cochrane was behaving near the cliff.

"You okay, sir?" the ranger called.

"I'm fine. Why? What's wrong?"

"We had an accident there a week ago. I have to ask you to be careful. Maybe you could step back a little."

The ranger took Cochrane's sleeve. It was more than a request.

"Sure," Cochrane said. "Sure. I'm leaving anyway. Plane to catch back East."

The ranger released him.

"That's good, sir," the ranger said. "Have a good flight. Thank you, sir."

Cochrane could distinctly tell that the ranger was relieved he was leaving.

It was *not* a good flight.

There was unusually severe turbulence crossing the Rocky Mountains, then another set of high altitude squalls near Missouri. For forty-minutes crossing the American Midwest, the plane shook so violently that the flight crew stopped serving lunch and strapped themselves into seat belts.

Cochrane felt a mounting fear. He remembered the van that had spun out of control in front of him on the Memorial Parkway and The Unicorn's promise to render him dead through an accident.

Twenty minutes into the second round of turbulence, he was terrified. The aircraft felt as if it were about to blow apart at thirty thousand feet, sending a hundred plus passengers into "No Survivors" oblivion.

Air travel might have been statistically safer than automobile travel, Cochrane reminded himself. But if your car flew apart you didn't plunge eight miles to your death. He kept looking out the window. They were bucking through something that looked like dark gray cotton. His hands were soaked with sweat. The aircraft seemed to be laboring.

Eight miles. Eight miles high. More numbers. Thank you, Unicorn. Cochrane felt himself haunted on all sides. The unnamed female ghost. The spirit of his father and the memory of long years spent in a Michigan mental hospital. The insane numerological Carl Einhorn. And then there was the madness of Washington and Gabe Lang.

No wonder Cochrane found himself teetering between so many different worlds. When he looked out the window at one point, he saw the female ghost sitting on one of the wings. He didn't know whether to take that as a good sign or bad.

Good sign, for example: She was an angel and would use her extraordinary powers to guide the aircraft to safety.

Bad sign, for example: She was an emissary of death, a demon. He would die soon.

And bad sign, again: She wasn't really there at all. So by seeing her, he was conceding that he was already crazy.

"Thanks, Dad," he said aloud.

A violent pocket of air walloped the aircraft again. Everything shuddered and even the flight crew seemed on the edge of panic. As if there were anything they could do.

Then, as abruptly as it had begun, the turbulence ended. The plane exited the gray and entered a stretch of blue sky. The flight was smooth as silk the rest of the way to Washington.

Cochrane returned home and put together his notes on his two interviews. The Acting President found time for him the next evening at the White House.

Gabriel Lang looked tired when Cochrane visited him in the Oval Office. It was 10 P.M. and the end of a nervous day in Washington.

Russian nationalists had mobilized part of the revivified Russian army and had positioned it close to the Baltic republics of Lithuania, Latvia, and Estonia. It was 1939 all over again. Since independence twenty years earlier, the little triad of Baltic States had quietly found health, democracy, and prosperity all at the same time. Baltic banks were brimming with assets and hard currency, and the leaders of the Russian Nationalist movement were suddenly calling for annexation.

Or as they called it, "reunification." Their excuse was that the tiny Baltic republics had never "repaid" Russia for the millions of rubles of investment made there in the Stalin and Khrushchev years. It was a neat trick of historical revision, as well as an alibi for an impending invasion.

But with the demilitarization of NATO in the late 1990s, Eastern Europe had been left to its own defense. Which, to the Baltic republics, meant no defense at all—other than dependence on the Americans.

George Farley had said many times that he would defend any Eastern European state that asked. Gabe Lang said that it depended on the alignment of planets. But the bottom line was that Latvia, Lithuania, and Estonia "probably weren't worth a drop of American blood. Where are they, anyway?"

If the latter line had been meant as a joke, the Russians hadn't taken it as one. They positioned two extra divisions fifty miles east of Riga the next day. Certain foreign governments, it seemed, were going to like this Lang administration more than they could have dreamed.

Meeting with President Lang that evening, Cochrane went through the details of his two visits. Lang almost seemed to listen absently, as if this were now all past history. It was as if he had greater things on his mind, which in fact he did.

He listened patiently for five minutes. When Cochrane reached his conclusion, that he couldn't find any link between the deaths of the two men, the President then surprised Cochrane with his only direct question.

"How did Patty Cassatt seem?" Lang asked.

"What?" Cochrane answered.

"Patty. How is she?"

"She seemed fine."

"Good spirits?"

"Reasonably good, considering she just lost her husband."

"Still pretty as ever?"

"I've never seen her before."

"Did she look nice?"

"Yes."

"Think she might want to visit the White House?"

Cochrane tried to control his disgust. "I didn't ask," he said.

"Maybe you could call for me and inquire."

"Is this a serious request?" Cochrane replied.

Lang laughed. "Patty gets around a bit," he said, sounding as if he might now let the matter drop. "You wouldn't have believed how she was coming on to me at a party in New York a few years ago. Tommy was right there. Some men just can't control their wives."

The Acting President shook his head.

"I wanted to ask you a question or two," Cochrane said.

"Go ahead."

"Remember how you used to draw the red queens from a deck of cards?"

"Yes."

"And you used to ask me about my belief in ghosts?"

"I remember. I remember," Lang said. "A silly period I was going through recently. I can't do the card trick anymore, and in point of fact, you can drop this whole investigation. I think it's gone as far as it can go."

"What?"

Lang repeated.

Cochrane voiced an objection, particularly with little Carl Einhorn, he of the mental fire bombs, in federal custody. Why not at least finish the investigation?

"I feel it *is* finished, William," Lang said.

"Not to me."

Lang scoffed. "Are you being difficult? Or has it just gotten under your skin? I thought you *wanted* out of it," Lang said.

"Not anymore. I want to see where it leads."

"Forget it," Lang said. "It doesn't lead anywhere."

"I think it might."

"Then you're as nutty as people accuse me of being. So drop it. I need you in this office."

Cochrane sighed. "I *am* hooked into it now. I don't want to drop it."

"Getting the best of you? Affecting your mind?" Lang teased.

"I just want to take it to its conclusion."

"I could care less what you want," Lang snapped. "*I* want you to drop it. And *I* am the President of the United Fucking States of America! Clear?"

After a moment to calm, "What about on my own time?" Cochrane tried.

"It's out of your orbit now, William," the President said succinctly. "You won't *have* your own time. I'll make sure of that. Anything further you do on this and I'll see to it that you're fired. Do you understand me?"

Cochrane stared at him. He had never seen Gabriel Lang so adamant about anything.

"I understand," Cochrane finally said.

"Good night, William."

Cochrane stood, bristling but silent, and left the President alone.

24

I am very sad.

Sometimes it surprises me that I can still be like that. But I have feelings and emotions. Maybe it shouldn't surprise me. After all, love and hate, happiness and sadness, are part of our spiritual being, are they not? So even though my physical presence no longer exists in a living form, perhaps it is not so unusual that my spiritual presence still bears certain emotions.

Qua, qua, qua.

I sometimes search for sounds and wonder why my sounds have meanings. Sometimes they do. Sometimes they do not. Once when I was living, a dear friend—a teacher in high school—lost her hearing through oracular degeneration. An electronic device was placed in her ears by doctors. The device picked up human sounds and translated them into a new language of electronic sounds. She spoke the same language as the rest of us, but she heard different noises.

Is that similar to what I am doing now? I float through your world. I see the same things as you. But my language sometimes is different. And the emotions I endure may be completely different from yours.

Or they may be the same.

And maybe that's why I am sad. My emotions seem to set me apart.

I had an instinct today. I went to see my parents. I'm not sure why I did this, but I had the feeling that I was in their thoughts.

I was.

They are still in the living world. They have a residence not too far from where I died. And I think I know why I am in their thoughts. You see, my mother is very ill. She has an advanced case of cancer. There are

*vibrations around her that living humans can rarely feel. Little spirits.
Almost like little angels, guiding her along her way.*

*I can see these little spirits. My mother can almost see them. Both she
and my father know the end of her physical life is very near. They know
this because they can feel the pull of the next dimension upon my mother.*

*When I came into the room, I think she sensed me. I think that, be-
cause they both started to talk about me. I was standing very close to them
and hoping they could feel me. See, the thing is, that even all these thirty-
one years after the fact, my death still unsettles them.*

You will learn why.

*There's a strange irony here. My mother stays alive and clings to life
because she wants to know about my death. Isn't that funny? If she would
just let herself go, she would pass through to the peacefulness of this side.
And she would know about my earthly passing. The death itself would
then not seem so bad; only the injustice of it.*

*Oh, if you could see what I know. Physical death can be traumatic,
but so often it can be a release.*

*Easy. Peaceful. Like passing through an old swinging gate in a coun-
try churchyard.*

*Easy. In my father's house there are many rooms. After death, it is so
smooth to pass from one to the next.*

If the door is closed, pass through the wall.

Go where you wish.

*Can you understand me? Is my logic too elliptical? I've lost my sense
of earthly logic and have this new one. I'm sorry if you can't yet follow
it.*

The time will come when you will.

I assure you.

*And I also assure you that I am sad. I am sad for the Forsythe fam-
ily. And I am sad for the Cassatt family. I led their fathers to their deaths.*

*There was some poetry in it. A certain geometry. I did, after all, wish
to avenge what had happened to me.*

*I do admit: When the Levins' hammering roused me, I was in one
fearsome mood. I think my mood has changed. Maybe it has changed because I led to their deaths two of the men who murdered me. But in doing
so, I claimed so many more victims.*

*I feel the sadness of Thomas Cassatt's son, who misses his father. I share
the grief of Ralph Forsythe's daughter, who saw his broken body at the base
of the cliff in California.*

*The other night I visited the Cassatts' house. I saw his son sitting at
his desk. The boy was supposed to be doing his homework. But instead, he*

was looking at his father's photograph. He was crying, though he wouldn't let his mother see. He is fifteen and trying to be a man. A few minutes later, I visited Vicki Forsythe, the dead man's daughter. She is a pretty woman and will survive this tragedy. But I share her sadness again.

I am not cruel. I only wanted justice. Maybe I am still learning about my own emotions and impulses. Who says a spirit must be predictable following death?

If guilt existed where I am, I might feel some for the Cassatt and Forsythe families. But it doesn't exist here, and I feel only sadness.

And I feel it twice.

I am sad that I still have unfinished business in this world. I cannot rest until all my accounts are settled. I have one more victim to claim and I might as well claim him.

I like the Levins, by the way. I hope this is not too uncomfortable for them. When I was alive, I had many Jewish friends. They were always thoughtful compassionate people. I liked that. And they encouraged me when I said I wanted to write a fine story.

I'm going to travel now. I have events to precipitate. Places to be. I am getting anxious to pass along.

Oh, yes. My mother will die in one week. I can see that from here.

Mother, don't be so sad.

I look forward to your embrace. I am capable of love here, too.

25

Elm Hill Veterans Hospital was a sorry place by anyone's standards. Built in the sixties for a wave of wounded veterans coming home from America's midcentury misadventures, it originally had all the charm of a tacky new motel. Now, however, the facility had deteriorated along with its neighborhood in northwest Washington. Currently, it was like a deteriorating motel in a bad neighborhood. All the good furnishings and medical equipment were gone and so were all the good doctors. And they didn't practice medicine there so much as psychiatry and human warehousing.

Originally, from the outside, there had been an intention to make this an attractive place. Elm trees had been planted around Elm Hill to replace the ones that had been bulldozed when the hospital went up. But most of the new elms hadn't been as hearty as the old ones. By now they had all died from disease or been cut down. But not completely. Several huge stark dead trunks—thirty, forty feet high apiece—still stood around the facility. To Cochrane as he drove toward the hospital, the tree trunks resembled a legion of stationary frozen robots, a brigade of massive unsparing inhuman guards.

Psychiatric Section C-2 was on the Richard Lamoureux wing. The wing was named in honor of a dedicated psychiatrist who had worked at Walter Reed with Korean War vets in the 1950s. There had once been a small bronze statue of Dr. Lamoureux in the lobby.

But a patient had gotten loose one night in the 1990s and, acting on instructions from a fourth century B.C. pharaoh, had decapitated the statue with a fire ax. A statue of a headless physician sent the wrong signals to anyone visiting, it was theorized by the staff. So the rest of the statue—now nicknamed "Louis XVI"—had been removed. It had never been replaced.

Just arriving at a place like Elm Hill made Bill Cochrane cringe. He cringed a second time to be visiting someone like Carl Einhorn. If the government was Big Brother, then the nut wings of the sixties-style vet mental hospitals were the Holding Company. And little Carl Einhorn was the genie in the bottle.

There were two concentric fences around the hospital, each with a double dose of electrified concertina wire atop cinder blocks. There was a guardhouse at the entrance, staffed by two policemen at all times.

C-2 Lamoureux housed the criminally insane—both convicted and awaiting trial—in maximum security, and there were two more layers of insulation that Cochrane needed to pass through once he was within the facility. Half of the security measures were designed to keep the inmates in; the other half were designed to keep the neighborhood out.

In the last few years, the government had been quietly warehousing the criminally insane here with the disabled veterans, a floor apart from each other. Years ago, Cochrane could remember, there was a fear expressed in certain political quarters that the government would become socialistic and paternal. Elm Hill Hospital was proof positive that such a thing had never taken place. Old soldiers in Elm Hill would have laughed bitterly at the notion.

Many of the men who had fought in Vietnam were in their late sixties and seventies now. Dozens were now doing their final tour on wings of veterans' hospitals, with nowhere else to go. They would sit all morning, all afternoon, all evening and all night in sullen little klatches. Some hadn't dressed for years. Some never went to bed, but rather slept in their wheelchairs. They discussed long-lost battles or comrades who had died decades earlier. They told the same stories to each other every day. They, too, were ghosts, but they were still alive.

It was the second week of December. The President remained in and out of comas at Bethesda. The weather made Cochrane long for the milder winters of California. The climate had played a cruel trick this year, or so it seemed. After a long mild October and a temperate November, the daily temperature had plummeted after Thanksgiving.

Cochrane couldn't help it. He associated the cold and the frost with Carl Einhorn, because the two had arrived in his life at the same time. Same as his ear disorder.

Or as he referred to it privately, his "fucking ear disorder."

He had been to two different doctors. There was nothing wrong with the inner ear, the first ENT man said. Same as the President. There's nothing wrong with him either, according to the best team of doctors around. He's just on a big snooze somewhere. Might come out of it, might not. Same as your ear.

The second doctor had done exactly the same examination but had come to a further conclusion. The ringing might not even exist. Psychosomatic, the physician suggested. Was Cochrane sure that he really heard something? Or was he so stressed that he actually wished to speak to another form of doctor?

Like a psychiatrist.

Cochrane had angrily answered that yes, he really heard a ringing, and no, he didn't want to talk to a shrink.

But all of that was immaterial this morning, even though he was surrounded by shrinks. This morning was a visit to Elm Hill.

Just a visit.

As Cochrane entered the main hospital building, he saw a man with his father's face staring at him from the reception desk in the lobby. But as he advanced, his father's face melted into that of a black policeman. Cochrane showed his parking pass, was logged in, and was allowed past another check point to a large steel elevator that would take him to C-2.

He rode the elevator by himself. When he arrived at the proper floor, he stopped at a water fountain. He took a fresh paper cup and filled it. Then he passed by a final security checkpoint. In the antechamber to where he would visit Carl Einhorn, he blinked when he saw a familiar face.

Agent Bradley of the United States Secret Service was camping out at Lamoureux, along with a civilian guard who controlled the steel gate that led to the corridor.

"What the hell are you doing here?" Cochrane asked the young agent.

"I seem to be the official guard for this prisoner," Bradley said sullenly. "Been guarding him for eight days."

"Why you?"

"Luck, I guess. Bad." The young man shrugged. "Got to have pull to get the good assignments in Treasury," Agent Bradley said. "That or pay your dues. I guess I'm paying my dues."

Cochrane nodded. "I understand," he said.

"How's the prisoner?" Cochrane asked.

Bradley made a pained expression, then tapped his head. "He gets creepier and creepier."

"Yeah? How?"

Bradley shrugged. "I don't know. Just things he says."

"Does he threaten you?"

"All the time."

"Just don't turn your back to him," Cochrane said.

"Yeah," Bradley shrugged. "We have to take him out for exercise thirty minutes each day. That's all I'm here for. Thirty minutes."

"As I said. Just don't turn your back."

"He gives me a headache," Bradley mumbled, "just thinking about him. Sometimes it feel like he follows me around. Mentally, you know?"

Bradley added something and Cochrane didn't ask him to repeat. The uniformed guard unlocked the electronic metal gate.

"Window six," the guard said.

Cochrane walked down the empty corridor of C-2 Lamoureux to a bank of visitors' booths. He sat down, still carrying a small paper cup of water. On the other side of a solid sheet of plate glass, Carl Einhorn was already in place.

The prisoner's wrists were chained and Cochrane assumed his legs were, too. The side of his face was swollen, as if he had fallen or been hit. He wore the orange hospital jumpsuit mandatory of prisoners, as opposed to patients.

He stared at Cochrane. Cochrane smiled back.

Then a smile emerged from Einhorn. It was the strangest smile Cochrane had ever seen. It was ominous, adding a new dimension from when Cochrane had seen Einhorn previously. It reminded Cochrane of a shadow emerging from sunlight.

"I didn't expect *any* visitors," Einhorn said. "Nor do I want any, as long as they have me dressed up like a Creamsicle."

"I thought I'd see how you were doing."

"What do you care, fuckface?"

Cochrane shrugged. "Let's say I'm interested. How are they treating you here?"

"Like an animal."

"In what way?"

"They keep me in a cage and feed me when they feel like it. I think they're fattening me up for a slaughter. Like a Christmas capon."

"Why would they do that?"

"I'm not meant to leave here alive. I can see it."

"You know the future?" Cochrane queried.

"Don't you?"

"How could I?" Cochrane asked.

"We all follow in our father's footsteps," said Einhorn.

Cochrane's eyes narrowed. "What do you mean by that?" he asked.

"*Tel père, tel fils,*" The Unicorn said. "The apple doesn't fall far from the tree."

Cochrane flinched. Was Einhorn intentionally mocking him, Cochrane wondered, or was it just the demented little man's usual scattershot approach to being difficult?

"So *you* can see the future?" Cochrane asked.

"Sometimes. Sometimes I can see it and control it. It's all mathematical. An ordered universe, if you comprehend it, which I'm sure you can't. And I can read your mind, too," Einhorn said, rambling onward. "Or what remains of your mind. You're *more* than interested in me, my sweet ass. You're in awe. You *know* that I control things with my head."

"Does that make me special, Carl?"

"Yes. You are the only one who secretly believes me, although that stupid Secret Service man is scared of me. And you want to know how I do it. Don't you?"

Cochrane made an expansive gesture. "So tell me."

"No."

"Please?"

"You wouldn't under-fucking-stand."

Cochrane sipped the water again. He put the cup by his elbow.

"Try me," Cochrane said.

"Nope."

"When will you make the President better?" Cochrane asked.

"I won't. Not while I'm alive."

"Are you planning to die soon?"

"I might. I'll probably be murdered in here. I'm a dangerous individual. Someone will try to kill me."

"No one's going to harm you."

"Horseshit!" snapped the little man. "That's what you say! I know better. I can hear them talking about me. When I'm asleep, they talk about me."

"Who would hurt you?"

Einhorn thought about it, then seemed to pick an answer out of the air. "I can't see it exactly. But probably you."

"Why would I hurt you?"

Einhorn shrugged. "A rage of spirits."

"What?"

"A rage of spirits. That's what you're in the midst of, Cochrane. Agitated animi—live ones, dead ones. Swirling all around you. Chaos, my man. Lovely beautiful chaos. And you can't explain it within any ordered logic that you recognize."

"And how is it going to affect me?" Cochrane asked.

"As I'm alive, you cannot succeed or live happily. Your job is to find out what's wrong with the President. Why he can't think. So you'll want me to die."

"That's nonsense, Carl," Cochrane said.

"No it's not. I see you coming to kill me. Not today, but soon."

"With a gun? A knife?"

Einhorn focused on something in the distance, then sailed back.

"No. Couldn't get those things past security. You'll choke me to death with a garrote. Unless I get you first." He grinned. "It's okay. I understand that you get a fierce erection and ejaculate when you're being strangled."

"Carl, I don't like this discussion," Cochrane said.

The Unicorn folded his arms. "Then what's the frequency, Kenneth?"

"What?"

"Do you remember Daniel Rather, who used to do television news for CBS?"

"Yes. Why?"

"Six letters in each of his names. He used to get his news straight from Satan. C.B.S. Corporation Broadcasting for Satan."

"Tell me how you affect the President," Cochrane asked again.

"No."

"What if I begged you?"

"Plop, plop, fizz, fizz. Oh, shit, what a fucking relief it is," Einhorn sang. "Alka Seltzer. I'm going to kill the President. I'm going to kill that guard out there and I'm going to kill you."

"Why the guard?"

"Why not?"

"Why me?"

"Same reason."

"And you'll kill me telepathically?"

"Yes. Probably an accident arranged telepathically. I'd like you to bleed and suffer."

"Why don't you do it now?"

"I am. I've already started."

"Why don't I feel anything?"

"You do. Your brains are coming out of your head. Like stuffing in an old sofa. And you won't admit it."

Cochrane drew back, sweating heavy at each of his armpits.

"Actually, I've just recently figured my chronology. First, Bradley my S.S. Inquisitor. Then George Farley. Then you."

Einhorn looked back at him, that horrible glimmer in his eye again. Cochrane moved slightly. Einhorn made a little teasing gesture with his lips, then puckered them and sent Cochrane a mock kiss.

"Want to blow me?" Einhorn asked.

Cochrane recoiled slightly. He thought his elbow must have caught the paper cup next to him because it suddenly flew from the ledge. It seemed to hang in the air for an abnormal extra split second then splashed downward onto his lap, soaking him.

Einhorn smiled. "Bravo."

Cochrane looked at him in shock.

"Wet your pants?" Einhorn asked. "Bad boy. Spanky, spanky."

Looking up, still in amazement, Cochrane glared at the little man behind the glass. "Did you do that?"

"Yes."

"Do something else!"

"No."

"Prove your power to me."

"I just did."

"Prove it again."

"Clumsy oaf. You did it yourself and you blame me. Couldn't hold your water till the end of my class, but you have to blame the math teacher."

"Explain what you just did!" Cochrane insisted.

But Einhorn chose to babble, tauntingly with just a trace of melody. "Are you going to Wheelbarrow Fair? Parsley, Sage, Rosemary, and Slime," he said.

"Carl . . . ?"

"Don't believe in a link between women and drugs?" Einhorn chirped in euphoria. "Then why is the little word *bitch* to be heard in the big word *barbiturate?*"

"I looked at your personnel files from Atlanta and New York, Carl," Cochrane said.

"All the more reason for me to kill you," Einhorn snorted. "Half the people you worked with disliked you. The other half hated you."

"Their problem. Not mine."

"It *was* your problem, in that you lost your job."

"I've never been broke," he said. "Always had money. 'Dennison, a Men's Clothier in Union City, New Jersey. Open Till Four A.M. Money talks, Nobody Walks.' "

"A couple of your students referred to you as 'a demon.' "

"Hmp!" Einhorn snorted. "And they were right, weren't they?"

"Were they?"

"Maybe they meant 'lemon,' and the Board of Ed couldn't read their handwriting. Couldn't tell an *l* from a *d*." He cackled in pleasure. "Do you know the nursery rhyme about the Golden Spinning Wheel and Rumpledforeskin?" Einhorn asked.

"No, but I know about 'grue,' " Cochrane tried, referring to one of Einhorn's mathematical writings.

"Oh, true. Grue! Grue to you, too, Jew! Hoo, hoo."

"Tell me about it."

"Grue as a concept is the key to a system of inherent logic that can't be proven."

"In what way?"

"Grue is a term for an item which will be green until the year 2100, then blue thereafter."

"Is there such an item?"

"Think there could be?"

"You're the expert."

"And I'm not telling," said Einhorn. "Maybe even I don't know. Prove it one way or another. All green items might be grue. Or none of them. Hardest thing to prove, My Ass, is the existence of something that *might* be present, but which we can't see. Grue might exist and might not. As you wish."

"Like your telepathic powers," Cochrane said, taking the point.

"Fuckety fuckety fuck you," chirped Einhorn. "And congratulations on understanding me in some small way."

Einhorn, relishing the plate glass between them, grinned like a gargoyle. From Cochrane's perspective, it was a taunting sardonic smile, combined with a wicked feral expression in the eyes, while still being cunning and intelligent.

Cochrane's gaze was arrested. He had the impression that he was looking at a giant rat in an orange jumpsuit.

"Christmas is coming, the geese are getting fat," Einhorn recited. "I'm sure starting to wonder where my guest's brains are at."

Then, Cochrane felt his whole body jolt in shock.

From Cochrane's perspective, the facial features of Carl Einhorn further flew apart. First, Cochrane saw his father as a young man, the way he looked when he had first married Cochrane's mother . . . then as the features quickly rearranged themselves, Cochrane saw some horrible beast. . . . and then finally he saw Einhorn again, his white skull exuding like a mask below the flesh of his face.

Then everything flashed back to normal—

"What the *fuck* are you staring at?" Einhorn snapped.

—or something approaching normal.

The little man barked and then spat angrily, his saliva thick and foaming white as it hit the other side of the glass.

"You're crazier than I am!" Einhorn yelled. "So, fuck you! What am I doing in here when I could be controlling the God-damned world?" He howled like a wolf.

Cochrane felt a frustration and a rage building within him.

"Answer me that!" the little man yelled. "I rule the universe and these mortals *lock me up!* And it's *you* who should be in here, not me!"

Something snapped within Cochrane.

He made a fist, stood, and punched at his tormentor. But Cochrane's hand stopped short of its target, coursing with pain as his knuckles struck the bulletproof plate glass.

By that time, Einhorn was on his feet and turning away. On the other side of the glass, a huge blond man appeared in a guard's dark blue uniform. The guard was trying to see what had happened. Einhorn, his feet in shackles, was waddle-hopping like a penguin toward the guard.

But Cochrane also heard a voice behind him. It was Bradley, the Secret Service again, who had also been summoned by the sounds of shouting and a thumping fist.

"Hey! You okay in here?" the young man asked.

Cochrane was standing, holding his right fist in his left.

"See?" Bradley asked. He must have known what had happened. "See how he gets to you?"

Cochrane watched Einhorn disappear through a door beyond the plate glass partition.

"Yeah. I see," Cochrane said.

"I don't talk to him anymore. I just guard him. Maybe you should do the same."

"I have to talk to him," Cochrane said. "I don't have a choice." He paused. "Now we're both on his death list," Cochrane said.

The young agent smiled ruefully.

"I'm not scared," Bradley said. "But as I said, it sure gives me the creeps." He looked down. "Need some ice for your hand?" he asked. "They have ice on the first floor. Downstairs with some of the nutty vets."

"I'm okay," Cochrane said after a moment. "Thanks."

Cochrane's hand was still throbbing several minutes later when he was back out in the parking lot, walking to his car.

"Antechambers to death," Lisa McJeffry had once called these federal hospitals, when she had visited one as a reporter. And Cochrane looked upon them much the same way. Cochrane found himself constantly replaying the specifics of his father's demise. His father had checked into a parallel institution and never checked out, a resolute downward physical and mental spiral under the careful scrutiny of the best doctors the government chose to afford.

"We all follow in our father's footsteps," Einhorn had said, keying Cochrane's anxieties for the day. How could Einhorn have known? How could the little madman have *possibly* known?

Unless . . .

To Bill Cochrane, mental hospitals were more sinister than graveyards. Having to visit one made him wonder whether some divine fix was in to drag him into such a place—perhaps for keeps.

Then, on the way out, Cochrane thought he saw his father standing near his car. It was the third time that day that he had endured such a vision. But then when he moved closer, rationality temporarily prevailed. He saw that the individual was not his father, but a D.C. policeman.

It was Sam, the Levins' cat, who first noticed something strange. It was seven in the evening, a Tuesday a week before Christmas. Lindsay was seated in the den watching campy ten-year-old reruns of *Melrose Place*. But Richard and Barbara Levin were in their living room. Classical music played softly from a big table radio. It was a quiet time in their day. Rich was reading a novel. Barbara was catching up with the morning newspaper. There had been two weeks of peace—no poltergeist tricks, no disruptions in the library, no music playing, no nightmares.

Suddenly Sam sprung onto his feet in the living room. The Levins had scarcely ever seen him so animated. The cat crossed the room and leaped up onto a table which allowed him a view of the outdoors. He caught the eye of both Barbara and Richard Levin. He paced back and forth, his tail wagging in anticipation of something pleasant.

A returning friend, perhaps. But Sam, being a cat, wasn't divulging any secrets either.

Sam leaped down from the table and hurried toward the kitchen. Rich and Barb watched him. He left their line of vision. Then they heard something. It was the sound of a door slamming in their kitchen, the door that led to the garage.

Mr. and Mrs. Levin could see the kitchen and were convinced that someone had just come in.

Someone has.

They looked at each other, poised for trouble. "What's that?" Richard called.

It's me.

The Levins both thought they had heard footsteps. But there was no verbal answer that they could hear.

"Anyone there?" Rich called.

I'm back.

"Now what?" Rich muttered.

"Oh, brother . . ." sighed Barbara.

Richard rose from his chair and walked tentatively to the kitchen. The room was dark. He turned on the light. The room appeared empty. For a moment he felt a cold draft. Accompanying it was a feeling he didn't like, something that made him uneasy.

He walked through the kitchen to the door that led to the garage. It was locked, just the way he had left it.

So it couldn't possibly have opened. Or closed. Examining the situation further, he saw that the screen door beyond the kitchen door was also latched. No way anyone could have opened and shut these from the outside.

I'm standing right next to you.

"The only way one could have gone through them," Richard found himself thinking, "would be to—"

pass through them!

"—pass through them."

Richard shuddered. Then when he turned, his heart kicked a second time. The cellar door, which had been closed when he had just passed it, was closing again.

Very quietly. Very slowly. As if this had been meant to happen outside his line of sight. He had only caught it, almost by mistake.

He felt a cold chill shoot through him. This cold wasn't from a draft. This chill was from the knowledge that he had seen something that most living people never view.

He sighed. He braced himself. He drew a breath.

He walked back to the living room, mildly shaken. Barbara was waiting.

"Well?" she asked.

"I don't know what we heard but the kitchen door was still shut," Richard said. "So was the screen."

Barbara tried to mask her own anxiety.

"Juliet again?" she asked.

"Who knows?" he said. He looked around. He didn't mention the cellar door. Not then, and not a few minutes later when Lindsay appeared from the den.

"Dad?" she asked.

Rich looked at his daughter. "I just heard something funny downstairs," Lindsay said.

"Funny how?" Rich asked. "Funny like what?"

"Well," Lindsay asked. "A woman's voice?"

Richard Levin blew out a breath. "Shit," he said. "She's back."

"Who?" Lindsay asked.

"Juliet," Richard said. "That's who. Our ghost."

Then he admitted he had seen the cellar door shutting on its own accord. It was sort of like hearing a skeleton rattling in the attic, then finally seeing the skeleton.

A family discussion followed. What to do?

Go downstairs immediately? Go downstairs tomorrow? Never go downstairs again? Evacuate the house?

The Levins took the scariest, boldest, and most aggressive route, trying to reclaim their home. Rich carried a baseball bat. Barbara carried her fears, plus a giant flashlight in case the electricity failed. Lindsay carried a rapid heartbeat.

And they all walked down the cellar steps together, one happy family.

They encountered a sweet smell. Almost a perfumed aroma combined with an aging mustiness. But they didn't see anything. Aside from fear, they didn't feel anything.

They also—

Hey! You're following me! Stay away!

weren't able to hear anything. And Sam the Cat, who was already down there, didn't seem apprehensive at all. Sam seemed pleased.

I love cats. His name is Sam? I've missed Sam.

"I don't see anything," Rich finally said, relieved but still anxious. "Shit! Maybe the door was just playing tricks. I don't know. I know I saw something, though."

Me? You saw me?

"All you saw was a door closing, Rich," Barbara tried.

Would you like to see me?
Maybe next time!

"Let's get out of here," Lindsay finally pleaded.

The Levins went back upstairs. They carefully closed the cellar door. Rich tried the latch and found it secure.

Barbara attempted to convince her husband that the thump could have come from something other than the kitchen door. Maybe some animal—like a dog or a raccoon—had been on the property. That would have explained Sam's reaction also, she said. And the old cellar door wasn't a perfect fit to the door frame. The weather was colder and Richard *could* have dislodged it as he passed. Then it could have swung shut again.

Rich looked at his wife.

"Sure," he said. "But let's sleep with the lights on tonight anyway."

Lindsay and Barbara looked at him.

"Let's be realistic," he said. "I know it's spooky, I know that it seems like something's here, but none of us have ever been harmed. Okay? We just have to concede that Juliet is back."

"Dad?" Lindsay finally asked.

"What?"

"Where do you suppose she is when she's not here?"

"How am I supposed to know that? I don't even know who she is." He paused. "I mean, I'm in advertising, not ectoplasm."

"Maybe," Lindsay said, "we should find out."

No way to research it that evening. So they slept with the lights on. And nothing further happened.

"She seems," Barbara said the next morning, "to live in our basement. I don't think I'll be going down there by myself anymore."

Lindsay knew a man who was a professor of American folklore at Northeastern University. His name was Dr. Lyle Walsh. He was sixty-two years old and one of the experts in his field. Dr. Walsh had made a lifetime study of folklore and hauntings in eastern Massachusetts. He had his theories.

When Lindsay told Dr. Walsh the story of what had been transpiring in her home over the last few weeks, he told a recent story that was even stranger.

Back in 1997, the body of an apparently wealthy old woman arrived at the city morgue in Boston. She had been pronounced dead in a parking lot a few minutes after collapsing, apparently of heat exhaustion. She had no identification with her, although her purse did yield a few good luck charms that she had apparently carried with her for years.

One of the charms was in the shape of a shamrock. It was silver with green enamel and appeared to have been minted to celebrate the birth of the Irish Free State in 1920. This being Boston, it wasn't much of a stretch to guess that the old woman was originally from Ireland, and it was further speculated that she was about as old as the Irish Republic itself. But that was less significant than the fact that the woman had been wearing tens of thousands of dollars' worth of now-antique jewelry when she died. And she had had no heartbeat when the ambulance crew brought her in.

When her body lay in a body bag in the morgue, two maintenance workers quickly went to work picking the lock on the body bag. A third stood lookout.

Once past the lock, they unzipped the cadaver sack to steal the old

woman's jewelry. This was one of the well-known perks for maintenance workers at city morgues, so they did not feel as if they were
doing anything wrong. This was their part-time job. One just had to
work rapidly when "good" bodies came in. Opportunity was not
there indefinitely.

When they had the bag open, they gasped. They could not believe
their good fortune. On the woman's left hand were two rings—a
beautiful old diamond and a glistening deep-kelly emerald the size of
a pea. But when they jarred her hands to get two rings off her fingers,
the woman's arm lurched reflexively. Then her whole body moved.

Whereupon, a modern Lady Lazarus, she started to sit up, as if
from a deep sleep. One of the robbers collapsed and died of a heart
attack on the spot. One other fled and never came to that job again.
The third, the sentry who was least involved in the aborted theft, lived
and was deeply shaken. He would recount the event to the newspapers and TV stations.

Meanwhile, the old woman got to her feet and walked to a telephone. She called her grandson's family in South Boston. The family
came around in a pick-up truck and got her.

But she was never "right" again.

She had previously lived alone. But now she lived a strange half-
life with her relatives in Southie, rarely speaking, never smiling, always
in a distant dream. She eyed other human beings very strangely. It was
as if, her grandson observed, she had never come completely back.

Then, ten months later, she died again. This time she was successfully buried. Her shamrock good luck charm went into the grave
with her, and her other jewelry was sold. But her spirit, according to
her family, kept coming back to their home, disrupting things, particularly in the room where she had slept and kept her things. One
morning the entire dresser top had been knocked onto the floor, as
if the arm of a disturbed old woman had swept it during a fit.

The family theorized she was looking for her rings. They discussed
the matter with their priest, who would not acknowledge that the
woman's spirit could still be walking, spiritualism and formal Christianity being at odds with each other. But the woman's granddaughters—Shauna Ryan and Mary Beth Quinlan—were into holistic cures,
alternative medicine, and meditation. They also enjoyed a little sor-
cery here and there. So the girls seemed to know what to do.

The granddaughters moved everyone else out of the house one
evening and burned conifer-scented smudge sticks in a wok in the living room. They permeated the house with a pungent cedar incense

and, still in keeping with an ancient Celtic pagan ritual, seated themselves around the incense like a little coven of latter-day witches. Then they recited incantations from the Celtic Tome of the Dead, which for some reason, was available at local health food stores.

"Maybe it was merely the power of suggestion. But it worked for them," Dr. Walsh, the Northeastern forklorist, told Lindsay Levin. "And it might work for you."

"*What* might?"

"Purgation. A cleansing ritual in your home."

Lindsay related the story to her family. Rich was skeptical. Barbara was willing to try anything. Sam wasn't polled. The smudge stick theory carried the day.

On a spur, Barbara added some sage and cinnamon to the pine cones in concocting the Levins' own smudge sticks. Neighbors were invited in for "cleansing evening." The Levins tried to make a party out of it. No one would join them, though Lindsay's friend, the folklorist, did come and preside.

The sticks were burned. So was some cedar incense. The Levins braced themselves for some reaction. None came.

They waited for some violent explosion from the cellar, some new installment of the owl in the stovepipe, a recurrence of the typing or tapping sounds.

Still nothing.

Days passed.

Nothing at all.

Then four days before Christmas, Lindsay's friend the folklorist died in a tragic accident. He had been hanging Christmas lights in his apartment house when he suddenly lost his balance and plunged through an eighth-floor window.

And on the same day, a few minutes after Lindsay received that terrifying news, Sam disappeared into the cellar.

The Levins never saw their cat again alive. Nor did they particularly enjoy Christmas. Juliet, they felt, was angry with them and lurking somewhere. The nightmares about Lindsay's death came back into their thoughts and they finally started to approach the unthinkable: abandoning their home to the vengeful ghost.

26

If a man is to go crazy, the best companion he can have is himself. Said differently, it is easiest to lose one's mind by oneself. It was like the old bit of playground doggerel from childhood:

Going crazy?
No thanks.
I've already gone.

Cochrane sat in his town house and laughed out loud. He could hear these little snippets of messages now. It wasn't enough that he was seeing the ghost woman from time to time. Why, he was confident that he could even summon her when he needed to. What he also knew was that The Unicorn was sending him messages. He could hear Carl Einhorn's voice in his empty house.

Live and direct from Elm Hill Psychiatric.

Einhorn.

Now controlling his fate. Or trying to.

It was all so clear.

The Unicorn had made that van spin out and nearly take Cochrane's life. The Unicorn had caused that wicked turbulence on the last flight back from California. And it went without saying that The Unicorn was controlling the health of George Farley.

Entire vistas of deceit formed in front of Cochrane. His friends, his ex-lovers, his employers, his peers, formed and reformed in patterns of intrigue and deception.

Gabe Lang was in cahoots with the little demon, Einhorn, for example. Einhorn would incapacitate the President, Lang would assume office, New Age mysticism would greet the first years of the second millennium, and the whole fucking country could go to hell in a handbasket.

Cochrane considered this theory as he sat in his den that evening and sipped a beer from a bottle. He watched the television news. Cochrane liked the theory so much and disliked the news so much—more Russian build-up in Eastern Europe, complete with a ho-hum response from President Lang—that he impetuously flung the beer bottle across the room at the television screen.

No matter. It was the fourth brew of the evening, so he was no longer thirsty. And fortunately, Cochrane's hand-eye coordination was as bad as his logic. The bottle sailed wide of the screen. It hit the wall and shattered, beer and glass flying in every direction.

"And it can fucking stay there," he said to himself.

"Hand-eye coordination," replied a voice from within him. "The world's best example of hand-eye coordination is masturbation."

He laughed out loud. Now there was another message *direct* from Elm Hill Hospital. C-2 Lamoureux. Cochrane was receiving loads of messages from the little man. Loads. He was almost on overload. Einhorn was the transmitter. Cochrane was now a receiver. Just like the President.

He thought he heard Einhorn talking to him. "Ready for another?" the voice asked.

"Sure, Carl."

Luckies separate the men from the boys . . .
But not from the girls!

"Oh, yeah, of course," Cochrane answered. "Lucky Strike. *L.S.M.F.T.*, right there on every pack. 'Lucky Strike Means Future Tracheotomies.' Coed cancer wards. Coed cardiac care, too!"

"Not what I meant," Carl's voice answered. "I meant fuckety-fornication. Fellatio. Cunnilingus. All the fun things."

"Well, screw you, Carl," said Cochrane. "I don't care what you meant. You've probably never been laid in your life, Carl. Probably got a dick the size of your little finger."

Downstairs, something in the house thumped in response. Or at least that's how it sounded to Cochrane.

By his side was a deck of cards. *The* deck. The one the female ghost had brought back from incineration.

Cochrane picked it up. He cut the deck.

Queen of diamonds.

He cut it again.

Queen of hearts.

He shuffled, mixed the cards, and repeated, spreading the cards on a tabletop. Same result a second time.

"Fuck it all!" he exploded. He gathered the deck up and pitched it hard across the room. It cracked against the wall. Fifty-four malevolent little angels fluttered to the floor. In the center, when the cards landed, all four queens fell contiguous to each other facing straight up, mocking him.

"Odds on that, Carl?" Cochrane asked. "Odds on four ladies landing together, much less four ladies agreeing on anything?"

"One in seventeen billion. Approximately," he heard Einhorn answer. "Now! Will you come visit me again soon? Here in the nut house?"

"Of course."

"You never visited your father."

"Shut up! He didn't recognize me!" Cochrane snapped, sullen, angry and increasingly drunk. "When he stopped recognizing me, I stopped going."

Carl's voice rang again in the empty house. "No-o-o-o! You stopped going. *Then* he stopped recognizing you!"

Cochrane got to his feet. He looked for his beer, then remembered that he had flung it. That was why he could smell it so distinctly.

"It was not like that!" Cochrane barked back to Einhorn. "Not like that at all. You're pissing me off when you say that!"

The entire night was the sound of Einhorn's chilly laughter.

"Never mind," Einhorn said. "Now *you* have another visitor."

"What?"

"A lady. I can smell her."

Cochrane lurched into the next room, supported by the door frame. He searched. He wanted a female companion, even if she was dead.

"The ghost, Carl?"

"No. A living woman."

"Hope not. This place is a mess. Rather have someone dead."

"You'll be that way yourself real soon."

"Not if I get you first," Cochrane snarled.

Cochrane surveyed his living quarters. It was every bit of how he had described it. A mess. He hadn't picked up anything or cleaned in several days. Blame it on this year's pre-Christmas depression.

"I hope you fuck her. I'd like to watch you fuck a woman," Einhorn said. "Can you get hard? That's why the last one left you, wasn't it? You couldn't get hard?"

"There's no one here," Cochrane said evenly.

Einhorn's voice a final time. "That's what you think. I know all."

Then Cochrane recoiled. His doorbell rang.

Jesus! His insanity was right there in the open. Telepathically, Einhorn had presaged a visit!

Clumsily, uneasily, he navigated his way down the stairs. The evening had focused on three and a half beers and a conversation with a man who wasn't there. No wonder he had to steady himself. He went to the door and, tossing all precaution aside, flung it open without even seeing what lurked on the other side.

Then he was startled a second time.

A beautiful female face came into focus. Tall and blond, dressed in a navy wool coat against the winter. The most beautiful woman he had ever seen.

"Hi," Lisa McJeffry said.

Cochrane blinked four times. Then a fifth.

"I'm a mess," he said, trying to gather himself fast. "I'm sorry. I'm a real mess tonight."

At the edge of his consciousness he could hear Einhorn laughing like a hyena.

Lisa studied him. "So I see. You okay?"

"I'm all right. Just a mess."

"Drinking?"

"Yeah. Some. Not too much."

"Looks to me like you might be drunk out of your mind."

"Maybe."

"May I come in? Or do I stand here in the cold all night."

"Of course. I mean, you may come in."

"Thanks."

She came in.

When he fumbled with the door, she took over. She led him back to the living room and set him down on the sofa. Easing onto it, he felt himself on the point of collapse.

He blew out a long breath and looked at her. For some reason, Lisa seemed like his one remaining lifeline to reality. He wished she would stay indefinitely.

"So?" she asked.

"Going crazy. Want to come?"

"You mean that literally, don't you?" she said.

He lunged at rationality. "Tell me why you're here," he said.

She wouldn't tell him why she had come over, not in his current state. Instead she waited. She indulged him in small talk and stayed for several hours, only talking.

He grew more and more tired, exhausted spiritually as well as physically. It was then that she told him that she had done some research for him, running the names that he had mentioned at their last dinner at Alan H's in Georgetown. Cassatt and Forsythe. Lisa had put them through her database at her network. She had come up with something interesting, she said, and in the sobering light of the next morning—or afternoon, or whenever he woke up—he should look at it.

Cochrane insisted that there was nothing wrong with him right now and he could look at it immediately. She told him that was fine, but she wanted to see him shower and lie down in bed first.

This sounded like an excellent idea. She helped him. In fifteen minutes he was cleaned up and on his bed. In seventeen minutes, he was sleeping soundly.

The next morning when he woke, the evening was but a disjointed foggy recollection, though he did recall events in the order that they seemed to have happened.

Coming home from work, frustrated and depressed. The beer. The conversation with Einhorn. The visit from beautiful Lisa.

And the clippings.

Where, he wondered, were the clippings?

When he thought about it, he reasoned that she would have put them on his desk. When he went to his desk at 7:30 A.M., he found them.

Cochrane shook them out of an envelope.

Yes, she had run the names of the Acting President's roommates through a database and she had uncovered some interesting stuff from three decades earlier. Four short clippings from the *Boston Globe*. Lisa had photocopied the originals.

Cochrane looked at the clippings and felt his blood begin to boil. It wasn't just that his initial instincts about Gabe Lang were being confirmed. It was that they were being confirmed so flagrantly. He uttered a low curse and wondered how this had never popped up in Gabe Lang's past before. And then he knew the reason. Lang wasn't mentioned in the articles. But his associates were.

HARVARD STUDENTS QUESTIONED

March 17, 1972. Wareham. Local police today questioned two Harvard seniors in the disappearance of twenty-year-old Juliet Voiselle of Wareham. The two students, identified as Thomas Cassatt of New York City and Ralph Forsythe of Lake Forest, Illinois, were asked if they had any knowledge of the whereabouts of Miss Voiselle, who disappeared last weekend after driving into Cambridge. Friends said that Voiselle had been planning to meet the two Harvard men.

The young woman's car was found on the Harvard campus. She has not been seen since the weekend.

Cassatt and Forsythe said, through an attorney hired by their families, that they did not know the current whereabouts of the young woman. They further stated that they had never seen her the previous weekend. A third Harvard student, the roommate of the other two students, was detained by Cambridge police but not formally questioned.

Cochrane felt something like a knife cutting through him. Then he heard Carl Einhorn's voice, laughing. That was followed by a pair of cold but delicately comforting hands on his shoulders. The feeling was so tactile that it raised the hair on the back of his neck.

"I know you're there," Cochrane said aloud. "And your name is Juliet."

Yes. And their roommate?

Juliet asked.
"Gabe Lang."

Yes,

she said again.

He thought back to what Elizabeth Vaughn had said, "Something very dark in Lang's psyche." "A deal with the Devil." Or something. He continued to read, moving through two updates until he reached the final clipping:

MISSING GIRL DECLARED DEAD

April 27, 1979. Juliet Voiselle, a pretty twenty-year-old art and literature student who disappeared at the edge of the Harvard University campus seven years ago, setting off a local missing persons case, was declared legally dead today in court papers filed by her mother, Mrs. Helen Sabato of Weymouth.

Police conjecture that Ms. Voiselle was murdered. No charges were ever filed in the case. At the time, several Harvard students were questioned, but no leads emerged.

"What happened?" Cochrane asked the ghost. "What did they do to you? *What happened?*"

There was no answer. He looked everywhere for Juliet. But she was gone.

27

O *h, my!*
They're going to come here for me!
I haven't finished my story yet and they're going to take me away from here. Or try to.
Is this sadness that I feel? Sometimes human emotions still confuse me. Physical pain is impossible for me. But spiritual pain still does exist.
My story: It is a sad one, and I still do not know how it should end. True, I returned to the world of the living and sought retribution against certain men. I remain sad about that. There is so much suffering in the world, and now I have caused more of it.
The Cassatts. The Forsythes. As I told you. Wreak your revenge upon the guilty and more innocents suffer. Why does the world of the living have such geometry? I don't find any such geometry in death.
I must concoct an ending for my story. Something grand. Something with balance. See, I am the author and I am a leading character. So much is in my power. And you have seen how I can also manipulate events when I want to.
So why can't I think of what to do? Maybe it's because so many of the other characters—the Levins, George Farley, Gabe Lang, Bill Cochrane—are not of my invention. I am writing the story but I am not completely able to guide it.
Then again, that is what a good novel is supposed to be—an arena of thought, largely evocative of real life—in which the characters attain a reality and a credibility of their own. Thus they act on their own. The author, me in this case, can only record their actions to form her story. The inmates take over the asylum, in other words. The privates run the war.

Unlike the real world of the living. There the most vicious animals run the zoo.

After all this, you now believe in me, don't you? I will demonstrate something. When you close this book, I remain in your thoughts. So my spirit is in your head. You believe in me.

But if you believe in me, I can come very close as a spirit. I can watch you as you sleep. I can lean over you while you are dreaming and hold my teeth to your throat. If you are a man, I can place my hands on your erection while you fantasize of copulation. If you are a woman, I can slide my thoughts into your mind and make you wake wishing a man would press his weight upon you and then slide his hardness between your legs.

I never had good sex when I was alive. What about you? Think of the strangest thing that ever happened to you with a sex partner. Hold that thought. Offer it up.

There! Now I know it, too! I will put it in my book, attached to your name.

Are you picturing that? Are you envisioning your friends reading about you in such a position of physical pleasure, debauchery, or compromise?

Yes? You pictured it?

Good. That means that you believe in me. I am in your head. When you are alone at home tonight, or taking a shower, or drifting to sleep, I will come back into your head.

Know why? Because I am real. I am not just in this book. I am part of your reality. And I will be right next to you when you think of me, long after you have closed this book.

Feel those eyes watching you? They're mine.

Feel that draft. That's me.

Hear that creak in the wall or the floor or the ceiling. That's me, too!

Ah, I am ever so restless tonight. I know that Bill Cochrane knows part of my story. I know that he will come here to dislodge me.

Will I fight? Will I be afraid to move to the next step beyond death? Will I bring Cochrane into the realm of the dead with me?

Maybe. Maybe not. That is the part of the story that I can control.

I feel like circulating, particularly since I know that a man is coming to put my spirit to rest.

I am traveling. I am passing upward through the floor of the Levins' home. I am in their living room, examining the nice fixtures that they have in the building. I like their books and their music. I have even grown to like them personally, if that is possible. They know that I am here and they no longer seem so alarmed.

They even know my name.

What's this?!

I am looking at two eyes gleaming in the dark! They approach me like the eyes of a tiny demon in the blackness of the afterlife.

But I know that these eyes do not belong to a demon. They belong to Sam, the Levins' cat. He can see me all the time. Don't you wonder what cats sometimes see? They see little spirits darting around the periphery of their vision. If you looked closely and believed, you would see the same. But you must try.

I am going up the stairs now. But I am doing it ever so quietly. Not like the night when I toyed with the Levins by slamming a door and mocking them as I stood in the doorway to their bedroom saying:

Look at me if you dare!

Tonight I just want to roam undisturbed. The night is very still and the darkness lends itself to my travels.

I am on the second floor of the Levins' home now. I can hear heartbeats of all three members of the family. Barbara and Richard are sleeping very soundly.

What's this, though?

Lindsay is a restless girl. Her dreams have deserted her. She is upset. Is there some way in which she has sensed me?

There is a clock in this hallway. It is four forty-five in the morning and this is a time of the night that is normally mine. Ghosts walk at night, my friend. They walk in every house. Yours and the Levins'.

And I am more than a little indignant because Lindsay is waking when she should not.

I am in the hallway a few feet from her room. I wonder: If I show myself, could she become my friend? If she sees me manifest myself before her eyes, would she have a greater understanding of spirits and how they inhabit the same realm but a different plane as living humans?

Perhaps this is the night to be seen.

I wonder.

Qua, qua, qua. Tap, tap, tap.

I will finish my story as I wonder.

Lindsay lay in her bedroom and listened to the quiet of the house around her. No creaking on floorboards or inexplicable tapping from within the walls.

So why was she awake? What had roused her from sleep?

Why did she have a sense of the impending, a sense of something unsettled around her?

She looked at the clock near her bed. It was 4:45 A.M. Why, to paraphrase the familiar religious service, was this night different from all other nights?

Outside, the night was dark and cold, but still. A light snow had fallen earlier. Lindsay rose from where she lay in the bed and went to a window. She pushed aside the curtain and glanced out.

Two days had expired since Sam had vanished.

She felt very lonely. She felt terrible about Dr. Walsh having that horrible accident just before Christmas. In the darkest recesses of her mind, she wondered if there had been something unnatural about it.

Something linked to the recreation of the old pagan Celtic service they had had in their house. She wondered if Sam was dead, too.

Lindsay looked at the freshly fallen snow. How beautiful it was when one didn't have to shovel it or drive in it. She pulled her hand away from the window. The curtain silently glided back into place. She turned and stood.

She knew. Something was beckoning her. She knew that if ghosts existed at all, they ruled the night and the darkness. Juliet's spirit had not manifested itself since the evening of the "spiritual cleansing" of the house.

But that didn't mean there wasn't something still there.

Lindsay walked to the bedroom door. She stood in it for several seconds.

Then she raised her eyes and stepped through it into the hallway. Where was Juliet now? *Who* was Juliet?

Meanwhile, further questions besieged her. Why didn't the ghost just appear if it desired attention? Lindsay wondered if the spirit could be summoned. Was there something she could do to provoke Juliet into becoming visible?

And who was she anyway? Lindsay now wanted to know more than ever. She had a pretty good inkling that the ghost was still there. Somewhere.

It was nearly 5 A.M. Kicking around this old house waiting for something to happen was spooking her. How could she hold on to her own thoughts much longer?

She stood there for several minutes, she realized, when she became aware that her eyes hadn't moved. They were set upon the half-open door that led to the guest room on the second floor.

Lindsay was aware of movement.

A flickering change in the lighting. A shadow crossing the floor. She couldn't see into the room because the door was blocking her vision. But she knew something had moved.

Something surged inside her. She walked quietly across the hallway and approached the room. She arrived at the door and listened.

What had she heard? That tapping that sounded like a distant typewriter?

No.

A voice? A heartbeat?

No. Not that either.

In fact, nothing. Dire silence. Why, then, did she know that something was there?

She pushed the door open. The hinges uttered a little tortured wail, but the door gave way easily.

Lindsay braced herself, waiting to see a human figure standing before her. But again, there was none. And now she realized what she had seen affecting the light in the room. It was a reflection of the moonlight through the branches of a large tree outside. The light from the moon filtered through the wavering branches and then through the window. A cloud may have passed over the moon to affect the brightness.

Or so it appeared.

She stepped into the room. Lindsay still had the sense of something.

"Anyone here?" Lindsay asked softly.

Just me.

"Can anyone hear me?"

I can.

Lindsay walked to the center of the room, then turned in every direction. She knew exactly what she was doing. She was trying to lure the ghost into communicating.

"Come on," she said aloud, her words echoing in the quiet house. "Talk to me. Make yourself known. We don't want to have to move from this house. Let's be friends."

Silence answered, a painful ironic silence because now silence was exactly what Lindsay did not want. There was too much silence in her life now. Then at the fringes of her consciousness, as she tried very hard, she thought, she *thought*, she heard something.

You're a young woman, too. Just as I was.

"What?" Lindsay asked. "I think. . . . I think I heard you."

You're almost the same age as I was when I died. I wish I could inhabit your body.

" 'Inhabit my body'?"

Yes! That's what I was saying!

"It's Juliet," Lindsay said aloud. "You're here, aren't you?"

Yes.

"Stop hiding! I want to see you," Lindsay insisted. "Whatever spirit is in this room. Juliet? Is that who you are? Whatever soul haunts this house. Please. . . . come forth. *Make yourself known.* "

A creak responded on the wooden floor before Lindsay. A creak that made her heart soar but which led nowhere.

She stared upward, toward the ceiling. "Juliet?" she asked. "Come on. Please come forth."

She cocked her head. She listened more intently than ever.

Oh, how she *wanted* to hear a silky quiet voice now.

Damn! How she would have liked to have felt that strange sense of something invisible sweeping by her or the cold draft.

Then a thought came to her from somewhere.

Are you sure you are ready?
Not everyone can accept the final reality of a ghost.

"Juliet?" she asked aloud. "Did you just ask me a question? Did you send me a thought?"

There was another creak over her head.

A response? Or a tick in the old floorboards.

Lindsay felt a shiver.

Then quickly another image was upon her. That of herself as an old lady, wandering from room to room in a haunted house, complaining of voices heard only by her. Lindsay had seen daffy old ladies in the streets. They wore tattered coats, their buttons were crooked, their hair was askew, and they talked to people unseen, as they begged for spare change.

Was this her future, she wondered. Was this how it started? Craziness?

"No. You'll be fine."

"What?" Someone had answered!

Again the house was still. But that answer had been as clear as the clapper on a new bell. She had heard a nearby voice.

Heard? Out loud? Or in her mind?

She wasn't certain.

But it had been a female voice. Human. Or spiritually human. Whatever. She had heard it! She knew she had. Or was this, too, part of the incipient lunacy?

"Talk to me!" she demanded, her voice loud and vibrating through the turret room and the still hallway beyond. "Where are you? Say something again!"

"You will be fine."

"*Who* are you? *Where* are you?" Lindsay asked.

Lindsay saw something move slowly along the floor. It was dark and it was very tangible. Her heart kicked and she uttered a short, staccato gasping scream.

Then she caught herself, though her heart was still raging.

She could recognize the movement.

Sam! The cat! He was back!

"Sam! Where the—?"

The cat sauntered to her, lurching slightly. He mewed and purred loudly. A friendly spirit, this Sam.

A nearby voice whispered again. *"Sam is dead now. He's with me."*

"What?" Lindsay answered. This was like dream logic. But this wasn't a dream. "That makes no sense. That makes absolutely no—"

The cat was leaning against her. Purring. Very happy. Very content. Lindsay leaned down to pet the cat and reassure him. Her hand traveled directly through Sam's body.

It was as if Lindsay had stuck her hand into a bucket of ice water. Her hand had passed into a previously unknown dimension of life and death.

Lindsay felt a scream in her throat. She caught the scream and stopped it. In a moment that had no measurement in real time, her lowered eyes caught something else in the room.

A pair of feet. Attached to a body. A female.

A woman.

Lindsay let her eyes travel. They rose and found Juliet and stayed there. The ghost was pale and shimmering and very clear, standing directly in front of her.

Confronting her.

White as marble. Cold as death.

The dead girl.

Sam's new custodian. Sam's new mistress.

Lindsay smelled the perfume. She caught the scent of death. Saw the white dead eyes. Felt the fear.

Juliet's mouth curled slightly into a smile. A smile for all eternity.

"Hello."

Lindsay's astonished eyes went wide. She had told herself that she would not be afraid if this moment came. But now the moment was there and she had deceived herself.

"Now can we become friends?"

Something welled inside Lindsay.

It started in the pit of her stomach and rose up out of her lungs and her throat. It was the most bloodcurdling scream of terror that anyone in that house—living or dead—had ever heard.

Lindsay's eyes remained on the ghost.

The cat fled.

The little smile at the corner of Juliet's lips dissipated. Her expression went flat, fading into something of deep hurt and abject sadness.

At the same time, Lindsay heard voices from within the house. Her parents. Scared as hell. Calling her name.

Running from their bedroom.

The moment seemed frozen. No transition from one world to the next.

At one instant Lindsay was staring at a specter returned from the grave. The next moment, the room lights flashed on.

There was no Juliet and no Sam. Just a terrified twenty-two-year-old Lindsay, continuing to scream while her father burst into the room.

He grabbed her. He held her. He shook her till she stopped screaming. Barbara Levin stood in the doorway.

"I saw her! I saw her! I saw her!" the terrified girl shrieked over and over. "She was right there and she had Sam! Right there! Right there! Right there!"

Barbara and Richard Levin looked at the empty spot in the room. There was no sign of Juliet. No indication of Sam. Only empty air at a few minutes past five in the morning.

"I *saw* her!" Lindsay kept insisting. "She appeared right before me! I *know* she did. I know what I saw!"

Single children weep longer than their peers, comforted as they are by two parents. Over the course of the hour that followed, Barbara Levin stilled her daughter's pain. At the same time, her father addressed her fears.

There was no point, they decided, to live in a state of terror and constant alert, no point to further deny that there was something malevolent within the house, no point to risk their daughter's life, much less her mental health.

They discussed what they would do and how they could rearrange their living accommodations. Somehow, they all reasoned, they would have to ease their lives out of this house. This place was not going to work for them.

Eventually, dawn came and with it a bright dose of sunshine. Unaccountably, the arrival of a new day brought with it a wave of sorrow for all of them. It was as if the terror of the sighting was made all the worse with the reality of dawn. No longer could they speculate on what might be in the house.

Now they knew. It was daylight and the terror would not go away.

A storm of anxiety and sorrow seized the entire family. And this time they were unable to console each other.

28

Agent Richard Bradley of the Secret Service was finally home after doing a double shift guarding Carl Einhorn at Elm Hill Hospital. This was the type of work, he thought to himself as he came through the door, that could cause agents to quit.

Long tedious hours. Lousy working conditions. Not even the glamor and excitement of guarding a visiting dignitary or his family. All he was doing was sitting around a nut house preventing access to a mental patient.

He went to the kitchen and found some beer in the refrigerator. He hadn't eaten all day and had picked up some sandwiches on the way home. But he had also brought home more than he had expected.

Bradley lived in a characterless one-bedroom apartment in a new high-rise in Silver Spring. It was nothing special, but it got him to work quickly and served his purposes. He rubbed his tired eyes as he tried to make himself comfortable. He supposed that if Einhorn hadn't gotten into his head, something else would have. There was never a moment's peace in this world for a conscientious policeman, something his father, a policeman in Omaha, Nebraska, had warned him about. The presence of Carl Einhorn was really starting to unnerve him. And there wasn't anyone he could dare tell.

Admit a weakness in Treasury? Might as well resign. Admit that he was sitting up at night imagining that Einhorn had physically followed him home? Forget it.

And then there were the death threats.

Einhorn had concocted a new one.

"Uno, duo!" Einhorn would yell from his cell. "Uno, duo, trey!"

It was to the opening words of an old song called "Woolly Boolly" by Sam the Sham and the Pharaohs. Einhorn would yell one, two, three in Spanish, then follow with "Bradley! Cochrane! Farley!" his intended one-two-three victims.

It wouldn't have bothered him quite so much if it didn't seem clear that Einhorn was fully intending to carry out his threat. Some way.

Well, Bradley cautioned himself, maybe he was overreacting. He wasn't a psychiatrist, after all. And they kept Einhorn hog-tied and behind steel bars most of the time. Was there really anything to worry about?

Bradley finished his dinner. He placed a glass and a plate into the dishwasher, where they would keep company with the utensils of the previous two days. He fed some soap into the washer and turned it on. Why not wash things at least twice a week, he reasoned. Then he walked into the next room.

An anxious feeling came over him again. More Einhorn? What exactly was bothering him?

Then he placed it. He stood in his living room and realized—or thought he realized—that things were not exactly as he had left them that morning.

It was the little things he was noticing. An overturned automobile magazine that he had left face up. Two pencils that had rolled off the table and onto the floor, as if dislodged by an intruder's hand. And spookiest of all, two window shades that were down about a foot more than usual.

For a moment, Agent Richard Bradley stood motionless in cold fear, assessing the violation of his apartment. Instinctively, he drew his pistol. What was there? Who was there? How had someone gotten past the locks on his front door?

His Treasury Department training kicked in. He did a thorough search of the premises. When he found nothing, no intruder or any evidence thereof, he relaxed slightly.

He put his weapon away. He sat down on his bed.

That little one-horned-horse creep sure had gotten into his mind, he told himself. The shades could have slipped down by themselves, the pencils could have rolled off the table through some vibration in the building, and who knows how he had actually left that magazine. He was getting hyper, Bradley told himself, because he had made the mistake two days earlier of engaging in a conversation with Einhorn about his living quarters. Having no one else to talk to all day, Bradley had revealed a little about his apartment.

A silly mistake, he told himself. But in the end, a harmless one. Bradley lay back on his bed and relaxed.

He relaxed very quickly and fell asleep with his clothes on. He dreamed he was eight years old again and back in Nebraska, running through a field with his dog, Freddy.

Freddy had been a wonderful animal. Had been hit by a car and killed when Richard was eleven. Young Bradley had cried and cried over Freddy's death.

It was so wonderful to see the dog again.

At the same moment, south of the capital, Bill Cochrane wandered through his own living quarters. He examined again the incomplete oil portrait of Lisa, the painting he had started long ago and remained stymied upon. He spent several minutes looking at it and the photographic studies. To him, the project remained stillborn.

He could paint it, he reasoned. Technically and physically, he could complete it. But it would be so lifeless, he reasoned. So much without spirit.

"What to do?" he said aloud.

"Finish what you have begun," a male voice said.

He looked to his left. His father was addressing him.

He saw not the decrepit shell of his father that had vegetated in a mental hospital. Rather, he saw his father as a much younger man. One his own age. The way he remembered his dad when he was a teenager, as a college lecturer, telling him also about the thrill and challenge of journalism in the 1960s and 1970s. Such father-son talks had shaped Bill Cochrane's professional ambitions in college.

"What about my heart?" the son asked the father. "What if my heart is no longer in it?"

He watched his father shrug. "How do you think I feel?" the father asked. "My heart stopped beating."

"But your spirit . . . ?"

"We are all at the edge of your senses," the father answered. "All you have to do is look. And believe."

"Where's the sanity in that?" Bill asked.

He heard his father laugh. "You stand there and you see me?" he asked. "And you still ask that question?"

Then his father faded and was gone. Cochrane set aside the paints. He walked downstairs and sat down at the table in the living room. The lights in the room were dark, because he knew that Juliet pre-

ferred the shadows. He waited for a moment, then eyed the deck of
cards that was now on the table.

Calmly, methodically, Cochrane reached to the deck.

He cut it twice. He waited. He could feel a change in the room
pressure. He was aware of an incipient chilliness in the room. Then
he caught a faint suggestion of her perfume.

When he raised his eyes in the room, he saw her again.

Juliet. The ghost.

Then she came to him. He felt the touch of her hand on his shoulder. On his cheek. Then for the most fleeting of moments he thought
that she had leaned over and kissed him.

"So?" he asked.

"You've entered my plane of existence, haven't you?" she asked. *"You
see me. You want to feel my presence."*

"Yes," he said.

His eyes again found the mirror across the room. Again the mirror told him he was alone. But he knew much better.

"You care," she said.

"I care," he answered.

He could tell that her mood was similar to his. Bittersweet and
moody. Great depths of sadness. They both knew they would need to
move on from the worlds they were in.

"Will you help me find peace?" she asked. *"Will you help put me to
rest?"*

"Yes," he said.

For an instant the entire room was the off-white color of old marble. Her face was before his. Her lips met his and they seemed to be
warm. He felt as if she had drawn him further into some arena. Some
new level of existence.

"Then I will tell you what happened," she said. *"And I will tell you
where to look."*

Cochrane's eyes flickered. He wanted badly to follow the ghost
wherever she was leading him.

His eyes flickered a second time. The last thing he remembered
before he started his journey was the feel of Juliet's hands upon his.
Then he felt as if he were flying somewhere—or his consciousness or
his spirit was. He had a sense of being weightless, outside of his own
body, and soaring through the air. In his experience, there were no
previous parallels to what he now felt. It was somewhat like the sense
of liftoff one has in an airplane on departure—but without the airplane.

He didn't dare open his eyes. He wanted badly to break through the boundaries that she had set for him.

He felt as if he had drifted into a light trance.

He was aware of Juliet guiding him.

"Think of this, Bill Cochrane. A tunnel," he heard the ghost say. *"Think of a long familiar friendly tunnel. A tunnel through the sky. Or through the ocean. Or through everything you've known as reality. Come with me."*

He obeyed.

There was an image before him of his life running in reverse, like a familiar old film being shown backward, from the present day in Washington quickly back through California and Massachusetts.

He could hear Juliet's voice. The inconsistency of her voice superimposed upon the events of his life didn't bother him. He was a youth again, with his mother and father in the old family home.

Still hurtling backward, time in reverse . . .

Scenes from his life were like the exit signs on the highway in Massachusetts the day he had visited Mrs. Vaughn. And then he realized that's where Juliet was taking him.

Lawrence. Wareham. Weymouth. All the old places.

He saw a million autumn days yet again, all rolled into one. Hockey rinks and hamburger places and the laughter of pretty college girls. He was speeding by in a car, seeing things as if returned from the dead.

Which in a way, he was. Returned *by* the dead.

Suddenly he was jolted, as if his vehicle had come to a skidding, snarling halt. It was as if he were on a roller coaster and someone had hit the emergency brake. He feared being catapulted forward. He hung on.

"It's all right," he heard her say. *"You're where I want you to be."*

He had the sense of breaking a sweat. But he knew her hands were still upon his. He again was conscious that he could open his eyes, that this wasn't physically happening, but he was definitely traveling to a place only available through his mind.

Opening his eyes, he felt, would ruin everything.

Then he had another sense. He felt that his eyes *were* open. He was walking and waking somewhere in the past.

Somehow he knew. It was 1972. And he was following along on an evening of physical and psychological brutality.

He resisted.

"Hey! What the hell *is* this?" he asked. He felt his own voice speaking aloud. "Something horrible is going to happen! I don't want to see it."

"You must see it to understand," Juliet said.

As if by her command, he saw three young men. Cassatt, Forsythe, and Gabe Lang. They were Harvard students. And they were meeting a young local girl

—me—

on the edge of the Harvard Campus. It was a cold March night almost three decades earlier.

"I am in uncharted land," he thought to himself. "I've been here before but I haven't been here before."

Juliet was a plain girl but sexy. Attractive in a bookish way. She was carrying something under her arm. Her novel.

It was a novel on witchcraft, and she was a witch. A good witch, she postulated, and her spirit had come forth from the evil that had occurred at Salem three centuries earlier.

She liked these Harvard boys, Forsythe in particular. Juliet had told them that she, too, was a witch, and endowed with a spirit that could travel across time. That is what she had written in her novel. That was what she felt about herself.

"Will you read it to us in a haunted house?" one asked. "That would be exciting."

She had agreed. And one of them had known about an old house in Hillsborough, ten miles north of Salem. It had everything the three young men needed. Beer and drugs. Atmosphere. A mattress and a naive young girl who was sincerely into the supernatural.

They took her to the old house on Warren Street. The house was under reconstruction. The basement was half dug up and the walls were being refurbished on the first floor. The house had a legend of spirits, but so did every other structure dating from the 1700s.

The boys broke into the house from the back door. Workmen had left the place unguarded. Entrance was easy.

They hung drop cloths over the windows in the room of the downstairs that would eventually become a den. There was an old potbellied stove in that room and they discovered that it still worked. They burned newspapers and bits of plywood for warmth.

They lit candles around a mattress and asked her to read her book. Her novel was unfinished, as it would be for years, but what she had was good.

The book was called *The Red Queens*. It was a spooky novel. Juliet seemed to know a lot about spirits and demons. She had illustrated the cover with two playing cards, taken from an old deck.

Queen of diamonds.

Queen of hearts.

"And how do you know so much about witchcraft?" Gabe Lang asked, intrigued.

"From my previous life. As a witch," she explained.

The boys laughed. But the book was effective. It established a mood in the old house.

Part of the story was sexy. Juliet read through this part without hesitation. The witch in her book had a foot in two different worlds, the living and the dead. The Queen of hearts represented the world of the living. The Queen of diamonds was the mistress of the dead.

These two domains were part of the personality of the woman who narrated the book. She had two voices. *One in the first person, from the world of the dead.* Another in the third person, from the land of the living.

The witch in the book drew power from sexuality. From her own sexuality and from the sexuality of the men around her. She would recharge herself by taking new partners.

Cassatt, Forsythe, and Lang liked this part. Juliet aroused them with her evocative writing. They asked her if she would like to recharge her own sexuality with them. At first they were kidding. But as the beer and the marijuana passed its way around among the four of them, the sexual levels increased around the room.

At one point she giggled. "I'm getting wet," she said. "You know? Between my legs?"

She pulled a long drag on a reefer and closed her eyes. The next thing she knew, the cigarette was out of her hand and Tommy Cassatt was trying to kiss her.

For a moment she responded, thinking he was fooling around. They were nice young men from good families, she reminded herself, so how could this go badly wrong?

Then she asked him to stop kissing her. He wouldn't.

Ralph Forsythe pushed her manuscript aside and held her, allow-

ing Tommy to kiss her more firmly. Then one of them started grop-
ing at her body. Another was pulling at her clothing.

"Are you a witch?" Gabe Lang asked.

"Yes," she murmured.

"Then satisfy us," Cassatt said.

"No," he said slowly in response. She sought to evade their hands
and push them away. "I want to read my manuscript."

They kept pressing her. There were hands on her breasts, then
other hands under her skirt. She thought they were still fooling
around.

They weren't.

They undressed her by candlelight until she was completely naked.
Juliet was too far gone from alcohol and cannabis to offer much re-
sistance. Her head pounded and a different horror than any she had
imagined was soon upon her. All three young men raped her on the
dirty mattress.

Afterward, they asked her again if she was a witch.

She was beside herself in revulsion and indignity. But she still insisted that she was. The concept had arrested the three young men,
coming to them within the haze of their alcoholic and chemical delir-
ium. They kept asking for a confession.

She wouldn't give them one. Juliet wanted to believe she was a
witch. Now they were even trying to take that from her.

"I know what we can do," Ralph Forsythe finally said. "I know how
to make her confess."

They dressed her again and took her outside. There were railroad
tracks that ran nearby, he said, and there were ways to make an alleged witch recant.

They carried her to a clearing in a wooded area not far from the
old house. The railroad tracks ran through the area. Juliet pleaded and
cried for help. But no one heard her.

They put her head on the railroad track and they laid a heavy
wooden railroad tie across her back.

"Recant," one of them said. "Tell us you're *not* a witch."

"I'm a witch," she said, groggily. "I'm a witch and I'll have my revenge. On all of you," she said between gasps and sobs. "I'll have my
revenge on all of you."

A yellow light appeared on the horizon, down the tracks.

The boys retreated. They stood several yards behind her and one
of them—she thought it was Forsythe—yelled again.

"Recant!" another of them yelled.

She wouldn't. She was crying too hard.

The train approached. She began to scream. How fast could the train go? Eighty miles an hour? It would be there in a few seconds.

The light grew larger. She could hear the train coming.

"Confess you're not a witch!" one of them shouted.

She was crying too hard, too terrified, to confess anything. She faced her death.

Then suddenly there were hands upon her and hands pulling at the railroad tie. The weight of the wooden tie came off her. There were strong hands on her arms, lifting her. Drawing her body up. Pulling her back.

The train was two hundred yards away. Then a hundred. Rushing toward her. They were in its headlights.

They hauled her backward and drew her away from the tracks. They stood her upright and she felt the rush of the train going by, the air so heavy that it nearly sucked her under. Her heart was in her throat. Her face was streaked with tears.

They had forced sex upon her. They had shown her terror unlike any that she had never known. They should all have had enough. But they hadn't.

"I'm not a witch," she finally sobbed. "I just want to go home."

"We'll see," one of them said. "We'll see."

They took her back to the old house on Warren Street. They took her to the basement again and laid her in a pit in the cellar that was shaped like a makeshift grave. There were high piles of soft dirt and clay beside the pit.

Juliet was crying and sobbing uncontrollably. How could any human beings be so cruel? How could any men treat an innocent girl this way?

They left her in the grave. They asked her to promise not to tell the police what had happened. They told her that they would give her some time to think about it since they didn't feel it would be safe to let her go right away.

They might have to keep her till morning, one of them said.

"My mother . . ." she pleaded.

"Who cares?" said one of them.

"If you ever talk about what happened here," Tommy Cassatt said, "we'll have people testify that you were a slut. You screwed us all voluntarily, and you made up the rest of the story."

Juliet again pleaded to be released. To mock her, they ripped the two red queens off the front of her manuscript.

And they threw the cards into the would-be grave with her.

The cards landed together, face up. Little red sentries. Little crimson angels.

The boys went upstairs to have a conference. It was slightly past ten o'clock. Even they knew the evening had gotten far out of hand. They drank some more and did some more marijuana. At about ten thirty-five, they heard a noise from the basement. A soft thumping sound, sort of like a movement of dirt.

"Maybe she's free," one of them said.

They laughed and expected to hear her steps on the stairs. They didn't.

So they came back downstairs after an hour. It was time to release her, they had decided.

When they approached the grave, they were stricken with their own terror. They could barely believe what they saw.

The walls of the makeshift grave had collapsed, burying Juliet alive. That must have been the sound they had heard thirty minutes earlier, one of them said. And it had been.

Gabriel started to paw the ground with his hands, trying to dig her up. But if she had been down there half an hour, Ralph Forsythe pointed out, she was already dead.

Bill Cochrane had the sense of watching all this from above, and then there was a further sense of listening to Juliet's screaming from the grave. He heard cries and pleas for help and mercy which were suddenly muffled by a small avalanche of collapsing earth.

And then Bill Cochrane felt another blackness settle upon him, a blackness formed not just by mood but empathy with a buried spirit upon whom the daylight would never again physically shine.

Then there was a tiny light in the blackness, like someone illuminating a penlight in the middle of the field in the middle of the night. And the penlight gave birth to stars which were above him.

Cochrane had the sense of traveling again, of soaring, of making a return trip.

"Are you in darkness?" a kind female voice asked.

Bill Cochrane heard his own voice answering. "Yes. I'm in darkness."

"And you're still traveling?"

"I am. But I see some dots of light."

The vision was like looking out of an airplane on a pitch black night. Nothing visible other than little dabs of light, and a clear sense of forward motion.

Juliet again. "Excellent! Those are other spirits. Don't be alarmed. They're friendly. They will remain all around you forever."

"How will I find my way back?" he asked.

"Back to where?"

"Washington. The present."

"The present day will find you, Bill Cochrane," Juliet said. "Wait for it. Let yourself fall into the present-day light."

He was again aware of her ghostly hands clasping his. They clasped tightly. He was in darkness, save those dots of light. The darkness swirled now. He almost had a sensation of plunging. Then that, too, stopped.

"I'm coming to lightness," he said.

"Keep going," she said. "Welcome it. It's the current world."

"It's what? It's *what?*" he asked.

"Don't question," she advised gently. "Go with it."

Bill Cochrane had the image of sailing up over a horizon, over a blue ocean and bursting upon a brilliant landscape. He soared euphorically, gliding into a sunlit reality.

Then he felt himself coming to earth. And with reality, his spirit became very heavy. An unbearable sadness was upon him as he knew what three young men had done to Juliet. Their evil was pulling him downward, reaching into his soul and asking for him to do something in the name of justice and decency.

"I hate this. I hate what they've done to you!" he called out.

He felt Juliet's hands upon his for a final moment, calming and reassuring as her voice narrated his voyage to a conclusion.

"Of course you do," she said. "Of course."

He felt his momentum come to a halt. He was aware of being back in his home in Virginia.

Everything was silent.

He felt the ghost's hands leave his.

Yet, he was afraid to open his eyes. And she knew it.

"It's all right," she said. *"You can look."*

He had traveled across the room. He was on the floor, his back against the wall. She was kneeling before him as he slowly opened his eyes.

Much of the torment was gone from her face now. She was shimmering and very pretty. He had the sense of being naked with her, but couldn't be sure. It had the same sense a man might have in the minutes after making love. But it was somehow different. More spiritual and thus more intense.

There were different degrees of intimacy in the world, he knew. And this was a level he had never previously reached. He wondered if he would ever find it again.

She kissed him again on the lips. He opened his mouth and her tongue entered him. Then she withdrew from him.

"When you find me," she said. *"I want to be cremated."*

"And the ashes?" he asked.

"You are my guardian. And the closest thing to a lover that I now have. So you'll know what to do."

Then she faded. She was gone. His shirt was soaked with perspiration.

He was left feeling very alone. And deeply saddened.

He drew a long breath and looked at his watch. Three hours had passed since he had sat down at the table and cut the cards. He had no idea where he had been.

But he did notice that the cards were again neatly stacked.

Had he put them back together. Or had she?

Or did it not matter?

29

Two days later, absent from work without permission, Bill Cochrane stood on Warren Street in Hillsborough, Massachusetts, and gazed at the house that he had only once before seen in a different level of consciousness.

He looked at it with anxiety and a lingering sense of unreality. He heard voices that beckoned him to the place and he recognized it from the visions within an unorthodox journey that he had been taken on within the last days.

His thoughts were scattered in many directions. Hatred for the men who had committed so many crimes upon an innocent girl. Lack of comprehension for the new world that he had now entered. A small amount of concern for his own welfare—when he returned to Washington, there would have to be explanations.

And the explanations would barely matter, because no one would ever believe them.

He went to the door and found the house deserted. This was not unexpected. He went across the street. A suspicious woman named Catherine Maloney met him at her door. She had Christmas decorations in her hand and Cochrane guessed she was cleaning up after the holidays.

But one never knew. He had been to hundreds of doors in his life seeking information. All he knew was that one should expect anything, however unreasonable. Like Christmas displays being put up a month late.

"I know the family who lives across the way is named Levin," Cochrane began. "Know where I might find them?"

"Moved out. Had some sort of trouble."

"Know where I might find them?" he repeated.

There was a motel at the end of town, Catherine said. She had seen their car there. He might try that. Or he could ask the real estate broker who was listing the house.

"The Levins," Catherine said, "must be kinda disappointed 'cause they're talkin' 'bout movin' again."

Catherine was a real font of knowledge once she got uncorked.

"Must be real disappointed if they're living in a motel," Cochrane offered. Working a case, working a story, the old newspaperman's lucidity came back to him, he knew just how to push.

"Ah, who knows?" she answered. "Maybe they had a hole in the roof."

"Sure," said Cochrane.

"I know their cat disappeared. They were pretty upset about that."

"I would think they would be," Cochrane said.

He could tell that Catherine was quickly talked out.

He found the Levins at the motel that evening. Barbara first, then Richard, then Lindsay when she came home from her graduate classes in the evening.

"Lindsay Levin," Cochrane said. "Pretty name."

"A lot of people think she's named after former Mayor Lindsay of New York," Barbara said.

"Is she?" Cochrane felt compelled to ask.

"Lindsay Buckingham," Richard said. "You know, we were big Fleetwood Mac fans."

Cochrane nodded. No one, *no one in the world,* he decided, was completely balanced.

He then found himself slipping into the usual ruses and gimmicks, the old harmless mistruths for when he needed cooperation during an investigation.

The old lies.

"I used to work in this area as a reporter," he explained to the Levins, "and I recently received a tip on a very old case. It involves a murder. I know this may upset you, but I have reason to believe that a woman's body may be buried under your house on Warren Street."

The Levins looked at each other only in mild surprise.

"Why do you think that?" Richard Levin asked cautiously.

"Obviously, I can't identify my source," Cochrane said. "But I believe that it's very trustworthy. Or I wouldn't be here."

"What do you want to do. Dig?"

"I'd like the police to dig, yes," Cochrane said.

The Levins looked at each other again. Cochrane tried to nudge them toward a decision.

"I don't know how you feel about such things, and of course there are legalities involved," he said. "But you might be happier in that house if the body—if there *is* a body—is removed."

It was Lindsay Levin who spoke up next.

"Was her name Juliet?" Lindsay asked.

Cochrane was legitimately surprised.

"Yes," he said.

"You can dig," said Barbara Levin.

"The sooner the better," Richard added.

Cochrane eased back in his chair. "Maybe you know more than I do," he suggested.

"Maybe," said Barbara, with a tight nervous smile.

With that, and a nod from her mother, Lindsay started to talk. And the three Levins, hopeful of regaining their home, told Bill Cochrane a ghost story that was in no way at variance with the one he already knew. In every way, it complemented his own perfectly.

It took another day to obtain the proper writs and warrants. Then Cochrane accompanied a police forensics team from the Massachusetts State Police into the house on Warren Street. He wanted to explain exactly how he had obtained this dark vision and who had given it to him. But he knew the time was not yet right. The proper exhumation would have to happen first.

The house perfectly reflected the vision that Juliet had brought to him—the layout of the main floor, the den with the old potbellied stove, the steps down to the cellar, the corner of the antique basement where the grave had collapsed upon her.

The police dug, led by a crusty thick-browed lieutenant named Kim Crowe. It took the diggers only forty minutes to find the remains of a woman. As there was a heavy salt and lime content to the clay beneath the building, a stunning part of the body had been preserved.

Cochrane, however, left the basement when the police unearthed their grisly "discovery." He had seen the victim in a better light and could not bear even a glimpse of something so lovely in its physical ruin. Had he remained in the basement, and had he watched very carefully, he also would have seen two other small items emerge from the earth.

Two playing cards.

The cards were *remarkably* preserved. They were almost pristine, a condition that forensic experts in the cellar could in no way explain. It was as if they had been somewhere else for many years, then dropped into the grave relatively recently.

But that would have been impossible. So the police attributed the condition of the cards to some quirk in the universe. One of those things that happens in old houses.

"Look at that," Lieutenant Crowe said, himself an amateur poker player of local renown. "Two red queens. The lady was holding a good hand when she died."

"Looks like a losing hand to me," said one of the bulls with the shovels, commenting on the sad end of the woman.

"Sometimes," Crowe said, "a pair of red queens is enough to win."

Upstairs, had he heard the conversation, Cochrane might have agreed. As the evening lengthened, he heard Lieutenant Crowe talking about the proper routine from here on with the cadaver.

First there would have to be identification. Then scientific records could be taken. Eventually, there would be burial.

"The county tends toward cremation unless there are some other instructions from a family," Lieutenant Crowe said.

Cochrane nodded. "Cremation is what the family would want," he said.

"How would you know?" Crowe asked.

"Take my word for it," Cochrane said.

Crowe shrugged. "It's a thirty-one-year-old case," he said. "Your word is as good as anyone's."

Back in Washington a day later, Cochrane felt the final fragile state of his mental health start to tremble. President Farley had sunken deeply into a coma now. He was on a respirator at Bethesda. Drs. Katzman and Gundarson had finally allowed all sorts of specialists to see charts of the world's most famous patient. But at this late hour it was to no avail.

The international situation worsened also. Gabriel Lang made clear to the world that the United States had no interest in involving itself in any conflict in the Baltic. By issuing such a statement, the resurgent Russian Republic seemed to have carte blanche to reoccupy some of the fragile democracies in Eastern Europe. First it had been 1939 all over. And now it was 1941.

Cochrane's concerns were more immediate, however. He drove to Elm Hill Hospital to view again his small nemesis, Carl Einhorn. Cochrane was twice surprised on arrival.

First, Agent Richard Bradley was gone and a new man was standing guard. Second, Einhorn's security status had been downgraded. Cochrane now met him in a hospital yard. They could sit at a table, across from each other, one rational man to the next, and discuss things.

"I still want to know how you do it," Cochrane said. "You use your mind, you use numbers, you use something, and you can affect things and people."

Einhorn was subdued this day. Cochrane figured he was on some sort of sedative. He was also slightly more talkative.

"It's just something that comes to you one day," Einhorn said, "when the atmosphere is clear, when the timing is right, when your mind is perfect, and when you're ready." He smirked. "You still believe me capable of such things, do you?" The Unicorn asked.

"Yes."

"You're the only one who does."

"Maybe you're right. And maybe you're as loco as anyone on Starship Earth."

The Unicorn nodded. "And maybe, following my death, I should bequeath my enormous powers to you."

"I'm not sure I would want them," Cochrane said.

Einhorn grinned. "That's part of my point. I'm not giving them to you because I like you. I'd want to see you destroyed. Just as you'll destroy me."

Cochrane paused and let The Unicorn's words sink in.

"Why would I destroy you?" Cochrane asked. "You're all locked up here. You get medication. You can't get loose. Why should I want to do anything to you?"

"To get even. For that ringing in your ears."

Once again, Cochrane found himself reining back his temper.

"What about the ringing?" he asked.

"I'm causing it."

"How do you even know about it?"

"I'm causing it."

"I never mentioned it here."

"Yes, you did, Sweet Cakes. Plus, as stated, I'm causing it."

Cochrane stared. The Unicorn grinned.

"That much I *don't* believe," said Cochrane.

"No?" Einhorn laughed. "Pity."

"Should I?"

No answer.

"Should I, Carl?"

Einhorn puckered his lips and blew him a mock kiss.

"My beer is Rheingold the Dry Beer," Einhorn chirped in his off-key singsong. "Think of Rheingold whenever you buy beer. . . ."

"Come on, Carl. Talk to me!"

"It's not bitter, not sweet, an extra dry flavored treat . . ."

"Carl!"

"When you *die,* I will *buy* Rheingold beer."

"Jesus Christ!" Cochrane snapped.

"Rheingold Brewing Company, Brooklyn, New York." Einhorn paused. "You're bitter and you're sweet, Cochrane. Have a nice evening."

Cochrane stood, disgusted, and turned to leave. Einhorn remained seated, preening and proud of himself, like a frog on a lily pad.

"Hope you like my new guard, Cochrane," Einhorn said. "I got rid of that stupid young blond one."

"Good-bye, Carl," Cochrane said. "I'm like Bradley. I've had enough of you, too."

"You'll be more like Richard Bradley than you might imagine. You and Farley within the next few days! Uno! Duo! Uno, duo, trey!"

It was only upon leaving that Cochrane cadged the news from the replacement agent in the corridor. Young Bradley had apparently slipped in the shower in his apartment and had taken a terrific blow to his head upon falling.

The young agent was dead.

Cochrane felt the final vestiges of his sanity quickly slipping away. He drove madly back to his home in Virginia, angrier on arrival than when he had left the hospital. He barged into his home.

He saw spirits all around him. They wouldn't leave him alone. Nor would Einhorn.

"Problem?" Juliet asked.

"No problem. I'm going to kill him."

"Kill who?"

"The Unicorn."

His father chimed in. "Son, no. That's the wrong thing to do."

"It's the right thing to do," Cochrane answered. "He killed Bradley. He's killing the President. He'll kill me."

Cochrane turned to Juliet. There was something very heavy about her spirit. Something grave and foreboding. She shook her head.

"No," she said. *"You mustn't."*

"You'll spend your life locked up. In a prison," his father warned.

"It doesn't matter."

Cochrane looked at his watch. Einhorn would take his exercise in the early evening, he thought. And Cochrane could get access now.

So how to kill him? How to slay The Unicorn?

A gun or a knife couldn't get past security. But Cochrane knew what could.

A garrote. The little madman had even suggested it himself. So much for poetic justice.

Cochrane went to a closet and found a short line of heavy rope. He knotted it carefully in the center. Just perfect to break the little maniac's neck.

He folded it carefully and concealed it within his shirt. He went back to his car, jumped in, and drove.

The parking lot guards at Elm Hill were surprised to see Cochrane twice in the same day. And he knew they would tell that to the police after the murder had occurred.

He walked steadfastly past the attendants in the lobby, who, used to seeing him, waved him through. He didn't go to C-2 Lamoureux, however. He went to the exercise yard, where he would wait.

Fifteen minutes passed. Then half an hour. Einhorn was late coming out of his cell. Cochrane wondered why. Then he heard some sort of commotion within the building and went back in to investigate.

He might have been the only person on the premises to fully understand what had happened.

About an hour earlier, just when Cochrane was starting out on his trek back to Elm Hill, there had been some terrible screaming in Einhorn's cell.

Screaming in the cell of a madman was not unusual at this place. It was normal. And so the guards had paid only cursory attention. Then it stopped. When silence returned, one guard wandered by for a look. Einhorn was lying on the floor, very still. When he didn't move for a quarter hour, a guard went in and poked him.

But he was dead. An apparent heart attack.

His cell had been under surveillance by cameras. When the tapes were reviewed, and Einhorn's shouts were taken more seriously, he seemed to be in a deathly pas de deux with some unseen force in the cell. The time print on the videotape said 6:27 P.M.

He had screamed that it was a woman, an evil spirit come to do him in. And he accused Bill Cochrane of sending her.

"The last paranoid demented act of a paranoid demented little man," said one doctor, looking at the tape in Cochrane's presence. He turned to Cochrane. "I guess we won't be seeing *you* here anymore, huh?"

"Yeah," Cochrane said. "Looks like you're rid of us both." He paused. "Good thing, too. I came here to kill him."

He then produced the garrote to the astonished staff. They put it in the incinerator before anyone could cause trouble with it.

Cochrane walked back to his car.

He drove home in a much calmer state of mind. He was perfectly calm and might have even regained his rational mind, except that news bulletins broke into the music on the radio.

Miraculously, at six twenty-seven that evening, President George Farley mysteriously sat up in bed. He came roaring out of his coma, his trance, his bewitchment, or whatever one wanted to call it.

He asked where he was and what in hell was going on. Thirty minutes later, he was dressing and demanding to go back to the White House.

He went back that evening, but was not sworn back in for two more days. He passed the physical exam perfectly, just as he had in early November. The nature of his "illness" was to remain a mystery not just to his own doctors, but to the rest of medical science altogether. Nor did the Russian nationalists ever understand the abrupt change in American policy that put seven divisions of American troops in Eastern Europe on Farley's first day back in office.

His illness was over. And so was the Presidency of Gabriel Lang.

30

"**I** don't have all the answers," Bill Cochrane told his visitors, "but I have some of them."

"Three Harvard students murdered a girl named Juliet Voiselle in 1972," he explained. "It wasn't an intentional homicide. Just one of those mindless college experiments in terrifying someone weaker. Except in this case the victim died."

Another brush stroke. He stood in the loft of his town house working at his easel. Lisa McJeffry sat to one side. He glanced at her from time to time as he painted. He also glanced to the other side of his easel just as much. She had brought with her a friend, Dr. Willard Lawrence.

"She was buried alive. I led the police to the grave, the grave was exhumed. The girl was cremated."

"Where are the ashes?"

"I have some of them," he said, glancing at the portrait and adjusting an eyebrow. "But I won't tell you where. The rest I buried."

"Uh-huh," she said. "This is one of the strangest stories I've ever heard in my life."

"You're a reporter," he said. "Do with it what you wish." He paused. "The thing is, how would I have ever known where the body was buried if Juliet Voiselle's ghost hadn't told me?"

"Why did you have a rope when you went to see Einhorn?" she asked.

"The Unicorn?" Cochrane asked. "He had found a way to manipulate the feelings and health of other people," Cochrane said. "Was going to do it with objects, too. Made a cup of water fly into my lap. Made a van nearly kill me on the Washington Memorial Parkway." He paused. "Bradley didn't die of natural causes either, Lisa. Einhorn did it."

"Uh-huh."

"Slipped and fell in a bathtub. Awfully suspicious," Cochrane said. "My bet is that Einhorn made him fall and made sure he fell hard."

"And how did Einhorn die?"

"The coroner said suffocation," Cochrane answered.

"He swallowed his tongue. He choked himself."

Cochrane laughed. "Sure. Believe that if you want. The truth is that the ghost, Juliet, went into his cell. She either scared him to death or choked him. Spared me from becoming a murderer."

"Which was it?"

Cochrane glanced at Juliet.

"Choked," he answered.

"How do you know?"

"She's here. She just told me."

"Oh," she said with a sigh. "Say hello for us."

Cochrane addressed the unseen presence and said hello.

"Unconvinced?" Cochrane asked.

"Sorry. Yes."

"And you?" Cochrane asked Dr. Lawrence.

"I'm afraid I'm unconvinced, also."

"Pity." Cochrane shrugged as he continued to paint. "And I'm a little surprised, Lisa. You helped convince me about the reality of spirits," he said. "Remember the story you told me about the voice of the crying child? At Dee Dee's house? In California?"

"I remember," she said. "This is different."

"Like hell it is," he said.

She sighed.

"Know why the number 33 is on the Rolling Rock bottle?" he asked.

"Why?" she answered, thinking it was a joke.

"Christ's age upon his crucifixion," he said. "Plus three plus three is six."

"So what?"

He smiled. "Just sort of the mysterious but perfect geometry of the universe," Cochrane said. "Just one of those things. Sixes running wild."

He stepped back proudly.

"I think that's it. I'm finished," he said. He glanced to the empty place on the other side of his easel. Juliet faded out. "The paint has to dry, but you can look."

Lisa came around to look. So did Dr. Lawrence. They were both stunned.

Lisa kept blinking. The woman in the portrait looked nothing like her. The portrait showed a woman who was attractive, but nowhere nearly as pretty. But she was striking in a homely way, hair much darker, a brilliance but a sadness also. Cochrane had caught more character in this painting than any other he had ever done. Maybe it helped to be mentally askew. And the eyes of the girl in the painting were positively alive.

"It's not me," said Lisa.

"No. It's not. It started out to be, but it's not. This is her. Juliet." He smiled. "And know how I got those great colors for her hair? I have some of her ashes from her urn. I mixed them in with the oil paints. This way, she's always with me."

"Billy, have you *completely* lost your mind?"

He only laughed. Dr. Lawrence couldn't take his eyes off him. Or the portrait.

"I asked you to sit while I painted," Cochrane said. "Of course the portrait's not of you. Not anymore. Why would it be? It's of her. She was right there the whole time. I just had you here to tell you the story."

She looked at the painting and felt rage seize her.

"Jesus!" she said to her former lover. "You jerk!"

She stormed out. Dr. Lawrence went with her.

"Angry?" he called after her. "I hope so."

Cochrane laughed himself silly that night. And the portrait, the best he had ever done, would be set in a place of honor in his home after the ash-tinged paint dried.

But the story didn't end there for Bill Cochrane.

Perhaps in retribution, perhaps out of genuine concern, Lisa returned with Dr. Lawrence several times. Eventually, they convinced Bill to check into a local medical and psychiatric facility in Arlington.

For observation. He would be there for several months.

There would be different doctors and various medication. There would be a search among relatives for someone to sign papers committing Bill Cochrane. There would be a notation that he should never again have a position with a high-stress high-anxiety level because—let's face it, everyone said—this was his third nervous breakdown.

Juliet came with him, at least in spirit. It eased his pain considerably during his hospitalization that her portrait could be with him. One day the Vice President came by to see him. There must have been a jinx to the portrait because Lang was thoroughly shaken by it—so shaken that he attempted suicide a month later. An astrologer told him that death might be the best way out.

The suicide failed, but the Twenty-fifth Amendment helped provide a new Vice President.

While hospitalized, Bill Cochrane knew better than to tell anyone else about mixing the paint with the ashes. Yet the story about the painting—and the events that surrounded it—were the hottest Washington rumor of 2004. And the eyes on the portrait, seen from a certain angle, were positively alive.

Looking at all of these events afterward, it had all been an extraordinary time for Bill Cochrane, the centerpiece of his life in the middle of his life. Reflecting back upon it, examining what had happened, thinking how he had moved across the surface of events, then prowled into their soul, he felt as if the entire journey had taken place in some immeasurably long single day. And as he did that, the different facets of the day began to take shape.

Dawn, when he was first called to the Vice President's residence to hear of the occult threat to George Farley.

Morning, when he had first met Elizabeth Vaughn.

Afternoon, when The Unicorn had first drawn him into his realm.

Evening, when The Unicorn had gotten into his head.

And then the long black night, one which he had never known existed, when ghosts walked and tiny Carl Einhorn declared his evil genius.

But then, Cochrane admitted cheerfully to himself, there had been yet another dawn. A dawn, a new day unlike any other, when he accepted the new world around him, even though others didn't.

What was rational anyway?

He had heard the questions before. Was a world of starving children rational? Was a world of religion and superstition a rational place? What about the inhumanity of three affluent young men toward a creative young woman? What about the listings of human indifference and cruelty in every day's newspaper?

Eventually at the hospital, Cochrane had a room of his own. He was considered a danger to no one. He fell strangely quiet, but was able to discuss things with the doctors. He had learned the answers to give.

And with time, Bill Cochrane responded to what they called "treatment." He became more alert again, his eyes sharpened, and his thoughts—to the doctors, at least—became clearer. The shadow of recent events withdrew, and he no longer rambled endlessly about the real psychic powers of Carl Einhorn, how Einhorn had been killed by a woman who was no longer living, and how Einhorn's extraordinary telepathic powers were accessible to anyone who believed and wished to discover them. Nor did he discourse how spirits were everywhere around if one just bothered to communicate with them.

April came. A long cold winter ended. So did May and with it sunshine and warmth.

Carl Einhorn: Cochrane sometimes had nothing else to do except reflect on the little mathematician and his extraordinary powers.

To amuse himself sometimes, Cochrane would set some dominos on their small ends across the room. He would stare at them and think about them. On some occasions the staff would see a domino lose its balance and fall. They didn't think much about it. A slight imbalance in the table, perhaps. A breeze. A vibration.

On another occasion, not far from his window, Cochrane watched as some deliverymen stacked four cartons of canned goods that they were unloading from a food truck. The cartons were piled five high, about six feet in all.

As Cochrane watched and concentrated on the stack, the cartons swayed suddenly and fell. The workmen were incredulous. Then again, they had been careless. Almost anything could have knocked them over.

Cochrane had a half-sister who lived in Kentucky. Her name was Kimberly. She took an interest in his case after his third nervous breakdown and worked with the doctors on her brother's health.

She came twice to visit and renewed the old family ties. She began to call once a week. Her interest proved therapeutic.

When the doctors thought he was well enough, they finally decided, he could move to Kentucky under his sister's supervision. There he could continue to be monitored by doctors at a local institution in Lexington. It was a more-than-reasonable arrangement. Cochrane, no longer wishing to be confined, stopped seeing his spiritual friends in the room. Or so he said. And even he admitted that follow-up psychiatric care might not be the worst idea.

Shortly before his discharge, a young doctor visited him. The doctor's name was Henry Marvin. He must have been about thirty-five. Dr. Marvin was in charge of making an independent assessment of Cochrane's case. Passing meant discharge.

Cochrane passed perfectly. The doctor could hardly believe that Cochrane had been confined here. Concluding his examination, Dr. Martin rubbed at his own ear.

"You okay?" Cochrane asked the doctor.

"I've got the damnedest earache," the young man said.

Cochrane smiled. "I'm sorry to hear that." He paused. The doctor was writing something on a memo pad.

"I had a bad one several months ago. Mine ended the day a certain little math teacher died." He paused. "How long have you had yours?" Cochrane asked indulgently.

"About seven days."

"Think there's any cause and effect?" Cochrane asked. "That's as long as you've been seeing me."

The doctor looked up and smiled. "Don't even joke about things like that," he said.

"I apologize," said Cochrane. "Couldn't possibly be a link, could there?"

"No."

"I was only kidding."

"I know you were."

Cochrane watched as the doctor struggled with the ear pain in some discomfort.

"Maybe it will just go away," Cochrane said.

"Maybe."

Cochrane smiled. There was a pause. Dr. Martin looked up.

"That's funny," the psychiatrist said.

"What's funny."

"It just did. It stopped." He looked at Cochrane with an indecipherable expression. "Thanks," he said facetiously.

"Don't mention it," Cochrane said.

A week later, Kimberly Cochrane arrived at the hospital. She checked her brother out. They walked out from the institution into the sunlight.

Her car, a Honda with Kentucky plates, was parked by a grassy sidewalk and the curb.

Cochrane drew a long breath of freedom. He smiled.

"I can't tell you how thankful I am," he said. "Freedom's wonderful. It's like a new world out here."

"Think of it as a fresh start," she said.

"I will."

He drew a breath of sweet summer air. He savored his newly won freedom and a bold new outlook onto a world different from any one that he had seen before.

He smiled.

Juliet Voiselle stood not too far from the car. He could see her. Across the street, his father stopped raking leaves just long enough to wave. Little Carl Einhorn was standing in the middle of the road, truculent as ever, the traffic driving right through him, and letting fly with the vilest torrent of obscenities that Kimberly Cochrane had never heard.

Cochrane ignored The Unicorn completely. He acknowledged his dad and Juliet, however. But only in his mind. That was all that was needed.

They understood.

"You okay?" Kimberly asked.

"I'm fine. Just enjoying being out," he said. "Among friends and family."

"That's good," she said. "That's good."

They got into the car and she began their drive.

What a bizarre universe it was, Cochrane thought to himself. If only everyone else could see what he saw. If only everyone could realize the many new worlds which existed just beyond the periphery of most people's view.

In the trunk of the car was the portrait of one Juliet Voiselle. Cochrane had a feeling that she was going to be with him for a long time. It's just that he had now learned to keep his thoughts to himself and his many new spiritual friends out of sight.

The last thing he wanted, after all, was for anyone to think he'd lost his mind.

He knew damned well that he hadn't.